I0613928

EMILY FITZORMOND;

OR,

THE DESERTED ONE.

A TALE OF MYSTERY.

BY THE AUTHOR OF "ANGELINA," "GALLANT TOM," "ERNNESTINE DE LACY," "THE DEATH GRASP," "MARY CLIFFORD," "ELA, THE OUTCAST," "THE MANIAC FATHER," ETC., ETC.

———————

"And who so cold as look on thee,
   Thou lovely wand'rer, and be less?
Nor be, what man should ever be,
   The friend of beauty in distress?

Oh! who would think that form had past
   Through danger's most destructive path,
Had braved the death-winged tempest's blast,
   And 'scaped a tyrant's fiercer wrath?"
                                        BYRON.

———————

LONDON :

PREFACE.

The story of "Emily Fitzormond," romantic as it may appear, is partly founded in fact, although the situation and names of the principal actors have been changed by the Author for obvious reasons.

Flattered by the encouragement it has met with, the Author feels gratified that this has been one of his most successful efforts to please—a circumstance he cannot but attribute to the indulgence of his readers, more than to any merit in the work itself.

"Emily Fitzormond," as well as most of the former works of the Author, has been dramatized most skilfully by Mrs. Denvil, and played for three months with the most rapturous applause at the Royal Pavilion Theatre; and here the Author feels it due to G. Denvil, Esq., to acknowledge the honour done him by the spirited manner in which it was presented to the public.

For the kind manner in which the other works by the Author, now in progress of publication, are being received, he gladly avails himself of the present opportunity to return his most sincere thanks, and begs leave to subscribe himself

THE PUBLIC'S MOST DEVOTED SERVANT,

THOMAS PREST.

January 30th, 1842.

EMILY FITZORMOND;

OR,

THE DESERTED ONE.

BY THE AUTHOR OF "ELA, THE OUTCAST," "ANGELINA," ETC.

CHAPTER I.

THE BALLAD-SINGER.

It was on a dreary evening, in the month of January, that Sir Felix Mandeville, and his amiable wife, were seated in the elegant drawing-room belonging to their spacious mansion, in St. James's Square. The fire blazed cheerfully, and the comfort everything around denoted, contrasted sadly with the misery without. It had been a most inclement winter, and the snow was falling fast, and the wind blew so violently, that it might be said to be a perfect hurricane. The severity of the weather had caused much distress amongst the poor people, and Sir Felix and Lady Mandeville had been engaged, for many days past, in the philanthropic task of

No. 1

looking out for worthy objects of charity, and relieving their distresses.—
Many were the prayers and blessings that were heartily breathed for those
benevolent individuals, by the tongue of honest poverty ; many were the
sad hearts they had the satisfaction to lighten of their woe, and to make
rejoice, and most amply rewarded did they feel in the satisfaction, which
the consciousness of their having performed their duty to their fellow-
creatures engendered in their bosoms. In them, the poor ever found the
best of friends, and integrity and industry were never suffered to go unre-
warded, or without encouragement. In fact, the principal portion of their
time was past in doing good, and their charity was dispensed in that unostentatious way, which rendered it doubly valuable.

"How awfully the wind whistles," remarked Lady Mandeville to her
husband, looking towards the window, the blinds of which were drawn ;
but the snow could be heard pattering, as it was driven with great fury
against the glass; "alas! what must be the sufferings of the houseless
poor in such terrible weather as this ?—How thankful ought we to feel to
that beneficent Being, who has so amply provided for our necessities, and
saved us from the griping misery attendant upon penury and want ?—We
can never be sufficiently grateful, Sir Felix."

"You are right, my dear Emmeline," replied her husband, "and the
only way in which we can evince our gratitude, is by endeavouring to relieve the distresses of our fellow-creatures, and by making those who are
deserving of it, participate in those comforts which we enjoy. But, hush!
—there is somebody singing outside; what a beautiful voice—it is melody
itself!—It is evidently that of a young female."

"Exquisite," ejaculated Lady Mandeville, in a tone of admiration, as
she listened to the sweet notes warbled with such delightful taste and
judgment, by the minstrel outside; "poor creature!—wretched, indeed,
must be her condition, to be compelled to wander forth to endeavour to procure a scanty and precarious livelihood in the streets, on such a night as
this. Listen!"

The female having sung one of the popular ballads of the day, in a
style of simplicity, and neatness of execution, which immediately rivetted
the attention, after a brief pause, broke into a different air, and Sir Felix
and his lady were enabled to distinguish the following words :—

> "Listen, gentle ladies pretty,
>   Listen to my simple lay;
> The ballad-singer claims your pity—
>   Then turn not scornfully away!
> Though in rags she's doom'd to wander,
>   And comforts few to her impart;
> Deign upon her fate to ponder,
>   And let soft pity touch your heart!
>
> Fast the chilly snow's descending,
>   No garments warm, her limbs enfold;
> Grief and want her heart are rending—
>   No shelter has she from the cold!
> Then listen to her tale distressing,
>   The ba'lad-singer grant relief;
> And she will pray for you a blessing—
>   Pray Heaven to shield you e'er from grief."

The female again ceased; but Sir Felix and Lady Mandeville were so
enraptured by what they had heard, and the last simple, but impressive
appeal which the ballad-singer had made, that they could not speak for a
moment or so, and stood listening attentively, still imagining that the
charming tones of the female's voice were vibrating in their ears.

"I never heard anything more beautiful in my life!" observed Lady

Emmeline; "this poor girl certainly must have received some cultivation. And, then, to be exposed to the inclemency of the weather, on such a night as this, perhaps, hungry, and half naked, and without a place of shelter, or any place where she can stretch her weary limbs; I must summon Laura, and see in what manner we can best relieve her wants. I hope she has not gone away."

"I sincerely hope so, too," returned Sir Felix, as Lady Emmeline arose and pulled the bell, "for she has inspired me with no common interest and curiosity, and I have a great wish to see the individual who has so surprised and entranced us both."

At this moment, there was a gentle tap at the door, and without waiting to receive an order from Sir Felix, or his lady, to walk in, it was opened, and there tripped lightly into the apartment, not Lady Emmeline's waiting-maid, Laura, but Arabella Mandeville, her lovely and amiable daughter. Her beautiful blue eyes sparkled with even more than their usual animation, and the eagerness of her manner shewed that something had deeply interested her, and that she wished to impart some intelligence to her parents.

"Oh, my dearest papa and mamma," began the charming girl, "did you hear the ballad-singer just now, who sang so sweetly, that——"

"We did, my dear child," interrupted her mother, "and I rang the bell to desire Laura to tell her to walk in, that we might see her, and try to ascertain whether or not she is an object worthy of our relief."

"I am delighted to hear you say so, mamma," returned Arabella, "I have anticipated your wishes, for I knew you would not be offended at my asking a poor distressed object in to sit by the fire, on such a shocking cold and stormy night as this. The poor young creature is in the kitchen, and I have ordered the cook to give her something to eat and to drink."

"You have done perfectly right, my dear Arabella," said her father, "and I commend you for your humanity. We must see this unfortunate."

"I am certain you will be astonished, my dear papa, when you do see her," observed his daughter—"for I never beheld such a lovely creature in my life before. Notwithstanding she is so meanly attired, there is something so superior in her appearance altogether, that I can never believe that she was born to fill the miserable station of life she at present occupies. She has got one of the most interesting and handsome countenances that I ever saw, and, as for her figure, it is really grace and symmetry itself."

Thus expatiating on the charms of the forlorn stranger, Arabella preceded her father and mother down the stairs, and they descended into the kitchen, where the ballad-singer was warming her benumbed limbs by a roaring fire, and eating greedily of the victuals which the cook, by the instructions of Arabella, had placed before her.

Upon the entrance of Sir Felix and his lady, she arose, and while a modest blush of bashfulness overspread her features, she curtseyed low to them both, and with a grace which was perfectly captivating.

Never had they gazed upon a more interesting-looking object; and they started back, with no small share of amazement, little expecting—notwithstanding the glowing description which their daughter had given of her—to see so much beauty concentrated in one being.

She was evidently not more than seventeen years of age, and the regularity and beauty of her features came as near to perfection as anything could approach. Her eyes were hazel, and beamed forth rays of lustre that penetrated to the soul. Her skin was delicately fair, and, notwithstanding that care and hunger had fixed their marks upon her cheeks, a delicate tinge suffused them, which added greatly to the fascination of her appearance. Her mouth was most exquisitely and beautifully formed ;— her hair, which was a dark auburn, hung down her shoulders in negligent tresses, caused by the wind, and her eye-brows were arched, and of a glossy silken texture. Her dress was old and patched, but very clean ;— and the graces of her form shone forth pre-eminent, even from beneath her humble garb. Her legs and feet were entirely bare, and her elegantly-turned ancle would have formed a model, which the most eminent artist might have been envious to obtain.

"Unfortunate girl," said Lady Emmeline, in accents of pity, "and have you no other means of obtaining a living than this ?"

"Alas ! I have not, lady," replied the girl, in a voice of sweetness, while a tear started to her eye, as she marked the compassionate expression of Lady Mandeville's countenance ; "I am driven to it by the most abject distress."

"But, have you no parents ?"

"None, that I am aware of, lady," was the reply ; "I have neither parents nor home ; I had not tasted of food since yesterday morning, until now, and, but for the kindness of this young lady, I verily believe I must have perished in the streets."

"And, how long have you been in this distress, my poor girl ?" asked Sir Felix.

"More than two years, sir,—and a dreadful two years has it been for me."

"But, have you no friends ?" inquired Lady Emmeline.

"None but those who relieve me, and they are but few, indeed," answered the ballad-singer, with a sigh.

"Poor girl ! then you are quite deserted ?"

"By all, but the Almighty," said the girl, with energy, and her countenance brightening up with hope as she spoke—"by all, but the Almighty, who, I sincerely believe, will not abandon me while I put my trust in Him !"

Sir Felix and his lady were much touched by the girl's answer, and stood gazing at her with admiration, for a short time, in silence.

"And what is your name, pray ?" asked Lady Mandeville.

"I have ever been instructed to call myself Emily—Emily Fitzormond," replied the ballad-singer.

"What do you mean by that, my girl ?" said the lady.

"Why, I have some suspicion that that is not my right name, madam," returned Emily—(for so we shall in future call her.) "Indeed, there is a mystery attached to my birth, which I have never been able to penetrate, and I probably never shall."

The interest of Sir Felix and his lady were now more than ever excited ; and they were convinced from the girl's manner that she spoke the truth, and was not attempting to arouse their sympathies by any false representations.

"In what part were you born ?" inquired Lady Emmeline.

"My first recollection of myself, was in a humble cottage, in a small village, in the County of Suffolk," answered Emily, "where I lived under the direction of an old woman, whom I was instructed to call my grandmother : her name was Fitzormond. She was the only relation I ever saw to my knowledge. She has been dead nearly three years."

"And did you never hear of a father or mother ?" said Sir Felix.

"Never," answered Emily ; "my grandmother was always very reserved towards me, and answered any questions I asked (with the simplicity of a child,) concerning my family, and why I had not a father and mother as well as the other children around us, with a peevish anger that effectually prevented me from resuming my inquiries, till lapse of time, causing forgetfulness, led to an inadvertent repetition of my fault."

"But how did you live?"

"My grandmother, I understood, had a small annuity," replied the ballad-singer, "which was allowed by some person in London; and, upon one occasion, a gentleman called at our cottage, and gave her a sum of money. He took particular notice of me, and the expression of his countenance made me shudder—for I could not help thinking that he was a very cross and spiteful-looking man."

"It is very remarkable!" said Lady Emmeline, "if what you have spoken be the truth, there is, indeed, a very singular mystery attached to your fate. But what made you take to the wretched course of life you are now pursuing?"

"Mine is a very long and melancholy story, lady," answered Emily,— "and I fear it would not interest you. However, if you will permit me to call again, to thank you for your kindness to me this night, I will, if you wish it, relate it to you."

"But, my poor child, you say you have no home—no shelter," said Lady Emmeline, tenderly, "and think you I would turn a fellow-creature forth such a night as this?—No, my poor girl, here you shall remain for to-night, and when you have warmed yourself, you can retire to bed as soon as you like. In the morning I will see you, and talk to you further upon this subject."

The eyes of the ballad-singer filled with tears, and her heart was too full to speak. Arabella, too, with the sweetest looks, bespoke her gratitude to her amiable mother, for her kindness to the unfortunate stranger.

"Oh, my dear good lady," said Emily, at length, while her cheeks were suffused with blushes, "how have I deserved this kindness?—Alas! how few are there in the world who possess the same gentle—the same benevolent heart as your ladyship. Seldom do the votaries of wealth deign even to bestow a look upon the less fortunate object of their charity, unless it be one of scorn and disgust. Many blessings attend you, lady, for this, and rest assured that Emily Fitzormond will never forget the debt of gratitude she owes you!"

"Nay, nay, no more of this, my poor girl," said Lady Emmeline, with increased kindness, "you are heartily welcome to all that I can do for you. Martha, you will see this poor creature to a comfortable chamber, when she wishes to retire, and get a change of clothes by the morning."

Emily was again about to express her thanks, but Lady Mandeville, taking the arm of her husband, left the kitchen, followed by Arabella, and returned to the drawing-room.

CHAPTER II.

THE DYING SECRET.

ON the borders of a dreary heath, in the County of Suffolk, at the time our narrative commences, stood a small hamlet, the wretched hovels of which were inhabited by the poorest people. There was one, however, much larger than the rest, which stood apart from them, and had a more comfortable appearance than any of the others, although it had not been inhabited for many years, from a supposition that it was haunted. This was called "The White Cottage," and had formerly been occupied by a man named

Luke Stanton, his wife, and two children. This man was a ruffianly-looking fellow, and report spoke of him in no very favourable terms; he associated with no one in the village, and it could never be ascertained in what manner he contrived to live—for he did not work, and yet he never appeared to be in any kind of distress.

His wife was a remarkably pretty woman, apparently much younger than himself, and her countenance was always overcast with a cloud of deep gloom and melancholy, which shewed plainly that her breast was the abode of some heavy care. She seemed fearful of contracting any acquaintance with her neighbours; and if she accidentally met them in the village, she never, by any chance, exchanged a word with them. Yet, as much as Luke Stanton, her husband, was hated, so was she respected and pitied—for it was the firm opinion of most persons, that he brutally ill-used her, and that he held her under the restraint which she evinced in her conduct.

Two or three years elapsed, when Luke Stanton was suddenly missed in the village—neither had his wife or children been seen for several days past; and, as the shutters of the cottage were closed, and the door quite fast, suspicion was excited, and permission having been asked of the Lord of the Manor, the door was burst open, when a dreadful spectacle presented itself. The lifeless body of Mrs. Stanton was stretched upon the floor, mangled in a most appalling manner. Luke Stanton and the children had disappeared. There was no furniture of any consequence in the cottage, and they could not find anything which could lead them to the discovery of the assassin. Every possible inquiry was immediately set on foot, but without success; all traces of the murderer or the children, were, ever after, lost. The cottage was immediately closed, and no one would take it—for it was said that the spectre of the murdered woman constantly haunted it; and many of the neighbours declared that they had heard such dreadful shrieks and groans issue from it at night, that were enough to appal the stoutest heart. The lord of the estate had been several times requested by his tenants to pull it down; but, although there seemed to be no chance of its again letting—for some reason, which every person was at a loss to imagine—he obstinately refused to comply, and there it stood, a source of terror to all the inhabitants around.

Several years had passed away, and still "The White Cottage" remained the same as when the murderer had left it; even the stains of blood had not been removed from the floor; and the rustics who lived on the spot, protested that the noises were continued nightly, and some went so far as to assert that the spectre of the murdered woman had been seen to walk forth from the cottage, at midnight, dressed in long flowing robes of white, which were stained with blood in several places. In the truth of these stories, of course, it was only the vulgar and the superstitious that placed any reliance. One night, however, some labourers, returning from their work, in passing the cottage, observed an unusual light reflected from the casement—the shutters being unclosed—and it had every appearance of being inhabited. As they passed by the casement, they caught the glimpse of a dark form, moving in the room, and concluding it at once to be some evil spirit, they took to their heels, and scampered away as fast as their limbs could carry them.

The next day, much to the astonishment of the neighbours, it was discovered that "The White Cottage" was occupied—not with preternatural, but human beings—for an aged woman, neatly attired, and accompanied by a sweet pretty child—a little girl, apparently about three years of age —was seen to totter from it, and take the direction to the steward's house.

The form of the old woman, although now bent with age, had, evidently, been stately and graceful, and traces might be easily discovered in her wrinkled countenance of former beauty. Poorly as she was clad, there was an air of superiority about her, which immediately excited attention, and created a feeling of interest in the beholder.

The little girl, as we have before said, was remarkably pretty; and its countenance sparkled with childish mirth and innocence, as it skipped and frolicked before the old woman, who hobbled slowly behind, with the assistance of a stick.

The most indescribable amazement prevailed among the inhabitants of the village, at this singular circumstance, and they followed the old woman and her young companion, with wondering eyes; and, then assembled together to consult upon the matter, and to endeavour to conjecture who the woman was, and what could ever induce her to seek a shelter in "The White Cottage." The opinions formed were as various as they were erroneous, and they separated in the same state of uncomfortable mystery as they had assembled. One thing was certain, and in which they all agreed, namely—that the woman was a perfect stranger in that neighbourhood, and that none of them had ever seen her before; but, that she could be no good, they were all positive of, or else why should she assume so much mystery in her behaviour, and why take possession of the cottage in so secret a manner?—The sages never for a moment took the trouble to consider that it was not the slightest business of theirs, and that they had no right to heap such suspicions upon one to whom they were utterly unknown. Their surprise was increased, when they understood that it was the intention of the aged female to make "The White Cottage" her future abode; and, for that purpose, she had entered into the necessary arrangements with the steward to the estate. Her name they also soon ascertained was Fitzormond—at least, that was the one by which she had chosen to be recognised.

The neighbours were, at first, completely horror-struck at the idea of any person having the hardihood to inhabit a place in which so dreadful a crime had been perpetrated, and which had been so long supposed to be haunted; but every other idea was soon absorbed in the anxious curiosity they felt to become acquainted with who she was, and what motives could have induced her to take to such a life of comparative seclusion. Notwithstanding the poverty of the old woman, and the plainness of her garb, there was an inexpressible something in her manner, and an air of gentility in her demeanour, which denoted that she had not always lived in obscurity. As by degrees, the neighbours became more familiar with her, and would stop and speak to her when they met her taking her customary walk with the child, Emily, to whom she said she was grandmother;—this has been remarked in her presence, but she never uttered a syllable that could in the least tend to gratify their curiosity in that respect, and kept herself as distant as possible from their society, without degenerating into downright incivility.

Towards Emily she behaved in the same mysterious manner, and, although she generally treated her with the most affectionate kindness, as she grew older, and began to have judgment to reflect, whenever she questioned her as to who were her parents, and whether they were alive or dead, the old woman would become dreadfully agitated—her countenance would turn ghastly pale—and, in a voice of mingled wrath and terror, she would exclaim:—

"Girl, forbear!—you know not how you torture me by such questions! —As you value my love, never mention the word parents to me again, upon any account, or I may be tempted to——but no matter, no matter; do not so again, child; the name of those who gave you being you must never know; be contented to bear that of Emily Fitzormond, and be happy in your obscurity, where you will probably be spared those troubles that too often beset those who move in a higher sphere."

In vain did Emily seek to penetrate through the veil of mystery with which her fate was enveloped, and many an hour of grief did it cause her; but the society of her young companions, among whom her sweetness of disposition soon made her a great favorite, by degrees wore it off, and she endeavoured to become contented in her present situation, trusting that time would unravel the mystery, which her grandmother now refused to solve.

Their means of living were very limited; their dwelling was lowly, but very clean; their fare was frugal, and their clothing such as is usually worn by English cottagers. How they contrived to subsist, was, for some time, unknown to Emily; but she, at length, managed to elicit from her grandmother that they were allowed a small sum yearly by a relation in London; and she then recollected upon one occasion, when she was very young, a gentleman calling at the cottage, of a morose and haughty demeanour, and repulsive countenance, who had a long conversation with the old woman, and, at parting, gave her a sum of money, making use of the following words, which made such an impression on the mind of Emily— young as she was at the time—that she had never been able to forget them since :—

"I should like it better if I had not much longer to pay this money for the *present* purpose; although I should not mind doubling it, could what I have before mentioned to you be accomplished."

The old woman turned from the stranger, with a shudder, when he thus spoke, and muttered some words which Emily could not comprehend; and soon afterwards the stranger took his departure, bestowing upon Emily a look of the utmost hatred as he left the cottage. From that time, he never came there again; but Emily never thought upon him without a feeling of disgust, so strong was the impression his stern and forbidding countenance, and the words he had made use of, together with the manner in which he behaved to her, made upon her mind. More than once, though, when Emily had grown older, an idea darted across her brain, which filled her with terror. Could it be possible that the stranger was her father?— That she was the child of shame?—And that, discarded by her unnatural parents, she had been left to be brought up in poverty and obscurity, by Mrs. Fitzormond, while they were most likely in affluence? But, no!— she could not bring her mind to believe that she was the daughter of that man who had excited in her bosom such feelings of abhorrence; any fate, she thought, would be preferable to that of ascertaining so painful a fact! —Rather would she remain unknown, and endure every hardship and privation, than to learn that the stranger possessed any paternal authority over her. She forebore to question her grandmother upon the subject, for fear of incurring her displeasure, and exciting her emotion; but many an hour of racking thought did it cause her—many agonizing and perplexing reflections did it give rise to.

As Emily increased in years, so did her beauties expand; and she was the universal admiration of every one in the neighbourhood, being commonly called "Pretty Emily, of the White Cottage." Her disposition was gentle, kind, and mirthful. She was the very life and soul of her young companions; and when she was absent from their little parties, everything seemed dull and cheerless. Mrs. Fitzormond, who was an intelligent woman, had taken great pains with her education; and Emily, whose quick perception soon imbibed all that she sought to inculcate, became at once the village pride, the village envy, and the village wonder. Emily shewed an early taste for music, and Mrs. Fitzormond, who was

herself accomplished in that science, encouraged her in it; and the sweetness of her voice, and the silvery melody of her tones, as she would sing some simple ballad, for the amusement of her grandmother, frequently attracted numerous admiring listeners round that cottage, which they had formerly shunned with terror, under the supposition that it was haunted.

Years passed away in this manner, and Emily had now attained her fourteenth year, and had never yet left the protection of her grandmother, on whom Time had now heaped his hoary honours, and who had become so feeble, that she was seldom able to walk out; and when she did, it was not without the assistance of Emily. One day she had left her for a short time, to go on an errand to the nearest town, where she was detained a longer period than she expected, much to her vexation—for her grandmother had seemed to be more indisposed than usual, all the morning, and if any thing were to happen to her while she was away, she should never forgive herself. Filled with many dismal forebodings and apprehensions—as soon as she had settled the business she had gone upon—Emily hurried away towards home, with all the precipitation she could; and had no sooner reached the cottage door, than she heard the deep moans of her grandmother, who was evidently suffering the most excruciating agony. With delirious haste, she burst into the room, and beheld the poor old woman, stretched upon the humble pallet, apparently writhing in all the agonies of death.

In the greatest state of agitation, Emily called in one or two of the neighbours to render assistance, and then threw herself on her knees, by the side of the couch, and pressing her grandmother's hand between her's, implored her to look up and speak to her poor child. The old woman knew her; and, motioning her to come nearer to her, she fixed upon her

No. 2

a ghastly look, and, after several ineffectual efforts, said, in a hollow voice :—

"Emily, you see in the poor, dying wretch before you, a guilty—a terrible sinner.—Nay, do not weep for me; I am unworthy your tears; I have injured you, deeply—perhaps, irreparably injured you. Listen to me, and, ere it is too late—ere my eyes are for ever closed in death—let me impart to you a secret, on which your future fortune and happiness depends. Know, then, that you are——"

Just at this critical moment—when Emily was listening with breathless attention, and her future fate probably hung upon a few words—her grandmother was seized with strong convulsions, and in less than ten minutes, she was a corpse, and the secret she was about to divulge, had died with her.

CHAPTER III.

THE VISION.—THE SPECTRE.

It would be impossible to describe the powerful emotions which distracted the bosom of poor Emily, as she stood over the corpse of her who was the only friend she had ever known in the world, and who was now taken from her for ever. Scalding tears of bitter agony streamed down her cheeks, and when she reflected upon her lone and desolate situation, she became the perfect image of despair. Who could she now look to for protection—for comfort, under her affliction?—Whither could she go—how subsist?—She was almost driven to madness, and was quite inconsolable—although a compassionate neighbour, to whose cottage she was conveyed, did all she could to soothe her anguish, and to impart consolation to her bosom.

But that which agonized her more than all, was the remembrance of the death-bed scene—the last words of Mrs. Fitzormond—and the secret which death had prevented her from revealing. Here, then, was all chance of the mystery, in which her fate was involved, being unravelled, lost for ever, and nothing but a dreary prospect of misery and suffering was before her.

"Oh, God !" soliloquized the poor girl, wringing her hands, "am I then born for nothing but misfortune?—Am I marked out by Fate to be its sport?—If so, how much better had it been, had I died in childhood; ere a knowledge of my affliction, or my destitute condition, were made apparent to me !—And whither can I now go?—Where shall I find a friend? Alas ! I am, as it were, alone in the world. Oh, cruel, heartless parents, thus to desert your unfortunate offspring, and leave her to the mercy of an unfeeling world !"

Her tears flowed with increased violence, as these reflections flashed across her brain, and her heart felt ready to burst. The poor woman at whose cottage she was staying, reasoned with her, in her homely manner, on the folly of giving way to excessive grief, at an event that might be reasonably expected, from the advanced age to which her grandmother had arrived; Emily made no reply, but, in vain, endeavoured to check the effusions of affectionate regret that would burst forth at every turn of painful thought.

The woman, and her neighbours, were surprised to find that Emily literally knew no more relative to the affairs of her deceased grandmother than themselves; not even the gentleman's name who brought the annuity —the only time she remembered seeing him, and consequently could not apply to him. Besides, the bare idea of pleading for assistance from that man, whose image was so indelibly stamped upon her memory—and whose stern and forbidding aspect had created in her mind such disgust and abhorrence—made Emily shudder, with horror and repugnance; and she felt as if she could perish sooner than she could submit to it. Again, the terrible idea that he was probably the only being upon whom she had any lawful claim, rushed upon her brain, and filled her bosom with the most overwhelming grief.

A minute investigation was made through the drawers, trunks, and closets, for papers that could cast any light upon the subject; but none were found that could give Emily the least clue to guide her in her actions, or tell to what family she belonged; nor was there money sufficient to defray the expenses of the funeral.

In consequence of this, it was thought advisable to insert in some of the morning papers, an advertisement, purporting that, an aged woman, named Elizabeth Fitzormond, was now lying deceased, at a cottage, near —————— heath; and, in consequence of that event, her grandchild, Emily Fitzormond, was left destitute of a friend, or even a shelter, for her tender years, —requesting, that, if she had any relations, or an individual who had a right to protect her—as, from circumstances, there was reason to suppose such a being existed—that they would lose no time in attending to that notice, and relieving the hapless Emily.

The time that intervened, before there was any answer to this advertisement, was past by Emily, in a state of doubt, uncertainty, and despair, which it was truly lamentable to behold; but it was, at length, answered. A letter arrived, without any name or signature, enclosing a bank note for ten pounds, which, the writer stated, was to defray the expenses of Mrs. Fitzormond's funeral; and he added, that Emily was to hold herself in readiness to attend a person, who would be sent down in a few days to take charge of her.

This letter filled the mind of Emily with a number of agonizing thoughts, and she shuddered at the bare idea of being placed under the care of strangers. And who was it to whom she was in future to be consigned?—Was it a relation?—Was it those parents, who, it appeared to her, had so unnaturally abandoned her in her infancy; and who, destitute (as she felt convinced they must be,) of all affection towards her, what treatment could she expect to experience from them, but such as would, most likely, render life a burthen to her?—The form of the stranger, who had visited her grandmother during her childhood, came fresh upon her recollection; and when she thought that it was probably into his hands she was about to be delivered, her heart sunk with the most serious alarm. Whatever authority he might possess over her, she could not form any idea; but she felt that she could never view him with any other feelings than those of fear and detestation, and she would willingly submit to any suffering, however severe it might be, rather than find herself in his power, or that she was bound by duty to obey him. So strong was the prejudice she entertained towards him, that she was confident, notwithstanding he should prove to be her father, that she could never esteem—much more, love him; and sooner would she continue in ignorance of the authors of her being, than discover that man to be one of them. There was something so terrible to Emily's imagination, in this probability—although it was a feeling which she was at a loss perfectly to comprehend—that she could not dwell upon it for a moment without experiencing the most acute anguish: but it was with the utmost difficulty she could divert her thoughts from the subject.

The woman with whom Emily was staying, affected great tenderness and complacence towards her ; but she had, in reality, only assumed a mask of duplicity for interested motives.   Herself, and her gossiping neighbours, with whom she was intimate, conjectured that her prospects would turn out most prosperous ; and that the person who was about to call for her in a few days, would prove to be the gentleman who she had once seen at "The White Cottage," and her father—from whom Mrs. Dartmouth, (that was the woman's name,) expected a handsome present, for the care she had taken of Emily ; and, very likely, if he did not choose to have her in London, that he would make some arrangements for her to board with her.   That Emily's parents, whoever they were, were wealthy people, they had not the least doubt ; and so sanguine was Mrs. Dartmouth, and her neighbours, upon the subject, that the fortune of the former was completely established already.   But they did not dream, at that time, how soon all these air-built castles were to be destroyed.

Mrs. Fitzormond was buried decently, and Mrs. Dartmouth took upon herself the management of it, and paid the undertaker. In this she did not fail to indulge her cupidity, charging a pound or two more than the funeral expenses came to ; at the same time, that she made a great boast of her kindness ; and Emily, ignorant as she was at that time of the ways of the world, had no suspicion of the hypocritical part Mrs. Dartmouth was playing, and really felt very grateful for what she thought to be such disinterested kindness.

But nothing could efface the deep melancholy which the death of her grandmother, and the uncertainty of her future destiny, had caused, from the mind of Emily ; and the time which intervened, prior to the arrival of the individual, to whose charge she was to be committed, was passed by her in a constant succession of distracting ruminations.   More particularly than all, were the last sad moments of her grandmother recalled to her memory ; and when she remembered the mysterious words she had uttered, and the secret which she had, in vain, tried to communicate to her, she became lost in the labyrinth of conjecture. The secret must have been something of a terrible nature, or it would not have agonized the old woman so violently !—She had also confessed that she was a guilty wretch—that she was unworthy of her's (Emily's) tears—and that she had greatly injured her—and every word tended to convince her that Mrs. Fitzormond was the agent of those who, it seemed, doomed her to misery, and not a relative, as she had represented herself.

A terrible feeling came over Emily, as these ideas darted upon her imagination · and something seemed to whisper to her that the spirit of the deceased, Mrs. Fitzormond, could never rest until she had been permitted to divulge the dreadful truth, which had weighed upon her conscience at the awful moment she was called into the presence of her Almighty judge.

"And, oh, may Heaven pardon her for the errors, whatever they may have been, of which she acknowledged, with her dying breath, that she was guilty," exclaimed the poor girl, her eyes filling with tears as she spoke, and the fervour with which she raised her clasped hands towards Heaven, shewed at once her sincerity ; "may her soul rest in peace ; and if her spirit is allowed to look down upon this earth, it will see how earnestly I pardon her for whatever injuries she may have inflicted upon me ; and——"

It was night, and Emily was alone in the little room which was allotted to her to repose in, when she was thus soliloquizing : and at the word, where we have so abruptly left off, she suddenly paused, and looked fearfully around her—for she was almost certain that she heard a deep sigh breathed near her, as if from some bosom heavily afflicted. She could see nothing but her own shadow, which was reflected on the walls by the beams of the lamp which gleamed upon the table. All was silent as death in the cottage—for Mrs. Dartmouth had gone to bed—and nothing was to be heard, save, at intervals, the melancholy howling of a dog, which was chained up on one of the neighbour's premises, and which was by no means calculated to dissipate the feeling that was stealing over the senses of Emily. She was naturally of a timid disposition, and rather inclined to superstition—which she had probably imbibed through listening too readily to the marvellous and awful stories, which the old people of the village delighted to relate, when assembled around the fire in the evening; besides, she could almost have ventured to have sworn that it was no delusion, but that the sound was uttered close to her ear. The recollection of her grandmother again darted across her memory, a cold sweat came over her, and her limbs trembled violently, with an emotion she found it impossible to conquer. Again she cast her eyes fearfully around the room, and drew in her breath. She could not remain in the room by herself; and taking the lamp in her hand, with trembling footsteps opened the door, and descending the stairs, entered the room in which Mrs. Dartmouth slept, the door of which was unlocked. She was sound asleep, but Emily awoke her; and, apologizing for disturbing her, in a few words, related what had happened, and requested permission for her to sleep in the same chamber with her.

"Gracious me!" exclaimed Mrs. Dartmouth, starting up in the bed, with terror depicted in her countenance, at what Emily had related, "how you terrify me, child!—Well, I shouldn't at all be surprised if the ghost of Mrs. Fitzormond should haunt the neighbourhood—for she will never rest in the grave, depend upon it, until she has divulged that secret she was endeavouring to reveal when she died. Ah! she must have been a very wicked woman in her time, or——God bless my soul! what was that?—Did you not hear some one groan?"

Timid as she was, and naturally more nervous, after what had occurred in her own room, Emily's alarm was not to be increased, by what she considered to be nothing but imagination on the part of Mrs. Dartmouth, and she, therefore, replied that she had heard nothing, and that Mrs. Dartmouth must have been mistaken.

"Well, to be sure, I might be," said the latter, partially recovering herself; "but I could almost have sworn that I was not!—But come into bed, Emily; and I am very glad of your company—for I could not sleep alone, now, for all the *hinges* of gold!"

Emily complied with the request of Mrs. Dartmouth, who soon went off to sleep again, and snored loudly; but the former was too much agitated and occupied with dismal thoughts, to yield to the influence of the drowsy God, for some time; and, with her head beneath the bed-clothes, lay listening to the ticking of the old clock, which stood in one corner of the room. At length, however, sleep did light upon her eye-lids; but it was only to present to her imagination the most fearful visions. At one time, she thought she was wandering through the old village church-yard, and at every step treading upon mouldering bones, and the broken remains of coffins. Suddenly she came to the grave in which her grandmother was interred; and here her footsteps were arrested, as if by some supernatural power. She felt a dreadful sensation creeping through her veins, but she could not move!—While she stood, a terrific shriek rent the air; a sulphurous smell arose from the earth—the grave of her grandmother was split, as if by an earthquake; a blue vapourish cloud gradually arose from it; and when it had partially evaporated, Emily, to her horror, beheld, standing before her, the phantom of Mrs. Fitzormond, in all the ghastly cerements of the grave. Her awful countenance had an expression so terrible, that it was sufficient to freeze the blood to ice to gaze upon it; and her eyes darted forth even more than a supernatural fire. The expression of the spectre was of the most dreadful torment, and its appearance, altogether, enough to excite the greatest terror.

Shuddering with the intensity of her feelings, Emily imagined in her dream that she made a desperate effort to get away from the spot, but she tried in vain; she was transfixed, rivetted, spell-bound, and she had not the power even to remove her eyes from the countenance of the spectre;—which, at length, raised its hand, and pointing towards our heroine, its lips parted, and the following words, in a hollow, sepulchral voice, smote her ears:—

"Child of misfortune!—pray for the troubled spirit of her you believed to be your grandmother; all rest is denied to me, until I have imparted to you that secret my dying lips would fain have revealed. Listen!—and mark me!—You are the——"

At this instant, Emily imagined, in her dream, a loud peal of thunder shook the air; the spectre groaned, and in a moment there started from behind a tomb, the tall figure of a man, who, darting in between the phantom and Emily, seized the latter fiercely by the arm, and placing the point of a knife to her bosom, exclaimed in a voice of thunder:—

"Spirit!—fiend!—accursed!—avaunt!—The secret shall never be disclosed—for thus I rid me of the being to whom alone it is of interest, and whom I have to dread. Die!"

Emily imagined that the phantom vanished as the man spoke, and looking up with terror into his countenance, she recognised the features of the man who had visited "The White Cottage," when she was a child. She screamed frantically, as his upraised arm was about to descend to strike the fatal blow, and trembling violently in every limb, she awoke!

Whether it was the powerful and appalling effects of the frightful vision, that still worked upon her imagination, or not, we cannot say; but upon the instant she awoke, some invisible power appeared to raise her in the bed, and a sense of some approaching horror enchained all her faculties! Again a deep drawn sigh vibrated in her ears; followed by a low moaning sound, like the stifled agony of some person in great suffering. This time she was certain she was not mistaken; terror smote her heart; she endeavoured, but in vain, to awaken Mrs. Dartmouth; and then tried to throw herself back on her pillow, and to cover her face with her hands; but some inscrutable power seemed to prevent her from doing that. At that moment, the village church bell tolled the hour of one, and scarcely had its last solemn vibration died away on the air, when Emily once more heard a sigh, and a rustling sound in the chamber. Another instant, and the curtains of the bed were drawn back—and, oh, horror!—Emily beheld gazing, with an awful expression upon her, the spectre of Mrs. Fitzormond, exactly as she had beheld it in the vision. But a moment did she look upon the appalling sight, and then, uttering a loud scream, she became insensible.

When she recovered, she found that it was daylight, and that Mrs. Dartmouth, and two or three of her officious neighbours, were standing around her bed; but the remembrance of all the dreadful events of the night, rushed immediately upon her recollection, she uttered an exclamation of terror, and nearly relapsed again into a state of insensibility.

"Goodness me!" observed Mrs. Dartmouth, who was all anxiety and impatience, "whatever can have happened, to frighten the poor girl in this manner? Do, pray tell me, child!"

It was, however, some time before Emily was in a fit condition to gratify the curiosity of Mrs. Dartmouth, or her inquisitive neighbours; and when she did, she very prudently concealed the fact of the phantom she was positive she had seen, and merely stated that she had been alarmed by a frightful dream.

Mrs. Dartmouth, and her companions, seemed to be far from satisfied with this answer, and by significant hints and winks, passed among themselves, signified that they were certain that Emily had not told them the whole truth.

"It is very strange, child," remarked Mrs. Dartmouth, "that a mere dream should so frighten you; but you must not give way to this weakness—for, no doubt, unless you are more fortunate than many others in the world, you will have much more to alarm you than that before you die."

Emily shook her head and sighed. Alas! she felt too keenly that the woman spoke the truth, and a fatal conviction came over her, that it was, indeed, her fate to become the victim of misfortune.

She was so unwell, with the fright she had sustained, that she was unable to leave her bed all that day; and her thoughts were constantly fixed upon the terrific and remarkable vision which had haunted her pillow, and the spectre which she had afterwards beheld. She tried, but ineffectually, to convince herself that she had been deceived, and that it was only the recollection of the horrors of her dream, that had conjured up the ghastly form, which she imagined had haunted her in her waking moments. The more, however, she reflected upon it, the stronger became the conviction upon her mind, that she had really beheld the spirit of Mrs. Fitzormond, and her bosom became the abode of the utmost anguish and alarm.

The next night, Emily again slept with Mrs. Dartmouth, but nothing occurred to excite her fears, and she slept more tranquilly than, after the recent events, could have been anticipated. Mrs. Dartmouth arose, as was her custom, at an early hour the following morning, to prepare the breakfast; and she had not long done so, when Emily, who had arisen, heard the noise of a vehicle drive up to the door, and in a few seconds, the voice of a man, in conversation with Mrs. Dartmouth, in the front room.

CHAPTER IV.

THE JOURNEY AND THE LONE-HOUSE.

EMILY trembled when she heard this, but she was not long kept in suspense; the room door was thrown open by Mrs. Dartmouth, and the next moment she was ushered into the presence of the person who was sent to take charge of her, and who introduced himself as Mr. Chesterton.

He was an elderly man, short, and thick-set, but with a disagreeable cast of features—although he endeavoured to assume an aspect of benevolence. The dark and insidious hypocrite, however, lurked in every lineament of his features, and there was something peculiarly repulsive in the expression of his eyes, which were small and keen, and, at times, they were nearly concealed by his long, grey eye-brows.

Emily shrunk from this man with a feeling of disgust, such as she had only felt once before, when she saw the man, whose image had ever since been impressed upon her memory in such vivid characters. Mr. Chesterton appeared no less struck with the beauty of Emily than she was agitated at seeing him; and there was something in the expression of his countenance, which called the blushes deep mantling to her cheeks, and she averted her head. Mr. Chesterton, however, attempted to assume a look of kindness, and taking her hand, said—

"And so, child, you are Emily Fitzormond—are you?"

Emily could make no reply; but Mrs. Dartmouth, who was very offi-cious on that occasion, with the expectation of shortly receiving some liberal remuneration for the trouble she had been at, answered for her:—

"Yes, sir," said she, "this is her, poor girl; and I'm sure I don't know what she would have done—I cannot form any idea of what would have become of her, when her grandmother died—had it not been for me. I took her in, and——"

"It was very kind of you, no doubt, ma'am," interrupted Mr. Chester-ton, with an ironical smile; "and I am sorry that it is out of my power to reward you with anything but thanks. Now her grandmother is dead, Emily has no one but a distant relation in the world, and, certainly, none whose duty it is to support her; as for the annuity which Mrs. Fitzormond used to receive, it ceased from the moment of her demise—and, indeed, she had, for some years past, been paid a quarter in advance. Emily has, therefore, nothing more to expect than from the kindness and humanity of the distant relative to whom I have alluded, who has deputed me to put her in a situation, where, by perseverance and industry, she may probably do well."

The countenance of Mrs. Dartmouth fell when she heard what Ches-terton said, and which entirely crushed the sanguine expectations she had formed; while the heart of Emily was full almost to bursting, and while her eyes streamed with tears, and sobs, that almost choked her utterance, she said—

"Oh, sir, rather than I would be beholden to the charity of one, whom you say is *a very distant relation*—and who, at any rate, is a stranger to me—let me be left to my fate, and Heaven, I trust, will become that pro-tector which those who had an undoubted right to be, have neglected be-coming, and have so long, and cruelly deserted me."

"Nay, nay, my dear girl," said Chesterton, in even gentler tones than before, "you are inexperienced yet in the ways of the world, or you would not have made use of the rash expressions you just now gave utter-ance to. What, think you, a young girl like you, could do in it, left to yourself, and without friends or protectors?—Your destruction would be sure to follow!"

"And where are my parents?" said Emily, with more firmness than she had hitherto assumed; "what has become of them?—Why have they abandoned me—who are they—and what care can they have whether my destruction takes place or not?"

Chesterton seemed to be rather confused for a minute or two; but, at length, replied—

"When I told you just now that you had only one distant relation left in the world, you might have understood, child, that your parents were no more; but, upon that subject I cannot enter further. Let it suffice that the relation of whom I speak, has full authority to take charge of you, and that I am chosen to convey you to the place which he has selected for your future residence, where you will be treated with every kindness and in-dulgence; and you will have, I am certain, no cause to regret the change. Come, come, dry your tears, and prepare for the journey we must under-take directly."

Emily trembled more violently than before, in spite of the assurances of Mr. Chesterton, who, all the time, was eyeing her with looks of admi-ration, and with other demonstrations that were only calculated to excite disgust.

"Well, sir," observed Mrs. Dartmouth, who had been standing by, and biting her lips with vexation, and impatiently awaiting an opportunity to

speak, "I suppose, if you think the trouble I have been at in taking care
of the girl, and managing the funeral of her grandmother, unworthy of
any remuneration, you will pay me for the fortnight's board and lodging
she has had of me?"

"I thought you acted from disinterested motives, and entirely out of pure
kindness, Mrs. Dartmouth," returned Chesterton, with the same disagreeable, sarcastic grin, in which he was in the habit of clothing his countenance.

"Pure kindness, indeed," reiterated Mrs. Dartmouth, her face glowing
like fire—"pure kindness!—It's all very fine for your gentry folks to be
humane when they have got plenty of money, but poor people can't afford
to be kind without they are paid for it. I have got something else to do
with my money, for which I work hard enough, without squandering it
away in keeping a parcel of strangers!"

"What has become of the furniture of the late Mrs. Fitzormond?" demanded Chesterton.

"It remains in the cottage where she lived, to be sure," replied Mrs.
Dartmouth; "I haven't touched a thing. But, perhaps, you have an in-
ventory of the goods which she had, and, therefore, can satisfy yourself."

"That furniture I give to you," said Chesterton; "perhaps that will
recompense you for the trouble and expense you may have been at?"

"Recompense me!" cried Mrs. Fitzormond, "what, a few wretched sticks
like them, that are only fit to be burnt for firewood?"

"It is all that you will have, and quite enough, too, I think," said Chesterton—"come, my dear, are you ready to depart; for our journey is a long
one?"

N. 3

Emily's heart sunk within her, and she shrunk back with a feeling of terror, as Mr. Chesterton attempted to take her hand.

"Whither, sir, would you take me?" she asked, as with a sensation of horror she thought upon the man who had visited Mrs. Fitzormond at "The White Cottage," and she feared that it was to his power she was about to be consigned; "tell me, under whose protection is it settled by my unknown relative, that I shall be in future?"

"Be satisfied, my dear girl," answered Chesterton, "that you are going where you will be properly looked after, and that everything is being done for the best; more, at present, I cannot tell you. But, come, this delay is useless. We will partake of refreshment on the road, and I am anxious to pursue our journey as quick as possible."

Emily in vain tried to conquer the repugnance which filled her breast; but, seeing the utter uselessness of not complying with the request of Chesterton, she turned to Mrs. Dartmouth, and with much affection, bade her farewell, and hoped that some time or the other, it might please God to put it in her power to reward her for the kindness and trouble she had bestowed upon her. The woman returned only some disagreeable answer, and Chesterton taking the hand of the almost unconscious maiden, led her to the carriage at the door, into which he handed her, and they were then driven off with great rapidity, before Emily was scarcely aware that they had left the cottage of Mrs. Dartmouth.

The sun was shining in full meridian splendour, as the vehicle drove away from that scene where Emily had passed the days of her childhood —days which, while they brought to her memory many things that caused regret, likewise reminded her of many joyful associations, she could not quit without the most intense anguish. It was a beautiful summer-day, and Nature was clothed in her gayest attire; the pearly dew of morn yet trembled on the emerald carpet of the earth, and fragrance filled the air around. Not a cloud—not a speck was to be seen on the clear blue sky, to which the lark soared, making the air resound with the mellifluous notes he warbled as he ascended. Everything around seemed to be unusually gay; but, alas! how different were the feelings of poor Emily. To her, nothing could impart the least consolation; everything she gazed upon seemed to bear an aspect of gloom, for their gaiety was dissonant with the state of her mind.

As the carriage rolled its way along, the eyes of Emily rested upon every well-known spot and object, with sentiments that may easily be conceived. She noticed each lowly cottage, inhabited by some one who had been kind to her, or by one of her young companions; they were happy, although poverty was their only lot, but, alas! she was sad, for she should see them no more; and where should she look for companions—for such friends, as the young and simple friends of her childhood had been, in the cold and cheerless world?—No more should she behold those hills, those vallies, over which she had so often frolicked! From amidst the green foliage, which sheltered the road they were travelling, on either side, Emily caught a glimpse of the tall spire of the village church, and immediately afterwards, its bells chimed forth a merry peal. It was a day of rejoicing in the neighbourhood, for it was the anniversary of the Lord of the Manor's birth. Emily was affected to tears; how many times had she listened with delight to the cheerful sound of those bells; how often had she sat within the old church-porch, and become entranced with a sort of holy delight in their mirthful tones. And did she now listen to them for the last time?—Was she no more to behold that venerable structure, to which her and her grandmother never failed to go every sabbath, (although the latter seemed always in a dreadful state of anguish while she was in it, and every sentence which the clergyman gave utterance to, appeared to penetrate her brain, and rack her nearly to frenzy)?—Alas! something seemed to whisper to her that she was not, and that she would henceforth be a stranger to the small portion of happiness that had hitherto been apportioned to her. A dismal presentiment filled her mind that she was doomed to be the victim of misfortune, and a dead weight pressed upon her heart, and made her more wretched than could very well be expressed.

And whither was she going?—To whom had she entrusted herself?—To an entire stranger; to a man who refused to give any satisfactory explanation of his motives and intentions, and whose very looks, unacquainted as she was with human nature, convinced her that the hypocrite and the villain lurked in his heart! She shuddered with an indefinite feeling of terror, as she thus reflected. But how could she have acted otherwise?—What other alternative had she, friendless, homeless, and unprotected, as the death of her grandmother had left her?—None? Besides, Mr. Chesterton had stated that he acted only by the instructions, and upon the authority of the only person who was related to her, and she knew not that opposition on her part would have been of any avail. She could do nothing, therefore, but confide in the will and protection of Providence, who she trusted would prove to her a better friend than any earthly power.

They had soon left the neighbourhood in which the early days of Emily had been passed, and the scenery became changed. They were travelling a cross-country road, and the prospect was very romantic and diversified; but Emily's mind was too fully occupied with other subjects, to feel any pleasure in gazing upon it, and had they been journeying across a dreary waste, she would not have beheld it with more indifference.

Hitherto Mr. Chesterton had suffered her to indulge the thoughts that stole over her mind, in silence, but he had been gazing at her with earnest looks of admiration, which Emily had once or twice noticed with much uneasiness. She could not help feeling a secret dread in his company for which she was, at the same time, utterly at a loss to account.

After they had proceeded for some distance, however, Mr. Chesterton broke the silence, by inquiring of her, with an assumed look of sympathy, what made her so sad?

"Oh, sir," replied Emily, timidly, and endeavouring to conceal her repugnance, "can you wonder that I should be sad, when I am about to quit those scenes in which I have passed the greater portion of my life, to go among strangers?"

"You are no stranger to them, child," returned Chesterton, "although you may not remember them."

"And have they, then, seen me before, sir?" eagerly asked Emily, catching quickly at Chesterton's words. He seemed confused, and anxious to recall what he had said.

Emily sighed.

"For what reason," she inquired, "is there so much mystery preserved in everything connected with me?—Am I considered so hateful, so disgraceful a being, that neither my parents, or any other relations, will acknowledge me?"

"Nay, it is not so, Emily," returned Chesterton, "but there is a peculiarity attached to your fate, which renders it imperative upon those who know you, to preserve that mystery for the present, which appears to you so strange and unaccountable."

"For the *present*, you say, sir," eagerly ejaculated Emily; "oh, tell me, then, are there any hopes that the secret which hangs over my fate will be ever divulged?"

" That all depends upon circumstances, child," was Chesterton's answer ; " but you say that none of your relatives have acknowledged you, when, at the same time, have you not been brought up by your grandmother, Mrs. Fitzormond ?"

" Yes," returned Emily, with an incredulous look, "*if she was my grandmother !*"

" *If she was*," repeated Chesterton, with some surprise and confusion in his manner ; " and have you, then, any reason to doubt that she was— eh ?"

" Why," said Emily, in reply, " I do not know that I ought to doubt our consanguinity, for she ever behaved with kindness to me ; but, then, there was a mystery in her manners which created my suspicions, and raised thoughts in my mind that would not otherwise have entered it ;— and, then, the poor soul, on her death-bed, told me she had a secret to impart, on which depended my future happiness ; but before she could give utterance to it, she slept the sleep which has no morrow."

" Ah !" cried Chesterton, starting, and turning pale as Emily spoke, " and did the old woman try to——But, are you certain she did not reveal anything ?"

" Nothing," replied Emily, noticing, with much astonishment, the perturbation of her companion ; " but, alas ! I fear me that something weighed heavily upon her conscience, for she died in much agony—mental agony I mean—and she accused herself of being a guilty wretch, unworthy of pity."

" The old idiot !" exclaimed Chesterton, in a tone of passion, and with an expression of countenance, which rendered him still more revolting than ever to Emily, " after keeping her counsel for so many years, and about to blab after all !—It was lucky, however, that death prevented her."

Emily turned from him with a look which sufficiently explained to him the disgust his brutal speech had excited in her bosom, and Chesterton, after endeavouring to banish the demonstration of his emotion from his countenance, said,—

" But are you still positive that Mrs. Fitzormond never divulged anything which could lead you to surmise to whom you belonged, and what could be their reasons for wishing you to be brought up in so private a manner ?"

" I have before assured you, sir," answered our heroine, " that she did not."

" 'Tis well," muttered Chesterton, in a low tone to himself, but which Emily overheard ; " then, all is safe."

" And what danger have you to apprehend, sir," interrogated Emily, " from my coming to a knowledge of any of the circumstances connected with this dark mystery ?—Oh, surely where there is so much secrecy and precaution used, it must be prompted by some guilty cause."

Mr. Chesterton frowned, and made no answer for a few minutes, but it was evident that the words of Emily very much disconcerted him, and that he repented having entered upon the subject.

" Whatever are the motives (which you have been pleased to put the worst construction upon) that have prompted your friends to act in the manner they have done," at length, he replied, " rest assured that they originated in a sense of justice and prudence, and that time may, perhaps, unravel, what to you now appears so ambiguous and suspicious ; but enough of this for the present."

" One question more, sir," ejaculated Emily, with considerable agitation, as strange ideas flitted through her brain, " tell me, are the authors of my being still living ?—I implore you not to deceive me !"

"Have I not already informed you, child," replied Chesterton, in a voice of assumed sympathy; "have I not already informed you that you have now only a distant relation living? But do not let that afflict you; you have friends who will look after you and protect you, and while you continue to deserve it, there will be no moderate or reasonable enjoyment which you will not experience. Of this be satisfied, that among those friends you have not a more attached or sincere one, my dear girl, than Mr. Chesterton."

As he spoke, he endeavoured to take her hand, and an expression passed over his features, which filled the bosom of Emily with a sentiment of fear and disgust.

"Nay, child," he continued, after a pause, "you must not evince this coldness and indifference of manners, especially towards those who have sincerely your best interests at heart."

"If you really were sincere in your protestations, sir," answered Emily, "you would not hesitate to reveal to me all that you know of my family and connections, so that I might know on what I have to depend; but where there is so much mystery, there cannot be any good. Would to Heaven that I had not quitted that spot where I passed my early days, in the company of one whom I know not, and whose intentions, from the ambiguity of his conduct, I have so much cause to suspect."

"How much you wrong me, Emily," said Chesterton, in accents of reproach; "but time will shew you how little I merit the unfavourable opinion you have formed of me. Believe me, my dear girl, that although this is the first time we have met, the feeling I entertain towards you is one of the most ardent description, and that there is nothing in my power which I would not willingly do to contribute to your happiness. Pray, then, endeavour to stifle your unaccountable prejudices against me, and let this kiss——"

"Sir," exclaimed the blushing maiden, while her eyes flashed with indignation as she spurned Chesterton away from her—"this rudeness, and from one who has but just this moment boasted of being my friend. Forbear! or instantly suffer me to quit the carriage, and leave me to my fate; it cannot be worse than that I have reason to apprehend from a man like you!"

Chesterton was evidently abashed, confounded, and astonished, to hear such observations from one so young, while, at the same time, the beauty and dignity of her countenance and demeanour, as she gave utterance to these words, served to increase those guilty passions with which she had inspired him; he, however, quickly recovered his self-possession, and with a look, which could not conceal his dissimulation from the penetrating eye of the offended Emily, he observed,—

"Pardon me, child, I meant not to offend you; my conduct was only suggested by the feeling, of what I may call parental love, which I imbibed for you the moment I saw you. But I see that you have been brought up in that simple and secluded manner, as to render you entirely ignorant of the ways of the world, and which causes you to put such unjust constructions upon actions that are blameless. But, pray quiet your apprehensions, and I assure you that that which has offended you shall never be repeated again."

Emily returned no answer, but she averted her head with a sentiment of resentment, and the tide of feelings which rushed to her heart, when she thought upon her destitute condition, and the uncertain and dangerous situation in which she was placed, overcame her, and, covering her face with her handkerchief, she gave free indulgence to her grief. Mr. Chesterton watched her earnestly for a few minutes, but did not offer to inter-

rupt her; and, then, affecting to be regarding the country they were travelling through, he became buried in deep thought, and Emily was thus
left to herself.

The scenery they were now traversing was extremely wild and unpleasant, and the roads were very bad, and did not appear to be much frequented. Emily had not yet broken her fast, although they had been
travelling for some hours, and in the course of that time had passed several
inns; but her heart was too full to suffer her to feel inclined to eat, and
looking from the carriage window, beheld in every object, that her eyes
encountered, something to increase her melancholy and despondency. All
the sorrowful and mysterious events that had recently occurred to her,
rushed to her memory—more particularly the death of her grandmother—
the dying secret—the awful vision—and the phantom which had afterwards appeared to her, and her breast became the abode of the most perplexing and dismal apprehensions and terrors. She had several times
questioned Chesterton as to whither, and how much further, they were
going; but he had always returned her some evasive answers, and which
only served to increase her doubts and suspicions. At length, Chesterton
did order the driver of the vehicle to stop at the door of a road-side inn,
and himself and Emily were shewn into a private room, where the former ordered refreshments—the landlord not seeming to take the least notice of our heroine, although she was so meanly attired, and, as it might
have been imagined, would have excited some curiosity, being seen with a
person clad so respectably as Chesterton. However, it soon appeared that
the landlord knew him, for Chesterton saluted him by his name, and they
exchanged compliments together, nothing more transpiring than a wink
which Emily observed him direct, first, to her, and then towards her
companion, and having placed the repast on the table before them, bowed,
and left them to themselves.

The fears of Emily now increased; but Chesterton treated her with the
most respectful kindness, and did not offer to renew that rudeness. which
she had before repulsed. He urged her to eat, but she only partook very
sparingly of the meal, and Chesterton having despatched his with the
greatest expedition, and fresh horses having been put to the carriage, he
conducted her once more towards it, and they renewed their journey with
the same speed that they had commenced it.

Chesterton tried frequently to engage Emily in conversation, upon different subjects, but she answered him with coldness, and shewed by her
manner that she wished to be left entirely to the indulgence of her own
thoughts.

"But tell me, Emily," at length, asked her companion, "have you no
recollection of anything which happened to you previous to you and your
grandmother going to the village from which I have just taken you?"

"Why, I was not more than three years old, at that time," answered
our heroine, "and, therefore, it can scarcely be expected that I can remember much. Yet, I have some faint idea of living somewhere else, although
it is like a dream to me!"

"Ah!" ejaculated Chesterton, eagerly, "this is strange. But, can you
recall to your memory the kind of place you inhabited, or what persons
were with you?"

"All that I can remember," returned Emily, "was sleeping in a very
large and gloomy apartment, which had the portrait of a man suspended
to the wall, and which, as well as I can call to my mind, represented features so repulsive, that my grandmother used to frighten me with it, whenever I proved refractory."

"And did no one live in the house but you and your grandmother?"

demanded Chesterton, after a pause, during which he appeared to be seriously ruminating upon what Emily had said.

"Oh, yes," answered our heroine, as fresh recollections darted across her mind, "I well remember, now, that there was a man, of whom both me and grandmother were afraid; for he was so savage in appearance, and used to swear so dreadfully, I used to scream with terror whenever I saw him, and for that reason, I suppose, we were seldom in his company, and used to confine ourselves to the old gloomy room, of which I have before spoken."

Chesterton muttered a few words to himself, which were inaudible to Emily, and his countenance became gloomy.

"And, think you, you should remember the place, or the man again?" he asked.

"Why, it is so long ago, and being but a child, that I do not think I should," replied Emily; "but, why are you so particular in questioning me?"

"Nothing, nothing," returned Chesterton, trying to conceal the emotion which the answers of Emily had evidently occasioned him. Our heroine turned away from him with a look of suspicion, and soon became immersed in the reflections to which his questions had given rise in her mind.

They continued to journey all the afternoon, and when night had set in, they entered upon a dreary wood, whose thickly intertwining branches rendered it almost impervious, and their way was only illumed by the partial rays of the moon, that penetrated between the foliage.—Here the fears of Emily increased, and she again inquired of Chesterton, in terrified accents, whither they were going. Chesterton, in his usual manner, requested her not to be alarmed, as they should soon be at the end of their journey, and that no harm was intended her; but Emily was not to be quieted by his assurances, and numerous terrible ideas darted across her imagination, which almost overpowered her.

"Good God!" she thought, "should it be the design of my enemies to murder me; and this man, who has pretended to be my friend, be the miscreant employed for that cruel purpose!—I am lost!"

A deadly sickness came over her, and her limbs trembled so violently, that she could scarcely keep from fainting. She, however, uttered up a mental prayer to Heaven for protection, and soon afterwards, when the carriage emerged from the wood, she became more composed and reassured.

They had now entered upon a wild and barren heath, and had not proceeded any considerable distance, when Emily, looking from the carriage window, perceived a light glimmering some way off across the heath, in the direction of which they were evidently proceeding.

"Ah, there is the place of our destination," said Chesterton, pointing towards the spot from whence the light issued; "our journey will soon be ended."

"And is it on this gloomy, this awful-looking spot, where I am in future to reside?" asked Emily, with a shudder of horror, as she looked with dismay upon the dreariness of all around.

"It is, child," answered Chesterton; "but, what do you fear?—The place is not half so dismal in the day-time as it appears now."

"Oh, Heaven! what will become of me?" exclaimed the trembling girl, clasping her hands together, and unable any longer to conceal the terror which filled her breast; "why am I brought to such a place as this, so lonely, and so frightful, if some harm is not intended me?—Oh, sir, if one spark of pity still remains within your bosom, suffer me to depart, and I will never appear to trouble you, or those by whom you are employed."

"Silly girl," returned Chesterton, "thus to give way to groundless terrors ; I tell you again that no harm shall befall you ; on the contrary, you will receive every comfort and attention from those into whose care I am going to commit you. There—there—be composed, my poor child, and all will be well."

Chesterton really did now seem to speak sincerely, and Emily became more composed ; and soon afterwards the vehicle stopped before a large stone house, built in the gothic style, the front of which was nearly concealed beneath the moss and ivy, which grew thickly upon it. A light (which was the one they had seen on the heath,) glimmered from a small, pointed upper-casement, and the whole aspect of the place, standing as it did on the borders of the heath, with no house near it, was dismal in the extreme. Emily could not help feeling a renewal of her fears, as she looked upon this gloomy fabric, and once more she implored the pity of Chesterton, who again tried to re-assure her, and alighting from the carriage, he advanced to a low porch, and knocked loudly at the door of the lone house. A second or two elapsed, and then the casement, from which the light issued, was slowly opened, and a man's head protruded from it, and a surly voice demanded who was there, and what they wanted.

CHAPTER IV.

THE RECEPTION.—THE PLOT OF BLOOD.—THE VILLAIN UNMASKED.

"Come, come, open the door, Gerald," said Chesterton, impatiently, in reply to the man's interrogatory, "don't keep us here all night, for the wind blows pretty keenly across the heath. I thought you would have expected me."

"Oh, it's you, Mr. Chesterton, is it ?" said Gerald ; "I beg your pardon—but, you see, I was not to know what sort of a visitor it was coming to me, and it behoves me to be rather cautious, or the traps——"

"Psha !" interrupted Chesterton, in a stern voice, "have you lost your senses, Gerald ?—But, make haste to the door."

Gerald left the casement, and soon afterwards made his appearance at the door, with a lamp in his hand. During the short colloquy which we have quoted above, Emily had been trembling in the vehicle, and the appearance of the man was by no means calculated to abate her terrors. He was a tall, stout man, dressed like a game-keeper in a dark velveteen coatee, with immense pearl buttons, light corded breeches, and long leather gaiters. He appeared to be about fifty years of age, and his features were strongly marked, and very irregular. There were several scars upon his face, which added much to its repulsive character, and a pair of immense sandy whiskers, nearly covered his cheeks, and extended beneath his chin. This unprepossessing object whispered a few sentences to Chesterton, which the latter replied to in the same low tone, and then approached the carriage and offered his arm to Emily to alight, but she shrunk back in the vehicle with terror.

"Oh, do not place me in the power of that man," she earnestly supplicated, while her tears flowed so fast that she could scarcely speak ; "his very looks are sufficient to strike terror to my heart ! In pity, spare me, and I will for ever bless you for the action !"

"Nay, my dear, this is ridiculous," observed Chesterton ; "once more I

repeat, you have no cause to fear any danger; Gerald Darnley is a homely, plainly spoken man. but you will find him and his wife, I assure you, two very worthy sort of people, who will do all that is in their power to make you comfortable.

"The lass seems to be very timid," said Gerald Darnley, advancing to the vehicle, holding the lamp up, and staring boldly in our heroine's face; "come, come, my girl, do not be afraid; you will find everything very comfortable inside, although it is called the Old Lone House of the Heath."

Emily shuddered at the mention of the name of the gothic pile of building, and the tones in which Gerald Darnley delivered himself; in fact, the aspect of the house, which was large and gloomy, and the wild and dreary character of the country around, were not calculated to inspire any other feeling than that of terror, especially in the bosom of a young and timid girl, who had never been among strangers before; and, in spite of the dread and repugnance with which she viewed Chesterton, she clang to him with fear, and looking up in his face with earnest expressions of supplication, she exclaimed,—

"Oh, sir, why am I brought to this frightful-looking place?—And what are the designs of those who call themselves my friends against me?—For pity's sake, tell me, and pause ere you plunge into misery, perhaps destruction, an unfortunate girl, who is totally unconscious of ever having injured you!"

"Humph!" ejaculated Gerald, surlily, and scowling upon her, "the young lady appears to be rather particular · but she may think herself very well off, if she never has a worse roof than that of the Lone House to live under, or such friends as Gerald Darnley and his wife. But I am

No. 4

not going to stand here like a fool all night; are you coming in Mr. Chesterton, or not?—if not, say so; go somewhere else to-night, and call upon me, if you like, in the morning."

" Come, come, Gerald," said Chesterton, "be not so impatient; the poor girl is naturally alarmed, for she has not been used to travel among strangers, but always been brought up tied to her grandmother's apron strings."

" Her *grandmother!*" repeated Gerald, emphatically, and an ironical smile overspread his repulsive features. Chesterton gave him a significant look, and then observed,—

" No doubt she will soon grow contented and happy enough when she finds how kindly you behave to her."

" Aye, aye," said the man, " I dare say she will."

" Now, my dear," remonstrated Mr. Chesterton, " pray arouse yourself; I tell you again, you have nothing to fear. Come, come, the night air is chilly standing here. Just hold the light up a little higher, Gerald; it is rather awkward footing here, and you have suffered the rank weeds and furze to grow so in the door-way, that a person can hardly make their way in."

" This way, this way, gently," observed Gerald, as Chesterton led the trembling Emily from the carriage to the ancient porch of the Lone House, which fully answered the description he had given of it. She felt an icy chill upon her heart as she crossed the threshold of this dismal place, and an awful foreboding, of she knew not what, crossed her mind.

Having traversed a dark passage, Gerald Darnley threw open a heavy oaken-door, and ushered them into a room of such capacious dimensions, that part of it was buried in darkness, notwithstanding the light which Gerald carried in his hand, and the remains of a large fire which was in the grate. It had a most ancient and dreary appearance, and was hung around with portraits, in a state of decay, whose originals, from their costumes, appeared to have lived about the reign of Queen Elizabeth. The tables and chairs were of oak, and of the most massive description, being probably co-eval with the date of the building, and, in fact, all the furniture corresponded with the Gothic appearance of the house.

" You ought to consider yourself a happy fellow, Gerald," observed Chesterton, looking around him ; " you have this old mansion all to yourself, and ought to feel as independent as one of our old lords in his strong and impregnable castle; you are not frequently troubled with visitors, I presume."

" Oh, no," answered Gerald, " and the less the better ; the set that we might expect would, doubtless, be more free than welcome. But the young lady had better draw up to the fire; it is none too warm to-night, and the wind begins to howl without at a rare rate. Well, e'en let it rattle; it cannot injure these old walls; they are strong as rocks, and seem likely to remain so for many ages to come yet. There, there—that's it; make yourself quite at home; oh, we shall become better acquainted by and by, I warrant. I will call old Madge, and she'll prepare some supper, you must be hungry with travelling."

" Where's Will?" asked Chesterton; " I want him to assist in putting up the carriage."

" He's out on a *little business,*" answered Gerald, winking his eye significantly at Chesterton, " and it is uncertain what time he may return.— But the men who drove you can manage to put up the vehicle, I should think, by themselves. What, ho! Madge! Madge!"

While Gerald Darnley was speaking, Emily had been watching his countenance narrowly, and its savage appearance smote her heart with terror. Was she then to be left to the care of such a man as this, the very sight of whom filled her bosom with the most unconquerable dread? Alas! what would become of her?—Shut up, too, in such a frightful place as the Lone House, where there was no habitation near, or any person of whom she might beg protection, should she be exposed to danger or ill-treatment!

She was interrupted in these reflections by the entrance of Madge, as Gerald had called her.

She was a tall, bony, masculine woman, about fifty, with very prominent cheek-bones; a large nose, small, cunning-looking eyes; a wide mouth, and teeth that projected far over her lips. She was a Scotchwoman, and spoke with a broad accent.

When she beheld Emily, she started back a few paces, and gazed with a rude look of curiosity upon her, and then addressing herself to Gerald, she said,—

"Th' deil, laddie! an' wha ha'e ye got here?—What chiel is this?"

"Why, I should have thought you might have guessed who it was, Madge," replied Gerald; "there, don't stand staring and gaping like a fool; this is the young girl, Emily, whom Mr. Chesterton wrote to us about."

"Oh, I ken now," said Madge, advancing nearer towards our heroine, and looking still more narrowly upon her; "she be muckle welcome, an', thof I say it mysel', she will nae find a better woman in a' th' warld than Madge Darnley."

"There, let's have no more of your nonsense, Madge," exclaimed Gerald, impatiently, "but put some supper on the table, for the young girl, I dare say, is hungry. I'll back you, for length of tongue, against any other woman in the country."

"Ma conscience! Gerald," cried Madge, "I ken ye be getting daft, or ye would nae talk sae silly, laddie; I were only——"

"Damn what you were doing!" interrupted Gerald Darnley, passionately; "go and do as I tell you, or we shall have a quarrel."

"Come, come, my good people," observed Chesterton, in an expostulatory tone, as he observed the terror evinced by Emily, at the coarse language of Gerald and his wife; "don't be angry with one another, for I'm sure there is no occasion for it. Nay, nay, Gerald, don't be so hasty; Madge meant no harm, and all women will talk you know."

"Yes," said Gerald, "and some will talk rather too fast, where they ought to hold their tongue. She had better mind that she don't do so some of these days, that's all."

"Ma conscience!" cried Madge, with a stupid expression of countenance. and raising her hands and eyes as she spoke; and she then immediately made her exit to do her husband's bidding.

"While she was gone, Gerald walked to one corner of the room and took up a gun that was standing there, tried the lock, replaced it, and resumed his seat by the fire-side. Chesterton fixed his eyes upon Emily, and addressed a few words to her, which were meant to re-assure her, and inspire her with confidence, but she returned him no answer; her heart was too full to suffer her to speak, and she averted her head.

In a short time Madge returned with the repast, and attended by a young girl of about sixteen, of rather a pretty and interesting appearance. A ray of pleasure darted into the bosom of our heroine when she saw her, for she hoped in her to find a companion, and one who might sympathize in her misfortunes. While Madge and her were spreading the cloth, the eyes of Emily and this girl frequently met, and the former thought she could discern an expression of kindness and pity in the countenance of the latter, which inspired her with hope, and she longed for an opportunity to speak to her. She soon ascertained that she was the only daughter of Gerald and Madge Darnley, although there was such a vast disparity in their appearance, that it seemed almost impossible.

Emily partook sparingly of the supper, not because she wanted it, but for fear of exciting the displeasure of those in whose power she now was; and when that was over, and Madge and Patty had cleared the table, Chesterton and Gerald drew their chairs closer into the chimney corner, and commenced talking to each other in an under tone, the purport of which conversation Emily could not understand, and, in fact, could only catch a word here and there, and that was so unconnected, that it was perfectly unintelligible to her.

It was not long before they were interrupted by a loud knocking, and accompanied by the tones of a man's voice, who requested them to open the door.

"It is my son, Will," remarked Gerald, rising; "he has returned sooner than I expected."

Gerald Darnley quitted the room, for the purpose of admitting the new comer, and soon afterwards returned, accompanied by a tall, powerful-made young man, who was dressed exactly like his father. His countenance, which was good-looking, was, nevertheless, determined in its expression, and when he entered the room, Emily perceived a frown upon it, as if something had occurred to vex him.

"Well, Will, my boy," said Chesterton, familiarly, "I have come to see you again. What success now?"

"Oh, don't ask me," said Will, dashing his hat on the table, and throwing himself carelessly into a chair; "confounded bad luck; I have been disappointed to-night."

"Ah!" quickly exclaimed his father, starting to his feet, and gazing intently upon his son; "how's that?"

"He did not come!"

"Damnation!"

"Aye, so I say," returned Will, "for it has disappointed us of one of the richest——"

"Hush!" hastily interrupted Gerald, nodding his head, and directing his son's attention to Emily, who was sitting in a corner, where Will could not perceive her on his first entrance into the room; but when he beheld her, he jumped up with an exclamation of surprise, and approaching close up to her, looked in her countenance with evident astonishment and admiration.

"Why, who have we here, father?" demanded Will.

Gerald Darnley briefly informed him; and his son evidently heard that Emily was about to become an inmate of the house, with a feeling of pleasure.

"Well, as I live," remarked he, "she is a fine wench—even prettier than sister, Patty—and that's paying her no mean compliment. How are you, my dear?—I'm glad to see you!"

Chesterton frowned, and was evidently displeased at the tone of familiarity in which Will spoke; while poor Emily felt her situation becoming every minute more painful.

"Why, bless her blue eyes, how bashful she is," observed Will; "nay, Mr. Chesterton, you need not look so black; there is no harm in a young man admiring and complimenting a pretty girl, only you old men——"

Mr. Chesterton frowned more deeply than he had done before, and interrupted Will by saying,—

"Hold your tongue, Will Darnley, or I may be offended; Emily has not been used to hear such language as this."

"I dare say not," replied Will, with a significant smile, "if she has been long in your society. You are not quite insensible to female beauty yet, although you are not so young as you were formerly."

"Hold thy peace, boy!" commanded Gerald, peremptorily; "Mr. Chesterton, perhaps the young woman is tired and fatigued, and would like to go to rest; so Patty shall show her to a chamber."

Emily gladly availed herself of the opportunity to escape from the disagreeable situation in which she was now placed, and having intimated her anxiety to seek repose, after the fatigue of her journey, she arose, and, making a powerful effort to conquer her agitation, she faltered out 'good night,' and advanced towards Patty, who was standing with the lamp in her hand, ready to conduct her to the chamber allotted to her.

"The blue chamber!" said Gerald, addressing himself to Patty;— "don't you understand?—What do you stand there staring for, as if you were silly?—The blue chamber, I say."

"I beg pardon, father," replied Patty, in gentle accents, "but, had not the young girl better sleep with me?—There is plenty of room, and it will be company."

"Will you do as I tell you?" demanded her father, in a coarse voice. "What the devil business have you to interfere?"

"Oh, I would much rather sleep in the same chamber as your daughter, sir," said Emily, as she noticed the increased kindness of the former's looks; and a secret dread came over her at the idea of being left to sleep alone in one of the dreary apartments of the Lone House; "if it is convenient, you would much oblige me if you would permit me to do so."

"But it is not convenient," returned Gerald, frowning at Patty;— "besides, you cannot have a more comfortable chamber than the one I have allotted to you; only that little fool is always interfering where she has no business."

"Ma conscience!" ejaculated Madge, "I should muckle like to ken where ye wad find a better room than that; an' didna I clean it all over, wi' my twa precious han's, only t'dee?—Ye wadna see sic anither clean room in a' th' country, lassie."

"Good night, child," said Chesterton, with his usual affectation of kindness and affection, "you need not be under any apprehension, but that Mr. Darnley and his good dame will do everything for your comfort and accommodation. Good night!"

Emily could not respond to this wish; but, placing herself under the guidance of Patty, she was glad to hurry from the room as quick as possible, more especially as she beheld the eyes of Will Darnley fixed upon her with an expression, which created an unpleasant sensation in her bosom.

Patty unlocked a door in the wainscotting of the room they had been sitting in, and a flight of stairs were immediately revealed. They ascended these, and came directly to the door of the chamber mentioned by Gerald Darnley, which they entered, and Patty sat the light upon the table.

The room was a small one, and certainly had not an uncomfortable appearance; it was furnished in the same old-fashioned style as the apartment below, and in one corner was a bed, which was remarkable for the cleanliness of its appearance.

Emily having taken a hasty survey of the chamber, turned her eyes once more upon Patty, and perceived that she was gazing at her with looks of sympathy and the utmost affection

"Oh, tell me!" exclaimed Emily, encouraged by these demonstrations on the part of the girl—"oh, tell me, what am I brought hither for?—What are the intentions of——"

"Hush, Miss, for goodness sake," interrupted Patty, fearfully, and placing her hand upon Emily's lips, "should my father overhear us, I know not what might be the consequences Good night, and God bless you!—You will find a friend in me Some other time I will tell you all I know, and——"

"Are you going to stay there all night, Patty?" at that moment, exclaimed the gruff voice of her father, "come down stairs, I say!"

"I must go," whispered Patty, in great haste, "good bye, and Heaven protect you from all harm!"

Having given utterance to these expressions, Patty smiled kindly upon our heroine, and then hurried down the stairs

For a minute or two after she was gone, Emily sat herself down on the side of the bed, and gave way to the numerous reflections that arose to her mind, upon her present strange situation, and the consequences that, in all probability, might result from it What were the real characters of Gerald Darnley and his son? From many words that escaped them, and their behaviour altogether, she was inclined to put the worst construction upon their characters, and the calling they pursued in fact, there were several words that had come to her ears, that filled her mind with the most dreadful suspicions, and it was, therefore, not too hasty in her to conclude that she was brought there for some sinister purpose, and had everything to dread from Gerald Darnley Mr Chesterton, too, she remembered his behaviour to her on the journey, and the strange looks he ever and anon fixed upon her, and when she weighed all these circumstances in her mind, she was filled with the most serious doubts and fears The words, too, and manner of Patty, did not tend in the least to alleviate her anxiety and suspicions, for it was very evident the girl was aware that she was not altogether safe there, and that she had been brought thither for no good purpose, or else she would not have expressed so much commiseration for her, for if she was in a place where she would be treated with the kindness and indulgence Mr Chesterton had described to her she was not by any means an object of pity, but ought rather to feel extremely happy to find such a home, and such friends, in her otherwise destitute condition

The dreariness of the prospect from the casement in her chamber—which was barred across, and only commanded a view of the dismal heath, upon the borders of which the Lone House stood—was not by any means calculated to lessen the terrors under which she laboured, and the idea of sleeping in the same house, and at the mercy of those who had inspired those fears, increased her uneasiness ten fold The melancholy circumstances of the last few weeks, all passed in retrospection before her mind's eye, the death of Mrs. Fitzormond, the mystery—the painful mystery—attending her last moments, the appalling dream, which had afterwards haunted her imagination, and the still more appalling phantom of the old woman, which she was confident had appeared to her, the letter from her unknown relative—the arrival of Chesterton, the boldness of his address, and his behaviour on the journey, and as they did, she could not help thinking that she had every cause to feel that poignant anguish which at present racked her mind, and distracted her brain

Again, what could have been the motives of Gerald Darnley in refusing the request of his daughter to suffer her (Emily) to sleep with her, unless it was that he had some evil intentions towards her, which he was fearful that Patty would divulge?—Yes, yes, it was too certain; she was the victim of some cruel plot of iniquity, and as she thus reflected, the agony of her mind became so intense that she could scarcely support herself. Oh, that she was once more at liberty, even in the hopeless, friendless, unprotected situation, which her grandmother had left her; anything would be preferable to her present situation, where she was in the power of those whose intentions she could not fathom, although their mysterious behaviour, and many other circumstances, all tended to convince her they were no good.

"Alas!" she soliloquized, "what a terrible fate is mine, so young, and yet it seems that I am destined for misfortune. Almighty Father, rather take me hence, than suffer me to remain in the world merely to be its sport."

A loud talking from below interrupted her, and excited her curiosity.—She listened, and distinguished in the tones, the voices of Gerald Darnley and Mr. Chesterton, who appeared to be engaged in loud altercation. She advanced to the door on tip-toe, and, after listening attentively, ventured to open it gently. For a few moments her agitation was too great to suffer her to understand the theme of their discourse, but, at length, the voice of Chesterton vibrated on her ears, and gave utterance to the following words in a conciliatory tone,—

"Psha! Gerald, what is the use of your getting into such a passion?—We should not quarrel about such a trifle as this; I should have thought we had known one another too long for that —You shall have everything in reason which you may demand, and——"!

"I will have it," interrupted the other, fiercely, "and neither you nor your master dare refuse me! If you dare, look to it, that's all!"

"You talk like a madman, Gerald," said Chesterton; "who is going to do anything of the kind?—Of course, we all three know each other too well to wish to divide friendship. Come, come, man, have a little reason in you; I'm sure I offer you fair enough; fifty guineas, in addition to the money his lordship agreed to give for the assassination of the girl, to save her life, and accede to my wishes, by retaining her for the indulgence of those desires her charms have inspired me with, and——"

At this moment a faint scream of horror, which Emily found it impossible longer to repress, escaped her bosom, and she immediately heard the two villains below, start, after which the voice of Gerald Darnley exclaimed,—

"What noise was that?"

"It sounded like a scream," was the reply from his companion.

"So I thought," returned Gerald; "should——but, nonsense, we are alarming ourselves to no purpose; it was only one of the owls who have taken up their habitation in different parts of this building, I dare say."

"Ah! no doubt of it," observed Chesterton; "and now, Gerald, let you and I understand each other. Two hundred guineas is the sum his lordship offers you, to rid him of this girl!"

"Well!"

"The two hundred guineas are yours—I add fifty more to them; save your conscience a deed of blood, and yet you refuse."

"To be sure I do, and will refuse; as for the deed of blood, I think nothing of it, and would rather it was done out of the way; for, should his lordship afterwards discover I have deceived him, and that the girl is living, I should lose a good customer. On the other hand, if this young and beautiful girl is not worth more than fifty guineas, why, she is not worth having at all."

"What do you require, then?"

"An equal sum to that which his lordship has offered for her destruction" answered Gerald Darnley, boldly, and in a determined manner."

"What! two hundred guineas?"

"Aye; not a farthing less; if that is not paid, she dies."

"Hear me, Gerald——"

"I have told you my resolution, and have nothing further to say upon the subject," interrupted the villain, Gerald Darnley; "do you agree?"

"Think better of it, Gerald; your demand is unreasonable."

"Psha!"

"One hundred I will give, and take all the responsibility upon my own shoulders, should it be found out that you have not made away with the girl."

"Not a shilling less than I have demanded; as for his lordship, you need not think that I am going to let him off so cheaply. He shall add many a bright guinea to the two hundred before I have done with him.— Come, decide at once; I am not going to stand parleying here all night."

"I suppose I must yield to your demands," said Chesterton; "I have fixed my mind upon the girl, and will have her; although it is a great deal of money."

"A mere trifle to a man of your resources," replied Gerald Darnley, sarcastically; "you know his lordship will have to pay for all!—Ha! ha!"

"Bah! I am not in any humour for jesting, Gerald."

"Indeed it is no joke, as his lordship's coffers must feel," returned Gerald.

"Well, no matter," hastily observed Chesterton, "then, it is an understanding?"

"You are to give me two hundred guineas?"

"The life of the girl is to be saved?"

"Of course."

"You are to make his lordship believe that she is no more?"

"Exactly."

"You will also behave kindly towards her, and use all your best endeavours to promote the success of my designs upon her?"

"Aye, aye."

"Enough, then, it is a bargain!—Here is the money. I will remain in the neighbourhood for a short time, (having written his lordship a letter, informing him that his fears are at rest,) and will pay occasional visits here; if I fail to persuade her to yield to my desires, you must then admit me, some night, to her chamber secretly, and my triumph will be certain."

"It shall be so!"

Language would be too weak to pourtray the feelings of horror that harrowed up the soul of Emily, as she listened to this base and guilty plot; supporting herself by the door-post, she was again unable to restrain a louder expression of terror than before.

"Did you hear that?" ejaculated the harsh and discordant voice of Gerald Darnley.

"I did," replied Chesterton; "that was not the screech of an owl, I am certain; it seemed to proceed from the room up stairs."

"Ah! by Hell! should she have been listening, her life shall pay the penalty of her curiosity!" cried Gerald. "Fools that we were

to act so incautiously. Follow me, Chesterton; I will ascertain the truth of this !"

How the distracted Emily trembled when she heard the wretches move across the room, and approach the door, opening upon the flight of stairs which led up to the chamber in which she was. A deadly faintness came over her, but yet she did not lose her presence of mind. She heard the door at the foot of the stairs unfastened, and in an instant she stepped lightly into the apartment, and silently closed her own, extinguished her light in a moment, and jumped into bed with her clothes on, pulling them over her, and feigning a deep sleep. She had scarcely done so, when she heard the two villains at the door, and the following moment, Gerald Darnley said,—

"All is still; we must have been again mistaken. Ah !—she has not fastened the door; we will, therefore, soon ascertain whether we have deceived ourselves or not."

"Great God assist me, or I am lost !" mentally ejaculated the agonized Emily, as her chamber door was thrown open, the two wretches entered, and advanced towards the bed on which she was reclining. She had the greatest difficulty in the world to repress the utterance of her terror, and to act in a manner which was at all likely to deceive Gerald Darnley and Chesterton. It was, indeed, a moment of horror, and Omnipotence alone could have empowered her with strength sufficient to endure it.

Gerald Darnley passed the light two or three times across her eyes, and turning to his companion, said,—

"She sleeps sound enough; so it is very clear that we have been again mistaken. Come, come, Chesterton, let us to the room below, and dissolve this meeting, since it now appears we perfectly understand each other."

No. 5

"By Heaven !" ejaculated Chesterton, "I could gaze on her for ever, and with each glance would my transport increase. How beauteous she looks in sleep, and yet she is very pale; probably from the fatigue of the journey, and the state of agitation her mind has been in for the last few days. Sleep on, fair maid, for the present, in peace; ere long these arms shall clasp you to my bosom, and revel in the enjoyment of your innumerable charms !"

" 'Psha !" testily exclaimed Gerald Darnley, as he laid hold of the aged libertine's arm, and hurried him out of the room. They closed the door after them, and Emily had no sooner heard them descend the stairs, than she rushed from the bed, and falling upon her knees, with streaming eyes, she poured forth her gratitude to the Almighty, for her preservation from the dreadful fate which had only a minute or two before threatened her. She then carefully locked the door, and listened to hear whether any one was stirring below, but all was still, and she, therefore, concluded that the wretches had separated, and had retired to their chambers.

CHAPTER VI.

THE OLD ROOM.—THE ATTACK.—THE RESCUE.—THE OATH.

THE distraction, the agony, the suffering, which Emily's mind underwent, after the event we have described in the foregoing chapter, may be imagined, but cannot, by any possibility, be properly described. To retire to bed, she could not think upon, and, involved in complete darkness, she traversed her chamber, and gave vent to the powerful emotions, which the horrors she had overheard had given rise to in her bosom.—Then, this relation, this *friend*—as the wretch Chesterton had described him to be—had doomed her to a horrible death, from which it appeared she was only to be saved to meet with a still more dreadful doom. Good God ! could there possibly be such monsters in existence ?—And who was this lord, to whom she was apparently so obnoxious ?—Why should he wish to take her life, when she knew him not, and had not any means, therefore, of annoying him ?—What relation could he be ? Her heart recoiled from the bare idea of being connected by the ties of consanguinity with such a monster ?—And, yet, perhaps that wretch, that miscreant, was her father ! The thought drove her to madness, and her anguish became almost insupportable. But the villany of Chesterton and Gerald Darnley exceeded all that she had ever heard of before, or had formed the slightest conception that it could exist in the human mind. Was it possible that that hoary-headed man, who affected so much kindness and benevolence, should contemplate the violation of a poor, friendless, deserted girl, to whom he was old enough to be a grandfather. The thought was so revolting, that, for the sake of human nature, she would have discarded it immediately, had not the evidence of her own ears convinced her of its certainty. But what chance had she to escape from the fate with which she was threatened ? Alas ! none—not the slightest !—She was surrounded by horror and despair.

"Oh !" she exclaimed, while a flood of tears gushed from her eyes, and somewhat relieved the terrible weight which oppressed her heavily surcharged heart, "how far more preferable would death be to that dreadful fate ! But alas ! what can save me from it ?—Yes," she added, as a ray of hope and fortitude beamed upon her mind, "there is *one* who can,—

who will save me if I put my trust in Him, and I will not entirely despair!"

Inspired with a feeling of religious hope, the poor girl knelt down, and prayed the protection of Heaven, after which she felt more composed.

All was silent in the Lone House, save, at intervals, the dreary screech of the owl, which had taken up his abode in some of the upper apartments that were not inhabited, and were suffered to fall into decay.— Sometimes, too, the wind would come in hollow gusts across the heath, and make the ivy-covered casements rattle, while the dismal clanking of the chains of a gibbet that stood not far from the house, could be plainly heard. The place was calculated to excite the utmost feelings of awe, and when she looked out between the iron-bars of her casement, on to the wild heath below, as far as her eye could stretch, and could not behold any object on which to place her attention, she felt as if she was alone in the world ; a wretched, isolated being, doomed to endless suffering by an offended God !—And, yet, what had she ever done to deserve a fate so appalling?—Of what crimes had she been guilty, that should incur the retribution of the Almighty ? Never had she harmed, by word, by thought, or deed, any of her fellow-creatures; but, on the contrary, had felt an universal love for all. It was awful to be in this old house, under such circumstances as those which racked her brain, and involved in utter darkness. In spite of all her efforts to the contrary, the most terrific ideas would dart upon her imagination, and make her shudder to look around her. She threw herself on the bed, and closing her eyes, tried to shut out the horrors that arose to her mental vision ; but every fresh effort she made to that effect, only increased them, and she again arose. By the faint light which was emitted through the casement, and which might be said only to make "darkness visible," her disordered imagination created a number of strange and hideous shadows upon the wainscot ; and several times, to such a pitch of fear was she excited, that she could scarcely help rushing from the chamber and calling for help. Among other horrors which she endured that night, was the recollection of the dying moments of Mrs. Fitzormond, and the phantom which had afterwards appalled her sight ; and she could imagine that she could again hear the old woman's dying sigh, and see her ghastly countenance, and filmy eyes, fixed upon her. Such thoughts were almost insupportable, and a thousand times did she pray for morning, yet dreaded its approach, as she should again have to meet those wretches, who were her greatest enemies, and had so cruelly plotted her destruction.

In the midst of these painful reflections, a sudden idea occurred to her, and with a feeling of renewed hope, she opened the room-door cautiously, and descended the stairs. Here, however, all her hopes were again turned to despair ; the door, which was at the bottom, was strongly secured on the outside, and she, therefore, returned to her chamber, nearly heart-broken.

At length, however, the long-wished for morrow broke,—and, in a short time afterwards, she heard the inmates of the house bustling about in the room below. She trembled as she recollected the awful occurrences of the night ; but endeavoured all that she could to conquer her feelings, so that she might not betray herself, and thus excite the suspicions of the villains.

In a short time there was a gentle tap at her chamber door, and Patty made her appearance to inform her that breakfast was awaiting below. It was very clear to Emily that Patty observed her pale looks, and the agitation of her manner, and she was about to speak to her, when the latter placed her finger significantly on her lips and enjoined her to silence, at the same time evincing by her manner, how sincerely she sympathized in her sorrows ; and preceding her down the stairs, they soon afterwards entered the room in which Gerald Darnley, his son, and old Madge, were already assembled. How the poor girl shuddered with horror, when she again beheld the wretch, Gerald,—the miscreant who had been paid to shed her blood, and who had since bargained for her violation with the villain, Chesterton. For a moment she averted her head, and such a deadly sickness came over her, that she could hardly support herself. She was aroused, however, into recollection, by Will Darnley, who, approaching her, offered her his hand, and with the same insolent air of familiarity as he had assumed when he first saw her, greeted her, and handed her a seat.

"By Saint George," exclaimed the young man, "the circumstance of this fair lass coming will put fresh life into us here, at the Lone House of the Heath, as it is called. Nay, don't look so shy, my girl; you will have a rare time of it here, and never fear but that you will soon be quite at home. But, how's this?—How pale you look!—Are you not well, my dear?"

"I—I—I am not quite well, sir," faultered out the trembling Emily; "but, doubtless—it is—that is, I have not been well since the death of my poor grandmother."

"Ma conscience!" exclaimed old Madge, "an' I can judge by her pale looks, an' her sunken een, I should think it unco strange, if the poor chiel ha' had ony sleep last nicht! Is it nae sae, lassie?"

Emily felt confused, but quickly recovering herself, she replied,—

"I certainly could not sleep much; but that I attribute to my being in a strange place."

"But did you not sleep at all?" hastily and fiercely demanded Gerald Darnley, partly rising from his chair as he spoke, and darting a keen and penetrating look into her countenance.

"Yes, for more than two hours, I should imagine," replied Emily, with greater firmness than she had given herself credit for being able to assume.

"Ah!" growled Gerald, with a look of satisfaction, and he then muttered to himself, "'Tis well. But," he added, after a moment, "did you not hear anything in the night?"

Emily trembled, and she could feel the colour mantling in, and fading from her cheeks, alternately; she did not like to tell an untruth, and, yet, if she did not, her life would most probably be sacrificed; at length, she hit upon an evasion, which answered the purpose just as well,—

"I heard the owls, who seem to have taken up their abode in this old house, screech several times, sir," she replied; "but what did you expect me to hear?"

"Nothing, nothing, particular," returned Gerald, "only some of the foolish rustics who live across the heath have reported this place to be haunted, as is generally the case with all old buildings. However, it is no bad thing for me, seeing that it enables me to get a spacious dwelling for almost as little money as it would cost me for a hut." He then muttered to himself—"I was right in my conjectures, then; the girl did sleep, and it was only the owls that we heard."

It was astonishing to notice the firmness and self-possession which Emily so suddenly acquired, under the existing circumstances; and the breakfast past over without anything particular occurring to disturb her, although the abhorrence and disgust she felt at being in the company of a man whom she believed to be a robber and murderer, may be easily imagined. The insolent looks and observations of young Will Darnley, too, were quite sufficient to discompose her; but she seemed, as it were, imbued with fresh courage, and passed them off with that indifference and contempt, which often abashed him.

Chesterton did not make his appearance at breakfast, and she was very happy to think he did not. He had arisen early in the morning, as she afterwards understood, having some business to transact in the town, and thus she was fortunately saved the pain of his presence. During the repast, our heroine and Patty frequently exchanged glances together, and she could see by the looks of the latter, that she sincerely pitied her, and longed anxiously for an opportunity to speak with her. It was a great consolation to think that she had one person near who could sympathize in her sufferings, and Emily felt that she could love the poor girl as if she had been her sister.

As soon as the breakfast was over, Will Darnley arose, and, after exchanging a few words with his father, in private, he bowed to Emily, with more politeness than he had ever done before he quitted the house. Gerald Darnley, however, stayed behind; and, after remaining for several minutes in silence, and with his eyes fixed upon Emily, he thus addressed her,—

" If you want amusement, young lady, you may find plenty in rambling over the ancient rooms of this house; there are some books in one of them, which I found when I first came to reside here; they may, probably, afford you some amusement. In fact, as far as the range of this building goes, you are at liberty; but, beyond those walls, I have particular reasons, for the present, not to suffer you to go!"

" A prisoner!" ejaculated our heroine, darting a look of indignation and astonishment upon Gerald. " And by what right, sir, let me ask, do you thus incarcerate me?"

" As for right," sneered the villain, Gerald, " it is a matter of very little consequence to me; it is sufficient for you to know that it is my will, and that it would be the height of madness in you to attempt to oppose it."

" And is this, then, a sample of the kindness which Mr. Chesterton promised me, under your protection?" demanded Emily, and tears, in spite of all her efforts to restrain them, filled her eyes.

" Mark me, Emily," said Gerald, in softer accents, " I possess uncontrolled power over you,—a power which nothing can deprive me of; did I think proper, I could place you in a loathsome dungeon for life, where you would never again behold the light of day; but it is not my wish to go to these extremities, while you do not obstinately and foolishly seek to oppose me; nay, more, you shall meet with every indulgence which has been promised you, (liberty excepted) that this place can afford you; you will, therefore, best consult your own interest and happiness, by endeavouring not to arouse my displeasure. Here are the keys of some of the apartments, and you will find sufficient to amuse you in them, I'll be bound. Come, I must desire you to retire from hence for the present; I have business to transact which it would not be meet for you to hear."

Emily took the keys which Gerald offered her, with a deep sigh, and without uttering a word, but casting an expressive look upon Patty, she quitted the room by a door which the villain, Gerald, pointed out to her.

Buried in profound meditation upon what had taken place, and the injunctions of Gerald Darnley, she traversed a long passage, and began to ascend a spiral staircase at the further end, before she was scarcely conscious of what she was doing, or whither she was going. The staircase was lofty, and appeared to ascend to the upper rooms; but, as it was a matter of indifference to her what part of the building she visited, she proceeded, and, at length, found herself in a kind of gallery, round which hung several full length portraits, dropping to pieces with age and damp. Everything she saw denoted the former comfort, and even magnificence of the place; and, as she proceeded, the curiosity excited by what her eyes encountered in the different rooms she traversed, for awhile diverted her thoughts from her own miseries. The furniture did not appear to have been disturbed for many years, and dust and cobwebs had been suffered to gather thick upon it. In some of the rooms, it was in an excellent state of preservation, while in others, it was rapidly falling to pieces.— The apartments were, most of them, very spacious, and it seemed remarkable that an edifice of that description should be built in such a lonely and unfrequented part of the country,—for, from whichever direction Emily gazed, she could behold nothing but the wild uncultivated heath, or the gloomy shade of the distant wood beyond. Well, did she imagine, had it gained the appellation of the Lone House of the Heath. At length, after wandering from room to room, until she was almost tired, she came to one, the casement of which opened upon a kind of terrace. She walked on to it, and looked down below—it was a great height from the ground— but all at once a dreadful idea rushed across her brain. Here, at once, was the means of escaping the loathsome caresses of the hated Chesterton, by death,—which was by far, in her estimation, the less terrible fate of the two; and as she gave indulgence to this thought, her bosom felt a sensation of hope and relief.

She was aroused from the train of thought into which she had fallen, by a gentle voice repeating her name, and, turning round, she was pleased to behold Patty at her elbow.

"Well, I have found you at last," said Patty, " I have been looking for you everywhere, for I was so anxious to see you that I might speak to you. Emily, you will not think bad of me, will you, because of the behaviour of my father and brother ?"

Emily could not help melting to tears at the kindness of the girl's manner, and taking her hand, she pressed it fervently between her's; but was unable to give utterance to what she felt.

"I can understand you, my poor girl," said Patty; "I knew you would not blame me. From the first moment I beheld you, my heart warmed towards you with the affection of a sister, and, oh! you cannot imagine how sincerely I pity you, for the trouble and misery into which you are brought. Would that I could serve you; but I am afraid it is out of my power to do so, any more than to offer you my sympathy."

"This is kind—very kind, indeed," said Emily, "and gladly do I accept your friendship. But, oh! tell me, I beseech you, do you know anything of my origin, who I really am, and who are those that pretend to be my friends, but are, in reality, my persecutors ?"

"Alas! I do not, Miss," replied Patty; "I never saw Mr. Chesterton but once before, and my parents but seldom, before lately, for I was brought up by my aunt. Perhaps it is wrong in me to say so, but, indeed, I have too much reason to believe that my father and William are two very bad men; I cannot feel that affection which I fain, in consistency with my duty, would. Oh, that I had been suffered to remain with my aunt, who behaved very kindly to me, and had never known that I had a father or a brother in existence."

"We are both the children of misfortune, I can see, Patty," said Emily, "and earnestly, sincerely can I feel for you. But tell me, in what way do your father and brother exist ?"

Patty evinced extreme emotion at this question, and shuddered. It was some moments ere she could make any reply, and when she did, her voice was half stifled with agonized sobs.

"Oh, do not, pray do not urge a question, which I dare not answer," she said; "I must not, dare not give utterance to those terrible suspicions that have lately been all but confirmed."

"I will spare your feelings, Patty," returned our heroine, again pressing her hand—"feelings which I can, and do duly appreciate; but, tell me, was you aware of my coming hither?"

"I was," answered Patty; "about a week since, my father received a letter, which I understood was from some great lord, whose name I have never been able to ascertain, but to whom, I am told, Mr. Chesterton is steward; and the next day I heard my father and mother talking about you, and the former told me that in a few days I should have a young female companion, and gave me many cautions as to the particular behaviour I was to manifest towards you. Although I could not help feeling a degree of pleasure at the prospect of having a female companion of my own age, in this lonesome place, it was greatly diminished by the certainty I felt that you was the victim of persecution, and was, probably, going to be sent hither only to endure fresh miseries."

Emily sighed; and as the remembrance of the conversation she had overheard, on the previous night, between Gerald Darnley and Chesterton, occurred to her, all the horrors she had then endured, were rekindled in her bosom.

"Patty," at length, she said, "I will not ask you whether I can confide in you, for I am certain I can; but, have you strength of mind to support the relation of certain facts, of the most revolting description, in which your father is principally concerned, and which have accidentally come within my knowledge?"

Patty looked at her with astonishment.

"What can you mean, Emily?" she demanded, in a tremulous voice;— "I will listen; and endeavour to do so with firmness to anything you may have to impart. But let us first be certain that there are no listeners,— for, should we be overheard, I would not answer for the consequences that would follow to us both."

As Patty spoke, she walked in from the terrace, and gently opening the room door, she looked out; all was, however, perfectly still, and in a minute or two she returned to where Emily was awaiting her.

"It is all right," she said; "I am obliged to use this caution, Emily, and you would not wonder at it, if you knew the real character of my father, and what reason I have to dread his resentment."

"Oh, Patty!" exclaimed Emily, with emotion, "too well, alas! do I know the real character of your father, and that——"

"What mean you, Miss?" interrupted Patty, betraying violent agitation.

"That your father is a wretch!—a villain!—a most cold-blooded villain!" answered our heroine, vehemently, and shuddering with horror as the recollection of what she had overheard between him and Chesterton, on the previous night, and the infamous plot they had concocted together against her, recurred to her memory; but, perceiving the pain her observations evidently occasioned Patty, she added,—"nay, my poor girl, pardon me if I have spoken too harshly—too abruptly: I can duly appreciate your feelings, and sincerely do I pity your situation, which is even as deplorable, or nearly so, as my own. But, believe me, I have good reason for applying the epithets I have made use of to your father: and so you will, I am certain, acknowledge, when you hear the awful facts I am about to impart to you."

" For goodness sake. Miss," said Patty, impatiently, while her countenance became deadly pale, and flushed by turns, as a feeling of shame and
degradation, at the thought of her being the daughter of such a man, shot
across her brain, " do not keep me in suspense ; for I anticipate something
even more dreadful than your words would give me cause to imagine."

Emily paused for a few moments to regain her composure, and then, in
as succinct and brief a manner as possible, she related to Patty the conversation she had overheard between Gerald Darnley and Chesterton, which
revealed the dreadful villany of them both, and shewed plainly that she
had everything to dread from them.

Frequently did Patty interrupt her during the time she was detailing it,
to give utterance to an expression of the most unqualified horror ; and
when our heroine had concluded, she exclaimed, in accents which fully
evinced the violent emotion under which she laboured,—

" Good God ! and can I, then, have heard aright ?—Oh, my wretched.
guilty parent, what anguish, what bitter anguish do you cause your child !
Heaven turn your heart, and render you penitent, after the crimes, I fear,
you have already been guilty of."

" Heartily do I respond to your prayer, my poor girl," ejaculated Emily,
taking her hand.   " But, tell me, am I not awfully situated ?—Am I not
to be pitied ?"

" You are, you are, Miss !" replied Patty, eagerly, " and I tremble for
you ; the wretch, Chesterton—that man whose grey hairs should remind
him that he totters upon the brink of eternity, and—but what is to be
done ?—I have no power to aid you to escape ; and if I had, whither could
you fly ?—Where seek refuge, and a shelter—friendless—destitute as you
are ?"

" Oh, Patty, for that I care not," returned our heroine, " could I but
escape from this dreadful place, and the power of Chesterton, who will,
there is no doubt, persist in his infamous designs, I care not whither I go !
—Let me wander a houseless beggar ; that would be a life of happiness,
compared with the fate with which I am threatened.   I would put my trust
in Providence, who would not, surely, abandon me to utter misery and
despair !"

" Put your trust in Him now, dear Emily," said the poor girl, " and
rest assured something will happen to frustrate the diabolical schemes
that are devised against you, and to restore you once more to liberty and
happiness !"

" Happiness !" repeated Emily, with a melancholy smile—" alas ! I fear
me, that happiness is never fated to be my lot ; I am the child of misfortune—the victim of sorrow ; but, oh ! let me but escape dishonour, and I
will not fear to encounter any other calamity, however severe, which the
Almighty may think proper to inflict upon me."

" Something must be done, and, yet, how ?" said Patty, placing her
hand to her temples, as if in meditation ; " alas ! I cannot think of anything, for the present, that is likely to succeed.   Oh, my wretched father,
wicked as I really thought you, little did I imagine that you possessed so
base a heart as you do."

" Alas ! then, there is no hope for me but one," said Emily ; and as she
spoke, she looked earnestly at the terrace, and the open space beyond.

" What hope is that, Emily ?" eagerly demanded Patty.

" Death !" replied our heroine, solemnly, " and, by Heaven, sooner than
the villain Chesterton shall triumph in his diabolical design, I would
cheerfully meet it."

" I am sure, Miss." said Patty, while a tear of sympathy glistened in
her eye ;—" I am sure that I have no occasion to repeat to you how sin-

cerely I pity your situation, and grieve that, at present, I see no means of rendering you any assistance, or, how cheerfully would I do it. But pray do not give way to despair; something may occur, and that sooner than you expect, to render abortive the designs of those you are plotting against your peace, and to rescue you from their power. I will watch narrowly any opportunity that may present itself, to enable me to render you that service I so much desire, and rest assured that no personal fear shall prevent me from running any risk to save you!"

"You are a good, kind girl, Patty," said Emily, bursting into tears, "and I know that you will do all you can to accomplish your wishes;— Heaven's blessings light upon your head for your kindness. But your brother?—Say, surely he cannot be so bad, so cruel as your father?—Were you to appeal to him, would he not, think you, join with you in endeavouring to save me from destruction?"

Patty shook her head and sighed. "Alas! no," she replied; "William, I have too much reason to fear is as bad as his father; and were I to hint such a thing to him, he would be sure to reveal it all to your enemies, who would then use such precautions as to destroy all our hopes. Is it not a dreadful thing, Miss, to be situated as I am, to have a father, a brother, whom I am disposed to love, but whose guilt makes me view them with horror, and to shudder in their presence? Oh, how often have I prayed for them—now pray for them—and sometimes my mother has caught me doing so, and has mocked at, and scolded me for it,—for, although not naturally depraved like her husband and son, she possesses a heart callous to feeling and sympathy."

"Your fate is little less terrible than mine, Patty," said our heroine; "but it is strange that there should be such a difference in a family; I can
No. 6

scarcely believe that you are the daughter of that bad man, Gerald Darnley."

"Why, Miss," said Patty, in reply, "I have often thought so myself; but, then, I have lost myself in a labyrinth of conjectures, without being able to arrive at any satisfactory one; still I cannot help fancying, after all, that there is some mystery connected with me, which time will unravel, and which will place me in very different circumstances to what I am in at present. This may be a romantic, a foolish idea; but still I confess that I cannot entirely banish it from my mind, and the more I reflect upon different circumstances of my life, the more strongly impressed does it become upon my imagination. My heart felt a strange and dreadful foreboding the first moment I beheld this gloomy old house, and——"

"Know you to whom this house belongs?" interrupted Emily, "and how your father came into possession of it? It has evidently been no insignificant building, formerly, and, even now it exhibits undoubted proofs of the wealth and station of its original inhabitants."

"This old house," answered Patty, "belongs to the nobleman to whom Chesterton is the steward, by whom my father is allowed to inhabit it.— Before we occupied it, it had remained empty for some years, and had never been inhabited but a very short time, I believe, by the family to whom it belongs. Any further particulars concerning it, I am entirely unacquainted with, more than the wild reports that are spread about of its being haunted; but, although I am certainly not one of the most courageous in the world, I am not so superstitious as to place any belief in the preposterous stories that are circulated about the ghosts and hobgoblins that are said to wander through its dreary apartments."

"But is not your father and his family looked upon with an eye of suspicion and curiosity, for residing here?" asked Emily, "and have not strange conjectures, of the manner in which he lives, ever been indulged in by the persons in the neighbourhood?"

"Of that, of course, I cannot know anything, Miss," replied Patty,— "as I am never in communication with any but our own family; and the nearest village is seven miles from this place, so, that you may very well imagine that we have very little opportunity of judging how far the curiosity of its inhabitants extend. This is a strange old fabric, and you have not seen it half yet; it has vaults and subterraneous passages, just the same as you may have read of in a romance, and they would actually frighten you to look upon; and there are many dungeons underground, where, formerly, no doubt, many hapless wretches have been confined, and, perhaps, lingered out a life of misery and torment, the victims of tyranny and oppression."

"Ah!" hastily exclaimed Emily, as a latent ray of hope darted across her mind, "and know you not of any secret outlet, from whence I might——"

"Oh, no, Miss," interrupted Patty, "there is no hope that way, all the underground places are well secured. There might have been a chance formerly, but since my father has made them the receptacles of such property as——" Patty checked herself suddenly, and endeavoured to recall her words; exhibiting, at the same time, much confusion and emotion.

"What property, Patty?" quickly inquired Emily, who noticed the confusion and agitation of the girl; and immediately caught at the truth.

Patty turned pale and hung her head in shame, and our heroine, who pitied her feelings, forebode to urge the question further—but she could perceive in a moment that her surmises were just, and her horror, at the situation in which she was placed, increased.

" I cannot—I dare not answer your question, Emily," said Patty, after a pause ; "and, yet, why should I hesitate ?—Do you not already know enough of my unhappy father and brother to excite your horror and abhorrence of them ?—But suffer me to drop that subject—it is one that racks me—tortures me to dwell upon. Come, Emily, let us away from here, and I will take you to the library above ; there, perhaps, you may sometimes find the means of obtaining a temporary relief from the cares and miseries it seems to be your lot to endure."

Emily made no reply, but followed Patty out of the room, and ascending a flight of stairs, they came to a heavy oaken door, where the latter paused, and taking from her companion the bunch of keys which Luke Stanton had given her, she prepared to unlock it. Emily looked up and around the place with an expression of the deepest interest and astonishment, and then drawing her hand across her temples, as if endeavouring to recal something to her memory, she observed,—

" It is strange—what can this mean ?—but the more I look at this place, the more familiar does it seem to me,—and I could almost persuade myself that I have seen it before !"

" Indeed !" said Patty, " you astonish me, Emily ; when, and under what circumstances does it occur to you that you have before seen it ?"

" It is like a dream to me, now," answered our heroine, " and—— ah ! that room !" she screamed, as Patty unlocked the door, and threw it back on its hinges ; " it rushes forcibly on my recollection now, although I was so young at the time ; it is the same room ; the same dark, frightful-looking place, in which I and my grandmother used to sleep when I was a very little child ! —I remember it as well as if it were but yesterday I saw it before !—There is the same grim, and ugly-looking portrait, gazing on, which I have been so often terrified. There is the old clock, with its broken hands, and worm-eaten case ; the same old broken chairs ; the low wooden pallet, and humble mattress ; I could swear to the place !— Good God ! this is wonderful !"

Emily's gaze remained fixed upon everything this well-remembered apartment contained, and the more she looked, the more was she convinced of its identity, that it was the same in which, with that astonishing memory, which circumstances of a peculiar nature are likely to create in the mind, she had been, and inhabited when quite a child !—Many circumstances connected with it, and the persons she had seen in it, now rushed upon her recollection, and filled her bosom with an indefinite feeling of terror ; and when she thought upon the manner in which she had again been brought thither, and under what dreadful circumstances, she could not repress an idea that entered her imagination, that the Old Lone House of the Heath would, some time or the other, become her tomb.

" In the name of goodness, what do you mean ?" asked Patty, who had been a silent spectator of the amazement and emotion which our heroine had evinced immediately on her opening the door ; " to judge from your observations, any person would imagine that you had seen this apartment before ?"

" Yes, I have, indeed, beheld it before," said Emily, " but it is many years since, and never did I expect to see it again !"

" You astonish me !" cried Patty ; " but are you sure you are not mistaken ?"

" I am positive that I am not," replied Emily ; " this is the same room, and——but know you how long your father has inhabited this house ?"

" I believe about ten years," answered Patty ; " but why do you ask ?"

" Ah !" remarked Emily, " it was before that time ; it could not be him, and yet his features are not unlike——"

" You speak in problems, dear Emily," said Patty, whose curiosity was excited—" to whom do you allude ?"

" You shall hear," returned Emily, and she immediately informed her.

" It is strange," observed Patty, " but, yet, I do not think it could have been my father whom you mean. This room, however, has never been inhabited by one of our family, since we came to the house, and everything has remained undisturbed in it."

" I know it; I am certain of it," cried Emily ; " it is the same, I could almost swear, as when I and my grandmother quitted it; nothing but the mattress, in which I used to sleep, and the bed-clothes seem to have been——Merciful God ! what is this ?—Look ! look, Patty !—The sheets are stained with blood !—Some dreadful crime has been committed here !"

Patty uttered a scream of horror, as she fixed her eyes upon the sheets which Emily had turned down, and beheld them clotted and marked with blood, which appeared to have been there for some time. There was the print of a hand plainly discernable, and the sheets were cut in several places, as if they had been perforated by some sharp instrument.

They both stood aghast for some moments, and continued to gaze upon the object which had so excited their horror, without being able to utter a word !

" Gracious Heaven !" at last ejaculated Patty, " what deed of blood has been perpetrated here ?—Who has been guilty of a crime so fiendish ?"

A deadly chill fell upon her heart, as the name of her father rushed upon her thoughts ; but she recoiled from the dreadful thought with a sensation of sickening horror, and became paralyzed to the spot.

" Some unfortunate wretch has evidently here met with his death," said Emily, " and if his murderers still live, may the Almighty bring a just and fearful retribution upon their heads. Let us quit this dreadful place —come, come, my blood runs icy cold in my veins while we remain here."

Thus speaking, with ghastly looks, Emily was about to hurry her companion from the room, when her foot kicked against something on the floor, and stooping down, she picked up a black morocco pocket-book, with the clasp torn off, and looking at the contents, she noticed nothing but a few memorandums in different places, and on the back of the cover were marked the initials " J. D."

" This, probably, belonged to the murdered man," said Emily ; " and if it did, it is very clear that the assassin committed the deed for the purpose of robbery. I will keep this in my possession; and should I ever escape from this place, it may serve to further the ends of justice."

" I am quite appalled at this dreadful discovery," said Patty, " and shall be fearful in future of moving about the house, lest I should encounter the ghastly spectre of the murdered being. But, for Heaven's sake, Miss, do not give the slightest hint to my father or my brother of what we have seen, or even that we have visited this apartment at all ?"

Emily hastily promised to obey, and they then hurried from the mysterious chamber, and closed the door after them, Emily having taken care to conceal the pocket-book in her bosom.

They had scarcely descended the first flight of stairs, when Emily was astonished to hear her name pronounced, and the next moment she was struck with a feeling of disgust and unconquerable horror, when she beheld Chesterton ascending the stairs. She paused and trembled; while he, with an insinuating look, came to meet her, and having endeavoured to take her hand, which she hastily withdrew from him, he said,—

" My dear Emily, where the deuce have you and Patty been ? I have been making many inquiries after you of Mrs. Darnley, for I heard that you were looking very pale this morning, and I was fearful that you might be ill after the fatigue of travelling, or that —"

" Hold ! Mr. Chesterton !" exclaimed our heroine, with a look of hatred and scorn; "your pretended kindness will not deceive me; how think you, I can believe in the sincerity of a man who, since I first saw him, has so grossly deceived me in everything he told me ?"

" How ! deceived you, Emily ?" repeated Chesterton, with some confusion ; " I do not understand you."

" I dare say not, sir," answered Emily, sarcastically, " but I understand you ; of that rest assured."

Chesterton could not avoid scowling, and he bit his lips with vexation.

" You can go," he cried, sternly, speaking to Patty ; " I do not want your attendance,"

" And I, also, will go," observed Emily, " to my own chamber ; I am not disposed for conversation at present."

" Stay," cried Chesterton, placing his back against the room door, and preventing her egress; " I will not suffer this, Emily. What mean you by saying that I have deceived you ? Did I not tell you that you would be confided to the care of friends ? That you would be treated kindly, and ——"

" Did you tell me that I was to be made a prisoner, sir ?" interrupted Emily ; " did you tell me that I was to be confined within certain limits, for what purpose, or with what design, you may, perhaps, be best able to explain ? Unhand me, sir; young and unprotected as I am, you shall find that Emily Fitzormond has the spirit to resent an insult ; and that she will be enabled to oppose and defy the insidious artifices of her enemies, she trusts in the goodness of Heaven."

Mr. Chesterton could not return any answer immediately, he was so abashed and astonished at the dignity and firmness of her manners ; but, at length, he somewhat altered his tone, and with an air of haughtiness, said :—

" The insinuations you have thrown out, young lady, but ill become one, methinks, who, but for the attention and kindness of those whom she has thought proper to designate her enemies, would even now be without a shelter or a home, and whom it is their anxious wish to make happy."

" If you would, indeed, make the poor destitute girl, of whom you speak, happy," said Emily, " oh, permit her to take the care and anxiety to which you allude off their minds ; suffer her to depart from hence, and take no farther trouble about her fate, and she will bless you for so doing."

" Why, the child must be mad," said Chesterton, again softening his manner ; " why should you wish to be exposed to such misery, when here you will receive every comfort you can wish for, with the exception, that you will not be permitted to leave the house, and which is done from motives of kindness, for it would not be safe for you to walk about the neighbourhood, which is infested with numerous bad characters, and from whom the worst is to be apprehended ; but you will have an agreeable companion in Patty, and an ample store of books to amuse and improve your mind. Come, come, Emily, your nature is very suspicious, and you must endeavour to conquer it, or it will cause you more trouble in the world than you can at present imagine. I request you will attend me below, I have something to say to you before the return of Gerald Darnley and his son, which is of the greatest importance to you. Nay, I will not be refused."

" If you would wish me to believe in the sincerity of your protestations of friendship and esteem for me, sir," said Emily, who began to be seriously alarmed at his manner, "you will allow me to retire to my own room for the present; I am not well, indeed I —"

"This is a mere obstinate excuse, and will not have any effect with me," said Chesterton, still remaining with his back against the room-door; "Emily, I would not appear harsh, but I cannot, and will not, neglect the present opportunity afforded me, of talking to you upon a subject on which my happiness and your own depends. Nay, you must excuse me, and blame yourself, if your obstinacy compels me to use a little gentle violence."

Emily trembled with terror as Chesterton spoke, and, grasping her hand, forced her from the spot, and compelled her to accompany him down the stairs into the parlour. When they had entered which, he closed the door at the bottom of the staircase, led her to a chair, into which she sunk, exhausted, with the exertion she had made, and the alarm she underwent, while he stood gazing at her for a short time with looks of admiration. At last, however, Emily so far conquered her fears as to be able to rise from the chair, and, in tones of firmness, she demanded,—

"What mean you, sir, by this strange, this violent behaviour? What would you of me? If your intentions are honourable, or you really are the friend you wish to appear to be, you surely would not act in this ambiguous and violent manner."

"Emily, dear Emily," cried the hoary villain, in a tone of rapture, "consent but to one request which I have to make, and you shall not only be restored to liberty, but have every thing your heart can wish for. Oh! avert not your face, most beauteous girl, nor seek to conceal your maiden blushes, but listen to the vows of a man who is prepared to adore you; who, from the first moment he beheld you, became ardently, irrevocably devoted to you, and who would now willingly make any sacrifice, to hear those lovely lips pronounce a confirmation of his hopes, his desires. Emily, I love you—I worship you—say, then, that you will return my passion, and command me your devoted slave."

As Chesterton thus spoke, he sank on one knee, and took the hand of Emily, and pressed it with passionate vehemence to his lips, she being too much agitated, frightened, and bewildered, to be able to offer any resistance.

"Emily," continued the aged libertine, "you have the chance of every felicity before you; do not, then, rashly, madly reject the offer while it is yet at your command. Escape from your unprotected state, by accepting the love and protection of one who will make it his sole study to render you happy; think not of the disparity of our years; I will love you with all the ardour of youth, and with none of its evanescence. No fresh object shall allure my fancy; nothing shall ever alter my sentiments, or weaken the passion with which your young and blooming charms have inspired me. You shall have no care, no wish unstudied or ungratified. My whole soul shall be devoted to you, and no trouble shall ever darken your brow with the cloud of sorrow. Still you turn away from me; you scorn me; you hate me; you —"

"Cease, sir, for the love of Heaven!" exclaimed our blushing and terrified heroine, starting from the spot where she had hitherto stood, and turning upon him a look of reproach and indignation; "this language, addressed to a poor, friendless girl, to one who is but a child to you, is not only disgusting, but brutal. Away, sir, you have unmasked yourself: leave me; the sight of you is loathsome to me. Oh, how have I deserved this cruel fate?"

As the poor girl thus spoke, she burst into a torrent of tears, and wringing her hands, afterwards covered her face with them, and sobbed aloud with the emotion caused by wounded delicacy, and the fear occasioned by the danger of her situation.

" Silly girl !" ejaculated Chesterton, once more advancing towards her, " why should you thus afflict yourself ? Surely there is nothing so alarming in being offered the homage of a heart which beats only for you, and will continue to do so, until it shall cease to throb for ever. Nay, I cannot, will not, beauteous maiden, see you weep thus. Here let me kiss off those pearly drops caused by —"

" Wretch ! villain !" screamed Emily, retreating to one corner of the room as Chesterton attempted to fling his arms around her waist, and to press his lips to her's; " stand off ! pollute me not with your touch ! or the vengeance of offended Heaven shall be invoked upon your head ; that Heaven to which I now solemnly appeal, and which will not suffer the guilty to triumph over the innocent and the unprotected. Stand off !"

The countenance of the villain Chesterson was inflamed with the unruly passions of desire and admiration, which Emily's opposition only served to increase, instead of to abash; and as he rushed immediately towards her, he ejaculated,—

" By hell ! you resist me in vain ! Your beauty has created in my bosom the most ungovernable passions, and they must, they shall be gratified. Your cries are useless. Here there is no one at hand to fly to your aid. You are completely in my power ; you are mine ; you are mine !"

" Help ! help ! oh, God !" shrieked the distracted Emily, as she struggled in the arms of Chesterton, while her strength was nearly exhausted, and despair had almost settled upon her heart.

" There is no help nigh, girl !" shouted the villain, triumphantly ; " ha ! ha ! ha ! My success is certain."

" 'Tis false !" exclaimed a female voice behind him ; " release the trembling girl, or I will discharge the contents of this at your head !"

It was Patty who thus spoke, and who, having on the stairs listened to all that had passed between Emily and Chesterton, started forth just at this critical juncture, and seizing upon a loaded gun which stood in one corner of the room, placed herself in an attitude to put her threat into execution.

" Confusion ! death !" shouted the miscreant, staggering back to the further end of the room, when he beheld the attitude in which the heroic girl stood. Before he could utter another sentence the door was thrown open, and Gerald Darnley and his son entered.

" Hollo ! hell and the devil !" cried the latter, " what's the meaning of all this—Patty—Emily looking as white as a sheet, and Chesterton as stupid as an owl ;—what's amiss here ?"

" Psha ! it's nothing, I dare say, Will," remarked his father, who, no doubt, guessed the truth ; " I have often warned you against playing with that pop-gun, Patty, and some of these times you'll have reason to repent it, or else I'm much mistaken."

" I shall never repent having used it upon such an occasion as the present one," said Patty, " when it has stood my friend to save an unprotected female from the ruffian attacks of a——"

" Ah !" exclaimed Will Darnley, looking fiercely towards Chesterton ; " damme, if I didn't think so. Why, is it possible that a grey-headed old fellow like you, Master Chesterton, should——"

" Hold your tongue, boy, will you?" said his father, sternly and peremptorily ; " I have no doubt Mr. Chesterton has only been up to some foolish frolic or the other, and surely he can do that without being called to an account by you. These girls are so very squeamish when there's no occasion for it."

Will Darnley muttered something to himself, and scowling upon Chesterton, he placed himself by the side of Emily, who all this while remained fixed in the same attitude as she had assumed when Patty had so courageously come to her assistance, and saved her from destruction.

" What say you, lass," added Will, in gentler tones, and addressing himself to Emily ; " let's hear your version of the affair. D—n the man who would ill-use a female, I say ; and Will Darnley will always be the first to stand her champion against the very devil himself !"

. " Headstrong fool !" exclaimed Chesterton, with resentment.

" Ay, what ?" demanded Will, fiercely, and clenching his fist. " Fool, say you ? Damme !—but no ; it is lucky for you that you are an older man than me, or you might have to pay dearly for that compliment, mayhap."

" Hold your peace, Will," remonstrated his father ; " what the deuce do you want to quarrel about ? It is no business of yours, that you need take it up so warmly."

" Oh, if you are men, if your hearts are not quite steeled against every feeling of humanity," supplicated the weeping Emily, " you will pity me ; suffer me to depart, and go where I may no longer be exposed to the brutal treatment of this hoary ruffian."

' " Girl, beware !" exclaimed Chesterton, his eyes flashing with indignation ; " you had better endeavour to conciliate my friendship than to make me your enemy ; you may repent this language ; nor would you venture to repeat it, did you but know the power I hold over you. For the present I bid you adieu ; I shall see you again to-morrow ; and rest assured, that I shall not readily give up my designs ; if persuasion fail to make you assent to my wishes, force is sure to prove more efficacious. Perhaps by to-morrow, Will Darnley, your boasted courage may have cooled a little, and your father may have told you better than to give way to such intemperate language to one whom——"

" Whom I thoroughly despise," added Will, with a scornful look, as Chesterton quitted the house.

" No more of this nonsense, boy," said Gerald, with a frown ; " nay, I insist upon it."

Will Darnley turned sullenly away, and, throwing himself in a chair, folded his arms, and crossed his legs carelessly ; while his father, turning to Emily, observed,—

" You will do well, girl, not to make such a fuss in future, when a little harmless joke is played off upon you. Mr. Chesterton means you no harm ; but, on the contrary, would make you much more comfortable than a person in your station of life has a right to expect, and I should advise you not to repulse, but rather to encourage his addresses."

It would be impossible to describe the feelings of horror and disgust with which Emily listened to the words of Gerald ; and when she thought upon his character, the deed he was employed to perform, and the awful discovery which her and Patty had made in the old room, her terror and emotion exceeded all bounds. She returned him no answer, for she could not speak to him, and his looks filled her bosom with alarm and abhorrence. Will heard his father, apparently, with a feeling of anything but pleasure, and the glances he occasionally fixed upon the countenance of Emily excited the greatest uneasiness in her bosom. The charms of the beauteous maiden had evidently struck the heart of the young man, and such was the impression that had been made, it was not very probable it would be easily eradicated.

"You can retire to your own room, girl," said Gerald, after a pause, "I have something for your private ear, Will. As for you, Patty, I warn you not to make yourself so officious in future, or you and I, perchance, may quarrel."

Glad to escape from the presence of Gerald and his son, Emily was hastening to obey the mandate of the former, when the pocket-book, by some means or the other, escaped from her bosom, and fell upon the floor. The eye of Gerald became fixed upon it in a moment, and as it did, his countenance changed, his eyes rolled in their sockets, his limbs trembled, and in a voice of indescribable emotion, he cried,—

"D————n! what do I behold. This pocket-book; the infernal proof of ——. Girl! speak!—instantly—how came this into your possession? Ah!—the old room—you have been there—fool that I was to suffer you to have that key. You have seen all, and must pay for your curiosity with your life—die!"

As the wretch thus spoke, he drew a pistol from beneath his top-coat, and was about to draw the fatal trigger, when Emily uttered a piercing shriek of terror, and, with clasped hands and piteous looks, fell upon her knees, and Will Darnley rushing in between them, seized his father's arm, at the same time vociferating,—

"Hold! rash man! what would you do?"

"Destroy her, whose word might now doom us to the gallows," answered Gerald; has she not discovered the secret? She must not—she shall not live."

"Mercy! mercy! spare me! save my life!" screamed Emily, in frantic accents. "How can I harm you, when you hold me here a prisoner? I solemnly promise you, that what I have seen shall never be divulged by me to mortal ears."

No. 7

"Will you swear?" demanded Gerald.

"Ay, an oath will be quite satisfactory enough," said Will Darnley; "her countenance much belies her if she would ever break an oath once administered to her."

"Hark ye, girl," said Gerald, dropping his arm, and fixing a searching glance upon her countenance, "are you ready to take the vow required of you?"

"Name it; I will do all that you require of me."

"Swear, then, that you will never reveal to mortal ears what you may have seen in the old chamber; and if you break your oath, wish that every possible misery may attend you throughout life, and that eternal perdition may light upon your soul!"

"I swear!" said Emily, solemnly.

"Enough," observed Gerald. "Now rise, and away to your room; remember the warning I have given you; above all, remember your oath."

With a bursting heart the unfortunate Emily tottered from the parlour, and hastened up the stairs to her own apartments, where she threw herself upon her knees in a paroxysm of despair, and gave vent to her anguish in a violent burst of tears and sobs.

CHAPTER VII.

THE ROBBER'S BOOTY.

LANGUAGE would be far too weak to pourtray the state of Emily's mind after these multifarious, exciting, and painful events. Young as she was, and with such an alarming prospect before her eyes, it is a wonder that it did not turn her brain.

"My God! what will become of me?" she said, in a voice rendered almost inarticulate with grief; "in the power of robbers, murderers; wretches who glory in wading through human blood. I am lost! lost!—Chesterton, too, the miscreant. Oh! how my heart shudders when I repeat his name! How shall I escape the fate he has doomed me to? What can my girl's resistance do against him and Gerald? Alas! nothing. Situated as I am in this lone house, without the means of assistance nigh, how can I save myself from destruction. Oh, Heaven! in mercy look down upon me, and shield me. Rather let me die than suffer the wretch Chesterton to triumph in his guilt. I can meet death, but not the destruction of my virtue."

After indulging in the vehemence of her grief in this manner for an hour or two she became more calm, and placed her whole reliance in the mercy of Omnipotence, and she was enabled to appear at the dinner table with more composure than any one could have imagined, after the violent shock her feelings had sustained. Nothing particular was said during the meal, but Emily was fearful to look up from the table, lest her eyes should encounter the fierce looks of Gerald, or the still more disgusting glances of his son. She was glad when it was over, and she was permitted to retire to her own room, where she was not again molested that day.

In the afternoon she was joined by Patty, whose society, we need not say, was a great relief to her. In the most unbounded terms did our heroine pour forth her gratitude to this kind-hearted girl, for the courageous manner in which she had defended her from the guilty designs of the villain Chesterton, but Patty interrupted her, hastily; she was too much gratified in having been made the instrument in the hands of Providence of saving the unfortunate damsel from so imminent a danger, to need any thanks, and she joined her in praying to Heaven, that the further machinations of the villains might be as fortunately frustrated.

One circumstance afforded them much satisfaction, and that was, that Patty had never been suspected by her guilty parent of having been our heroine's companion in the old chamber when they made the discovery of the blood-stained bed and the pocket-book; and therefore, although Emily was bound down by an oath, Patty was not, and should necessity require it, the ends of justice could be as easily accomplished as they could had our heroine have remained unrestrained and unshackled as she had been before.

Many were the opinions and conjectures they formed upon this awful circumstance, and they could come to no other conclusion, after the agitation which Gerald and Will had betrayed when they saw the pocketbook, that a murder had been some time or the other committed, and that Gerald and his son were the barbarous perpetrators of the crime. What a dreadful conclusion was this for Patty to be obliged to come to in respect to her father and brother. But, alas! what other one would reason allow her to form, and, indeed, had they not by their own words admitted it? What horror filled her breast when she thought upon the ignominious death that one day or the other, sooner or later, would be sure to overtake them. What an indelible blot it would be upon her name. What an alien would it render her from all society. Too often, she knew, were the sins of the parents visited upon the children; and if it should happen so in her case, what prospect but one of unceasing, of unendurable misery had she before her? Taking all these things into consideration, the situation of Patty was scarcely less deplorable than that of Emily, only that she was not in such immediate danger as the latter; and good reason had the poor girls to sympathize in each other's misfortunes, and in trying to impart consolation, they somewhat blunted the keenness of the sorrow, which would otherwise have filled their bosoms with the most insupportable despair. One idea every hour gained more strength in the mind of Patty, and that was, that she was not really the daughter of Gerald; and oh! what a relief would it be to her could she but have that imagination confirmed. To believe herself to be associated by the ties of consanguinity to such wretches as Gerald and his son, was a most dreadful thing for a young girl, of the kind and virtuous disposition of Patty, to reflect upon, and many a wretched day and night had it cost her. She had, also, as may be supposed, much to endure from the savage treatment of Gerald, who had ever evinced a thorough dislike to her, and after the affectionate manner in which she had been brought up by her aunt, she felt it more keenly than she would otherwise most likely have done; but mild, patient, and forbearing, Patty endured it all, without so much as a murmur, and in the solitude of her own chamber, when there was no one to observe her, she only ventured to give vent to her feelings. Now, however, that Emily had become her companion in misfortune, she had a feeling breast to whom she could confide her sorrows, and who must feel reciprocal sentiments to those of her own.

Terrible, indeed, were the sufferings of Emily, after the startling events we have been describing, for, on every side to which she looked, nothing but danger met her gaze. Confined in this miserable, lonely abode, the prisoner of ruffians, who hesitated at the perpetration of no crime, however dreadful; what had she to hope?—Alas! she was left entirely to their mercy, and gave herself up to despair.

"Oh, Emily! wretched, unfortunate girl," she soliloquised, "thou art lost! thou art lost! But, surely thy fate is a cruel one, so young, and never having been wilfully guilty of any offence, thus to be made the victim of the most disgusting brutality and persecution; alas! is it not enough to make me almost ready to arraign the justice of Omnipotence! But, what am I saying? What is my sinful tongue giving utterance to? Oh, pardon me, Heaven, for what the wildness of my despair prompted me to say!—In the Most High I will put my trust, and hope again shall animate my bosom."

"Yes, Emily," said Patty, who was present when she thus spoke, "while you implore the protection of Heaven, there is still hope of your being able to triumph over the machinations of the guilty; and something whispers to me, that the time is not far distant, when you will once more be restored to liberty."

"Liberty!" repeated Emily, with a sigh. "alas! even should your predictions be verified, Patty,—whither should I go, what can I do?—without a home, without a friend in the world to assist me; oh, dear! mine is, certainly, a most melancholy fate."

"It is, indeed, Emily," answered Patty, in a deeply-commisserating tone, "and mine is scarcely better, for, can I call mine a home, or look up to my cruel parent for protection, with anything like confidence, when I know him to possess a heart callous to every virtuous feeling? Oh, no, no, and could I but escape from it, willingly would I run any risk, encounter any danger to do so?"

"Ah!" cried Emily, catching at her words with eagerness, "and cannot you do so?" Then suddenly bethinking herself, she added; "But, what do I say; I should persuade you to a dereliction from your duty, were I to urge you to such a course; besides, whither could we flee; where seek a shelter? And, to what dangers should we be exposed, alone in the world, and, probably, surrounded by such bad men as Chesterton!— Oh, how I shudder when I think of his name! No, Patty, I must endeavour to resign myself to the will of Providence; but, let me not make you a participator in those troubles that have fallen to my lot. I will, if it is ordained, that I shall ever be able to escape from this place, no matter where, or what situation I am, always think of you with affection,—with the affection of a fond sister, and remember, with everlasting gratitude, the sympathy and kindness you have bestowed upon me!"

Patty could not restrain her tears as our heroine thus spoke.

"And, believe me, dearest Emily, I will return your love with all the warmth and fervour that you bestow your's on me;" she ejaculated, in tones that bespoke her sincerity, "from the very first moment I beheld you, my heart warmed towards you, and I felt that I could love you with all that strength of feeling which I now do, and though nothing could afford me more sincere pleasure than to see you be able to escape from the clutches of those bad men; I am certain that I should be wretched, were I to be separated from you. I feel that I could, without hesitation, quit this house in your company, and I am determined to use all my endeavours to effect such an object, in spite of the arguments you have advanced against it; my father's cruelty does away with every sentiment of love and duty in my breast, and I know not how it is, but I cannot help thinking that something would occur to enable us to exist in the world in comfort and respectability."

"Alas! how?"

"I have a few pounds saved by me," said Patty, "and that would be sufficient to support us, until fortune turned up something in our favour; I know you would be willing to work, and there is nothing I would hesitate to do to enable us to get an honest living away from the power of your persecutors."

"But what could two young girls, like us do, exposed as we should be to the vices of the world, Patty ?"

"I would seek the protection of my aunt, who, I know, would gladly afford us a home, until we could procure a situation, or get some employ-ployment."

"But you could not resist the authority of your father, Patty, who would demand and force your aunt to resign you, and then his cruelty would, doubtless, be redoubled to you for having been guilty of what he would, perhaps, call an act of disobedience ; and, when I think of the desperate character of your father, and the threats he has held out to you, I cannot be so selfish as to wish you to run the risk of your own life to save mine ! No, no,—I will endeavour to meet my troubles with fortitude, and trust in the mercy of Heaven for the result."

Patty paused, and seemed at a loss what answer she should make to the observations of Emily, but, at length, she said :—

"I cannot, I will not see you fall a victim to the brutality of my father, or the disgusting passions of the villain Chesterton, Emily, and, therefore, am I determined, at all hazards, and in spite of the arguments you have made use of, to——"

At this moment, the shrill voice of Madge was heard calling upon the name of her daughter, and turning hastily to obey the summons, she said, in low tones :—

"I will see you again, if possible, this evening, and we will talk further upon the subject ; in the meantime, keep up your courage, and all may be well."

"Alas ! I see but little prospect of it, at present ;" sighed Emily, as Patty quitted the room ;—" and then to remain another night, even in this horrible place, after what has this day occurred ; my God ! the bare idea is sufficient to fill the mind with the most insupportable terror ! I tremble to look around, for fear my eyes should encounter the ghastly shades of some of the unfortunate beings who have, doubtless, fallen here by unfair means ! Murder seems to stalk through every chamber of this lone house, and despair to inclose me in on every side. Oh, God ! in mercy take my life into thine hands, or rescue me from this dreadful situation !"

She clasped her hands vehemently as she spoke, and raised her eyes with earnest supplication towards Heaven, then throwing herself into a chair, she covered her face with her hands, and again the fearful occurrences of the last few hours passed in agonizing review before her recollection. The old gloomy chamber, which she remembered so well to have occupied with her grandmother, when a child ; the blood-stained bed ; the myste-rious pocket-book ; the emotion of Gerald and his son, when they beheld it, and the terrible oath they had extorted from her, all held the most para-mount station in her thoughts, and filled her mind with horrible apprehen-sions and conjectures. That murder had been committed in that room, she had not the least doubt ; that the villain, Gerald Darnley and his son, had perpetrated it, she was equally confident ; and that she was in some way or the other connected with the unfortunate victim of their barbarity, she could not help imagining. A fearful sensation shot through her heart as she gave way to these thoughts, and she felt ready to faint. Then the disgusting vows of Chesterton, and the violent outrage he had committed, likewise the determination with which it was evident he would pursue his infamous designs, aided as he was by Gerald, all came to her mind with overwhelming force, and she had the greatest difficulty to support herself beneath the weight of the accumulated horrors that oppressed her heart.

She saw no more of Patty, but old Madge summoned her when the meal was ready, fearful, however, of encountering Gerald and his son again, (the strange conduct of the latter, and the looks he had fixed upon her, having filled her mind with fear and disgust), she made an excuse that she felt indisposed, and remained in her chamber. She frequently heard the voices of Gerald and his son, in loud altercation, and more than once she heard her name repeated, and she was, therefore, inclined to think that the subject of their dispute was the circumstance that had taken place, and the opposition which Will had evinced towards Chesterton ; but shortly afterwards all became still, and hearing the outer door close, she concluded that the two ruffians had left the house. Of this, she was soon enabled to convince herself, for, leaving her room, and peeping through the casement which was over the door, at the foot of the staircase, she beheld no other person in the place but old Madge, who was bustling about at her domestic duties. An idea, for a moment occurred to her, which was, to appeal to the pity of the old woman, but then the hard and repulsive features of Madge ; and the fear she seemed to entertain of her husband, withheld her, and believing that any such attempt would be unsuccessful, and might only be the means of inducing Gerald to behave with more rigour towards her, she abandoned all thoughts of it, and returned to her chamber.

As night approached, so did the apprehensions and the terror of Emily increase ; must she pass another night of horror in this chamber, after the villanous attempt of Chesterton, and the resolution he had expressed of obtaining his brutal desires by some means or the other ? And should he be admitted to the house for that purpose, what means had she of resisting him ? None ! A deadly faintness came over her, as she thus reflected, and she gasped for breath ! She examined the fastening of her door, and found it to be so weak, that the least force would prevent its being any obstacle to the entrance of any person, and this, of course, was an additional cause of terror to her, and served to increase her despair. She could, in fact, see no cause whatever to indulge in the slightest hope, and the dreadful excitement of her feelings in consequence, almost overpowered her.

Ever and anon, she would go to the top of the stairs and listen, but all was still, and although there was a light burning in the parlour below, she could not distinguish any person moving. Then she descended the stairs, and cautiously tried the door, which, however, she found was fast, and at length the voice of old Madge smote her ears, in querulous tones, singing the burthen of an old Scotch ballad. There was something in the idea of Emily, peculiarly dismal in listening to the tones of merriment in that gloomy place, which she had every reason to imagine had been the scene of many horrible crimes, and she returned to her own apartment, and closed the door. She seated herself by the casement, and leaning her head on her hand, gave free indulgence to the dismal thoughts that harassed her mind. All was so quiet in the house, that she could plainly hear the ticking of the old clock in the room below, and its monotonous sound had anything but a pleasing effect.

Hour after hour, elapsed in this manner, and still Emily did not retire to bed ; she feared to do so ; and the anguish of her thoughts, and the strength of her terrors, kept all signs of sleep from her eyelids. Presently, however, she was aroused by a loud knocking at the outer door, which she had, no doubt, was Gerald Darnley and his son returned. Her heart throbbed with alarm as she thought of the wretch Chesterton, and the probability that he accompanied them, and she was, for a moment or two, unable to move. At length, determined to satisfy her doubts, she once more quitted her room, and going to the top of the stairs, she looked eagerly through the casement before-mentioned, and which commanded a full view of the room, and her mind felt a great relief when she perceived that Chesterton was not there. The looks and manner of Gerald and Will, however, particularly rivetted her attention. They were attired in great rough coats, and seemed as if they had just returned from a long journey. They looked strongly excited, and the countenance of Gerald expressed considerable fear and agitation, and every now and then his eye would wander round the room in a restless manner. Will's demeanour was more bold, but, nevertheless, he likewise evinced a good share of trepidation, and his face was very pale. They were seated at the table, and were several minutes before they offered to speak to one another, until, at length, Gerald made a sign to his son, which he understood, and immediately arose from his seat, and going to the door, barred and bolted it carefully. He then returned to the table, and Gerald commenced pulling out several canvas bags, that seemed to be well filled, from his coat pockets, and deposited them on the table, and, as he did so, Will opened them, and emptied them of their contents, which consisted of gold and silver coin, and hastily counted it, in which his father assisted him when he had unloaded himself of all the bags. Besides this, Gerald took from his pockets a watch, several rings, and other articles of jewellery, and a brace of pistols, at the sight of which, our heroine could, with difficulty, repress a scream, and the certainty of what the two villains had been doing immediately flashed across her mind! She gasped for breath, and yet was afraid almost to respire, lest they should hear her, and discover her; and she had not the power to move from the spot!

"The wretches have been committing robbery and murder," she reflected, "and these are the fruits of their crime."

When they had finished counting the money, they returned it to the bags, and Gerald having deposited it in an iron chest, which was concealed behind the wainscot, one of the panels of which slid back upon touching a secret spring, returned to the table, and, addressing his son, Emily could distinguish the following words:—

"Well, we have not managed this business very badly, Will; and there's very little chance of suspicion lighting upon us."

"Suspicion!" reiterated Will, "to be sure not; why should it? No one will think of looking for the murderers of the old miser here, for our real characters are not the least suspected, and the mystery of his death, so long as we keep our own council, and act with our usual prudence, will never be revealed. The old fellow did not like giving up the ghost though, and the thoughts of being separated from his hoarded treasures, drove him nearly crazy. I did not want to take his life, but he clung so to his darling gold, and after all, I think it is much better, as dead men, you know, tell no tales."

"Well, we've made a very tidy booty, Will, and I warrant we shall circulate the money well," said Gerald."

"Ay, there's no doubt of it," answered Will; "but, I'll tell you what I have an idea of doing, but I don't know whether you will approve of it or no."

"What's that?"

"Why," returned Will, "the beauty of that girl, that Emily, has somehow, made a strong impression upon me, and——"

"Well, and what then?" interrupted Gerald, abruptly, and frowning.

"Well, and what then?" reiterated his son, "why you needn't be so sharp, father,—I see you will not be inclined to approve of my design; however, I shall tell it you, whether or no. The whole of it is, I have some idea of doing the matrimonial with that wench, and, as I want a

short rest from this sort of business, my share of the booty will enable me
to do so.   Why, you look as black as a thunder-cloud, father!"

"Fool!" exclaimed Gerald, fiercely, "know you not that I have already
bargained with Chesterton about the girl, and that she is to be his?"

"Then you must break the contract, that's all," returned Will, carelessly, "it will not be the first time you have done so; Emily is too rich a
prize for that hoary-headed old libertine, she must be mine."

"She must either be his or die," said Gerald, "you know well what
interest I have at stake in obeying the will either of the steward or his
lord!"

"And his lordship has too much cause to fear you, to be very ready to
withdraw his patronage from you;" said Will, in the same cool and careless manner; "become the mistress of Chesterton, or die,—psha!—she
shall neither do one nor the other."

"Ah! dare you?"

"Why, hark you, father," said Will, "you ought to know my character pretty well, and you are well aware that I will not easily be baulked
in anything that I have set my mind upon; besides, I have now arrived at
years sufficient to be capable of judging and acting for myself; and the
whole of the matter is, my mind's made up, the girl is mine!"

"Then it must be when Chesterton is tired of her," answered Gerald,
"since you seem to be so determined."

"Never!" cried Will, fiercely, "neither you nor any other person shall
move me from my resolution; and it will be well for those who do not
attempt to thwart me in my desires."

"You get bold and saucy, boy!"

"Perhaps I may, and if I do, I am indebted to you, I believe, for all the
excellent accomplishments I possess;" returned Will, in a sarcastic tone.

Gerald struck the table furiously with his clenched fist, then hastily
arose, and with compressed lips, and contracted brow, traversed the room
for a second or two with uneven footsteps, while Will crossed one leg over
the other, and shook his foot with the most consummate *nonchalance*.

"Will, I advise you not to arouse my wrath," at length observed
Gerald, walking back to the table, and fixing a look of deep resentment
upon his son.

"I wish not to do so," replied the latter, "but seek not to frustrate my
wishes."

"I cannot consent."

"You must."

"I must?"

"Ay, if you do not, I shall only take French leave!"

"Suppose I take means to prevent it?"

"If you study your own interest and safety, you will not attempt it;"
was the reply.

"What if I obey the injunctions of his lordship, and murder her?"

"You must first slay me!"

"Damnation!" cried the wretch Gerald, furiously, "this is inssupport-
able!   Will, beware, I repeat, how you exasperate me, or I will not answer for the consequences."

"I will risk them all, anything," replied Will, "but I will not abandon
my designs; I have taken a fancy to the wench, and have her I will, though
the devil stood in my way."

"Headstrong fool!" vociferated Gerald, "but you will think better of
this if you're wise."

"I am wise enough not to be easily intimidated, as you know," retorted
Will, boldly.

"Well, well, I see we shall not agree to night, and so we will say no more upon the subject at present. It's getting late, and—ah! see, you have not washed the old fellow's blood from your hands yet! Hark! what noise was that?"

"You had better go to bed, father," said Will, "our night's adventure has made you qualmish. I heard no noise, unless it was the wind."

"Ah! it might be so," said Gerald, looking very pale, and evidently enduring considerable terror; "I could almost have sworn that I heard a groan, just such a one as the old miser uttered before he died, close to my ear!"

"Bah! mere fancy, nothing else," observed Will; "the old man's quiet enough, and will utter no more groans, I'll warrant. Come, we will go to bed;—I will talk to you about the other business to-morrow."

"You may, but my mind's made up."

"And so is mine; so, upon that point, we agree, at any rate;" answered Will Darnley, in his usual careless manner. Gerald then took the light in his hand, and led the way to the door which opened to their chambers,—but he had no sooner unfastened it, than he started back again in apparent great trepidation, and stood trembling and aghast in the middle of the room.

"What's the matter, now?" demanded Will, "you seem quite panic-struck!"

"It's nothing," faultered out Gerald, endeavouring to conquer the fears under which he evidently suffered;—"I—I—'psha! What's come to me, to-night?—I'm as weak as a girl! This is an unusual thing with me! However, you take the lamp and lead the way, Will, I——"

"Ha! ha! ha!" laughed the ruffian Will, taking the light from his father's hand, and advancing towards the door; "why, any one would suppose you had seen the ghost of the old chap! Come along, there's nothing here to be alarmed at."

Will passed under the door-way, and Gerald followed, but with much apparent fear, and the next moment they both disappeared, and the room was involved in complete darkness.

Vain would be the task to endeavour to give even a faint idea of the intense horror, disgust, and alarm, with which our heroine had witnessed this scene, and listened to the discourse of the wretches;—her faculties seemed to be completely suspended, and she was unable to move from the spot on which she had been standing for several minutes after Gerald Darnley and his son had retired; at length, however, she staggered into her own apartment;—her limbs failed her; her head grew dizzy, and she sunk upon the couch in a state of insensibility!

When she recovered, she shivered with cold, and she was unable for a short time to bring to her memory any recollection of what had taken place. Happy would it have been for her, if this forgetfulness had lasted; what hours of mental agony would it have saved her! But, alas! in a few minutes it rushed upon her brain with overwhelming force, and she clasped her hands, and groaned aloud with the intensity of her feelings. Horrible as her situation was before, it was now, if possible, still more appalling and hopeless. Destruction seemed to her to be totally inevitable, surrounded as she was by the most awful danger. On one side, she was threatened with the loathsome passion of Chesterton; on the other, Will Darnley, a robber and a murderer, evinced his determination to obtain possession of her, and nothing but her ultimate murder would be the result of this two-fold persecution.

The dreadful account Will had given of the assassination of the poor old miser, had made her blood run cold with horror, and to be beneath the same roof with such bloodthirsty wretches, and who had perpetrated such a fiendish crime, filled her bosom with a sickly dread, that made her tremble to look around her, for fear she should encounter the ghastly features of the murdered man! The least sound that came to her ears made her start; and even her own shadow upon the wainscot, filled her with apprehension. Rest!—never again could she rest in that lone house! But what was to become of her, in what manner could she avoid the miserable fate with which she was threatened? She could perceive no way. She remembered the terrace!

"Ah!" she exclaimed, "should the door of the apartment which leads to that be open; if I cannot escape from it, I can, at least, end my life, and avoid a fate more horrible than death! I will venture to search."

She took up the lamp, and stepping forth from her chamber into the lobby, she proceeded by another door into a gallery, which led her round to the flight of stairs that ascended to the room mentioned. She was pleased to find that the door was unlocked, and, after first listening, and finding that not a sound disturbed the utter stillness of all around, placed her hand on the handle, and entered the room. She put her lamp on the table, for fear the wind should extinguish the light, and then walked on to the terrace. The keen air came fresh and reviving to her, and she felt more firm and composed than she had done for some time past. The moon was sailing through an ocean of clouds, and afforded her the means of distinguishing the objects around for some distance. The country it looked upon, as we have before stated, was wild and uncultivated, and its height from the earth was considerable. To leap from thence, would be to jump immediately into the jaws of death. Emily stood and gazed around her for some minutes, and awful as it was for one so young to contemplate self-destruction, she felt a sentiment of satisfaction, when she perceived that she had thus the means of escaping from the more to be dreaded power of her terrible foes, who would strengthen the pangs of death, by inflicting upon her shame and degradation.

Wrapped in these reflections, Emily still paced the terrace, uncertain in what way to act, when suddenly a thought darted across her mind, and hope again sprang up in her bosom.

CHAPTER VIII.

THE SUPERNATURAL VISITOR.—THE SKELETON.

OUR heroine thought, that by fastening the bed clothes together, and affixing one end to the balustrades of the terrace, she might contrive to let herself down, and elated with this idea, she was about to enter the room, when a strong ray of light darted across her eyes, and filled the apartment; the light from her lamp emitted a blue sickly flame, and with the most unutterable horror, the eyes of Emily rested upon the phantom of her grandmother!

Appalled—aghast,—she started back, and held by the balustrades, or she must have fallen, while cold drops of perspiration stood upon her temples, and every limb seemed paralyzed with horror.

The spectre stood in the centre of the room, and a thin vapourish cloud seemed to play around her. Her countenance had a melancholy and extremely ghastly appearance, and her hollow filmy eyes were fixed solemnly and intently upon Emily. The silence of the grave prevailed around, and, at the presence of the unearthly being, the wind seemed to be hushed, and not the slightest breath to disturb the solemnity of the awe-inspiring moment, could be heard. Transfixed to the spot—her feet, as it were, fettered to the earth, Emily still stood and gazed upon the phantom with distended eyelids, and was unable to give utterance to a syllable; her tongue clave to the palate of her mouth, and speech was denied her.

Suddenly the spectre slowly receded towards the door, and as it did so, it raised its hand, and motioned our heroine to follow it. Aroused by some instinctive impulse, Emily obeyed, and the phantom, with noiseless steps, passed from the chamber into the gallery, and seemed to glide along like a shadow, turning every now and then, and looking after our heroine, at the same time encouraging her to proceed by a ghastly smile.

Emily felt suddenly imbued with courage, she had never befor experienced, and followed the awful spectre along the gallery, at the extremity of which, it began to ascend a flight of steps, which our heroine firmly believed led to the old chamber. Here she paused, and felt again somewhat daunted, when she recollected the horrible spectacle she had there witnessed, but the spectre once more turned its head, and motioned her to follow, and without any further hesitation, she obeyed.

Emily's conjectures were right; and the phantom stopped at the door of the old chamber. It flew open as it approached, and Emily, with trembing steps, also entered the room. Here the shade of Mrs. Fitzormond again stopped, and fixed its eyes with a still more melancholy intensity than before upon the countenance of Emily, which was blanched with terror. At length, it approached the bed, and pointed to the blood-stained sheets, and as it did so, three sepulchral groans issued from its chest, and echoed awfully through the dismal place.

Emily tried to speak, but she tried in vain, and the phantom then glided towards the old clock, to the case of which it significantly pointed, and then gradually faded away, and our heroine found herself standing alone in the gloomy old chamber.

It was some time ere Emily could recover from the surprise, consternation, and awe, into which this mysterious and supernatural adventure had thrown her; but, when her reason was in part restored to her, she fell upon her knees, and clasping her hands vehemently together, exclaimed :—

"All merciful God! direct me how to act!—and instruct me what to do in this awful and mysterious affair. *Why are the dead thus made to revisit me on earth? What is the secret that my poor grandmother was not permitted to impart to me ere she died; oh, teach me, I implore thee, how to unravel this mystery!"

She arose from her knees with renewed firmness, and suddenly she recollected the strange and significant manner in which the spectre had directed her attention to the clock-case, and it occurred to her immediately that there was some secret attached to this, which she was destined to discover.

No sooner did this idea cross her mind, than she hastened towards the old clock, which she remembered had stood in the same situation when she was an inmate of the room, and held the lamp close to it, and examined it all round, to see whether she could discover any thing to verify her surmises.

It was some time before she could perceive anything at all to justify her suspicions; but, at length, her hand touched some cold substance in the wainscot immediately behind the clock, which, on closer inspection, she found to be a spring. She was, of course, unacquainted with the nature of it, but after trying it in various ways, she bethought her to press upon it with all her might, and almost immediately it took effect, and a panel in the wainscot flew back, and revealed to our heroine a small closet.

Emily felt a shuddering sensation come over her, and she paused ere she entered the closet, her mind predicting that some dreadful circumstance was about to be revealed to her. At length, however, she mustered fresh courage, and boldly stepped into the closet. But she started back with a piercing shriek at the dreadful object which her eyes immediately encountered.

It was a human skeleton, with the tattered remnants of apparel clinging to the fleshless bones, and from which it appeared that it was the remains of a man. It was stretched on the floor, and seemed to have fallen from an old chair which stood close by, and in its hand was clasped a prayer-book. On a small table in the room was an empty pitcher, and a pen and ink.

It would be a needless task to seek to depicture the feelings of our heroine at this terrific sight, as the reader must readily imagine them; alone in that silent place, at that solemn hour of the night, and after the appalling adventure she had but just before met with, it is a wonder that she could sustain herself for an instant; but she conquered her feelings as much as possible, imagining that she was the humble instrument in the hands of Omnipotence of revealing a frightful crime, and, probably, bringing the guilty wretches to punishment, and stepped forward towards the mouldering and ghastly remains of mortality, and examined it more minutely. With difficulty she took the book from the hand of the skeleton, and hastily turning over the leaves, could discover no other marks than those on the back of the wrapper, which corresponded with those in the pocket-book she had before found in the old chamber, being " J. D. 1721," and were written in the same elegant hand. From what she could see, it appeared to her, that the unfortunate man, whoever he might be, had been confined in this room, and there left to die of starvation by his fiendish murderers.

This, then, was, probably, part of the dreadful secret which Mrs. Fitz-ormond had endeavoured to disclose when death abruptly terminated her mortal career, and she was, most likely, in some measure connected with the unfortunate being who had met with so shocking a fate. Perhaps (and the blood ran icy cold in her veins as the idea darted across her brain) they were the ghastly remains of the author of her existence; but the thought was too horrible for her to dare to encourage it.

After another pause of a few minutes, she advanced towards the table, and, looking behind the pitcher, was astonished to behold a number of manuscript papers, that were greatly defaced by time.

" Ah!" she cried, as she hastily seized them, "these, these are the precious documents that will, probably, reveal the dreadful secret, and be the means of bringing retribution upon the heads of the guilty, if they are not already summoned to their dread account. From these, too, may I ascertain the mystery of my birth. Merciful Heaven! I thank you for this!"

As she thus spoke, she took the manuscripts and the prayer-book, and casting one more fearful glance upon the skeleton, she hastily quitted the closet, pushed back the panel in its place, and hurried from the room.

Astonishment, horror, and mystery had so bound up the faculties of our heroine, that after she had left the old chamber she scarcely knew what she was doing, and went the wrong way, taking that end of the gallery which led to that part of the building where Gerald Darnley and his family resided, and she did not discover her mistake until she laid hold of the handle of the door which belonged to the chamber of Gerald, and turning it, attempted to open it. It happened that Gerald had been in no humour to go to bed after the occurrences of the night, and was sitting up and rumi-nating upon the obstinate determination of his son, and endeavouring to imagine how it would be best to act to conciliate all parties, without com-promising his own interest. Startled by the noise, he jumped up, and in a voice of alarm, cried,—

" Hah! what noise was that?—Who's there?"

Filled with almost inconceivable terror, when she heard the well-known voice of the ruffian, Emily extinguished her light, and fled with breathless haste along the gallery, dropping the MS. and book in her way, and never stopped until she had gained her own chamber; where, completely over-come with the power of her terrors after the several exciting incidents of the last half hour, she hastily locked the door, threw herself upon the bed, and was unconscious of anything but her own fears for several minutes. Then she listened attentively to ascertain whether any one was approaching, but all was quite still, and she felt grateful to Heaven for giving her the pre-sence of mind to extinguish her light; for, had she not done so, she had very little doubt but that Gerald, seeing its rays through the crevices of the door, would instantly have come out, discovered her, and, in all probability, her life would have fallen a sacrifice to his savage wrath.

She now, for the first time, remembered the MSS. and the prayer-book which she had dropped in the course of her flight, and she was in a terrible state of agitation and alarm when she thought of this untoward circum-stance. At first she thought of returning and searching for them, but, then, the fear of encountering Gerald prevented her, for, should he see her, nothing, she was certain, would save her from his fury. But then, again, should he find them, his suspicions might be excited, and she would in that case be placed in the same dangerous situation as she would have been had he caught her on the spot. Besides on these MSS. probably her whole happiness depended; from these she might at last obtain that information respecting her origin and her relations she had hitherto tried in vain to become acquainted with, and without which the secret might remain for ever concealed; she doomed to perpetual misery, doubt, and anxiety, and the guilty be suffered to escape with impunity the punishment due to their crimes. Stimulated by these ideas, she arose, gently opened the door, and was proceeding to step forth into the gallery, when again her heart failed her; an irresistible dread arrested her intention, and she returned to her room, leaving the MSS. to chance, but resolving to search for them at an early hour in the morning, before she thought that Gerald would leave his chamber.

The awful events she had that night undergone now again came to her mind, and, being involved in utter darkness, they were more calculated to excite her horror; but, at length, exhausted nature could support no more, and she sunk into a sound sleep, from which she did not awaken until the morning had far advanced, when, remembering what she had resolved the previous night to do, she hastily arose, and, looking into the parlour, she beheld them all seated at the breakfast table, therefore, she knowing the coast was clear, stepped cautiously on towards the spot where she must have dropped the book and the manuscripts, but they were not there, a circumstance which not only excited the greatest consternation in her bosom, but filled her with the most unqualified regret and disappointment, as the hopes that had been excited in her mind of unravelling the mystery were thus almost as suddenly crushed as soon as they had been formed.

She returned to her chamber in a state of great uneasiness, and had not long been there, when Patty tapped at the door, and was immediately admitted.

"I am glad to think, Emily," said she, with a smile of satisfaction, "that you have been enabled to sleep so soundly; I have knocked twice before, but could not make you hear me. It seems, however, that your sleep has been anything but refreshing, for,—bless me! my dear girl, how pale you look, and how violently you are agitated; for Heaven's sake, what has happened to you?"

"Oh! I have many awful and wonderful things to tell you, Patty," replied our heroine, "but I am afraid to tell them here. Meet me as soon as you can on the terrace; but say, have you noticed anything particular in the manner of your father this morning?"

"Why, he seems rather out of temper and agitated," answered Patty, "but there is nothing extraordinary in that."

"Thank Heaven!" exclaimed Emily, "and yet it is strange; but, perhaps, he did not——"

"What in the name of patience, my dear Emily, are you talking about?" asked Patty.

"You shall know all, by and by," said our heroine, "but do not stay with me any longer, lest your father should grow impatient, and suspect that we are talking of something which——"

"Come, Patty! Patty! what the devil are you loitering about?" at this moment Gerald shouted out.

"But you will attend the morning repast, will you not?" asked Patty.

"Oh! no, no; pray make some excuse for me," said Emily. "I cannot, dare not, meet those wretched men; I——"

"I will tell them you are unwell," hastily interrupted Patty; "it will be nothing more than the truth, I am certain. They will be going out presently, and then I shall have an opportunity of joining you."

With these words Patty left the room, and descended the stairs, and our heroine closing the door, gave herself up to reflection.

She was completely at a loss what to imagine respecting the manuscripts and the book; could it be possible that they had not fallen into the hands of Gerald, and if not, who had found them, and what purpose would they use them? It was a subject that occasioned her the most poignant regret, to think that she had lost them, for, by the appearance of the phantom to her, and the manner in which the secret closet had been pointed out to her, she could not entertain any doubt but that they contained the secret, the unravelment of which might have been the means of altering her condition in life, and rescuing her from those dangers and difficulties by which she was at present so surrounded. It was most likely the melancholy task of the poor murdered individual, whose skeleton was mouldering to dust in the closet, and disclosed the dismal history of his life and his sufferings, and had she had them in her possession, she would have had indubitable proof of his name, whether he was related to her, and who were his barbarous assassins; but now they were gone, and the mystery upon which she had been told by her grandmother her happiness depended, would most likely remain for ever in the same impenetrable state that it had hitherto been.

A confused train of ideas crossed the mind of Emily after Patty had left, the principal of which were fixed upon the subject of the adventure she had met with in the old chamber, the skeleton, and the manuscripts, the loss of the latter she still continued to regret most poignantly, and she could never sufficiently blame herself for having been so careless as to lose them in the manner she had; but, above all, she was completely at a loss to imagine into whose possession they had fallen, and what might be the consequences of the same to her. Conjecture, however, only bewildered her the more, and, at length, she gave up the attempt, and awaited with impatience the re-appearance of Patty, whose sympathy was the only consolation she possessed under her sufferings.

Neither Gerald or his son, however, seemed at all inclined to leave the house; and Emily, who occasionally watched them through the casement above the door at the foot of the stairs, could perceive that the latter seemed to be sullen and taciturn, while his father appeared to be by no means in one of the best of tempers. Occasionally a word or two would reach her ears, and once or twice she heard her name mentioned by them both, but the thread of their discourse she was unable to catch.

Patty was in the room, assisting old Madge in her domestic duties, and every now and then Gerald would direct some surly observation to her, which, however, was nothing uncommon, as kindness to him was quite unknown.

How Emily shuddered as she gazed upon the countenances of these two ruffians, and recollected the conversation she had overheard between them on the previous night, and how dreadful was the idea that she should be under the same roof and in the power of two wretches, whose hands might almost be said to be yet reeking with the blood of the poor murdered old man. To know, too, that she was doomed to die, or to yield to the lascivious desires of Chesterton. The horror of these thoughts was almost too powerful for her feelings to support, but she endeavoured to stifle her emotions, to put her trust in Omnipotence, and to bear her troubles with sufficient fortitude, so that she might be prepared to act with coolness and self-possession upon any emergency. When she recollected the sentiments which Will had expressed as regarded herself, and the determination of his character, she had, indeed, very good cause for misery, and she was resolved, at every hazard, to endeavour to make her escape. Even should the worst take place, she could only lose her life in making the attempt, and she had better do so, than to meet with the still more terrible fate with which she was threatened by Will Darnley, and Chesterton. After what she had seen and heard, to remain another night in that Old Lone House, she could not think of, without a feeling which chilled her heart; and although she would rather not expose Patty to the danger she would thus encounter herself, yet such was the urgency of the case, that she had made up her mind to avail herself of the proposal which the former had recently made, to be the companion of her flight. To remain with such wretches, the constant perpetrators of crime, and who seemed to glory in the shedding of human blood, would be, in a manner of speaking, participating in their guilt, and she could, therefore, easily find excuses for Patty's deserting her home, especially when it was done with the best of motives, and with an idea of avoiding corruption, and to prevent her from being a witness of those scenes that to one of her gentle and virtuous disposition, must be so revolting. Indeed, such was the deep interest which Patty had excited in her bosom, and the affection which her generous commiseration had inspired her with, that she shrunk with a feeling of repugnance from leaving her behind, when she would most likely be accused of assisting her, if she (Emily) should succeed in effecting her escape alone. She could never imagine, that one so diametrically opposite in disposition as Patty, could be the daughter of Gerald Darnley and Madge, and she was unable to banish an idea, that there was some mystery attached to her birth which time might, probably, unravel. Perhaps she, too, had been abandoned by her unnatural parents, and left to the mercy of strangers.

She was interrupted in the midst of these cogitations by a noise below, and, hastening to the head of the staircase, she beheld Will had arose, and having put on his hat, and thrown his gun over his shoulder, he was preparing to leave the house.

"What time shall you return, Will?" enquired Gerald.

"Oh, I don't know exactly," answered the other, in a surly tone, "but I dare say I shall come back quite as soon as I'm wanted. My presence might not be altogether agreeable when Mr. Chesterton——"

"But," hastily interrupted his father, in a tone of vexation, "why will you persist in making yourself such a fool, Will?"

"Mayhap you may not find me such a fool as you think me," said Will, with a significant expression of countenance, as he left the house.

As soon as he was gone, Gerald gave some instructions, apparently, to his wife, and then left the room by another door. Emily re-entered the apartment in a state of great uneasiness. The mention of the name of the villain Chesterton had made her shudder, and she felt glad to think she had made an excuse to keep to her chamber, as it might be the means of saving her an interview with that old miscreant who had plotted her destruction.

At length she heard the light footstep of Patty upon the stairs, and immediately afterwards she tapped at the door of her apartment.

"I could not come before, Miss," said Patty, when she had entered and closed the door after her, "although I was most anxious to do so, especially after the mysterious hints which you threw out this morning. Oh, Emily, I am certain that something unusual has happened, from the dark insinuations and surly behaviour of Will, and the great perturbation of manner evinced by my father, but they are both out of the way now, and my mother is so deaf, that if she had her ear to the key-hole even, she could not hear what we are talking about. Do for goodness sake tell me what you have seen or heard."

"I have both seen and heard that which has smote my heart with

horror," returned Emily; " but have you fortitude, think you, sufficient to bear what I am going to tell you ?"

" Oh, yes," returned Patty, " I have—it cannot be more dreadful than my worst surmises suggest ; but this suspense is insupportable."

" My heart sickens with disgust and terror when I think upon it," observed Emily, once more looking timidly around her.

Patty again urged her to satisfy at once her anxiety and curiosity, and, at length, our heroine complied, being frequently compelled to pause from the power of her own emotions, and the exclamations of horror that escaped the bosom of Patty on hearing the shocking recital. When she had concluded, there was a dead pause for several minutes, neither of them being able to speak, and Patty's feelings were wound up to such a pitch of astonishment, disgust, and unqualified terror, by what she had heard, that her blood ran cold in her veins, and she had some difficulty in preventing herself from fainting. Had the terrific tale fallen from any other lips than those of Emily, she could not have believed it was true. Wicked and guilty, as she felt certain her father and brother were, she had not, she could not (although the circumstance of the blood-stained bed in the old chamber was a mysterious circumstance) make up her mind before to think them guilty of bloodshed, but now the conversation which Emily had overheard placed it beyond a doubt ; and it was too much to be feared, that the old miser was not the first unhappy being who had fallen by their hands ; and could she acknowledge them as relations again? Could she remain beneath the same roof with them, and share in the fruits of robbery and bloodshed ? " Oh, God !" she reflected, " what anguish, what unappeasable agony do those thoughts create in my breast ! How does my heart revolt from such

No. 9.

an idea!"—The very air of the place seemed to breathe contamination and guilt.

"Oh! Emily," observed the poor girl, "to what a tale of horror have I been listening. It seems scarcely possible that there can be such monsters in existence, and those monsters my —— no, no, I cannot, I dare not, call them by the names I have been taught. Heaven forbid that I should be linked with such wretches by the ties of consanguinity."

"You are not, you cannot be, dear Patty," said Emily ; "of that I feel confident ;—we are both the children of mystery and misfortune, and we will together share the same fate."

"We will,—we will!" eagerly cried Patty. "Dear Emily, whatever troubles may attend us, whatever dangers and miseries we may have to encounter, they cannot be greater than those we are now exposed to, and —— but I had forgot myself; Gerald is still in the house, and should he listen and overhear us, our lives would, most undoubtedly, fall a sacrifice. Let us hasten to the terrace, it is never frequented by him, and therefore we can commune there in safety."

Emily complied with the request of her companion, and they soon reached the room which opened on to the terrace.

"Emily," said Patty, in a low tone, when they had first looked round and ascertained that there was no one near them, "are you willing, are you ready to join me in attempting to make an escape from this frightful, this awful place?"

"Oh, Patty, why ask me such a question?" replied Emily; "how thankful should I be were the means placed in my power. But what mean you by making your escape? Have you not free egress from the house whenever you please?"

"No, Emily," returned Patty, "I am as much a prisoner as yourself. Since I have been taken from the care of my aunt, this terrace has been the full extent of my liberty."

"You surprise me! and yet, why should I feel astonished at any act of cruelty and injustice which such wretches may be guilty of?"

"The outer door," continued Patty, "is ever kept securely locked ; and whichever of the three, my father, mother, or Will, are at home, they keep it in their possession, so that all getting away by that means is out of the question."

"Then how do you propose making the attempt?" eagerly asked Emily.

"By this terrace," replied her companion.

"The way I was thinking of myself," said Emily ; "by tearing the bed-clothes and fastening them together, we might reach the earth in safety."

"We might," observed Patty; "but still I have a better method than that. Amongst the old lumber, in one of the uninhabited rooms of this building, the other day I found a rope-ladder, which has, in all probability, been used by Gerald and Will in some of their nefarious transactions, so that our descent might be effected without any difficulty. Oh! let the consequences be what they may, they cannot be half so terrible as to remain under the same roof as robbers and murderers. Even should I afterwards perish of hunger, I am determined that this night shall be the last I will remain here."

"And why remain here another night?" asked Emily, with a shudder, as the events of the previous night recurred to her memory.

"Believe me, were there any possibility of accomplishing it with prudence," answered Patty, "our flight should take place this instant; but, it cannot be ; I have arrangements to make, which I cannot, by any possibility complete, before to-morrow evening; for you know, my dear Emily, by being too precipitate, we may thwart all our designs."

"I cannot deny but that you speak both reasonably and justly," remarked Emily, "but, oh, Patty, the idea of remaining another night in this dreadful place, is more than sufficient, after the horrors, the unprecedented horrors I have witnessed since I have been a prisoner here, is more than enough to create alarm in the bosom of one much more courageous than I am myself. But, should we succeed, whither do you propose going?"

"I have already said, to my aunt's," replied Patty.

"But," observed Emily, "would not your father easily discover the place of our retreat; and, what could the opposition of your aunt effect against his will?"

"My opinion is," replied Patty, "that it is the last place he would suspect we should fly to, as he would consider that I should be sure not to imagine I should seek the protection of the only friend I knew in the world, and that is the very reason I have chosen it; we must, however, act with the greatest caution, or all our schemes will most assuredly be frustrated."

"Then, to-morrow night," said Emily.

"Yes, to-morrow night, if Heaven aid us, we will quit these accursed walls, I hope for ever," answered Patty; "and something tells me, that we shall not be left to destitution and misery, while rectitude and virtue guide our conduct."

"We shall not, I'm sure we shall not, dear, dear Patty," exclaimed Emily; "your words inspire me with redoubled hope and courage. Oh, how shall I ever be able to repay the debt of gratitude I shall owe you for being the means of releasing me from so terrible a fate as that which threatens me while I remain here?"

"Talk not so, Emily, I beg," said Patty, "am I not your sister in misfortune? What credit, then, can I take to myself for the performance of that in which I cannot but say I have been guided by something of a selfish feeling. Henceforth, I hope nothing but death will divide our affection, and that some day or the other, we may be as ample partakers of happiness, as we are now of misery."

"Heaven ordain that we may," fervently ejaculated our heroine, and her eyes beamed an expression of reciprocal affection upon Patty, which could not be misunderstood by the latter;—"by to-morrow night, then——"

"Everything shall be arranged," rejoined Patty, "and we will make the attempt to quit this hateful place, and the merciless wretches whom I dare not designate my kindred."

"At what hour?" asked Emily.

"I cannot, with any certainty, inform you," replied Patty;—"we must not make any attempt until they have all retired to rest; when you hear the house quite still, you may expect me."

"Enough, my dear girl;" exclaimed Emily her eyes filling with tears of hope and gratitude; "and oh, should we prove successful, there is no trouble, no labour, I shall consider too great to contribute to our mutual benefit. But think you, Patty, you will have fortitude sufficient to accompany me to the old chamber, where I will show you undeniable proof of the truth of part of the dreadful recital I have given you."

"Alas! I want nothing to confirm what you have related to me, Emily," answered Patty; "not only should I be unworthy of your love, should I doubt you, but entirely opposed to reason and my own conscience, when I recollect the desperate character of Gerald and his son. But, if it will not be harrowing up your feelings too much, I will attend you."

" I never harmed the unfortunate being ; but, on the contrary, I deeply, I sincerely deplore his melancholy fate, and earnestly trust his inhuman assassins will be brought to punishment ; and, therefore, what should I fear ?" said our heroine ; " it is a terrible spectacle, but, as we know not what, at some future period may occur, and how deeply we may be connected with this mysterious circumstance, I think it is decidedly necessary that you should witness the same as I have done, so that you may be able to corroborate the testimony I might be called upon to give. But, should your father discover us there ?"

" I think it is most probable that he has left the house," replied Patty, "for he said something to my mother when he retired from the room to that effect. Besides, I know that he never goes near the old chamber, of which he seems to entertain, (and it is very clear, not without good reason), the utmost dread. But, how know you that it is unlocked ?"

" It was unlocked last night," answered Emily, " and so, unless either Gerald or his son, have visited it since, it remains the same now."

" Then I know very well that they have not been near it," remarked Patty, "so that there is sure to be nothing to prevent our entrance ; come, then, I am ready to accompany you."

Emily took the arm of her companion, and with cautious steps, and frequently listening and looking round to see whether they were observed, they made their way towards the old chamber.

They found the door standing ajar, just as Emily had emerged from it on the previous night, and when she recalled to her memory the awful circumstances under which that visit was made ; the spectre of Mrs. Fitzormond, which she was certain had guided her thither, and the horrors that followed, she felt a dreadful faintness come over her, and paused, supporting herself by the arm of Patty, and trembled at the thought of once more encountering the ghastly object which had before so appalled her. Her companion did not evince so much terror as herself, and our heroine found that she had considerably over-rated her own courage, when she imagined that she could return to this scene with anything like strength of nerve.

Patty perceiving her emotion, would have persuaded her to return to the apartment they had just quitted, but Emily soon recovered herself, and they entered the old gothic chamber, which was impressed upon the recollection of our heroine by so many singular and mysterious circumstances. They found everything there in just the same condition as when they had before visited it, and the bed-clothes did not seem to have been disturbed in the least since they had turned them down, and discovered the marks of blood. This very much surprised them after the agitation Gerald and Will evinced, and any one would have thought that they would have taken care, either to have seen that the chamber was fastened up, or that the blood-stained sheets were removed.

Emily led the way towards that part of the chamber where the old clock stood, and having pressed upon the secret spring, the panel glided back, and they entered the closet.

Firm as Patty had imagined herself, she started back with a shudder of the most unconquerable horror when the skeleton met her gaze, and clinging to the arm of Emily, looked aghast.

" Oh, let us away !" she cried, " I have seen quite enough ;—this dreadful spectacle will never be erased from my memory."

Our heroine was proceeding to obey, when her eyes became fixed upon something which glittered upon the floor, close by the hand of the skeleton. She stooped down, and picking it up, discovered that it was a handsomely chased ring, with an emerald set round with pearls. It seemed as if it had dropped off the finger of the unfortunate being whose ghastly remains they were now gazing at, and had before escaped the observation of Emily. Like the pocket-book and prayer-book, it was marked with the simple initials "J. D.," and was evidently made for the finger of a man. From this circumstance, it seemed very certain that the closet had not been entered for many years before our heroine had been led there in so mysterious and awful a manner, for, had Gerald or his son been there, it is not likely that their cupidity would have permitted them to have left this ring behind them.

"I will take this," said Emily, carefully concealing the ring in her bosom," it may serve, at some future period, to forward the ends of justice, and be the means of identifying the unfortunate individual who has met with so horrible a death."

"God grant that it may !" firmly ejaculated Patty ; and then again urging Emily away, they left the closet, closing the secret panel carefully after them.

They retraced their way to the room which opened upon the terrace, and when they had got there, Patty, for the first time, gave free vent to the feelings of terror the awful sight she had witnessed, had excited in her breast.

"That the unfortunate man has been left to perish of hunger, I think is the most probable conclusion we can come to ;" said she, " but yet, is it not rather strange, that if Gerald and his son were aware of the skeleton being in the closet, and they were guilty of the crime, they should not have buried such an evidence of the horrid deed they had perpetrated ?"

"It does, indeed, seem remarkable," replied Emily, "but, still fancying, most likely, that this secret closet would never be discovered by any one, they imagined it would be secure there."

"Good God !" exclaimed Patty, "when I think of this horrible circumstance, and reflect that the probable perpetrators of so fiendish a crime are my father and my brother, I can scarcely contain my feelings. But, after the barbarous assassination of the poor old miser, which you heard them acknowledge last night, how can I doubt that they are capable of committing any bloody deed ? Would that all doubts of my consanguinity to them were removed. What misery, what racking anguish should I be released from."

At this moment, Emily uttered an exclamation of astonishment, and stooping down, picked up a bundle of papers that was lying close by their feet, and which they had not perceived before.

"By Heaven ! these are the very manuscripts I found in the closet ;" our heroine ejaculated, " and which I dropped in the gallery ;—how could they have come here ?"

"Wonderful !" cried Patty, gazing at the packet of musty papers which Emily held in her hand, with a look of astonishment and curiosity; " these may at once unravel the dreadful mystery. Surely the ways of Providence are wonderful ! Let us immediately peruse them, and——"

At this moment, the sound of horses' hoofs met their ears and arrested their attention, and looking forth from the terrace, they were greatly disconcerted to behold Mr. Chesterton riding towards the house. Emily turned very pale, and hastily concealed the papers in her bosom.

"Good Heavens !" she cried, "how shall I avoid meeting this man, whom I never behold but he inspires my bosom with a feeling of disgust and abhorrence, which is completely overpowering ? How can I patiently endure the presence, and listen to the hateful importunities of a man who has bargained for my virtue, and made up his mind to my destruction ? Oh, let us hasten to conceal ourselves, Patty ; for the love of Heaven ——"

"Nay, my dear girl," said the compassionate Patty, " pray be more firm, and you may set the villain at defiance.   Besides, of what use would it be for you to conceal yourself, as he would not leave again until he had seen you, and by such conduct, you would be sure to bring down upon you the wrath of Gerald?"

"But you can excuse me, Patty," said Emily, in a voice of great agitation, "you have already told your father that I am indisposed, and, therefore, it will not cause any surprise, if you add that I am quite unable to see company."

While our heroine was thus speaking, the object of her fears raised his head, and his eyes directly rested on Emily and her companion.   A smile of exultation and satisfaction immediately passed over his disagreeable features upon recognising the former, and he kissed his hand to her, with an air of familiarity which excited a feeling of the utmost disgust in her bosom, and called the blushes, deep mantling to her cheeks.   When, however, he saw Patty, he frowned, and directly afterwards he was hid from sight.

"It would be entirely useless now to offer any excuse, Emily," said Patty, "since he has seen you, and, as we were both together, should you refuse to attend the summons of Gerald, it would bring down upon me his anger, for he would think that you acted by my persuasions, and he might be tempted to do something which would be the means, probably, of frustrating those plans of escape which we have devised.   Come, Emily, endeavour to be firm, I repeat, and you will be able to repulse the detestable advances of this hoary-headed libertine."

Emily wrung her hands in despair, as Patty thus spoke, but could not offer any word in reply.   Her observations were too reasonable to be easily rebutted, and taking her arm, they walked away from the terrace, and hastened to Emily's apartment.   Here our heroine had only just time to conceal the manuscripts she had recovered again in such a singular manner, when the gruff voice of Gerald was heard calling his daughter.

Patty seeking to encourage Emily by a look, and enjoining her to silence, obeyed the summons of Gerald, and descended the stairs into the parlour.

CHAPTER IX.

THE INTERVIEW.—THE MANUSCRIPTS.

WHEN Patty had left her, our heroine burst into tears.   From approaching Chesterton she shrunk with disgust and fear ; but she had no means to avoid it ; to oppose the will of the ruffian Gerald, and the wretch who employed him in this villanous transaction, would have been complete madness, and could have had no other effect than to cause them to use immediate violence ; and could but her feelings have permitted her, she thought that to dissimulate a little, would be the most advisable plan, as it might obtain from them some indulgence and forbearance, until she and Patty could have an opportunity of putting their projected escape into execution. But how could she dissemble with such miscreants as them ?—she felt that it would be utterly impossible for her to attempt to prevent the expression of the real sentiments they had excited in her bosom.

In a few minutes, Patty returned to the room with a message from Gerald, commanding her to attend them down stairs immediately.

"I did all I could to excuse you, Emily," said her friend ;—"pleaded your indisposition, and several other things that suggested themselves to my mind, but it was all to no purpose, as I expected.   Mr. Chesterton had seen us together, and that was quite sufficient.   My father said that if you were not too ill to enjoy my society, you were quite well enough to see Mr. Chesterton, and, therefore, he insists that you will not raise any more objections, but come at once."

"Alas! what shall I do?" cried Emily, in tones of despair; "what a painful, what a terrible fate is mine."

"Courage,—courage, Emily, for goodness sake," entreated Patty; "should you delay, and remain here any longer in conversation with me, the suspicions of my father may be excited, and we know not then what may be the consequences."

Here Gerald demanded, in peremptory tones, whether his daughter was coming or not, and intimated his determination to come and fetch her, if she did not immediately obey. Emily, therefore, endeavoured to regain her composure as much as possible, and, with a faltering step, followed Patty down the stairs.

On her entrance, Chesterton advanced towards her with affected kindness in his demeanour, and attempted to take her hand, at the same time he said, in a voice into which he endeavoured to throw as much gentleness and affection as possible.

"Dearest Emily, I am delighted again to see you, and regret that you should be ill; I hope——"

Emily interrupted him.

—"Is it a matter of surprise, Mr. Chesterton, that I should be ill, when I find myself the victim of a cruel persecution; deprived of my liberty, and insulted by your hated passion? You have basely, wickedly deceived me in everything you have uttered; and have even plotted my destruction! Did you not tell me that here I should be treated with every kindness and indulgence? and how have you kept your word? But I waste my breath in appealing to one whose heart seems callous alike to virtue and honour."

"I suppose you can dispense with my company?" said Gerald, rising from his seat, and frowning upon our heroine, as she gave utterance to the last words; "the attendance of a third person, when matters of this kind are being transacted, are not generally agreeable. Patty, what do you stand there for, gaping? Away, girl!"

"Oh, no, I pray, do not leave me, Patty," exclaimed our heroine, with emotion; "do not let me be alone with this bad man," (Chesterton frowned)—"nothing should be said which would be improper for you to hear."

"I dare say you think so," said Gerald, with a bitter sneer, "but you see me and Mr. Chesterton happen to differ from that opinion, Come, come, girl, do you hear?" With these words, Gerald laid hold of Patty's arm with violence, and pulled her after him, and casting a look of pity and encouragement upon Emily, she followed her father from the room.

"Emily," said Chesterton, when they had gone, forcibly taking her hand between his, and compelling her to take a seat by his side, "will you ever continue thus obstinately blind to your own interest and happiness? Will you never listen to my sincere and ardent protestations of love with any other feeling than disdain and freezing coldness? Foolish girl! Could you but read my heart, you——"

"I do read your heart," interrupted Emily, with more spirit, "and know it, therefore, to be base and treacherous! I know you, sir, to be a heartless villain, or you would never thus brutally persecute a poor, friendless girl, whose tender years, innocence, and destitute condition, should plead for her in your eyes, and make you hate and despise yourself for having encouraged sentiments towards her that are only calculated to excite the utmost abhorrence. Unhand me, sir, and suffer me to depart, and if you would have me forget the past, and to pay you that respect which is due to your years, forbear to give utterance to your disgusting sentiments, and reproach yourself for ever having spoken them."

"Admirable!" exclaimed Chesterton, with the most provoking sarcasm; "I never beheld anything more exquisite in my life! Upon my word, Emily, these heroics become you amazingly, and will serve to amuse me, while they cannot avail you the least in the world. But, come, my dear girl, why do you take so much pains to make yourself miserable, when, at the same time, every chance of happiness is offered to you?"

"Happiness! happiness with *you!*" cried Emily, rising hastily, and fixing upon Chesterton a withering look of scorn and hatred; "but I waste my breath in appealing to one who is destitute of every principle of honour or humanity!"

"Upon my word, young lady, you pay me some very pretty compliments;" returned the villain; "I ought to feel highly flattered by them. But these are usually the expressions of a silly and inexperienced girl, who——"

"Who you would initiate into vice," hastily rejoined Emily, "and make familiar with crime! One whom you would bring to ruin and irretrievable misery. Oh, shame! shame! is there not one spark of virtue and pity left within your breast?"

"Emily," observed Chesterton, "this is only a silly waste of time. I have repeatedly told you, that your charms have excited such a passion in my breast, that nothing can extinguish it. Encourage it, and I swear there is nothing you can desire which shall not be at your command; continue obstinately to oppose it, and that which before was love, may be turned to hatred, or mere sensual desire, and that desire once sated, you would cease to hold any influence over my affections. You have now the power to rivet my very soul to you for ever; to make me your slave; your adorer; then, why reject such certain bliss, for such equally certain misery? Can you complain of my want of forbearance, when I have you here completely in my power, and could immediately enforce a compliance with my wishes? Here no one could fly to rescue you, and——"

"Unmanly ruffian!" interrupted the indignant and disgusted Emily, unable to control the resentment which the boldness and heartlessness of his speech created; "and is it thus you triumph in your iniquity, and exult over the forlorn and destitute condition of an unfortunate girl?— Shame upon your grey hairs! You may have children of your own, and think, then, what they would suffer if similarly situated to me."

"Psha! nonsense; I am tired of thus wasting time in bandying words to no purpose," said Chesterton, impatiently. "Emily, that man must, indeed, be cold and insensible who could resist the power of your charms. Such a one is not he who now sues your favours; and having once inspired such a sentiment in his heart, he will never rest until it is gratified. Every time I gaze upon you, my admiration, my love increases; the more I dwell upon your beauties, more deeply do my senses become entranced, enraptured. By all my hopes, I would not resign you for all the wealth of Golconda, or were I to be made emperor of the earth. No, lovely, all captivating Emily, here let me enfold you in my arms, and swear——"

"Hands off! you damned old poacher!" exclaimed a loud voice behind them, just as the villain Chesterton threw his arms round the waist of the victim of his persecution. He released her trembling form in a moment, and starting back in confusion and amazement, his eyes became fixed upon the countenance of Will Darnley, who had forced open the small casement, and was standing before it, with his musket presented at the steward, and apparently half inclined to fire at him.

"Back! back! old man!" added Will, in a determined tone; "if you

touch but a hair of Emily's head, may I swing from the highest gibbet that can be found in the country if I do not send you to your last account a short while before your time."

"Confusion!" cried Chesterton, "am I again thwarted and obstructed by this beardless boy?—Will Darnley, put down your gun, are you mad?"

"No, no, Mr. Chesterton," replied Will, "I am not mad, though, perhaps, you may take me to be so;—the whole of it is, I will not see Emily insulted by you, and——"

"Insulted, fool!" vociferated Chesterton; "you know not what you are talking about;—are you not aware that——"

"I am aware that you are an infernal old rogue!" interrupted Will Darnley, with the utmost coolness; "but I have made up my mind that you, at any rate, shall not annoy the girl. An old fellow like you must go farther a-field, and leave such young game for such as Will Darnley to become the master of. What, ho!—father, are you in? Open the door, and don't keep me standing here all day."

"Ma conscience!" cried old Madge, tottering from an adjoining room, "what be's th' matter wi' the bairn now? I ne'er heard sic a noise in a' ma life. Ma conscience, Willie, are you daft, or are you going to shoot us a'?"

"Open the door, mother," said Will, impatiently; "I have only been giving this old gentleman a bit of a lecture at the muzzle of the musket. I don't know whether he is satisfied; if not, I dare say I can find arguments sufficiently forcible to convince him."

"Insolent clown!" cried Chesterton, gnashing his teeth and frowning terribly, as Madge unlocked the door, and admitted Will; at the same moment Gerald entered from an adjoining room, and Emily having par-

No. 10

tially recovered from the confusion into which this circumstance had thrown her, and no one offering to obstruct her, she hastened up the stairs, and regained her own apartment, in a state of mind we need not attempt to describe.

She had not been many seconds in the room, however, when the loud war of words from the parties below arrested her attention, and excited her curiosity. She trembled at the wild recklessness and impetuosity of Will, who seemed prepared to go to any lengths to obtain the accomplishment of the object upon which he had evidently fixed his mind, and she apprehended even as much or more danger from him than the wretch Chesterton.

" Good God!" she mentally ejaculated, as the loud tones of Will Darnley's voice smote her ears, " there will be murder committed before they have done. Alas! what will become of me, thus placed in the power of such desperate and remorseless wretches ?"

Unable longer to resist her anxiety and curiosity, she cautiously took her old station at the top of the staircase, from whence she could see into the parlour below, and watched all that passed with the most painful interest. Will Darnley was standing with his arms folded, and leaning on the muzzle of his gun in one part of the room, and opposite to him was Chesterton, whose features were completely distorted with rage, excited by the bitter taunts and invectives which the former had been lavishing upon him. Gerald Darnley exhibited extreme wrath, which appeared to be directed against his son. The tall and bony figure of old Madge completed the group. She was, apparently, attempting the part of mediator, but it seemed without success, for, at length, Gerald pushed her sternly away, and commanded her in a gruff voice to quit the room.

" Will," ejaculated Gerald, passionately, addressing himself to his son, " beware, for if you arouse my wrath, you may repent it. This is the second time Mr. Chesterton has been annoyed by your interference in that which does not concern you, and if you again——"

" Hark you, father," interrupted Will, " you know you might as well whistle against the wind as to threaten me. I am not to be intimidated in that way. I told you· before the girl had taken my fancy; we are more suited to each other by years, and damme, if I don't have her in spite of Chesterton's teeth. Let him find some other girl, if he is still so attached to youth; he shall not have her; I have said it, and I will keep my word."

Chesterton laughed scornfully.

" Aye, you may laugh now, old boy," said Will, " but I doubt much whether you will be in so merry a mood by and by."

"· Will Darnley," said Chesterton, " you certainly must have taken leave of your senses, or you never would talk in this manner· Know you not of the bargain between your father and me ?"

" I care nothing about your bargains," replied Will; " had you acted faithfully to the instructions given you by that master you pretend to serve truly, you would never have made any such bargain at all; but as it is, why you must be content to take the consequences, and put up with the loss of your money."

" Idiot!" cried Chesterton, fiercely, " would you ruin yourself and your father ?"

" From incurring whose displeasure have we to fear ruin ?"

" Mine !"

" Ha! ha! ha!" laughed Will, scornfully.

" Will," again cried Gerald, " I command you to silence."

" Sorry I can't comply with your request, father," said his son, " but you see I happen to be in a talkative mood at present, so I can't stop my tongue when I like. At any rate, I shall not hold my peace for any such fellows as the old scoundrel who now stands before me!"

" Insolent boy! I will hear no more!" cried Chesterton, furiously, and rushing upon Will, he seized him by the collar, and attempted to deal him a violent blow. Will, however, shook him off with the same ease as if he had been an infant, and hurling him to some distance from him, he wielded the butt-end of his musket in the air, and would have dashed Chesterton's brains out, had not Gerald suddenly rushed forward, and arrested his arm.

" Mad! headstrong fool!" exclaimed the latter, " what would you do ?"

" Make him pay for his insult with his life," answered Will; " another second, and his blood would have been spilt for his boldness."

" This rash boy will bring ruin upon us all," said Gerald. " Chesterton, let me beg of you to leave the house for the present ; I will see you by and by at the place where you are staying, when this business can, and shall, be satisfactorily arranged."

The enraged steward gathered himself on to his feet, and speaking to Gerald, said,—

" Remember what you have promised, it will be well for you. As for this foolish boy, I shall see him swing from the gallows yet."

" Not if you do not quickly depart," replied Will; " for you will not live to see your prophecy fulfilled."

The steward frowned revengefully upon him, and again telling Gerald to remember, he quitted the house.

" Will," said Gerald, when Chesterton had gone; " I thought, after our conversation upon this subject last night, we should not have had any more of this foolery ; but it appears you have got something into your head which, if you persist in encouraging it, will bring a fine house about our ears."

" And e'en let it," answered Will, sullenly. " I tell you what it is, father, you do not like to be baulked in anything you have made your mind up to, and in that one respect, in particular, I am exactly like you ; as I told you last night (for I gave you then no reason to suppose you should hear no more of this subject, although you say I did), I do not care what the consequences may be, the girl has taken my fancy, and if a hundred Mr. Chestertons, or the devil himself, stood in the way, I would have her in spite of them."

" Psha! it is only a foolish whim, which will soon be banished from your mind," said his father; " why are you so obstinately bent upon having this girl? Are there not plenty more as good-looking as her in the world ?"

" There may be," replied his son, " but that's not the question; the whole of it is, that Emily has made a stronger impression upon me than any I have hitherto seen, and as I think it's not very likely I shall readily meet with another whom I could fancy so well, why I have made up my mind not to do as the old saying has it, namely, ' go further, and fare worse.' "

Gerald gave utterance to an oath, and walked sullenly away ; and Emily, satisfied with what she had seen and heard, re-entered her room, where she was soon afterwards joined by Patty, to whom, with many tears, she related all that had happened, and who saw at once the truly critical situation in which she was placed, and sincerely pitied her. She, however, endeavoured to soothe her feelings with the hope of the success of their design on the following night; but alas! to remain for one night, for one hour, in such a situation, was almost too dreadful for contemplation.

Patty, who well knew the determined character of her brother, could not hold out any hopes to her, that, while she remained there, he would desist from his designs, and she was only surprised that he had not ere now sought some means of getting an interview with her, making known his passion, and attempting to get her solely into his power. She trembled when she heard of the threats that had passed between Chesterton and Will, for she feared there would be murder before it ended. Will Darnley was a young man, who did not care what he did to accomplish any project he had formed, or to gratify his revenge against those who attempted to thwart him in his designs; and it was very evident that, had not his father fortunately been present, the life of Chesterton would have been sacrificed. He had been brought up in that brutal and reckless manner by his wretched father, that it had become a part of his nature, and no persuasion, no arguments, no threats could ever destroy it.

Night had set in, silence reigned in the Old Lone House, and Emily was seated in her chamber, immersed in the dismal reflections which the exciting events of the last few days had given rise to in her bosom; but paramount above all her other painful thoughts, was the guilty passion which Chesterton and Will Darnley had imbibed for her, and which had already been the cause of so much anguish to her, and would, doubtless, be productive of so much more misery. That Chesterton would persist in his hateful importunities,—from what she had already been able to judge of his disposition,—she had not the least doubt; and that Will was also of the most determined character, she was equally most firmly persuaded. Therefore, between them both, her situation was truly dreadful, unless her and Patty could succeed in making their escape from the house, which she at all times feared would not be attended with any success. But to make the attempt she was fully determined, at all hazards, for death was preferable to the life of suspense she was leading, and to the fate with which she was threatened. The scene she had lately witnessed between Chesterton and Will Darnley, and the violent conduct of the latter, had filled her breast with the greatest terror, and she feared that murder would be the issue of it; for to men like Will and his rival, crime was familiar, and they would not hesitate at shedding blood for the gratification of their vengeance. When she reflected, too, that the villain Gerald was bound to force her compliance with the wishes of Chesterton, or to take her life, she shuddered with the most sickly feeling of terror, and whichever way she turned, nothing but the most utter despair surrounded her.

She clasped her hands together, and raising her eyes to heaven, she ejaculated,—

"Oh, merciful Father! for what am I reserved?—What have I done, of what heinous sins am I guilty, that I should be visited with this terrible retribution?—But sinful wretch that I am, thus to arraign the justice of the Almighty!—Rather let me submit with patience to His all-wise decrees, and He will, in His infinite mercy, release me from the perils by which I am at present surrounded."

The impetuous passion of Will Darnley, she felt convinced, would induce Chesterton to become more urgent, and she, therefore, plainly saw, that unless she escaped from it, her fate would quickly be decided one way or the other. This was a terrible thing to reflect upon, and it was astonishing that she did not sink under it; but Providence often gives the weakest strength to combat horrors, which the most firm and resolute would shrink from encountering with the unconquerable alarm. The sympathy which Patty evinced in her sufferings, and the sincerity of her conduct hitherto, was a great relief to her, and she felt as deep an interest in her fate, or nearly so, as she did in her own. There was a similarity in their sorrows, which naturally caused them to commisserate each other, and there was a mystery about the origin of Patty, which often caused our heroine much reflection, for that Gerald Darnley was the parent of so much virtue and gentleness, she could not believe. It was this idea, and the certainty she felt of the cruelty she had been, and daily would be, exposed to while she remained at the Old Lone House, which induced her more than all to accede to her proposals, and to allow her to become the companion of her flight; and, although the project might be considered a wild one, it was fully justified by the critical situation in which they were placed, and the imminent danger with which they were surrounded. She looked forward to the following night,—which was the time they had fixed upon for their flight,—with the utmost impatience, and was in a state of the most horrible suspense and fear until it arrived, and she could ascertain the result; but that she would either succeed, or meet with death, she was fully determined.

It was a tempestuous night, and the rain pattered loudly against the ivy-covered casements of her dreary chamber, and the wind howled in fitful gusts through the different rooms and avenues of the ancient building. A cheerful fire blazed in the grate, by the side of which our heroine had seated herself, and again and again ran over in her mind the events of the last few days, which were marked with so much horror and cause for alarm, and ever and anon she cast her eyes fearfully around the room, as she recollected the spectre she had seen, the horrors of the old chamber, the blood-stained bed, and the skeleton; and every moment she was fearful that some fresh horrors would arise to her view. These thoughts gained such powerful ascendancy over her mind, that she shuddered at the slightest noise, and was afraid to gaze into the darkness of the further end of the chamber, and which the faint rays of her lamp would not penetrate, lest her eyes might rest upon some ghastly object. Yet, although she felt tired, she was not at all inclined to retire to her couch, on the contrary, she felt a secret dread of doing so, and remained in the chimney corner, unable to move, and listening to the dismal howling of the blast, which at intervals was acompanied by the dreary screech of the owl, which sounded like the awful omen of death.

What would she not have given, had it been in her power, to have had a companion?—What a relief would it have been to her if Patty had been with her, and why had Gerald refused her request to let her sleep with her, unless he had some evil design in view, which he knew that her presence would be the means of frustrating?

She now remembered the manuscripts, and considering this an excellent opportunity of perusing them, she arose and took them from the place in which she had carefully deposited them. She trembled when she took them in her hand, and a strange feeling came over her such as she had never felt before. She returned to the fireside, and trimming the lamp, she proceeded to inspect the papers, with the contents of which she could not help thinking she was in some shape or other connected. They were in a very mutilated state, in some places quite rotten with the damp, and in others they looked as if they had been gnawed by rats. A considerable portion of the writing was rendered perfectly illegible, but that which was distinguishable, was written in a bold and elegant hand. The papers seemed to have been thrown together promiscuously, and Emily was unable to find out any commencement to the matter upon which they treated, and the whole formed a mass of unconnected sentences, the spontaneous thoughts, it appeared to be, of some poor unfortunate, labouring under the most acute suffering.

Emily trembled when she prepared to peruse them, and a mist seemed to float before her eyes, and obscure her vision for a few minutes.

"What can be the meaning of this extraordinary emotion?" she ejaculated, "why am I thus agitated upon taking these mysterious papers in my hand?"

She started, and let the manuscripts drop from her hand on to the table, as she felt almost confident that she heard a deep moan, as if from some person in great agony, close to her ear. She looked timidly around her;— but nothing met her gaze, save the different things which the chamber contained, and she sought to combat the fears that would, in spite of her efforts to the contrary, steal over her, and to attribute the sound she had heard to the dismal moaning of the wind. The night was far advanced, and all remained perfectly still below. Emily having somewhat conquered her terrors, arose, and gently opening the door, looked through the casement below, into the parlour. A light was burning brightly upon the table, at which she beheld Gerald seated, and intently gazing upon something which he held in his hand, and which appeared to be a miniature. The expression of his countenance was stern, and his mind seemed to be entirely absorbed in thought. He never removed his eyes from this miniature,—for such our heroine soon discovered it was,—for several minutes; and his whole interest and attention appeared to be wrapped up in the contemplation of it. Suddenly, however, he burst into a loud and ironical laugh, which at that solemn hour, and coming from lips like his, sounded particularly awful. Emily shuddered, and then Gerald started and looked fearfully around, as though he was terrified at the sound of his own voice, and Emily could not help observing the awful and peculiar expression of his eye. He returned the miniature to a small box, which was upon the table, and having locked it, resumed his seat, and leaning his head on his hand, he appeared to drop off into a deep reverie.

Although Emily could not gaze upon this man with any other sentiments than those of the most unqualified terror, she found it impossible to help watching him; and a few minutes afterwards, she saw him again arise from his chair, and after having gone to the door which opened upon the heath, to see whether it was secure, and closed the shutters of the casement, he proceeded to the secret panel in the wainscot, in which was concealed his treasure, and unlocking the chest, brought from it bag after bag, and deposited it upon the table, until it was nearly covered. Then he folded his arms, and stood and contemplated the ill-gotten wealth before him with looks of the most unbounded satisfaction. Next he seated himself at the table, and commenced unfastening the different bags, and emptying them of their glittering contents, counting every coin as he proceeded, and piling them up in small heaps before him. Having emptied the whole of the bags, he again gazed at his treasure with an expression of indescribable delight, and once more his rude laughter resounded through the building. Suddenly, however, startled by the noise of the wind, which his conscience construed into a voice, he cast a hasty and fearful glance towards the door, and spreading his arms over the table, scrambled the money altogether in a heap, and seemed afraid that some one was endeavouring to enter the house, and that they would observe him. In a short time, however, he recovered himself, and commenced replacing the money in the bags. This task having been accomplished, he returned them to the chest, and, taking a seat in the chimney corner, folded his arms across his chest, and appeared again either to be deeply buried in thought, or to be half dozing. Emily returned to her chamber, and her mind felt more uneasy than it had done before. What could Gerald be sitting up for?—To be sure Will had not yet, she believed, returned home, and it might be that he was remaining up for the purpose of letting him in; but yet, she could not help indulging in the most fearful forebodings that there was some guilty plot upon the tapis, with which she was not wholly unconnected. To venture to retire her couch, she could not think upon, and as she listened to the storm, which still raged without, and was in such perfect unison with the state of her mind, she felt certain, had she done so, she could not have slept. She once more took up the manuscripts, and as she did so, the same mysterious sensation came over her which she had before experienced, and she hesitated, yet was she anxious to commence the perusal of them. A distant bell now tolled forth the hour of midnight, and its solemn vibrations fell upon the ear of our heroine with more than usual awfulness, her feelings being excited to the utmost degree by what she had seen and dreaded. Before she commenced reading the manuscripts she walked forth gently once more on to the staircase, and looked again through the casement into the parlour. The light still glimmered in the lamp, and by its feeble rays, she perceived that Gerald was in his former place, in the chimney corner, and did not seem to have altered his position, but appeared to be either sleeping, or wrapped in deep thought. She returned to her chamber, and after locking the door, and securing it as well as she could, she took up the manuscripts, and trimming her lamp, prepared to read them.

The first words her eyes fell upon were the following :—

"If the tear of pity ever dimmed thine eye, reader, whoever thou mayest be, into whose hands, perchance, these papers may fall, it will be shed in commisseration and pity to the unfortunate, much wronged individual, whose sufferings these lines trace. But alas! how fallacious is the hope that they should ever meet the eye of mortal, save those that will take care to destroy them! But, should fate ordain it otherwise, and some humane individual become possessed of these melancholy details, rest assured that every word herein written, is that of truth, and that the hapless writer, so far from exaggerating, has drawn but a faint sketch of the bitter sufferings which cruelty and oppression have heaped upon him! Alas! when will my miseries be at an end? When will these eyes be closed in death, and I be released from the dreadful earthly torments, it is now my fate to endure? Wretched! wretched Jerdan, what a terrible fate is thine; and yet, how hast thou deserved it?

"Long before these papers may meet the eyes of the world, should it be ordained that they should ever do so, the writer will, doubtless, be numbered among the dead! Yes, with the dead; for, what other prospect is there before me? And why should I wish to drag out this weary existence? Why not pray for death, as the only means of escaping from suffering? Am I not a miserable prisoner? The victim of unheard-of cruelty; the tool, the sport of a detestable monster, who——"

Here the manuscript became so defaced, that Emily was unable to make out only a syllable here and there for several pages, and they did not serve to enlighten her upon the subject the least in the world. The commencement of the melancholy diary of the unfortunate man, had completely rivetted her attention, and excited her deepest interest and compassion; and, trimming her lamp, she returned to the perusal of it with the utmost avidity. The next portion which she found at all legible, was couched in the following words :—

"Yes, it is he, the villain, who is the author of this. He whom I believed to be my dearest friend; he to whom I confided all my thoughts, in whom I * * * * * * He has visited me this day. He has unmasked himself. He has acknowledged that he is the author of this damned plot! He has bid me despair! He has told me that I must never more expect to quit this house alive! He had not the fortitude, the courage, or, I firmly believe, that he would have taken my life! But he seems to exult in my sufferings; he laughs at, and mocks my reproaches;

and for why? What have I ever done to injure him? Never! by word, by thought, by deed, so help me, Heaven! But ah! a thought rushes across my brain!—horror! horror! can it be correct? Forbid it, All-merciful Father, for the confirmation would freeze my soul to ice! The   * *

"They have torn me from my wife; they have taken me from my smiling infants, and here am I incarcerated in this lone house, with nothing but a horrid and lingering death before mine eyes. How dismal is everything around me! how horrible is this living tomb! How the fierce wind howls without, and the owl screeches through the ancient chambers. Fit place for deeds of blood; and the wretches who inhabit it! Their very looks are sufficient to fill the human breast with horror. They mock at my anguish; they revile my tears, my prayers, my supplications; they are instructed to insult and torture me!   *   *   *   *   Oh, my poor wife! Alas! my unfortunate children! What have become of them? Perhaps exposed to the same misery as myself! But how my mind wanders; I scarcely know what I write   *   *   *   *   *

"It was midnight when they brought me hither! I was so closely muffled up in the mantle which the ruffians threw over me when they seized me, that I could scarcely breathe. My heart sunk with horror when I looked upon the place, for the very walls seemed to frown despair and death! I implored them to tell me for what I was seized, why torn from my wife and family, and brought hither? But they bade me ask no questions, and lifting me from the vehicle in which they had conveyed me, I was led along a dark passage, and up a long flight of stairs, until we reached the old gothic chamber, which adjoins this closet. Here   *   *

  *   *   In vain I tried the door; it was secured by lock, bolt, and bar! I endeavoured to force open the casements, but in that effort I was equally unsuccessful! Alas! they had taken too many precautions for me to hope to effect my escape. I wrung my hands, and cried aloud in despair! The rolling peals of thunder alone answered me! The lightning glared fiercely in at the casements, and made the horrors of my prison more apparent.   *   *   *   *

"How the old clock ticks—and yet I feel a melancholy pleasure in listening to it. It is the only companion I have. I sit and gaze at its venerable face for hours together; and trace in its figures, and the movement of its hands, a source of amusement.   *   *   *   He has twice visited me. My God! is it possible that such a hypocrite; such a heartless, cold-blooded villain can exist in the world? And is it possible that that man, whom I have nurtured in my bosom; whom I loved as a brother, could have been such a consummate wretch? This day he racked my mind to madness; he told me that here I might make up my mind to remain for the rest of my days, and that the only release from my earthly sufferings which I might expect, would be death!"

Here, again, several pages of the manuscript were so defaced, that Emily could make out only a word here and there, and she was about to take up the other portion of the papers to peruse them, when she was startled by a loud knocking below, and her mind filled with the greatest apprehension, she hastily concealed the manuscripts where she had before placed them, and with a trembling hand, having unlocked her door, she stepped on to the landing, and the first object her eyes encountered was Chesterton, being let in by Gerald Darnley!

A deadly sickness came over her as she saw this, and fearing that the purport of his visit at that unseasonable hour, was for some terrible purpose, in which she was interested, she trembled violently, and mentally invoked the protection of Heaven.

Chesterton was attired in a great coat, and seemed to be very wet, so he

immediately took his seat in the chimney-corner, the fire still burning
briskly in the grate.

Gerald Darnley seemed in no very pleasant humour, and looked at the
steward with a surly expression of countenance. They spoke, and everything was so still in the house, that Emily could distinctly hear every word
they uttered.

"Where the devil have you been till this hour?" demanded Gerald,
"I thought you was never coming. It is well for us that that headstrong
boy of mine, Will, has not yet returned home, or he would, doubtless,
spoil the sport you have in view."

"I think Will is gone mad," answered Chesterton; "and had it not
been for the respect I have for you, I do not think I should have been
inclined to have looked over his conduct so easily as I have done. But the
girl?"

"Oh, she's right enough," replied Gerald; "she has been in her chamber for hours, and, doubtless, sleeps sound enough by this time."

"'Tis well," observed Chesterton, "then I have no time to lose. How
shall I gain access to her chamber? No doubt she has locked herself in."

"Oh, that don't matter," said Gerald, "for I have a key that will unlock it."

"Give it me;" demanded Chesterton; "quick, quick, I am all impatience for the accomplishment of my wishes.—The key!"

"It is here," replied Gerald, taking the key from a large bunch, and
giving it to the steward, "you don't want my attendance! You had
better not take a light."

In a state of the most inconceivable consternation, the distracted Emily,
with that presence of mind which seldom forsook her on the most trying

No. 11

occasions, extinguished her light, as she heard Chesterton unlock the door at the bottom of the stairs, and mentally implored the protection of Heaven. She heard him ascend a stair or two, and then he paused, apparently for the purpose of listening. It was a moment of terrible excitement to our hapless heroine, and she felt the same dreadful sensation as the wretched culprit must experience a few moments before his execution. "Good God," she reflected, "what chance is there of my escaping? None, none at all!"

Still all remained silent for a second or two longer, when she heard the villain Chesterton speaking apparently to himself:—

"All is quiet; there is no light in her chamber; she is, doubtless, therefore, asleep, and little dreams that the man she has dared to despise and hate, approaches to the certain consummation of his wishes. How fortunate that that headstrong boy is out of the way, or he would, doubtless, have frustrated my designs. Now, then, for the deed for which my soul has long panted!"

"Merciful God! protect me!" gasped forth Emily, as she heard the villain ascending the stairs with stealthy footsteps, "save me, Heaven, or I am lost?"

She stood for an instant in a state of fearful suspense and uncertainty in which way to act. She heard the hand of the hoary ruffian upon the handle of the door! He turns it; the door is partially opened; Emily with difficulty suppressed a shriek; when a thought, like lightning, flashed across her brain. She stepped behind the door, so that when the miscreant Chesterton opened it wide, she was concealed from view, and as he walked eagerly towards the couch, thinking to find her there, she stepped with the lightness of a sylph from the chamber, and flew along the passage beyond. She had only just reached the door which communicated with the apartments in that portion of the building, and which she found fortunately open when she heard Chesterton in a loud voice of fierce indignation, exclaim,—

"Damnation! the girl is not here! What, ho! Gerald!—Gerald Darnley! thou hast deceived me!"

What's the matter now," Emily heard the other ruffian demand, in a gruff voice, as he began to ascend the stairs on hearing the exclamation of the steward; "what are you making all this noise about?"

"I tell you the girl is not in this room," answered Chesterton, "and you was well aware of that. You have played me false, but you shall repent of it."

"Why, are you mad, or drunk?" cried Gerald, as he ascended the stairs with increased speed.

"I am neither," replied Chesterton, "and so you will find. Emily has escaped."

"Escaped! the devil!"

"Convince yourself," said the steward. A momentary pause ensued, and then our heroine heard Gerald give utterance to an expression of rage and astonishment. During this time she had passed into the gallery upon which the door opened, but, notwithstanding the danger of her situation, fear completely rivetted her to the spot.

The two miscreants now issued from the chamber, and the light from the lamp which Chesterton carried, streamed along the passage, but still Emily was unable to move from the spot. She tried to close the door, but found that it was impossible to do so, as the lock was broken off, and there was no bolt upon that side. By the lurid rays emitted from the lamp, she could behold the savage expression of wrath and disappointment in the countenances of Gerald and the steward.

"I tell you," said the former; "I tell you that she must be somewhere in the house. How the devil could she escape when I was below, and every door was secured?"

"How she did so I can't say," replied Chesterton, "but that she has done so is very certain; and, moreover, it strikes me very forcibly that you are not so ignorant of the manner in which she made her escape as you would seem to be. There has been some treachery in this business; that is the plain English of it."

"Treachery!" cried Gerald, in a voice of much wrath, and frowning ferociously upon Chesterton, "and dare you say that I——"

"There, there, come, perhaps I have been too hasty," interposed the steward, seeming to imagine that he had, in all probability, proceeded rather too far; "at any rate, it is very clear, that, as you lately observed, she must be somewhere concealed in the house, and while we are thus cavilling, it may give her the opportunity of obtaining her liberty."

"Impossible," remarked Gerald, "she cannot effect her enlargement, unless—— but ah, the terrace! Should she be bold enough to venture to make the attempt from thence, she may have succeeded; and yet I should not think she would be so mad, as almost certain death would, undoubtedly, be the consequence."

"It appears to me," remarked Chesterton, "that she has been listening to our discourse, and I cannot help thinking, that it was not at all prudent for you to place her in the apartments you did; in the immediate proximity of the parlour, and where she could not only overhear all that was spoken there, but, if she was inquisitive enough, view from the casement above the door at the foot of the stairs, all that took place.

"Why, certainly," replied Darnley, "I cannot deny but that your argument is very just; it was rather silly of me to put her in those rooms; but it is too late to say anything about the matter now; in the house she must be, and while we are talking here, we are only wasting time. Let us search the place, and if she is not to be found, I will not only give you leave to brand me with the name of traitor, but return you the cash you have given me for doing this business for you, and the money sent by you from my lord for——"

"Enough," interrupted Chesterton, with a shudder, "I don't like talking about these matters at this time of the night, and this is not one of the most cheerful places in the world into the bargain."

"You may think so, Chesterton," remarked the ruffian Gerald, with an ironical grin, "but use is second nature, you know, and my profession has inured me to it. I would not change my situation for a palace."

"I dare say not," was the answer, "unless you were out of danger, and had sufficient to keep you from following your *profession* in future. But, come, we waste time; your mad fool of a son will probably return soon, and then there will be an end to the business, for this night, at any rate. Let us immediately prosecute our search."

"Very well; I am ready;" quoth Gerald, and suddenly starting, as he directed his eyes towards the door behind which our heroine was standing, he added:—"Ah! the door; it is open; I remember that the lock is broken off; doubtless, that way she has fled! Follow me, and we shall soon find the fugitive, never fear."

It is needless for us to attempt to describe the horror of Emily, when she heard these observations, but they immediately aroused her into action, and she fled with the utmost precipitation, uncertain in which direction she was going; for it was completely dark, and she heard the footsteps of her pursuers close upon her heels. She made her way as well as she could, however, towards the room which opened upon the terrace, being determined to sacrifice her life, rather than fall a victim to the nefarious designs of the miscreant Chesterton. Terror gave speed to her feet; and she was fortunate enough to reach the turning in the gallery, and to enter one of the apartments, which led towards the old chamber, before the two villains entered the gallery, or the rays of the lamp carried by Chesterton would have revealed her in an instant. In the darkness, however, she was led astray, for it was not the old chamber to which so many horrors were attached, that she wished to gain; but the one which, as we have before stated, led to the terrace, and no sooner had she discovered this mistake, than she heard the two ruffians at the door. Terror almost overpowered her, and she gasped for breath; but, wound up to a state of desperation, she rushed into the old chamber, and finding here her further progress was impeded, she hastily crouched down in as small a compass as she possibly could, behind some old rubbish collected in one corner, shuddering as she reflected upon the awful situation in which she was placed, and the terrors by which she was surrounded. She had scarcely had time to do this, when she heard Chesterton and Darnley open the door of the outer apartment, and immediately afterwards, the former exclaimed :—

"Confound the wind! It has extinguished the light!"

"Thank God!" ejaculated Emily, mentally, "then they probably will not prosecute their search further, until they have obtained another light, and that will give me time to elude them."

She was too soon, nevertheless, undeceived, for the villanous steward almost immediately observed :—

"Never mind! we will not wait to get a light, for something strikes me very forcibly that she is concealed just at hand, and the delay might give her the opportunity she requires."

"Psha!" said Gerald, "she has not gone this way, I am certain, for beyond this, is the old chamber, where her further egress would be stopped, and having once witnessed its horrors, I do not think it is likely she would have the courage to brave them again. Besides, I gave Will strict orders to fasten up the door of that room, and consequently, she could not gain access to it."

"Nonsense!" returned the other, "I must still think you are leading me astray; for here, see, the door is wide open."

"Ha!" cried Gerald, "then by hell, Will has deceived me! But do not enter that room; I shudder with horror at the bare mention of it!"

"Fool!" exclaimed Chesterton, "you are getting as weak as an infant. What is there in that apartment that should so fearfully alarm you. Let me set you an example."

As he thus spoke, the steward threw open the door, and Emily felt a deadly sensation of horror come over her, when she heard him and Gerald enter. She endeavoured to compress her body into a still smaller compass, and scarcely ventured to breathe, lest it should meet the ears of those terrible enemies she had so much reason to dread.

The door closed after them with a loud bang, and immediately afterwards, Chesterton, in a voice of anger, exclaimed :—

"Curses on the door! Why did you not shut it more cautiously? We must return to the parlour for another light."

"Well, that will not occupy long," returned Gerald. "Give me the lamp, and I will be back in a minute."

"What, and leave me here?" demanded Chesterton, in tones of fear; "oh, no, I do not fancy being without company in this lonely place."

"Oh, then you are not quite so courageous as you would have given yourself credit for a short time since;" remarked Gerald, with a satirical laugh, which sounded particularly awful in that dismal place ; but, come, we will go together."

Emily, in breathless suspense, heard them moving across the room, and immediately after, a heavy weight fell upon the floor, which convinced her that one of them had fallen.

" Damnation !" cried the disagreeable voice of the steward, " what an idiot you must be to cause me to extinguish the light. Ah! what is this ? By hell, it is the fleshless bones of a skeleton !"

" Come, come," said Gerald, in accents of subdued terror, " let's away ; you know well what that skeleton means ; the secret panel must have been left open by whoever was last in here, and you have fallen into the closet."

" It must be so," remarked Chesterton ; " this is a terrible place, and I cannot imagine why such horrors have not been removed."

" They shall be," replied the other villain ; " but do not tarry ; some-how or the other I can't keep a limb of me still while I am here. Let us begone, and prosecute our search in another part of the house, for I can-not imagine that a timid young girl would choose such a place as this to secrete herself in ; and if I thought she had——"

" What then ?"

" Why, my dagger should instantly open a passage to her heart," was the terrible reply.

" Not so," said Chesterton, " at least not for the present ; she must first serve my purpose, and then you may dispose of her as you may think proper. Give me your hand, it is so confounded dark, that I shall be breaking my legs over some of the old rubbish, there appears to be such an abundance of here."

The two ruffians now again groped their way across the room, and the horror of our heroine may be readily conceived, when they once or twice approached so near the spot where she was concealed, that she was fearful they would fall over her. At length they seemed to have reached the door, and the heart of Emily was immediately smote with a feeling of the most indescribable dread when she heard Gerald exclaim,—

" Come along, and I will lock the door after us ; it is not likely I should want to visit it again in a hurry."

The idea of being locked in this awful chamber, surrounded by so many ghastly objects, and with the almost certain prospect of a slow and dreadful death, so completely overcame her, that, unable any longer to repress her terrors, she gave utterance to a loud scream.

" Ha ! what noise was that ?" cried the steward, turning back.

" Come, come," replied Gerald, in a hoarse voice ; " it was no earthly sound."

" By hell ! but I have my suspicions that it was," said the other ; " it was the scream of some one in terror, and I am much mistaken if the bird we seek has not flown hither. Stand by the door, and mind that no one passes from it, and I'll search the room."

" Lost ! lost ! oh, God !" mentally breathed Emily, in a state of the most frantic despair. The ruffian Chesterton groped his way round the apartment, and as every step brought him nearer to her, her agony was so great that it defies the power of language to do adequate justice to it. She feared to move, she feared almost to breathe, lest she should betray herself. Even the pulsation of her heart she dreaded would be the means of direct-ing the wretch Chesterton to the spot where she was concealed. He approached her so near, that his hand knocked down a portion of the rubbish behind which she was concealed, and once more he moved to the opposite side of the room, and she breathed more free ; but yet, should he not discover her then, what means had she of ultimately escaping, and would she not be left to a fate equally as terrible, in being locked up in that dreadful apartment, in which human blood had evidently been shed, and in which the spirits of the murdered seemed to stalk?

" Well, I do not find her anywhere, and yet I feel almost certain that the scream we heard proceeded from a human being, and from this room, too," said Chesterton.

" Psha!" returned Gerald, " are you mad? I tell you again, that it is not at all likely the girl would select a place of concealment like this. Let us begone; while we are wasting time here, she may be making the place of her retreat secure, and in the meantime Will may return, and spoil the sport you have in contemplation. If you are obstinate, and are determined to remain here, poking your way about in the dark, you shall do it by yourself."

At this moment Emily, having been cramped up by remaining in one position so long, gently moved herself, but, unfortunately, in so doing she disturbed some of the lumber, which fell with a loud crash, and left her completely revealed to the view, had there been any light in the room.

" Ah! by Jupiter she is here now," exclaimed Chesterton, springing immediately towards the spot where our heroine was on her knees, and grasping her arm, " I have her, by Heaven!" he added; " ah! damsel, you have in vain sought to elude me; I have destined you to become the mistress of my passions, and you must yield; resistance is vain."

" Oh! mercy, mercy!" shrieked the horrorstruck maiden, as the villain dragged her forcibly from the floor, and endeavoured to take her from the apartment.

" She has been listening to our converse, and she dies," cried the ruffian Gerald, fiercely, rushing, knife in hand, towards the terrified girl. Chesterton, however, interposed, and arresting Darnley's arm, he ejaculated, in a determined tone,—

" Hold! Gerald Darnley, or we are mortal foes. Harm her not; has not an oath of secrecy already been extorted from her? Besides, is she not in our power, and what have we then to fear?"

Gerald sullenly returned the knife to his belt, and said,—

" Well, well, I can't deny the truth of your last observations, so e'en let it be as you wish. But mark me, I will take especial care that she shall not have any opportunity of breaking her oath, should she be disposed to do so."

" Unhand me, villain!" shrieked our heroine, as she endeavoured to release herself from the hold of Chesterton; " are you not fearful that the vengeance of an offended God will overtake you for this brutal outrage upon an unprotected female? Unhand me, I say!"

" Perverse girl," answered Chesterton, " you supplicate in vain. Your charms have inspired me with passions that I find it impossible to resist; and even were the forfeiture of my life to be the immediate effect of such a course, I would not forego the chance that is now in my power of gratifying my wishes! Nay, nay, this resistance is worse than useless: I am determined, and your obstinacy but increases the desires you have excited in my bosom. This night shall witness the consummation of my wishes, let the consequences be what they may."

" Almighty God!" exclaimed Emily, as she in vain endeavoured to release herself from the ruffian hold of the steward, " look down upon me, and shield me from the infamous designs of this bad man. Rather abruptly terminate my existence than suffer me to meet with such a fate as that with which he threatens me. Gerald Darnley, in mercy perform the deed which you just now threatened me, and stretch me a corpse at the feet of this hoary miscreant."

"Away, Gerald," cried Chesterton, as he forced the now almost power-less Emily from the old chamber into the chamber beyond, his arm encir-cling her waist, and inflamed by the base passions that existed in his breast —"I need not your aid any further than to procure me a light. You will find me in the Blue Chamber."

Gerald Darnley departed without saying a word, and Chesterton suc-ceeded in forcing our distracted heroine from the room, and in spite of her shrieks, conveying her to the apartments she had occupied since she had been in the old lone house. It was a wonder, under the dreadful circum-stances, that she could retain her senses; but she did, and, having reached her suite of rooms, the miscreant Chesterton placed her upon a couch, and awaited with apparent suspense and impatience the appearance of Gerald with the light. The latter was not long in coming; and, having placed the lamp on the table, after bestowing a significant look upon the steward, in spite of the supplications of Emily, who wrung her hands in despair and wept torrents of tears, he quitted the room, and left her and Chesterton to-gether.

The steward, after the departure of Darnley, fastened the door, and having gazed upon Emily for a few seconds with glances of lewd desire, he took a seat by her side, and endeavoured to embrace her; but she broke from his hold, and throwing herself at his feet, looked up into his face with tearful eyes and looks of the most impressive supplication, as, with clasped hands and great energy of manner, she exclaimed—

"Oh, sir, if one spark of humanity remains within your breast—if your heart is not entirely callous to all sort of feeling, pity me, and forbear. I will pardon you for all the grief, the bitter anguish, the fear, the suspense, you have hitherto caused me, and even endeavour to forget that you have so far suffered the unruly passions of your nature to overcome you, and to treat you with respect. Imprison, confine me—nay, more; seek to gain my regard by honourable means, and I will try to make you a due return : but, for the love of Heaven, do not persist in this cruel, this brutal, this un-manly outrage, or the vengeance of Heaven will most assuredly pursue you."

"Lovely maiden," said the venerable libertine, "I would not appear the brute you seem to think me; but your charms, and the opposition you have evinced towards my passion, have increased my desires to an insupportable degree, and those desires must, and shall be indulged. Nay, do not turn away from me with that disdain—that air of repugnance; rather seek by a less freezing demeanour to conciliate my forbearance. Say that you do not hate me; promise me that you will try to look upon me with the regard I covet, and——"

"I will—I will promise to endeavour to do so," eagerly interrupted our heroine, "if you will now leave me. Oh, in pity to my youth, and my destitute, unprotected state, relent and leave me."

"On one condition I will," returned Chesterton; "I will give you a week to consider of my offer. If, at the end of that time, you will solemnly promise to yield compliance to my wishes, I will immediately depart, and will not seek your presence again until the expiration of that period. Do not hesitate, sweet girl; believe me, my love for you is sincere, and that there is nothing that I will neglect to perform to contribute to your happi-ness. You shall not have a single wish ungratified; my whole, my sole study shall be to make you happy! I will ever be your fondest, your most devoted admirer, and in your felicity find alone mine own."

"Oh, spare me, sir; for Heaven's sake spare me!" implored Emily, as the tears fell rapidly down her cheeks, now blanched with terror, as she beheld the increasing warmth with which Chesterton urged his hateful and lawless suit, and still endeavoured to enfold her in his loathsome embraces.''

" Will you promise me ?" impatientiy demanded the villain.

" Never !" firmly answered our heroine ; "never will I promise to make a sacrifice of my honour ; sooner would I suffer death—that death with which your blood-thirsty minion has threatened me, and which hideous crime he has been hired to perpetrate."

" Ah ! say you so ?" cried Chesterton, his eyes flashing with rage and savage determination ; "rash girl, then thy doom is sealed : this hour, this moment you shall be mine ! I heed not your cries : I mock your struggles—they are futile ! There is no one here to render you assistance. The time I have long panted for has come : prepare you, maiden, for this instant gives you to my arms."

" Help ! help !" shrieked Emily, as the ruffian threw his arms around her, and endeavoured to kiss her in all the wildness of his detested passion ; " is there no power to save me from this fiend in human form? Spirit of her who so long protected me, I invoke thee ! I solicit thy aid—thy inter- position ! Save me !—shield me from the power of the guilty seducer !"

Scarcely had Emily given utterance to these exclamations when the light seemed to burn blue ; a loud peal of thunder shook the ancient building to its foundation ; an unearthly shriek rent the air : the villain, aghast, re- leased his hold of the terrified damsel, and retreated to the other side of the room ; and in an instant there appeared, standing between him and our heroine, the shade of Mrs. Fitzormond, attired in all the awful parapherna- lia of the grave. Her hollow eyes were fixed with a look of severity upon the countenance of the hoary libertine, which seemed sufficient to freeze the blood in his veins ; and her long bony finger was pointed in a menacing attitude towards him, while, in a voice of sepulchral horror, the following words smote his terrified ears :—

" Forbear, villain ! The spirit of the dead riseth up to interpose between thee and the guilty deed thou wouldst commit. Forbear !"

" Horror ! horror !" cried the appalled ruffian, as he covered his face with his hands and rushed from the room, leaving our heroine alone. The instant he had gone, the phantom faded into thin air before the eyes of Emily, and almost immediately disappeared.

She had been rendered completely immoveable, enchained to the spot with horror, on this the third supernatural visitation ; but instantly after the spectre had vanished she regained her usual fortitude, and finding that the wretch Chesterton had left the room, she clasped her hands together, and, raising her eyes with solemn earnestness towards Heaven, she fervently returned her gratitude to the Almighty Power that had rescued her from the danger with which she had only a few minutes before been threatened.

She was suddenly aroused by hearing a loud noise below, and, in spite of the lateness of the hour, and the recent exciting events that had taken place, so much was her curiosity and interest excited, that she immediately forgot her terrors, and, leaving the light with which the villain Darnley had lately supplied Chesterton, and which the latter in his horror and con- fusion, had left behind him, she once more left the room, and took her usual station on the landing-place outside. A scene presented itself to her eyes for which she had not been prepared. The door which opened upon the heath was standing wide open, and Will Darnley, who seemed as if he had but that instant entered, had grasped Chesterton by the throat, and with fierce gestures, seemed to threaten his life. The repulsive counte- nance of the steward was distorted with rage, and he struggled hard to re- lease himself, but in the powerful grasp of the muscular young man, he was the same as an infant would have been. Gerald stood by, apparently

thunderstruck at the behaviour of his son, and perfectly unable to interfere one way or the other. The more that Chesterton struggled, the more useless he found his efforts to release himself from the firm hold of his antagonist were, so did his indignation increase, until he absolutely foamed at the mouth with rage, and his eyes seemed ready to start from their sockets. Emily could perceive from the flushed countenance of Will, and his whole demeanour, that he was labouring under the influence of liquor, and her terror may be easily conceived, especially after the exciting circumstances occurring to her, which we have related in the previous pages. From the desperate and ferocious demeanour of Will Darnley, she had every reason to apprehend murder, and well was she convinced, that such reckless ruffians as they were, would not hesitate a moment to perpetrate the most horrible crimes, to gratify their diabolical feelings of hatred and revenge. Still the miscreant Will retained his hold of his struggling foe, and with clenched fist, seemed to threaten him with instant annihilation, while Gerald Darnley remained in the same attitude, and appeared to be paralyzed to the spot, and deprived of the use of all his faculties.

"Villain! murderer! miscreant!" hoarsely cried Chesterton, "unhand me!—Cowardly ruffian, would you murder me on the spot?"

"Yes, I would!" cried Will, "and the world would have to thank me for the deed; for a greater villain than you are, never mounted a scaffold! Answer me, what do you here at this hour?"

"What matters that to you?" returned Chesterton with another violent but futile effort to release himself; "my business was with your father; I shall not explain it to you."

"Then by hell," exclaimed Will, with increased fierceness, "by hell, I

No. 12

will not release my hold until I have pressed the breath out of thy vile carcase. You have come here with some design upon the girl!"

"What boots that to you?—I have purchased her."

"Ah! you acknowledge it; then you shall not again quit this roof alive! —I have fixed my mind upon that girl, and I will not yield my choice to an old fool like you!"

"Gerald," gasped forth Chesterton, in tones that were scarcely audible, and his countenance becoming distorted with the violence of the young man, "come to my aid, and tear off this ungovernable bloodhound from my throat, or he will murder me!"

As the steward gave utterance to these words, Will, apparently tired of the hold he had hitherto retained of the steward's throat, released him, and hurling him violently from him, he was about to rush forward and place his foot upon his chest, when Gerald Darnley, at last, recovered himself, and darting forward, interposed between his son and the prostrate Chesterton.

"Back, back, boy!" he exclaimed in a stern voice, "what means this violence? Wouldst thou murder the steward?"

"Unless he abandons his designs against the girl, I would; nay, more, I am determined to do it; for I have before told you repeatedly that I have fixed my heart upon her. Yes, my heart, for I love her, father, and it shall not be a trifle that shall make me tamely resign my pretensions, especially at the suit of a man like Chesterton."

"But Emily has shewn thee no favour," remarked Gerald.

"And has she not evinced the greatest horror and detestation towards him?—However, favour or not, mine I am firmly determined she shall be, and if she cannot learn to love me afterwards, at any rate, I can make her fear and obey me."

"Rash boy, thou art determined to bring destruction on us all," said his father.

"I would as soon do that," replied the young ruffian, "as to be foiled in my designs."

"Ah!—and is this the affection thou owest to the author of thy being?"

"Affection," sneered Will; "ha! ha! ha!—thou didst never teach me that, or set me an example; therefore, thou canst not wonder that I should be totally unacquainted with it."

"Gerald Darnley," said Chesterton, gathering himself upon his feet, and retreating towards the door, "I will, for the present, leave thee and this ferocious young savage together; but I would advise thee to try some method of curbing his passions, or it may be the worse for thee both. A night's sleep may probably bring him to his senses, and he will then probably see the headstrong foolery of which he has been guilty. Good night, and remember the compact which binds us together."

"Nay," cried Will Darnley, with fierce determination, rushing to the door, and placing his back against it, prevented the egress of the steward, "thou shalt not quit this place, until thou hast satisfied me as to what purpose thou camest hither, and inform me whether thou hast taken an unmanly advantage of the girl, and enforced the gratification of thy desires. Come, no equivocation;—I am not to be trifled with, and nothing shall prevent me from forcing the truth from thee, ere thou quittest this place to-night. Nay, father, thou mayest frown; but thou knowest what I am, and it will be worse than useless to seek to oppose me."

"Will, Will," cried Gerald, "this madness will bring ruin upon us.— Let me conjure thee to appease thy wrath, which is without occasion. I give thee my word that the girl is safe, and that nothing wrong has happened to her. Come, come away from the door, and let Mr. Chesterton depart; you and I will talk this matter over together."

"Attempt not to deceive me," said the ruffian, fiercely, "for that will but increase my anger, and render me more desperate. Hast thou spoken the truth?"

"I have told thee so, boy," replied his father, sternly.

"Thou wilt swear it."

"Will," returned Gerald, "try not my patience too severely, or it may be worse for both of us. I again repeat that I have told thee the truth!"

"Am I to be suffered to depart," demanded Chesterton, whose looks shewed the terror under which he was labouring, "or am I to be murdered by this young ruffian?"

"Another word like that," exclaimed Will Darnley, "and it shall be the last thou shalt ever give utterance to. I will take the word of my father, so go thy ways, and thank thy lucky stars that thou hast escaped so easily; thou mayest be less fortunate on any future occasion."

Thus speaking, Will Darnley walked away from the door, and no longer opposed the departure of Chesterton. The latter, having opened the door, turned to Gerald, and said,—

"We shall shortly meet again, when I shall expect that I am not subjected to this interruption!"

"Thou mayest, in all probability, be disappointed," returned Will, with a look of mysterious meaning.

Chesterton made no answer, but frowning upon Will, he hastily retired, and closed the door after him.

When he had gone, Gerald and his son stood for a few seconds, and gazed upon each other in silence, and with looks of indignation. At length the latter coolly took a seat, crossing one leg carelessly over the other, and began humming a part of a popular flash song of the day.

"Will," Gerald at last broke silence, "what has come to thee within the last few days?—Hast thou gone mad?"

"No," answered the other, "I believe my wits are as keen as ever they were;—perhaps too keen for some persons."

"What is the cause, then, of the headstrong conduct you have lately evinced?"

"Thou mayest call it headstrong, if thou thinkest fit," replied Will, "but I tell thee now, as I have told thee at least a dozen times before, that the cause of my behaviour is simply because I have taken a fancy to a pretty girl, and think it would be much better for me to have her than such an old dotard as Chesterton."

"But she can never be thine."

"But I say she shall."

"Fool!"

"Perhaps I may be, father, but I rather think the fool has sense enough to outwit those who carry much older heads upon their shoulders. But come, thou knowest I am not one of the most easy tempers in the world, so that it is useless for thee to talk to me in this manner. If thou actest with the wisdom thou refusest to give me the credit of possessing, thou wilt not oppose my wishes."

"Impossible! are we not in the power of the steward?"

"And is he not as much in ours?"

"He would betray us to his master!"

"He dare not; for by so doing, he would only reveal his own treachery. Besides, there is a way of effectually preventing any danger of that kind."

"What mean you?"

"Oh," returned his son, with a frightful smile, "the contents of a pistol, methinks would not fail to do that service for us."

" Ah ! wouldst thou murder him ?"

" It would be a sure way of ridding us both of a dangerous customer."

" I like not the deed."

" Probably not," answered Will, " but it is not at all unlikely that I may have occasion to perform it without consulting thy taste upon the subject.   Art thou willing to aid me in my wishes with the girl ?"

" I will not."

"That's a positive answer, at any rate.   Well, then, I must e'en endeavour to do without thy help ; and I have no doubt that I shall meet with my usual success."

"Well," cried his father, "this boldness and obstinacy is unbearable, and can lead to no good end.   Mark me, I shall consider it my duty to oppose any designs thou mayest have in contemplation, to the best of my power !"

" Then thou may'st take the consequences," replied Will, " for by the infernal host, I swear, that neither the ties of nature, or any other earthly power, shall prevent me obtaining possession of the girl.   However, I have said enough for to-night ; thou understandest me well, no doubt, so I will now retire to bed ; perhaps you may think different to what you do now, by the morning."

With these words, Will arose, lighted a lamp which stood on the table, nodded slightly to his father, and disappeared by the door which led to the chamber in which he slept.

CHAPTER X.

THE ESCAPE.—THE RETREAT.

EMILY retired into her chamber once more, when the two ruffians, to whose savage discourse she had been a listener, quitted the parlour, and her feelings need no description from us.   Such accumulated horrors as she had endured this night, it would seem scarcely possible for any human being, especially a female to undergo, and yet retain her reason ; but in the midst of it all, a latent hope sprang up in her bosom that she should be able to escape the danger which threatened her, and that, in spite of the desperate characters of those persons by whom she was surrounded, she should be suffered by the Supreme Being to frustrate their diabolical designs, and ultimately to attain that path of happiness from which she had so long been estranged.   It evidentally appeared to her from the recent supernatural appearance of Mrs. Fitzormond, that the eye of Heaven watched over her, and when, as long as she put her trust in its power, she was threatened by the most imminent danger, it would interfere to save her from the power of the villans by whom she had been lately persecuted. Rumination upon her singular fate she had completely exhausted, and was unable to arrive at any satisfactory conclusion upon the subject ; she therefore abandoned it, and came to the conclusion that Providence in its own wise course, would bring about a proper adjustment of her affairs, and inflict upon the guilty that retribution which their crimes doubtless merited. It was now long past midnight, and, although her mind had been sufficiently agitated by the horrors she had endured, she, not feeling at all inclined for sleep, took up the manuscript which she had so abruptly left off, and having trimmed her lamp, prepared once more to peruse the continuation of the journal, which the unfortunate former occupant of the secret closet had penned. It was not long ere she discovered the paragraph at which she had left off, and then continued the perusal of it, which ran as follows :—

"One dreary night,—another wretched day has elapsed, and still I am alone ; no one has been to visit me ! Good God ! monster as I am convinced he is, he cannot be fiend enough to have doomed me to starvation ! My food is all exhausted ! There is not a drop of water left in the pitcher ; my throat is parched ;—a burning fever is upon me ;—water ! water ! oh —— * * * * * * *

How dismal is all around ; the midnight hour has long flown, and the owl screeches drearily !—Still no one has been near me ;—my worst surmises are correct ;—they have doomed me to an hideous death ! Alas ! how faint I am ! Nearly two days have elapsed, and still no food ! My hand almost refuses to guide the pen ! But yet amidst all this horror, and nothing but the prospect of an untimely and frightful end before mine eyes, my dear wife and children, are the principal objects of my anxiety. Could I but be sure that thou wert safe, methinks I could even die content. But, alas ! what hope of that is there for me ? Doubtless, the villain who holds me in his power, will have adopted secure means to prevent the possibility of your escaping from him ; and this renders me doubly wretched, and embitters the last sad hours which I feel convinced are only allowed me in this world ! * * * I loll back in my old arm chair, but in vain I seek to rest ; the fierce gnawings of hunger in the first instance, drive me to madness, and there are moments when I can with difficulty resist the temptation to devour mine own flesh ; and then the thoughts of my wife and two innocent babes rush upon my brain, and render me worse than a maniac. Rest,—rest for me,—there is none, but in the cold and silent grave, to which I am hastening. There, there, only can I now hope to be at peace. * * *

"Two more hours, and still no one comes near me ! Oh, God ! this is more than I can endure ; in mercy release me from my sufferings ! How awful is every thing around me in this place ; even the ticking of the clock in the old chamber adjoining this, seems now to ring nothing but the knell of death ; and through the moss covered squares of the casements, grim and frightful faces seem to smile ironically and exultingly upon me ! What a monster he must be to doom me to a fate like this ! He that I considered did possess every amiable quality, and viewed me with the regard of a brother ! But surely it must be some hideous delusion,—some horrible dream ! There cannot be such a monster in the world ! There cannot be so specious a villain, who with all the basilisk powers of a fawning hypocrite, could thus sneak into my bosom, not only to destroy the honour of my wife, but to take away the life of that man who has assisted him in his difficulties with the open hand of friendship, and to whom he ever vowed the attachment o a brother ! * * *

"I feel the hand of death upon me, and I welcome its approach with eagerness ! Oh, how terrible is hunger ! Not long since I gnawed greedily the flesh from my arm, and with gluttonous haste sucked the warm blood as it oozed from the wound ! It is wonderful how long the human frame can endure suffering before it finally sinks under the dreadful infliction !— I get very faint ; but a short time, and I shall be unable to guide the pen which fain would trace the particulars of the miserable fate to which I have been doomed ! Oh, Providence ! surely my misdeeds have never been so henious as to merit such an end as this ? But, wretch that I am, thus to arraign the mercy, the justice of the Most High ! Horrors increase around me ; strange noises seem to vibrate in mine ears ! Methinks I hear the inarticulate mutterings of myriads of voices;—some seem to laugh at my sufferings, and others to depicture to me the horrors of that which I have yet to undergo! Oh, how awful is this! Ah! who is it that offers me food—water—kind friend—surely thou art some saint from heaven. See, they offer it to my grasp. They invite me to appease my maddening wants! Thanks,—thanks. May the blessings of the Almighty follow thee for this. There—there—let me clutch thee! Horrors! horrors! 'tis mockery all! A terrible delusion, conjured up by my fevered imagination. Oh, death! death! thou art now the only friend to whom I can look for relief. Come, then, and end at once this suffering!"   *   *   *

Emily was here obliged to lay down the manuscript, for the tears which gushed to her eyes at the terrible sufferings of the ill-fated writer dimmed her sight, and she was unable to proceed until she had given vent to her feelings. But what tortured her more than all was, the mystery which the unhappy man, owing to the power of his emotions, maintained, as to who he was, or who was the miscreant who had doomed him to so cruel a 'fate. She could but commisserate in his sorrows without having the opportunity of obtaining that retribution, should chance ever present it, on the head of his oppresor which his wrongs demanded. Besides, she felt something more than a common interest or sympathy in the miseries of the unfortunate man, and the feeling every moment gained greater strength in her bosom, that she was more immediately connected with him than circumstances at present seemed to authorise, and her mind was so dreadfully agitated, that she had the utmost difficulty in being able again to take up the manuscript, and resume the perusal of them. However, she did at length somewhat conquer her emotions, and with trembling hands, took up the mutilated and scarcely legible papers: the first passage she was enabled to make out, was couched in the following words :—

"Hark! what terrible sound is that? It seems to proceed from the next room! It is the groaning of some poor wretch in poignant agony. There are lights too moving there; and I can hear the footsteps and struggles of two or three persons. And now again that piercing cry! Horor!—They must be perpetrating murder! There is some other wretched victim as well as myself! Another shriek! It is the voice of a woman! Hold! hold! ruffians, monsters! In vain are my cries. They will not avert their guilty hands! Another shriek—and now all is again still! It is all over; the wretches have accomplished their fiendish ends! Their victim is no more! Oh, enviable fate! Would that they would end at once my sufferings in the same manner! Ah! my poor wife!—Should it be her ——"   *   *   *

Here the light in the lamp of Emily, which had long been burning very dim, gradually sank in the socket, until it became entirely extinguished, and she was involved in complete darkness, and, not having the means to procure another, she was compelled to lay down the manuscripts, at the very moment when her interest was the most excited. The last words she had read filled her bosom with the most indescribable horror; the blood-stained sheets which she had seen in the old chamber, and the account which the wretched prisoner gave of the circumstances, left no doubt whatever upon her mind that murder had been perpetrated on the night to which he (the prisoner) alluded, and in the gothic apartment, which herself and Mrs. Fitzormond had formerly occupied, and which she had lately again been brought to behold in so mysterious and unfortunate a manner.

The stillness which reigned around, the deep melancholy of the place, the horror excited by the events that had recently occurred to herself, and the shocking circumstances she had been perusing, filled her bosom with a sensation of awe and terror which was almost insupportable, and entirely precluded from her mind all idea of sleep; yet, to remain up, would be folly. She secured the door of her chamber as well as she could, and then committing herself to the care and protection of Heaven, she threw herself upon her couch, and closed her eyes. Horrible thoughts rushed tumultuously upon her brain, which she was unable to arrange, and for some time entirely precluded all thoughts of sleep. She revolved in her mind all the alarming and awful events that had occurred to her since the death of Mrs. Fitzormond, and, as she did so, her anguish increased, and the mystery by which her fate was involved, became strengthened. Then she thought upon the conversation she had recently heard between Gerald Darnley and his son, and the determination of the latter to obtain possession of her person, caused the most intense agony and fear within her bosom.

At length, completely exhausted, she did fall off to sleep, but it was restless, for continual visions of the most frightful description haunted her imagination, and ever and anon she would start up in the bed, with the cold drops of perspiration bedewing her temples, and her limbs trembling as if she was suffering with the ague. At length, however, the morning dawned, and glad enough was she of it; she arose quite unrefreshed from the disturbed sleep she had met with.

The day had broken, upon which Patty had informed her she was determined to put the project they had concerted together to escape from the Old Lone House, into execution; or, at least to make the attempt, and she longed for the time to arrive when she should see her, to ascertain whether there was any chance of the same being made practicable. She had secured the manuscripts in the place where she had before concealed them, being resolved to restrain her curiosity in finishing the perusal of them to some more fitting opportunity, and she now endeavoured to regain her composure as much as possible before she was summoned to breakfast, for fear the suspicions of the villains, Gerald and his son, should be further excited against her, and they might adopt such means as might render the designs of Patty and herself completely abortive. If they did not succeed that night in escaping from the house, Emily had but little cause for hope, for it appeared to her certain that her fate would be sure to be decided either one way or the other, and that she should either become the victim of Chesterton, or else, to judge by his threats, Will Darnely would contrive some desperate means or the other to get her in his power, and frustrate the designs of the former. She had taken the precaution to put what few articles of wearing apparel she had in her possession, in readiness, so that she could take them without a moment's delay; and she eagerly awaited the time when she should see Patty, to learn from her whether or not her plot was likely to succeed.

She heard the people in the house moving about as soon as she arose, although it was yet very early, and not long afterwards Patty tapped at her door, and was admitted. Notwithstanding all the efforts of our heroine, her quick eye immediately noticed the agitation under which she laboured, and Emily was about to make her acquainted with the whole particulars of the many painful and alarming events that had occurred to her on the previous night, when Patty interrupted her.

"Say nothing about it for the present," she observed in a low voice, "I can very well guess that something unusual has happened, but inform me of it by and by, when I have a more fitting opportunity, lest they should overhear us from below—keep up your spirits, and endeavour to appear as composed as possible before my father and brother, or their suspicions will be sure to be aroused. They do not seem to be in a very good humour with each other this morning, and I am certain that something unusual has occurred."

"You are right, Patty," returned Emily, "something unusual has, indeed, happened, and which, when I think upon it, makes me shudder with horror. Alas! if I do not succeed in escaping from here—"

"Hush! hush! for goodness sake!" interrupted Patty, "or we shall be ruined; hope everything for the best; I have not been unmindful of our plot, and everything proceeds as well as we could expect. But come, they will grow impatient below. The breakfast awaits."

Emily made another effort to regain her composure,—as much as the ruffians could expect to behold her assume after the outrage which Chesterton had attempted upon her, and the awful event of the supernatural appearance, and, accompanied by Patty, descended the stairs, and entered the parlour.

She could not help an involuntary shudder as she entered the presence of men to whom bloodshed was familiar, and who had determined upon her destruction in one way or the other, but she quickly recovered herself, and took her seat at the table, and endeavoured to conceal herself from their observation as much as possible; but she could perceive that the scrutiny of Gerald was fixed intently upon her, and that Will was eyeing her with an expression of countenance which plainly evinced the passions that were raging in his breast. The meal passed over in silence, and as soon as it was ended, Will arose, and after an observation to his father, to which Emily paid no attention, he quitted the house, and she was about to return to her chamber, when Gerald laid his hand upon her arm, and arrested her attention, exclaiming:—

"Stop, girl, a word with you before you leave this room."

"A word with me, sir," said Emily in a tremulous voice, and trembling at his touch, "what mean you?—What would you with me ?"

"I would caution you against a repetition of the conduct you have hitherto shewn towards Mr. Chesterton," answered Gerald, sternly; "your obstinate opposition to his desires will do you no good, and may only exasperate him to use more violence than he might otherwise be inclined to do, and will not prevent him from enforcing the gratification of his wishes. I also warn you not again to be so curious as to listen to any conversation that may take place while you are in this house, between myself or any of my friends, lest you should have to pay dearly for your propensity."

"If," answered Emily, boldly, and for a moment forgetting her usual prudence, "if you expect me tamely to yield to the villanous desires of the detested miscreant, Chesterton, you will find that you deceive yourself; for by Heaven, death presents less terror to me than such a fate !"

"And yet you might alter your tone, young lady," said Gerald, biting his lips, "you might alter your tone if you were put to the test !"

"Never !" ejaculated our heroine, with increased firmness ; "there is no fate that I would shrink from rather than encounter such a fate as that! But think not that I yet despair of being able to escape from your power, for the all-seeing eye of Him above, never fails to watch over the innocent, and to protect them from the snares and artifices of the guilty."

"Thy words are bold, young lady," said the ruffian, scowling, " but thou mayest ere long be glad to alter thy tone; as for escaping my power, ha! ha! ha! thou talkest madly. But away with thee to thy chamber; remember the warning I have given thee, and if thou art wise, thou wilt profit by it."

Emily returned no answer, but, glad to escape from the presence of the villain, upon whom she could almost imagine she could behold the blood of

the murdered smoking, she hastened up the stairs, and entered her own apartment. A short time afterwards, Gerald, as was his usual custom, quitted the house, and no one but Madge, Patty, and herself, were left behind. In a little while, Patty rejoined her, and they then as usual, bent their way towards the chamber which opened upon the terrace, where they might converse without fear of interruption, or of listeners. When they had arrived there, our heroine, as well as her emotion, created by the recollection of the circumstances would permit her, related to Patty all the terrible circumstances of the previous night, and the danger she had so providentially been rescued from, but in so awful and supernatural a manner. She also imparted to her the conversation she had overheard between Gerald and his son, and the evil and determined designs of the latter, and expressed the little hope she had of being long able to uphold against such unprecedented and accumulated dangers, if they could not contrive to make their escape from the house.

Patty listened to her recital with the utmost horror, and after a pause, observed,

"There is indeed no time to be lost, for affairs as they now stand betwixt my father, (if such he really is,) William and Chesterton, must quickly come to a crisis. But I have got everything in readiness, and this evening, as soon as it is dusk, we will make the attempt."

"But should we be discovered, dear Patty," observed our heroine, "believe me, it is not for myself that I fear, but, alas! what would be your fate? and I should never forgive myself for being the indirect cause of leading you into such a dilemma."

"Oh, do not be uneasy about me, Emily," replied Patty; "I am willing to run any risk to escape from this terrible place, and I am in great hopes
No. 13

that the result will be everything we could wish. You know, my dear Emily," she added, with a smile, "that I am a little given to superstition, and last night I had a dream; however, I shall not trouble you with that now : let it suffice that no fate can appear half so terrible to me as that of remaining here; so, therefore, that at once decides the matter, and I will not hear any further objections upon the subject. In examining my golden hoard, I find that I have no less than thirty-five guineas, and, therefore, we shall not starve for a few weeks, at any rate; and I know that my aunt will do all that is in her power to assist us. As for my father suspecting that we have fled thither, it is the very last place he would think of, because he would be sure to imagine that I would never think of going there, where there was a probability of his so soon finding me out. From what I have heard, it is not likely that my father or Will will return this evening, so that we shall have a famous opportunity of putting our designs into execution. You see that I have secured the rope ladder in the room which opens upon this terrace, so that we shall have it handy at the moment we want to make use of it, and I will take good care to lock the door and keep the key in my possession, so that no one can enter this room till we do. Now, my dearest Emily, pray cheer up, and endeavour to hope for the best; and trust to Providence for the successful issue of this adventure."

" I do indeed feel more sanguine on the subject, Patty," returned Emily, "and heaven send that our hopes may be realized, and that it will direct our footsteps in the right way."

"Amen," ejaculated Patty; " and now, my dear Emily, I think it would be advisable for us to separate, for fear our being longer together might excite the suspicions of my mother, who is almost as much to be dreaded as my father and brother. In the evening I will be sure to meet you as soon as it is dusk, and then for our design."

" Farewell, then, dear Patty," said Emily, as they both quitted the chamber : "may the Almighty prosper our designs, and bless you for all your kindness to the poor deserted one."

" Oh, name it not, my dear girl," returned Patty, " even were I not deeply interested in this plot, there is nothing, I am sure that I would not willingly do to serve you, and especially to rescue you from the clutches of villany. But let us talk nothing about obligation, for you are under none to me. Now good bye, as soon as evening shall have thrown its shadows over the earth, and my father (oh, how I revolt from the bare idea, even of calling him by that name) and brother shall have left the house, I will rejoin you, and then to put our plot into execution."

Emily expressed by her looks more than words could have done, and Patty smiling sweetly upon her, quitted her and retired down stairs; having taken especial care to lock the door of the chamber in which she had placed the rope ladder, and put the key in her pocket. Our heroine retired into her own room, and then soon completed the trifling arrangements she had to make, after which she earnestly implored the kindness of Heaven to aid them in their plot, and then her bosom became inspired with more confidence and hope. She could not blame the resolution of Patty, which was a strictly prudent and reasonable one, namely, to shun that haunt of vice and those bad men, by which her morals were daily, nay, hourly exposed to contamination, and who behaved to her with such cruelty. The more, in fact, that our heroine reflected upon the characters of Gerald Darnley and his son, and compared them with the gentle and amiable disposition of Patty, the more doubtful did she feel of their being related to her so closely as they pretended to be, if, in fact, they were in any way connected with her by the ties of consanguinity ; and as these ideas crossed her mind, and the similarity of their fate occurred to her, Emily felt her affection for the poor girl hourly increase, she could love her with all the warmth, all the ardour of a sister. A sister!—at the mention of that name, a sensation shot through her heart, such as she had never felt before, and tears started to her eyes :—

"Alas!" she ejaculated, "I have no sister, no relation in the world; I am a solitary wretched being, with no one in the world that cares for me; no one who would lend a helping hand to relieve me in my misfortunes, or to soothe the anguish of my bosom. Oh, yes!—I do Patty an injustice; she, at any rate, sympathises in my sorrows, and is ready to run any hazard to serve me;—she shall be my sister; henceforth we will know each other by no other titles !"

These reflections were accompanied by a sensation of pleasure, which made the heart of our heroine rebound again ; and her mind had not felt so composed and even cheerful for considerable time.

After awhile she again took up the manuscript, although it was with the most poignant anguish she prepared to trace the dreadful sufferings of the ill-fated writer, in whom she felt so powerfully interested. Several pages were completely illegible, and the conclusion of it was written in characters less clear even than the others, as though the hand which traced them gradually became weaker, until death stopped the pen altogether. The sentences that she could make out also, were very much unconnected, and seemed to emanate from a mind disordered by suffering, and left the reader in the same state of mystery as to who the writer actually was, or the name of the heartless wretch by whom he was persecuted, or what could have been his motives for such conduct. Emily having come to the conclusion of the melancholy document, felt vexed and disappointed, for the whole circumstance had excited her to the most nervous state of impatience, and here she was left without knowing any more than she had done at first, namely, that an unfortunate being had been confined in the secret closet, and there left to die of hunger, and that another ill-fated wretch had been murdered in the adjoining chamber, but who that was, any more than it appeared to have been a female, according to what was stated by the writer of the manuscript, she was entirely ignorant. After the appearance of the spectre of Mrs. Fitzormond to her, and the manner in which the secret closet had been revealed to her, she did think that the manuscript would have been so explicit as to explain all, and disclose the names of the guilty persons ; and moreover, she had entertained an idea that it would also have been the means of unravelling, in all probability, the mystery of her origin, a mystery which caused her so much painful doubt and anxiety. One thing, however, these papers would prove, and that was that murder had been perpetrated by some person or persons within these walls, which persons, if they still lived, Providence might ordain should in due course of time be brought to justice ; and she, therefore, determined to take all possible care of them, hoping that she might be made the humble instrument of bringing about that retribution, which the blood of the murdered called aloud for.

One circumstance very much surprised Emily, and that was, that these papers which contained such evidence of guilt, should have been suffered to remain where they had done, evidently for so many years ; and that the guilty parties did not remove them, also the ghastly skeleton of the murdered man, and the blood-stained bed-clothes. Such neglect ; such a total disregard of danger, seemed to her to have been the work of either a madman, or one who seemed to care nothing whatever about concealment. Perhaps, however, she reflected, they had imagined that the secret would remain safe enough concealed in the closet until they were beyond the fear or reach of punishment in this world.

Emily having finished perusing them, folded the manuscripts up carefully, and concealed them in her bosom, and she then sat down and awaited impatiently the approach of evening. Never had the hours appeared to her so long and tedious. They seemed to move on leaden wings, and as the time she was looking so anxiously for approached, so did every moment appear longer. Her mind was in a state of great anxiety, alternately filled with hope and despair. Several times she had looked from the head of the staircase which led to her room into the apartment below, and at length she was glad to perceive that there was no one there but Patty and her mother.

Twilight had now also set in, and shortly afterwards she perceived old Madge retire from the parlour, which she had no sooner done, than our heroine heard the light footsteps af Patty ascending the stairs. The critical moment that required all her fortitude, had now arrived, and she trembled. She quickly, however, aroused herself, and by the time Patty entered her chamber, she was quite composed and collected. Patty put her finger to her lips significantly, and made a sign to our heroine to follow her; Emily raised her eyes towards Heaven, and mentally offered up a prayer for the protection of the Almighty in their undertaking, and this having been responded to by the expressive looks of Patty, they both with noiseless footsteps, quitted the room.

As well as placing the rope ladder in the chamber which opened upon the terrace, Patty had taken the precaution to have there in readiness also, such articles of dress as they would require, and she had also secured the money she had saved.

"Dear Emily," said the poor girl, when they had reached the terrace; "the time is now come, and thanks to heaven, everything seems to favour our designs; my father and Will are both from home, and from what I heard the former say, Chesterton is not expected here to-night. My mother is busy in another part of the house; so courage, courage, and in a few minutes we shall bid farewell to this horrible place, I hope for ever. Assist me to fasten one end of the ladder to the balustrades, we have not a moment to lose, for every instant of delay is fraught with danger."

"I am prepared to combat every difficulty, dear Patty," replied our heroine, "any fate would be preferable to that of remaining here, and in the power of the cruel and guilty wretches who are seeking my destruction."

Darkness had now entirely veiled the earth, and not a sound could be heard, save the wind, as it came in gentle murmurs across the heath. As far as their eyes could penetrate through the darkness, the coast seemed to be entirely clear. Emily and Patty soon fastened the ladder to the balustrades, but then they were sadly at a loss to secure it at the bottom. This, however, they were unable to accomplish, so that the descent by it would be a very hazardous one. Nothing daunted, notwithstanding, at the danger which presented itself, Patty determined to descend first, and then she could secure it, so that our heroine might go down it without danger. She would not listen to any persuasions that Emily could offer, to allow her to make the first attempt, and the next moment, after having commended herself to the care of Heaven, she placed her foot upon the ladder, and was swinging in the air, in a manner that made our heroine shudder, imagining every moment that she would be compelled to let go her hold, and would be precipitated to the earth, in which case she must have been killed upon the spot. For a few seconds, Patty hung in this perilous situation, and was unable to make any effort to proceed in her descent, but at length she did succeed in somewhat steadying the ladder, and slowly reached she earth in safety.

"Thank Heaven!" cried Emily, fervently, and clasping her hands, "she is safe."

At this moment, when Patty, to whom our heroine had thrown her bundle, was about to secure the bottom of the ladder, previous to the latter preparing to descend, the sound of approaching footsteps met her ears.

"Hist! hist! Patty, for Heaven's sake conceal yourself; some one is approaching; we shall be discovered and all will be lost."

Emily whispered this in breathless haste, and in accents that were scarcely audible. Patty immediately concealed herself in one of the porches of the building, and Emily pulling up the ladder, waited in a state of the most painful suspense to see what would be the result of this adventure, and to observe the person pass. It was not long ere he came, and the terror of Emily was so great that she could scarcely suppress a scream, when she recognized at once, the hateful person of the wretch Chesterton.

As he approached the house, he looked up towards the terrace on which our heroine was standing, and she drew back with terror, and trembled for Patty, who was concealed in the very porch towards which Chesterton seemed to be approaching, and she did not see how it was possible that she could escape his observation, and thus their scheme would be at once frustrated. Her heart throbbed heavily against her side with the agony of suspense, and her limbs trembled violently. To her great relief, however, when Chesterton had got to within a few paces of the building, he turned off, in a different direction, and passing round an angle, was hidden from the sight. Emily once more clasped her hands, and raising her eyes piously towards Heaven, returned her thanks, with all the fervour that her feelings prompted. After a few seconds had elapsed, Patty emerged from the place in which she had concealed herself, and in a voice of agitation, said ;—

"Quick, quick, dear Emily ; the ladder—the ladder !—Delay not a moment, or our scheme will be frustrated."

Emily immediately let down the ladder again, and Patty having made [it fast at the bottom, the former descended without much difficulty, and Patty and her threw themselves into each other's arms, and embraced each other affectionately, while tears of gratitude gushed to their eyes, and flowed down their cheeks. They were aroused into action, however, by the danger of their situation, and stifling their emotion as well as possible, with hasty steps they quitted the spot, and made their way in silence and precipitation across the heath. The heart of Emily bounded with joy and gratitude, at the success they had met with, but neither her nor Patty ventured to give expression to their feelings, and indeed, while they were on the heath they were still exposed to the most imminent danger, as there was no place of concealment, should their flight be discovered, and a pursuit commenced ; and they might likewise meet Gerald Darnley and his son on their way home. The heath was very extensive, and it would, Patty knew, take them at least two hours to cross it; but beyond that the country was better, and they might pursue such a course as would baffle their enemies. Some two or three miles beyond the heath, Patty knew that one of her school-fellows resided with her mother, who was a widow, and in their cottage she resolved that they would seek shelter for the night.

Sanguine with hope, and her heart elated, now she once more breathed the air of liberty, Emily felt more than her usual strength, and never once thought of fatigue. Patty also indulged reciprocal feelings, and they both walked with much vigour, and in a short time they had got far away from the Old Lone House, without meeting with anything since they had seen Chesterton, to excite their fears. In their whole progress across the heath, they did not encounter a human being, but frequently they looked back, as well as they could penetrate through the darkness, apprehensive lest their flight should have been found out, and their pursuers be at hand. Often the voice of the wind made them start, in fact, when persons are placed in similar circumstances, the most trifling things will excite their terrors.

At length they could perceive the lights from the village, but a very short distance from them, and again they poured forth their thanks to Heaven for their preservation. They, however, avoided the village, and crossed into the fields, for Patty thought it was not at all unlikely that her father and Will were there, and they would run in danger of encountering them. The path they chose was a circuitous one, but it was not much frequented, and, therefore, Patty acted very prudently in having taken it.

"Mrs. Burton I know will give us a lodging for the night," said she, "for she is a very good kind of a woman, and both her and Ellen, her daughter, are very partial to me. How astonished they will be to see me; and we shall be quite safe there, for my father knows nothing whatever about them, and would not, therefore, think of looking for us there."

"Heaven has, indeed, so far favoured our designs, dear Patty," observed our heroine, "but doubtless, ere this, our escape has become known, and I am apprehensive until we get beneath some place of shelter and concealment for the night. Is the cottage of the good woman you speak of far from hence ?"

"To the best of my recollection, it is about three miles," answered Patty, "it is in a very retired spot, and I feel confident that we shall be quite safe there."

They now redoubled their speed, and went on with renewed spirit, and in little better than another hour, they arrived at the cottage of Mrs. Burton, which was situated in the midst of a woody dell, and quite secluded from the village we have mentioned. The good woman beheld Patty and her companion with much amazement, as did also her daughter Ellen, who had come from service on a short visit to her mother, but they received them with much kindness, and offered to afford them all the accomodation in their power. Patty briefly related the melancholy story of our heroine ; the persecution and cruelty they had both been subjected to, and the manner in which they had effected their escape. Mrs. Burton, and her daughter were much astonished at all Patty had told them, and expressed in no very measured terms, their detestation and horror at the villany and cruelty of the steward, Gerald Darnley, and his son, applauded the resolution of Patty, and wished them every success. After sitting for some time in conversation, and having partaken of the repast which Mrs. Burton had provided for them, they retired to the chamber in which Ellen slept when at home, but which she now gave up for their accommodation, and made shift herself in the same bed with her mother.

Although they were very tired with the exertion they had undergone, Emily and Patty sat for some time after they had quitted the presence of Mrs. Burton and her daughter, conversing, and giving vent to those feelings of joy, which their deliverance from the Old Lone House had occasioned them, and trusted that Providence would still enable them to elude the vigilant search which would no doubt be set on foot after them.

They pictured to themselves in imagination, the rage and surprise which would fill the minds of the villains when their flight was discovered, and well calculated upon the vengeance they might expect, should they again fall into their power. This latter thought made them both shudder with terror, and they could not bear to dwell upon it with anything like composure.

"But I hope, dear Emily," said Patty, "that any fears we may entertain upon that subject may prove groundless ; I shall not feel very apprehensive when we reach the residence of my aunt ; for should my father and Chesterton think of looking for us there, which, in my opinion is not very likely, I will hazard the consequences ; and seek that protection from the law, which, of course, we can both of us demand ; and after what we have witnessed in the Old Lone House, neither my father or the others, I think, would feel inclined to incur the inquiry which might be made into their past and present actions."

" Your observations are very reasonable," said Emily, " and I only hope that they may be verified ; for my own part, however, I am determined to suffer death rather than to be forced back to that awful place, the Old Lone House, and left to the mercy of the villain, Gerald Darnley, and the hateful miscreant Chesterton ; both of whom, I have had sufficient proof, are capable of perpetrating any crime to answer their purpose, however hideous ; at any rate, as you have observed, the law of the land must protect me, and upon that, I am determined to throw myself, should things arrive at the extremity we apprehend. I cannot dwell upon the scenes I witnessed during the short time I remained in that old house, without a feeling of the most indescribable horror, and it strikes me very forcibly, that I am some day or the other, destined to be the principal cause of bringing those villains to justice, and to receive that reward, which, I am thoroughly convinced, has so long been due to their numerous crimes. Patty, I speak thus of those men, without for a moment, disguising my real opinion of them, neither do I think you ought to be offended at my observations, for I feel thoroughly convinced that they are neither of them, even in the remotest degree, related to you."

" I have always expressed the same opinion to you, Emily," observed Patty, " and I cannot divest my mind of the idea, although I will admit that it is a singular one, and one that, perhaps, will never be satisfactorily decided. Nature seems to revolt from the association ; and could I think otherwise, I should be even more wretched than I am already. But if Gerald and Madge are not my parents, who can they be ; and for what purpose have they thus abandoned me ?"

" It seems to me, Patty," said our heroine, " that we are both the children of mystery, and there appears to be a similarity in our fates, which makes it not at all surprising that our hearts should warm towards each other."

" You are right, Emily," said Patty, " you are perfectly right, and I sincerely hope that nothing may ever occur to put a stop to that friendship and attachment which has sprung up between us, in so remarkable a manner. It seems to me as if we were destined by Fate to be as sisters to each other. But it is getting late, and as I do not feel inclined to go to rest, perhaps you will hasten to bed, if you feel so disposed, and I will remain up, and, with your permission, peruse those manuscripts, which came into your possession in so singular a manner, and which have excited such a deep interest in your bosom."

" I have perused them three or four times," returned Emily, " and the oftener I read them, the more is my sympathy excited for the unhappy being who wrote them, and met with so untimely a fate, and the more do I become involved in the mystery of their contents. If it is agreeable, Patty, as I am also disinclined for sleep just yet, I will re-peruse them aloud."

" Very well, be it so," replied Patty, " and I shall be very glad of your company."

Emily trimmed the lamp, and then taking the manuscripts from her bosom, read the contents aloud to Patty. She was frequently interrupted by the tears and exclamations of terror that escaped the bosom of the latter, and when she concluded, she ejaculated ;—

" Good God ! and can it be possible that monsters such as these can exist, and that they have been hitherto able to escape the vengeance of offended Heaven ?—And who can the villains that have committed these atrocities be ?—Can those men, whom I have hitherto been led to suppose to be my father and brother, have had anything to do with these monstrous crimes ?

That William Darnley could not, there cannot be a doubt, for he was but a mere child at the time; but, I have too much cause to suspect his father. Oh, all merciful Providence, confirm my suspicions, I beseech thee, and let me no longer think myself the daughter of a robber and a murderer!"

"Abate your anguish, Patty," said our heroine, "and rest assured that something will ere long transpire, to bring about that explanation which you so much desire, and which none can more ardently wish than I do myself."

"I know you do, dear Emily," returned Patty, "and our thoughts are mutual. To see each other happy is a source of happiness to us both; and I firmly believe that our wishes will, one day or the other, either sooner or later, be realised. Poor, unfortunate creature, how dreadful must have been his sufferings, doomed to that horrible lingering death, and torn from his wife and children. It strikes me forcibly, Emily, that the other hapless victim to the enormities of this fiend or fiends in human shape, was the wife of that unfortunate man, whose mouldering bones we saw in the secret closet."

"Why, that thought has occurred to me," remarked Emily, "and I have never encouraged the idea, but my mind has been wrought up to a pitch of horror I have seldom, if ever before experienced. You may deem me romantic and foolish, Patty, but I have even been led so far at times to suppose that I am not wholly unconnected with the murdered man."

"Dear me, Emily," returned Patty, "that is indeed a singular idea; but there have been many more remarkable things than that happen before now; but although I should be glad of you to be able to learn the mystery of your birth, heaven forbid that you should discover your parents to have come to such a dreadful fate as that of the unfortunate Jordan. That, by the by, is a foreign name, I think."

"It is," answered Emily, "and that is the only hint we have in the manuscripts of the name, country, or rank of the ill-fated writer. Have you ever heard Darnley or his son, (for I will never again call them your relations,) have you ever heard them mention anything about any foreign acquaintance?"

"Never," said Patty, in reply, "not a sentence;—but it is not at all likely that they would do so in my presence."

"True," returned Emily, "I did not think of that."

"Nay," added Patty, "although, as I have before frequently told you, I firmly believed my father and brother, as I have been taught to call them, thorough bad men, and knew that they did not get their living in an honest manner, yet I never for a moment thought them capable of perpetrating half the heinous crimes they have done, and are, it appears, constantly in the habit of doing, until you apprised me of the fact which you ascertained from conversations which you had overheard between Gerald and Will."

"But knowing as we do, the guilty course they pursue, is it not strange that suspicion should never light upon them, and that they are not brought to justice?" said our heroine.

"Why, that certainly is strange," returned Patty, "and it has often been the subject of my thoughts. But they manage their guilty business with the most consummate skill and sagacity, otherwise they could never have carried on their nefarious practices so long with impunity, and without the slightest interference. Certain it is that, so far from any suspicion of their real characters being entertained, they are thought by many to be highly respectable persons, and men of some little independent property, and they have the skill, however ruffianly they may be at home, to cloak their real characters under such a specious mask, that they would deceive a person of much penetration. But hark; it is eleven o'clock, we had

better go to bed, Emily. Tnank heaven, we have so far been able to elude those individuals we have so much reason to dread."

" Aye," answered our heroine, " and I do not despair but that we shall ultimately be able to frustrate their designs altogether."

" At any rate we will try every means to do so," said Patty, " and if the worst should come to the worst, we know our remedy, and certainly they will find the iron arm of the law sufficiently powerful to prevent them from resisting it."

After some other conversation, of no interest or importance to these pages, the two friends retired to rest, and sleep, which they much needed, after the mental and bodily fatigue they had undergone during the evening, soon fell upon their eyelids, and was a source of the greatest relief to them. Sleep, the balm of rest to the weary traveller ; the transitory death of care, although often busy fancy is at work to render it worse than that of waking horror.

CHAPTER XI.

THE WOODBINE COTTAGE.—A TALE OF ROMANCE.

THE night passed away without anything taking place to disturb our heroine and her companion, and the blush of morn peeped through the casement with refulgent splendour, and they awoke much refreshed, and looked forth from the casement on to the scenery beyond, which was illumined by the golden rays of the sun.

Mrs. Burton and her daughter had been up some time, for they were No. 14.

early risers, and were seldom in bed after the first streak of day appeared
in the eastern horizon.   Our heroine and her companion had scarcely
finished the duties of their toilet when they were aroused by Ellen, who
came to inform them that the breakfast awaited their presence.   She enquired kindly after their health, and how they had rested ; to which Emily
and Patty replied in a suitable manner, and then followed Ellen down stairs
into the neat little parlour, where they found the frugal repast spread upon
the table, with that cleanliness, and precise attention to order, that appeared
to invite them to the meal.   The breakfast passed over in the most agreeable manner, and during the time it was going forward, Patty gave Mrs.
Burton and her daughter some necessary precautions as to how she should
act, if at any future time there should be any enquiries made of her concerning them.   But they needed no such precautions, for, independent of
both of them being naturally very shrewd, they so sincerely commisserated
with our heroine and her companion, that they were prepared to encounter
a good deal rather than betray them.   Mrs. Burton next enquired of Patty
how she purposed they should complete the remainder of their journey,
which was a considerable distance.   Patty had not yet come to any de-
cision upon this subject, and she was glad that Mrs. Burton had broached
it.   She informed her that she had not made up her mind, and she would
be glad of her advice.

"It would, however, not be prudent for us to remain in this neighbourhood a moment longer than can be helped," said she, "for fear that those
from whom we have fled should discover the place of our retreat, and get
us once more in their power."

"Of course, the distance is too great for you to think of walking it, and
were it not, it would not be safe for you to do so," remarked Mrs. Burton.

"Certainly," replied Patty; "but a public coach is a very little more
secure, when there are a number of passengers, and, perhaps, among them
the very persons we wish to avoid."

"Why, that is very true," replied Mrs. Burton, after a few minutes reflection, "but I'll tell you what it is, Miss Patty, my brother, who only
lives in the village, has got a post chaise of his own, which he depends upon
for a living ; he is a man whom you may safely trust, and I have no doubt
but that by my speaking to him, he would take you both to the place you
want to go to very reasonably.   If you like, I will send Ellen for him, and
you can speak to him on the subject."

Both Emily and Patty uttered their thanks to Mrs. Burton for her
kindness, and expressed themselves glad of the offer, which could not have
happened better, under the present circumstances.   Ellen left the cottage
to request the attendance of her uncle.

Sam Burton, as Mrs. Burton's brother was familiarly called, was an
honest, good-hearted fellow, and in every respect the prototype of his
sister.   He commisserated our heroine and Patty, on being briefly made
acquainted with their misfortunes, and the bargain being quickly struck,
they were soon on the road to the place of their destination.

We will pass over the journey of our heroine and Patty, during which
nothing took place worthy of any particular notice, and by the following
day, they arrived at the residence of the latter's aunt, which was very
romantically situated, and was a small, but very neat and compact building in the gothic style, with the ivy and honeysuckle climbing up its walls.

The astonishment of Mrs. Seagrove on beholding her niece, may be
very readily conceived, but she embraced her with the most unbounded
affection ; shed tears of compassion when she related what she had had to
undergo at the Old Lone House ; shuddered with horror at the guilty
course her brother and his son were pursuing, and welcomed her once more

to that home in which she had passed her early days, and promised to protect her all that was in her power. She received Emily with that cordiality which went immediately to the latter's heart, and made her accept the obligation with less repugnance than she might otherwise have done ; but when Mrs. Seagrove looked more narrowly into the countenance of our heroine, she started and turned pale, and then muttered something which was inarticulate, evincing considerable agitation which surprised both the young girls, and Patty, with much eagerness, enquired what was the matter ?

"Nothing, my child, nothing," answered Mr. Seagrove, still looking very earnestly at our heroine, "nothing particular, only your young and fair companion bears such an extraordinary likeness to one I have seen before—that, but, however, it is not possible that she can be any relation to her."

"Oh, my dear aunt," said Patty, whose deepest interest, as well as that of Emily's, was aroused by the seriousness of the former's manner, and the words she had made use of; "you know not; singular events are often brought about by the most simple and unlooked-for means, and it might be the case in this instance. Emily's is a strange history, as you will acknowledge when you have heard her relate it."

"Perhaps your friend will favour me with it, after we have partook of some refreshment," said Mrs. Seagrove, still scrutinizing our heroine with the utmost curiosity, "I shall be very glad to hear it, and believe me, if commisseration can afford her any consolation, such sympathy she shall find in me."

"I know she will, my dear aunt," said Patty, affectionately throwing her arms around the neck of Mrs. Seagrove, and kissing her vehemently ; "oh, you were ever so kind; so feeling."

Emily could not resist a tear at the kind manner in which Mrs. Seagrove had received them, and after warmly thanking her, they entered the little dining-room, where a plenteous and delicate repast was placed before them, of which they partook heartily. This being completed, and the things having been removed by old Peggy, (the faithful companion and housekeeper of Mrs. Seagrove, who had nursed Patty, and had been with the former ever since the melancholy death of her husband, who, being embarrassed in his circumstances, in a fit of despair, put an end to his existence) ; at the request of Mrs. Seagrove and Patty, Emily commenced her narrative, and detailed every particular that had occurred to her since she could first remember. She was frequently interrupted in the course of it, by an exclamation of surprise and grief from Mrs. Seagrove, and when she related the conduct of Gerald Darnley towards her, and the conversations she had overheard between him, Chesterton, and his son, from which it appeared that they were familiar with, and ready to perpetrate any deed of blood, her emotion was so great, that she could scarcely support herself. She arose hastily from her chair, and traversed the room with disordered steps, and frequently gave vent to such exclamations, as shewed the emotion which struggled in her bosom.

"Can it be possible !" she cried, "that, bad as I really believed, nay, knew him to be, he can be such a monster ! A cold, deliberate murderer, a robber, and—— Oh, horror !—horror !—What a stigma is this upon my name !"

"Oh, no, my dearest aunt, no one will be so unjust, so ungenerous, as to reproach you for the crimes and faults of your brother," said Patty ; "your amiable character is too well known. But, is it not strange that there should be such an extraordinary difference in the dispositions of real tions ? Who could imagine, for a moment, that you were the sister of that

ferocious, that guilty man, whom I shudder to call father, and whom I confess,
I cannot help entertaining doubts, of his being really related to me."

"Not related to you, my dear!" repeated Mrs. Seagrove, in a voice of
amazement and confusion; "whatever can have put such an idea into
your head?"

"I know not, my dear aunt," replied Patty, "but certain it is, that I
cannot divest my mind of it. You, of course, ought to know all about it,
for I was entrusted to your care from childhood, and before I can remember; you, I know, would not deceive me; tell me, then, I beg of you,
whether you know anything relating to me, to give strength and confirmation to my surmises?"

"Patty," at length her aunt observed, "now that I see your suspicions
are excited, I am ready to admit that I have always had my doubts as to
Gerald Darnley, my unfortunate brother, being your father; but, you
will, I am confident, believe me, when I assure you, that as to any direct
certainty upon that point, I have not the least proof."

"No," ejaculated Patty, in accents of disappointment, "you astonish
me!"

"I dare say I do, my child," returned Mrs. Seagrove, "but such, I
assure you, is the case. Listen to me:—I have never related to you the
particulars I am now about to detail before. My father was a man of
excellent principles, and in affluent circumstances, and he brought up
myself and Gerald, who was my only brother, with every care and attention. But Gerald, even from a child, evinced a morose, cruel, passionate,
and sullen disposition, and as he grew up, in spite of the good example he had had before him, and the excellent advice he had ever received from his parents, it grew with him. Our mother died when
we were both very young, and after some years, a bank failing, in
which my father had invested the greater portion of his money, we became nearly ruined. This circumstance, I have, no doubt, tended to
shorten his days, for he did not live but a very short time afterwards, and
was enabled to leave me and my brother but a very small annuity. Gerald
launched forth into every scene of vice and dissipation, and left me, and I
heard no more of him for several years afterwards. In the meantime, I
married the late Mr. Seagrove, of whom I was so unhappily deprived
only two years after our nuptials. I have no occasion to dwell upon that
melancholy subject. A short time after his demise, I recovered some
property which belonged to him, and which was sufficient to keep me in
future independent, if not in affluence. I made several enquiries after my
brother, but could not hear anything of him for some time. One day,
however, guess my astonishment, when he made his appearance before me.
He was very much altered, and his countenance bore testimony to the
intemperate course of life he had been leading. He was, however, well
dressed, and informed me that he had married a woman with some property, who had borne him two children, a boy and a girl. His wife, he
further stated, had been dead about two months, and——"

"His wife dead!" interrupted Patty, in accents of amazement; "what
can this mean? I always imagined that Madge was the woman who had
brought us into the world."

"If we are to believe Gerald," answered Mrs. Seagrove, "she was not.
But hear me out. Gerald informed me that he was, at that time, living in
the Old Lone House, which had belonged to the family of his wife, and
added, that the only thing which annoyed him was the girl, whom he was
fearful he could not bring up as he could wish. I felt interested in the
fate of the poor child, whom I was aware would have but a very bad
example set her. I had no children of my own, and I, therefore, made my

brother an offer to take it, and bring it up with the same care and affection as if it had been my own. He accepted of my offer with much apparent pleasure, and a week afterwards you were brought to me. I was struck with your beauty, and my heart instantly warmed with maternal fondness towards you. Gerald laid very strict injunctions on me about you, and cautioned me not to satisfy the idle curiosity of any one as to who you was, and how you had come into my possession. This, at the time, did not create much surprise in my mind, but it has done since, and the more I reflected on it, the more I became involved in mystery and doubt, as to what could be the cause of Gerald's being so fearful that it should become known that you were his daughter, and I must confess, that the idea has frequently occurred to me that you were not really his child, though whose could you be, and what could possibly be the motives of Gerald in asserting his paternity to a child that did not belong to him, I could not form the slightest conjecture. What followed, you are already acquainted with."

"My dear, dear aunt!" exclaimed Patty, once more throwing her arms round the neck of Mrs. Seagrove, and kissing her in the most affectionate manner; "my dear, dear aunt, if such, indeed, you are, what a debt of gratitude do I owe you for your unexampled kindness to me? I feel more than ever confident that my conjectures are not without foundation, and that Gerald Darnley is not my father; but the only cause for regret I have in this circumstance is, that you are not my aunt."

"And why should you regret that my dear Patty?" demanded Mrs. Seagrove; "should it, indeed, transpire that we are not really connected by the ties of consanguinity, you must ever have my most fervent love."

Patty expressed more by her looks than she could have done by her words, and they both remained silent for a few minutes, when Mrs. Seagrove, addressing herself to Emily, said,—

"You have, indeed, my poor girl, suffered much in the school of adversity, and your fate is one of great mystery and interests me much; as to who this steward can be, or even the title of his master, I cannot imagine, as I am entirely unacquainted with my brother's affairs, and, therefore, have no knowledge of his acquaintances. My firm belief, however, is, that you are of noble birth, and that some time or other you will be restored to your rights. I sincerely commisserate in your misfortunes, and receive you with the same hearty welcome as I do my niece."

"Oh, Madam," cried Emily, shedding tears of gratitude, "you are too kind, indeed you are, to a complete stranger."

"Stranger or not, you are the child of misfortune, and the victim of a cruel and unjust persecution," said Mrs. Seagrove; "and, therefore, it is the duty of every Christian to render you all the assistance in their power. I am glad you chose my place for an asylum, for I am of opinion, as well as Patty, that Gerald, or your other enemies, would never think of looking for you here. In the course of a few days I have not the least doubt but that I shall be able to devise some plan for your future security. In the meantime, you shall have every attention and comfort here, that my circumstances will permit."

Emily and Patty again thanked the good woman for her unexampled kindness, and our heroine assured her that she should never cease to remember it with feelings of the most unqualified gratitude.

"But, my dear Madam," said Emily, "you have not explained to us what occasioned the extraordinary emotion you evinced when you first beheld me."

"It was the remarkable resemblance you bear to one who is long since no more," replied Mrs. Seagrove, with a sigh; "and the more I look upon you, the greater does your likeness to her appear to be."

"And was the lady to whom you allude," asked Emily, whose interest was deeply excited, "was the lady to whom you allude, unfortunate?"

"She was of noble rank, but, indeed, unfortunate," replied Mrs. Seagrove; "but, excuse me, this is a subject I cannot bear to dwell upon—let us drop it."

Emily obeyed, but she felt a more than usual curiosity to be made further acquainted with the female of whom Mrs. Seagrove had spoken, and who had created an inexplicable sensation in her bosom which she, in vain, tried to conquer.

They now conversed freely upon other topics, and they were evidently all very much pleased with each other. Mrs. Seagrove was a remarkably sensible, accomplished, and intelligent woman, and Emily could not but most sincerely pity her for having the misfortune to be connected with such a wretch as Gerald Darnley. It seemed, in fact, totally impossible that the same blood should flow in the veins of two beings so diametrically opposite in disposition, habits, and every other respect; and appeared to be one of those singular vagaries of Fate, for which there is no accounting.

"And does the good Mr. Walton and his amiable family still reside in this neighbourhood?" asked Patty, in the course of conversation.

"He does," replied Mrs. Seagrove, "and in their society I pass many, many happy hours, that else might prove dull and languid. Ah! there is, indeed, a pattern of virtuous patience and perseverance under every misfortune that one would think it were impossible to attend the human race. You can see his beautiful little farm from this casement."

Emily and Patty walked to the casement, and looked in the direction to which Mrs. Seagrove pointed. The farm-house was situated on the skirts of a large wild common, with fields and pastures surrounding it, all well fenced, and cultivated with care, skill, and taste. The air breathed forth the sweet fragrance it inhaled from the bean-flower and clover. An orchard of fine young fruit-trees lay beyond the house, and before it a little garden gay with all the flowers of the season. On the southern side, sheltered by the honeysuckle and sweet-brier, was a stand of bee-hives. The farm-yard was well stocked with pigs and poultry, and everything denoted, in strong characters, the trouble and management which the possessor had bestowed upon it.

Emily was quite enraptured with what she saw, and expressed her most enthusiastic admiration of it.

"Yes, Mr. Walton is deserving of every praise," said Mrs. Seagrove; "but I will introduce you to him and his family, Emily, and you will, doubtless, be delighted with him, his amiable wife, and lovely daughters."

"Yes, that she will, I am certain," remarked Patty, "and I am very glad to think they are still such close neighbours of your's. How astonished and pleased they will be to see me again!"

"You are right, Patty, that they will," returned Mrs. Seagrove; "for they ever treated you as one of their own family, and were never happy but when you were at the farm with them."

Thus the day passed away in the most agreeable manner, and at night Emily and Patty retired to the chamber allotted to their repose, in comparative happiness. For the first time for many weeks did our heroine enjoy a night's repose undisturbed, and her and she companion arose in the morning in better health and spirits than they had experienced for some time.

They kept themselves closely confined to the house for more than a week, and no one in the neighbourhood knew that they were residing there, with the exception of Farmer Walton and his family, whom Mrs. Seagrove entrusted with the secret, and had introduced to them. The worthy farmer and his family were delighted with our heroine, and she was no less so with them. Mr. and Mrs. Walton had three charming daughters, who possessed all the virtues of their parents, and we need not, therefore, inform the reader with what pleasure they received the friendship of Emily.

One day, when the farmer and his family had been on a visit to Mrs. Seagrove, and they were all seated in the back parlour, the windows of which commanded a more delightful prospect than those of the front, at the request of Mrs. Seagrove, Mr. Walton consented to relate his extra-ordinary history, which Emily and the others listened to with the deepest interest, and sincerely sympathized with him in the vicissitudes he had undergone, and admired the virtuous fortitude with which he had borne up against them. He delivered his narrative in the following words :—

THE STORY OF FARMER WALTON.

" I was born in the county of Suffolk, and my father was a man of very good property, but of a most improvident disposition. His greatest care, and the only one, in fact, which I believe plagued his mind, was in what manner he should squander his fortune away ; and in that you'll admit he was rather successful, for he not only contrived to spend it once, but twice over. This can be very easily explained ;—the first time he disposed of it, it was bought in by a relation, who died not long afterwards, and bequeathed it to him. Any one would have imagined that this would have been sufficient to have cautioned my father, and to have learnt him how to take better care of his fortune in future ; but no such thing—he was not a man of that disposition, and the consequence was, that he launched forth into still greater extravagance than ever, and ended his property and his life together. He expired at the age of forty, and left his family in absolute beggary.

" My mother had a brother, who was master of a ship, and he under-took to take care of, and provide for me. To him, then, I went, and was apprenticed to him, serving several years, during which time I had my ample share of the hardships and vicissitudes of a sailor's life. He be-haved very well to me, and was so well satisfied with my conduct, that he made me his mate ; and we were going a voyage up the Mediterranean, when we were unfortunately wrecked on the coast of Morocco. The ship struck at some distance from the shore, and there we lay a long stormy night, with the waves dashing over us, and looking for death every moment. My uncle and several of the crew sunk beneath the fatigue and want we had undergone, and when the morning dawned, we found that there was only three of us surviving. The spirits of my two companions were so broken, that they were about to lie down and submit to their fate ; but I, who did not think it worth while to resign life without a struggle for it, persuaded them to cheer up again, and to join me in making a desperate effort to rescue ourselves from the jaws of death.

" The weather being calmer, of course it was all in our favour, and I, therefore, prevailed upon them to join me in constructing a raft, by the help of which, after much toil and danger, we were enabled to gain the shore. We had, however, not been long here, when we were seized by the barbarous inhabitants, and borne forcibly away up the country, to be made slaves to the emperor. Here again the weakness of my unfortunate companions sufficiently evinced itself ; for the bare idea of perpetual slavery, together with the brutal treatment we met with, quite overcame them. They did not long survive their hard lot, and drooped and died one after the other.

"The time we were compelled to work was about twelve hours per day, and we were allowed one holiday in the week. The manner in which I employed my leisure time, afterwards turned out to my advantage, as you will see. I learned to make mats and flag-baskets, and in which I soon became so expert, that I had a great number to dispose of, and by that means I got a little money to purchase better food and many other conveniencies, which my companions, for the want of management, spirit, and perseverance, could not.

"After this we were in a little time set to work in the emperor's gardens, and here I always evinced so much good will, care, and industry, that I quickly was taken notice of by the overseer, who treated me with a marked difference to any of the other slaves. I was unremitting in my exertions to become useful to him, and the consequence was, that I succeeded so well, that he treated to me more like a hired servant than a slave; and, what was more, he gave me regular wages. I studied the language of the country, and, in fact, I might have passed my time away happily enough, could I have driven from my recollection the land which gave me birth.

"I spent nothing in extravagance, and saved all the money I could, so that I might be able to purchase my freedom; but still the ransom was immense, and, consequently, it was many years to come before I could, by any possibility, have a chance of doing so. Fortune was, however, about to aid me in this respect. An occurrence quickly took place, which brought it about immediately.

"It was planned by some miscreants one night, to murder my master, and plunder his house. I slept in a little shed in the garden, where the tools lay, and being awakened by the noise, I saw four men break through the fence, and walk up an alley towards the house. I crept out, with a spade in my hand, and silently followed them. They made a hole in the house-wall, large enough for a man to enter it. Two of them had got in, and the third was about to enter, when I shouted aloud to alarm the family. My master and his son, who lay in the house, got up, and having let me in, we secured the villains, after a sharp contest, in which I received a severe wound with a dagger. My master, who looked upon me as his preserver, had every possible care taken of me; and as soon as I was restored to convalesence, he gave me my freedom. He was sorry to part with me, and tried hard to persuade me to stop with him, but I was so anxious to see once more my native land, that I would not assent, and immediately set out for the nearest seaport, and took my passage in a vessel going to Gibraltar. From this place I sailed in the first ship for England."

"As soon as we arrived in the Downs, and my heart was leaping for joy at the sight of the white cliffs, a man-of-war's boat came along side, and pressed into the king's service, all of us who were seamen.

"My nautical knowledge soon got me promoted to the post of a petty officer, and at the peace I was paid off, and received a good sum for wages and prize-money. I immediately made my way to London, and put my cash into the hands of a banker, and made up my mind to start into some new course of life to that I had been hitherto leading, and of which I was heartily tired.

"It happened to be my misfortune to be as ignorant as a child of many things, and among the most important of these was a want of knowledge of the tricks of London.

"Shortly after my return to England, my eyes fell, unfortunately, upon

an advertisement, offering remarkable advantages to a partner in a commercial concern, who could bring a small capital. I caught, unluckily, at the bait, and was induced to make inquiry upon the subject. It was an unfortunate day's work for me when I did so; for I was soon cajoled by a plausible, artful fellow, to embark my whole stock in it. The business I was completely ignorant of, being a manufacture; but labour had no terrors for me, and I, therefore, set about working as they instructed me, with great diligence, and thought that everything was going on with success. I was soon, however, undeceived; for one morning when I went to the shop, I found that my partners had decamped, and on the same day I was arrested for a considerable sum, due on the partnership. Any idea of my being able to procure bail, was quite out of the question; and, therefore, I was obliged to go to prison. In this place I should have been half starved, had it not been for my Moorish trade of mat-making, by the help of which I bettered my condition for some months, when the creditors, finding that there was nothing to be got out of me, suffered me to go at large.

"Behold me now in the wide world, without a farthing or a friend; but think not that I gave way to despair; no, I thanked Providence that my health and limbs were yet left me. I did not like the idea of returning to a sea-faring life, but gave the preference to my other new trade of gardening. I, therefore, applied to a nurseryman near town, and was received as a day-labourer. I set myself cheerfully to work, as I had always done, in every misfortune in which I had been placed, and took good care not only to be in the grounds the first man in the morning, but the last at night.

"I made my employer acquainted with all the practices I had observed
No. 15

in Morocco, and, in return, I got him to instruct me in his own. I improved wonderfully, and in the course of a very little time was considered a skilful workman, and my wages were advanced considerably. I was not only well fed and comfortably lodged, but saved money into the bargain.

"It was about this time that I became acquainted with that dear woman who is now my wife, and after a short courtship, soon finding that our sentiments and dispositions corresponded, we were united.

"My wife had saved a little money in service, and having taken a cottage, with an acre or two of land to it, we furnished the place, and bought a cow. All the leisure time I had I spent upon my piece of ground, and by perseverance made it very productive; and the profits of my cow, with my wages, supported us very well. It was impossible for any human being to be more comfortable than I was, after a hard day's work, by my own fire-side, with my wife beside me, and our little infant on my knee.

"In this manner we passed two or three years when a gentleman who had dealt largely with my master for young plants, asked him if he could recommend an honest, industrious man for tenant, upon some land that he had recently taken in from the sea. My master, who was anxious to serve me, mentioned me. The proposal pleased me, as the situation appeared to me to be likely to prove a lucrative one, and having gone down to view the premises, I took a farm upon a lease at a low rent, and removed my family and goods to it. It was situated at a distance of one hundred and fifty miles from London. There was ground enough for money, but much was left to be done for it, in draining, fencing, and manuring. Besides, it required more stock than I was able to furnish, and I was obliged to borrow some money of my landlord. I began with a good heart, and worked late and early to put things into the best condition. My first misfortune was, the place proved very unhealthy to us. I was attacked with a violent and lingering ague, which reduced me very much, and, of course, interrupted my business most materially. My wife fell into a slow fever, and so did my eldest child, and the latter died, and it was a miracle that what with grief and illness, my wife was able to recover. One sorrow, as the old adage has it, never comes alone, and to add to my misfortunes, the rot got among my sheep, and the greater part of my stock was carried off by it.

"These misfortunes following so rapidly one upon the other, were sufficient to break the spirits of many persons, but I was not one that easily gave way, as may be seen from what I have already related, and I, therefore, bore up against distress as well as I was able; and with the assistance of my landlord, who acted very kind to me, was in a short time able to recover myself pretty well again. We were restored to perfect convalescence, and began to be seasoned to the climate. But again was fate about to bring misfortune upon us; we seemed, in fact, to be particularly marked out to be the sport of Fortune.

"We had began to form the most sanguine hopes that better times were in store for us, when one night in February, a dreadful storm arose;— never will that night be effaced from my memory as long as I live;—the spring-tide was driven with such fury against our sea-banks, that they gave way. The water rushed in with such force, that all was presently at sea. Two hours before daylight I was awakened by the noise of the waves dashing against the side of our house, and bursting in at the door. My wife had lain in about a month, and she and I and the two children slept on the ground floor. We had just time to carry the children up stairs before all was afloat in the room. When day appeared, we could discover nothing from the windows but water. All the out-houses, ricks, and utensils, were swept away, and all the cattle and the sheep drowned. The sea kept rising, and the force of the current bore so hard against our house, that we thought every moment that it must fall. We clasped our infants to our breasts and expected nothing but present death. At length we espied a boat coming to us. With a good deal of difficulty it got under our window, and took us in, with my servant maid and boy. A few clothes was all the property we saved; and we had not left the house half an hour before it fell. Not only the farm-house, but the farm itself was gone.

"Again was I a ruined man. My wife and I looked at one another and then at our little ones, and wept. Neither of us could offer a syllable of consolation to one another. At last, however, I reflected 'at any rate I am not now in Morocco; here there are doubtless persons who will pity our case, and perhaps relieve us. Besides, I have not injured my character, I have a pair of hands left, and am both willing and able to work. I will not give way to despair, for although things are bad, yet might they have been much worse.' After I had thus soliloquized, I took my wife by the hand, and both kneeling down, we thanked the Almighty for His mercy in saving our lives, and prayed that He would continue to protect us. We rose up with lightened hearts, and were enabled to talk calmly about our condition. I had an anxious wish to return to my former master, the nurseryman, but having no money, how to convey my family so far, puzzled me. Not only was I without cash, but I was even in a far worse dilemma, being greatly involved in debt, which I owed to my landlord. He came down on the news of my misfortune, and, notwithstanding his own misfortunes were heavy, he not only forgave my debt, and released me from all obligations, but he also made me a small present. Some charitable neighbours did the like; but what affected me more than all was, the kindness of our maid servant, who having saved a guinea out of her wages, would insist upon our accepting of it. Poor girl! we had never treated her any otherwise than as one of ourselves, and she felt for us like one.

"When the weather would permit us, and we had provided ourselves with necessaries, we began our weary journey. My wife carried the infant in her arms, I took a bigger child on my back, and a bundle of clothes in my hand. We could only walk a few miles in a day, but sometimes we got a lift in an empty waggon or cart, which helped us on our way very much.

"It was upon an occasion of this kind, that we met with an old farmer returning from market, who suffered us to ride, and entered into conversation with me. I did not scruple to tell him all my adventures, with which he seemed much interested, and understanding that I was skilled in the management of trees, he informed me that a nobleman in his neighbourhood was making great plantations, and as he would very probably be glad to engage with me, he would, if I liked, convey me to the place. As all I was seeking was a living by my labour, I thought the sooner I gained that object the better it would be for me, so returning him my thanks for his kindness, I accepted his offer; and he took us to the nobleman's steward, and made known our case. The steward wrote to my old master for a character, which proving satisfactory, I was immediately engaged as a head manager of a plantation, and I and my family were settled in a comfortable cottage contiguous to it. He also advanced us some money to purchase a little furniture, and a home was thus once more mine.

"Forgetting all my past misfortunes, I entered upon my new employment with renewed spirits, and could not have felt more elated had I been taking possession of a wealthy estate. As for my wife, I kept her employed in her domestic duties, and she found plenty to do. To provide all devolved upon me, and you may rest satisfied that I was compelled to be industrious. Independant of the weekly salary which the steward paid me, I managed to make a little money at my leisure hours, by pruning and dressing gentlemen's fruit-tress. I was allowed a piece of waste ground behind the house for a garden, and it cost me much time and labour to bring it into order. My old master sent me down for a present, some choice young trees and flower-roots, which I planted, and they throve wonderfully. Everything went on almost as well as I could wish. The situation being dry and healthy, my wife recovered her lost bloom, and my children sprung up like my plants. Hope once more filled my mind, and that no further misfortune would attend me, but Providence had ordained it otherwise.

" In this situation about three years passed away, and another child was added to my family, when my landlord died suddenly ; and the one who succeeded him was a young man, wild, heartless, and dissipated, and deeply involved in debt, who was not long before he stopped the planting and improving of the estate, and sent orders to turn off all the workmen. This, as you may very well imagine, was a serious blow to me, but nevertheless, expecting that I should be allowed to keep my little house and garden, and to maintain myself as nursery-man and gardener, I did not entirely droop under the infliction. But as well as a new landlord, we had a new steward, one after his master's heart, and he had received instructions to raise the rents upon the tenants. This man, who had neither conscience nor feeling, asked me as much rent for the place as if I had found the garden ready made to my hands ; and when I remonstrated with him, and told him positively that it would be impossible for me to pay it, he immediately gave me notice to quit. What was more unjust and unreasonable than all, too, he would not even suffer me to take away my trees and plants, nor allow me anything for them. I soon discovered the principal motives for his conduct ; he had a favorite of his own whom he wished to put in, and start him in the world at my expence. It was only a complete waste of time and breath, my expostulating with him on this cruel injustice ; harsh words were the only return I could obtain from him.

" Seeing plain enough that it would be the ruin of me being turned out of the place in this manner, I resolved to go up to London, and to plead my cause with the new landlord, hoping that I might induce him to relent. My parting with my wife and family, was of a most melancholy description, and when I had torn myself away from them, I made my way to the next market-town, and took my place on the outside of the stage-coach.

" Nothing particular happened on our journey, until we were within twenty miles of the metropolis, when the vehicle was accidentally overturned. I was thrown violently to the ground on my head, and being taken up quite senseless, was conveyed to the nearest village, where, as I was unknown to everybody, I was carried to the parish workhouse.

" I was here confined for nearly a fortnight before I regained my strength, a period which was past by me in the most miserable manner, occasioned more by the anxiety which I knew my wife and family must endure on not hearing from me, for, of course, during the time that I was insensible I had no means of letting them know what had befallen to me, and where I was. At the end of three weeks after receiving a very affectionate letter from my wife, in which she expressed the deep anguish herself and her family had experienced at my strange silence, she informed me that she had just made up her mind when she heard from me, to go up to London to make inquiries after me, although it would have put her considerably out of the way, and to an expense which we could but very ill afford at that time.

" Although I was still very weak and ill, as soon as I could get about, I made the best of my way to the metropolis, where I saw the young gentleman who had come into possession of the estate, and in humble, but forcible terms, remonstrated with him on the conduct of his steward, and begged that he would shew me more leniency, as, in the event of my being turned out of my house, and no allowance made for the trees and plants, it would be the ruin of me. It appeared to me very soon, that the young gentleman was not near so bad as his steward, but that he was giddy, thoughtless, and extravagant, and was compelled to act in a manner contrary to his real principles, in order to indulge in his profligate habits. He was at first quite inexorable, but after awhile, he began to relent, and promised me that he would write to his steward upon the subject, and, if upon enquiry, it turned out to be as I had represented it, he might, in all probability, be induced to do something for me.

"Still this answer was far from satisfactory, and finding that it was useless endeavouring to get any other from the gentleman, I was about to make my departure, with a heavy heart, when a servant entered the room and announced the name of the gentleman whose tenant I had been upon the estate where I suffered so much from the flood. Remembering the kindness with which he had ever behaved to me, and particularly the benevolent part he had acted towards me, when the awful calamity I have alluded to took place, I thought if I could see him, he might be able to urge something in my favour with the young gentleman; I, therefore, lingered in the room, (although I am ready to admit that it was a great breach of good manners, and was evidently by no means pleasing to the gentleman to whom I was suing,) until [Mr. Harewood entered. He expressed much surprise at seeing me, but addressed me in the most familiar and friendly manner,—enquired kindly after my wife and family, and also the reason of my coming to London? This was just what I wanted, and in a few words I made him acquainted with the misfortunes I had encountered since the unfortunate affair which had driven me away from his estate, and the business I had come upon to the metropolis. He heard me with attention and patience, and it was very evident to me that he commisserated with me in my misfortunes, and would do all in his power to aid me. My conjectures proved to be correct; he pleaded for me with the young gentleman, who I afterwards learnt was a relative of his, and the consequence was, that he gave me a letter, addressed to his steward, and in which he ordered him to make me a handsome allowance for the great inconvenience and loss I had been put to by my sudden ejectment, and also for the various trees and plants upon the ground, which I had taken such pains to cultivate. Mr. Harewood also made me a present of a guinea, and with a much lighter heart than I had possessed a few minutes before, and a bosom teeming with gratitude to the urbane Mr. Harewood, I quitted the house, and hastened to the coach office, where I immediately booked my place to return home, for which I started in a few hours afterwards.

"I need not describe to you, my dear friends, the joy with which I was greeted on my return home by my wife and children, nor the delight they expressed when informed of the favourable result of my mission; they poured forth their earnest expressions of gratitude to heaven for its goodness, and implored its blessings upon the head of Mr. Harewood, through whose benevolent interposition the good had been effected. Our pleasure was, however, of course, greatly mingled with regret, at the thoughts of being obliged to quit the place where we had been for several years so comfortable; but we hoped that something might occur to put us in a place where we might be as happy, and meet with as much success as we had done in the present instance.

"The steward received the letter of his master with much vexation, and did not forget to give vent to his resentment against me, for having, as he said, the impudence to go to London upon such an errand, after I had heard his (the steward's) determination. However, I cared little for his resentment, since I had succeeded in my object, and made very little reply to his observations. We left the house, but continued to reside in the neighbourhood for a short time, until I could make some arrangements for the future, and it was not long ere the house I at present occupy was advertised to be let. The rent was low, and I was, therefore, enabled to accomplish it; I removed hither, where I have been for several years, and thanks to Providence, who has ever enabled me to support the many vicissitues I have encountered throughout my busy life with fortitude, I have met with success, and am as happy as those could be, possessed of wealth and independence. Thus, my dear friends, do I end my unvarnished narrative, and if the few simple incidents it contains have afforded you any amusement or moral benefit, I am more than repaid for the trouble I have been at in relating it."

Mr. Walton ceased, and his auditors, who had been highly entertained with his story, returned their thanks to him for the trouble he had taken, and expressed the most fervent wishes that those misfortunes he had so frequently encountered might henceforward be a stranger to him. Mr. Walton thanked them heartily for their good wishes, and the remainder of the day passed off very happily. The more that Emily remained in the society of Mr. Walton and his family, the more delighted was she with their amiable manners.

Mrs. Walton was a very agreeable, intelligent, and affable woman, one who had evidently been brought up in the utmost respectability, and who had performed the duties of a wife and a mother in the most exemplary manner. Under all the various afflictions with which they had been visited, she had never murmured nor given way to useless grief; but, on the contrary, had copied the fortitude of her husband, and endeavoured to console him under their misfortunes. To the education of her children, assisted by her amiable partner, she had paid the most sedulous care, and they had readily imbibed the excellent precepts their parents had inculcated. There could not possibly be a more happy family, and they were the admiration of all who knew them, for their intrinsic qualities, as well as personal attractions.

The family of the worthy farmer consisted of himself, his wife, two daughters, and a son. Grace and Ellinor were twins, and two more beauteous girls could not be imagined. Innocence, virtue, and transcendant loveliness beamed in every feature, and they were so alike in every respect, that it is quite unnecessary to describe them separately. They were not more than sixteen, yet with all the playfulness and freshness of youth, they possessed the mature judgment and prudence of womanhood. Brought up to habits of industry, their minds were entire strangers to pride, vanity, or affectation; and they were enabled to perform the domestic duties of the poor man's wife, with the more refined habits of the lady.

Henry Walton was three years the senior of his sisters, and to the excellent intrinsic qualities of the latter, he added all that manly beauty which is calculated to create admiration and esteem in the breasts of those who knew him, but more especially the fair sex; and Emily had not been many days acquainted with the family of Mr. Walton, ere she discovered that Henry had made an impression upon the heart of Patty. This the latter admitted to our heroine, and acknowledged that they had made a mutual acknowledgment of a reciprocal affection. They had passed many of their younger days together, and the impression they had made upon each other's heart, time had strengthened instead of decreasing.

By the industrious habits of Henry, the circumstances of the family had undergone much improvement, and they were now, as we have before observed, in a very prosperous condition.

CHAPTER XII.

THE MANUSCRIPTS.—THE MYSTERY.

SEVERAL days elapsed, and nothing whatever occurred to disturb the serenity of our heroine or her companion, Patty, nor did they hear of anything to lead them to suspect that Gerald Darnley or Chesterton had discovered any means which might lead them to trace out the place of their retreat. But still it cost Emily many hours of sorrow, when she reflected upon her low, dependant, and destitute condition, the mystery by which her fate was enveloped, and the melancholy prospect that was before her, without any protectors except strangers. Had it not been for the kindness she experienced from Mrs. Seagrove, Patty, and Mr. Walton's family, and the hopes with which they endeavoured to inspire her of happier days, she would have been truly wretched. Often did she catch Mrs. Seagrove watching her very earnestly, and with tears trembling in her eyes, and then she would sigh deeply and walk away to avoid any questions which Emily might put to her. This particularly excited the astonishment of our heroine, and there were times when she was half inclined to imagine Mrs. Seagrove had some suspicion of her real origin, but that some powerful reasons prevented her from speaking upon the subject. She remembered the emotion she had evinced when she first beheld her, and the observations she had made of the extraordinary resemblance she bore to some unfortunate lady, whose name she declined revealing; and these circumstances combined, raised a variety of conflicting thoughts in her mind.

Patty's ideas and her own perfectly coincided upon this point, but she was equally unable to form any opinion that was likely to arrive at the truth. The account, however, that her aunt had given her concerning Gerald Darnley, and her own suspicions that he was not really her father, eased her mind of a dreadful weight, while, at the same time, it added to the mystery in which all the circumstances were involved.

They had hitherto kept themselves as much secluded as possible, and their time had been passed more frequently at Mr. Walton's, than at Mrs. Seagrove's, and their friends thought it was advisable for them to continue to do so ; and, indeed, the rational pleasures that were provided for them within this little circle, left them scarcely a wish beyond. The horrors she had endured, and the many dreadful circumstances which had occurred to her, together with all she had seen and heard while she had been at the Old Lone House, were constantly the subjects of our heroine's thoughts ;— the blood-stained sheets—the secret closet—the skeleton, and the pocket-book ; and the more she dwelt upon them, and the circumstance of her remembering the old room to have been the place she had inhabited when a child, the more thoroughly convinced she became that she was connected with them. Upon the latter subject Mrs. Seagrove had frequently questioned her, and it seemed to make a deeper impression upon her than anything else.

"It is evident," she observed, "that if, as you believe, Gerald to be the same man who, at that period, was an inhabitant of the place, he must have seen you before, and I am fearful that he knows more about your origin than he would like to divulge."

"Oh, yes, there cannot be any doubt of that whatever," replied Emily ; "for the frequent conversations I have overheard between him and Chesterton, fully proved so ; and, moreover, that he was employed by some one to put me out of the way. It must, indeed, be something very desperate that could urge this nobleman, whoever he is, to such a course."

Mrs. Seagrove shuddered.

"Atrocious villains!" she exclaimed. "Providence surely will not suffer their cruel blood-thirsty deeds to remain much longer involved in their present mystery. It was strange, too, Emily, that your supposed grandmother should take up her residence in *The White Cottage*, a place made notorious by a deed of blood, which struck horror into the whole country when it took place. This was a murder perpetrated by a man who was known by the name of Luke Stanton. It is about sixteen years ago, I remember. The unfortunate wife of the villain was found in the cottage dreadfully mangled, and the wretch, with the two children that were supposed to be his own, had disappeared, and have never been heard of since, notwithstanding every possible endeavour was made by the officers, and a large reward offered for the apprehension of the assassin. It is more particularly stamped upon my recollection, because I noticed at the time, in the advertisements, the striking resemblance there was between the description of the man and Gerald Darnley; it fact, so remarkable was it, that had it not been for the difference of the name, I could almost have sworn it had been him. It is my horror and misfortune to call him my brother."

A sudden idea flashed upon the brain of Emily, as Mrs. Seagrove thus spoke, and she hastily observed ;—

" But might not the villain, whoever he was, have changed his name ?— I do not think it is probable that a man whose means of living were always questionable, would be likely to go in his real name."

"Ah!" ejaculated Mrs. Seagrove, " what terrible idea—what awful suspicion is it that takes possession of me ?—A man who has been guilty of other crimes equally as bad, and who is ready to do anything for money, would not hesitate to perpetrate a deed so atrocious."

" Oh, Heaven forbid, Madam !" said Emily, fervently; " Heaven forbid that your suspicions should be correct ; for then, indeed, would that man, whom you believe, but whom I can never think, is your brother, be a monster of ten-fold deeper dye than I already know him to be."

"The horrible idea gains still greater strength with me," continued Mrs. Seagrove, apparently taking no notice of what Emily had said, being completely absorbed by the thoughts which had thus suddenly taken possession of her mind ;—" I recollect now that it was not more than three months after this murder, that Gerald made his appearance before me ; and then the story he told me of the death of his wife, and her having left him two children—all, all corresponds so with the circumstances, that it almost brings conviction to one's mind."

" Of what sex were the supposed two children of the murderer?" asked Emily, hastily, and trembling with a strange and irresistible feeling of emotion ; " a boy and girl I think I have heard."

"You are right," returned Mrs. Seagrove, turning very pale, and her agitation greatly increasing ;—" ah! William Darnley and Patty !"

"Oh, no, for Heaven's sake banish such an idea !" remarked Emily, with a shudder ; " for the consanguinity of Darnley and his son with poor Patty would be almost established beyond a doubt; in spite of the terrible coincidence I cannot, dare not, believe that Luke Stanton and Gerald Darnley are one and the same person."

" God grant that it may be as you would believe," said Mrs. Seagrove, " but I cannot, and shall not, be able easily to erase from my mind, the powerful suspicions that have taken possession of it. We will, however, change this subject for the present, as we cannot come to any satisfactory

conclusion, and it will be the cause of the most poignant anguish, doubt, and uncertainty, to us both. Do not mention anything to Patty about this, for it would, I am certain, have the effect of making her truly miserable, when, at the same time, upon this point, she has not the least cause to be so. I have often thought of mentioning what I am going to say, to you before, but it has always slipped my memory. If I recollect aright, Emily, you mentioned something about the discovery of some manuscripts, but you did not describe to me the nature of them."

"True, I had forgotten that," said Emily, "and yet I wonder that I should do so; for on those documents I think depends a great deal of the unravelling of this terrible mystery."

"Did you bring them away with you?" asked Mrs. Seagrove, eagerly.

"Fortunately I did," answered Emily;—"I will go and fetch them immediately, and you will, doubtless, feel a melancholy pleasure in perusing them; although the dreadful recital is in such detached fragments, and in many parts so illegible that it is not possible to arrive at any conclusion as to who the victim was."

Emily left the room as she spoke, and soon returned with the manuscripts in her hand. Mrs. Seagrove took them with much avidity, but scarcely had her eyes fallen upon the first few lines, when her limbs trembled violently, and her face turned very pale.

"Gracious Heaven!" she exclaimed, "this hand-writing—the name, too—but no, it cannot be the same; she fled, and ——"

"Of whom do you speak, Madam?" enquired Emily, taking advantage of the confusion of Mrs. Seagrove.

"Of an unfortunate lady who bore the same Christian name as the one mentioned here, and to whom you have before heard me say, you bear such

No. 16.

a remarkable resemblance," replied Mrs. Seagrove. "I have hitherto avoided this subject, because it gave me pain, but I know not why I should wish to conceal the facts from you, whom, I am certain, possess a heart that will deeply sympathize in the lady's misfortunes."

"The lady and you were friends, then, Madam?" asked Emily.

"Friends!—oh, yes, we were, indeed, friends," answered Mrs. Seagrove ;—"we were more like sisters, in fact, at one time. Alas! did I ever imagine that the circumstances would have taken place which afterwards occurred to her, or that she could have become the guilty being she was represented to be."

"I think you said that the lady was married?" said our heroine; "I beseech you to pardon me for my apparent impertinent curiosity, because what you have already told me about the lady, has excited a deep interest in my bosom."

"Yes, she was married, and to one of the best of men," replied Mrs. Seagrove ;—"to a nobleman who adored her, and of whom she seemed to be doatingly fond."

"Had they any children?"

"Yes, two; but they both died soon after they were born—they were twins."

"But you say that the lady and gentleman were fond of each other; what, then, pray, was the cause of the misery at which you have hinted?"

"A short time after the death of the two infants," said Mrs. Seagrove, "the lady disappeared in a most mysterious manner, and no one was certain what it was that caused it, although it was reported that she had fled with a paramour. This would have met with a direct contradiction, (for the affection that existed between her and her husband seemed to increase,) had it not been confirmed by a letter which she left behind her for her husband, and in which she bade him adieu for ever."

"Strange!—most unaccountable!" ejaculated Emily. "Any person would scarcely believe it possible. But was not the name of the gallant ever ascertained?"

"It was not," returned Mrs. Seagrove, "but it was suspected that they had fled to the Continent."

"But what of the unfortunate husband?" demanded Emily.

"Why, as you may be sure, he was driven nearly to madness by this terrible and unexpected blow; and when he had sufficiently recovered himself, he went in pursuit of the fugitives. He never returned."

"No!"

"No ; a body was picked up in a river in France, in a state of great decomposition, which, from the description of the dress it had on, was supposed to be the unfortunate nobleman's; and it was imagined that, having failed in his endeavours to find out his wife and her paramour, in a fit of despair he had committed suicide, by precipitating himself into the water."

"But was there no further inquiry made into the affair, by any of his relatives?" asked our heroine.

"He had only a very distant one living, who had been his constant companion, and of whom he was as fond as if he had been his own brother. He seemed to exert himself very much, but it was all no use; some time afterwards it was found that the unfortunate nobleman had left a will, which had evidently been made after the elopement of his wife, and in which he bequeathed the whole of his wealth and title to his friend and relative."

"And does that friend and relative still live?"

"He does; but he has sold the estate which originally belonged to his relative, and resides chiefly in London.'

"Would it be too much to ask his name?"

"For certain reasons I would rather not for the present reveal it," answered Mrs. Seagrove.

"There is a terrible mystery about the affair which you have just detailed," said Emily, " of which I cannot form any satisfactory conjecture; but I am almost inclined to think that the unfortunate lady was wrongfully accused, and that her husband died not by his own hands. What was the character of the relative?"

"I liked him not, although he ever appeared in the character of a real friend; yet there was something about him which I used often to think spoke of hollowness and hypocrisy, and I did not consider that he seemed to be so much distressed at the supposed melancholy end of his relative as might have been expected."

Emily became wrapped for a few moments in deep thought; and several singular ideas flashed across her brain, which she did not think fit to express to Mrs. Seagrove.

"Well," she exclaimed, " heaven will, I hope, in due time unravel the mystery, establish the innocence of those who may have been wrongly accused, and bring the guilty to punishment."

"Most earnestly do I respond to that prayer, Emily;" said Mrs. Seagrove, " but never can I believe that my ill-fated friend was the guilty woman she was suspected of being. But I had almost forgotten the manuscript."

Emily being glad of the opportunity to indulge in her own thoughts, seated herself oposite to Mrs. Seagrove, and did not offer to interrupt her, while she proceeded to peruse the melancholy documents which had come into her possession in so mysterious a manner. Frequently did Mrs. Seagrove pause, and give utterance to an exclamation of surprise and horror, and when she had arrived at the conclusion, she arose from her chair, and traversed the room with disordered footsteps, and kept muttering incoherent sentences to herself.

"What a strange coincidence;" at length she she said aloud, " the names, the handwriting, the other characters so much alike. But what a horrible story is this; alas! unfortunate being, whoever you were, may justice, may the retribution of Heaven overtake your monstrous assassins, and bring to light the dreadful truth."

"Amen," cried Emily,—" but although there probably may be a great similarity in the two cases, it does not appear that the victim of the Old Lone House could have been the ill-fated nobleman of whom you have been telling me; for in the manuscript he raves of his children, and you say the children of those unfortunate people died as soon as they were born."

"True," observed Mrs. Seagrove;—" that does seem at once to contradict the supposition; but then in the distracted state of mind which the writer was at the time he penned these documents, it would not at all be surprising if his brain should wander, and he should fancy his children were still living, The idea of the sufferings that poor unfortunate being must have undergone, makes the blood run chill to think upon it. Shut out from nearly the light of day; entombed as it were in that narrow space; each day the gnawings of hunger becoming more insupportable, and no one near at hand to pity or relieve him. How terrible must have been that lingering death; how maddening his anguish. I shrink with fear and disgust from the bare contemplation of it. But did you not discover anything else, Emily, by which you might be able to judge who the murdered man was?"

"No, there was nothing more that I could see, which could throw any more light upon the matter;" answered Emily;—"to be sure I found a pocket-book, which Darnley afterwards took from me, and a prayer-book in the secret-closet, both of which were marked with the initials J. D., on the cover."

"J. D!" exclaimed Mrs. Seagrove, eagerly, "and in the same handwriting as these manuscripts?"

"Yes!"

"Gracious Heaven! they are the very initials of his name!—My heart again misgives me;—he must have been the wretched victim."

"Who;—what the husband of your friend?"

"The same! Oh, Heavens! Can it be?—What terrible suspicions haunt my mind?"

"Still this cannot be," observed our heroine, "for if you again read the manuscript, you will find that the unhappy writer raves of his wife as living, and again that he hears the groans of a female in the apartment which adjoins his prison, and which he imagines is his wife, whom his enemy or enemies are murdering."

"All this is very true," observed Mrs. Seagrove; "but still it does not serve to banish my surmises. But let me intreat you, Emily, not to say a word to any one about what has this day past between us. Not even to Patty."

"You may depend upon my secrecy, Madam," returned our heroine.

"Above all, take particular care of those manuscripts; for they will probably be the means of doing justice to the innocent, and bringing the guilty to punishment."

Emily promised to obey, and after a few more observations of no particular interest, they separated.

Our heroine hastened to her own chamber, where she again perused the manuscripts, and compared them with the circumstances which Mrs. Seagrove had related, and, although she agreed that they very much corresponded in some of the facts; yet, upon the whole, she could not make up her mind that the unfortunate being who had perished by such cruel means in the Old Lone House, and the nobleman Mrs. Seagrove had given an account of, were one and the same person. The narrative of Mrs. Seagrove had made a very great impression on her, and she longed to be made acquainted with the names of the different parties, which she could see no reason for Mrs. Seagrove wishing to conceal. The horrible event which had taken place at the White Cottage, and which had been so forcibly recalled to her memory by the before-mentioned lady, next occupied her attention, and the more she reflected upon it, the more convinced did she become that Luke Stanton, the assassin of the *White Cottage*, and Gerald Darnley, the ruffian of the Old Lone House, were one and the same individual. This opinion was accompanied by the most painful thought, when she remembered how fully it seemed to establish the fact of Patty being the daughter of Gerald and the sister of Will Darnley, and confirmation of such an unnatural connection as that, filled her bosom with the most unbounded regret.

Patty had been by herself that day to Farmer Walton's, as Emily had felt rather indisposed, but she now returned, and in better spirits than our heroine had seen her for some time, so that she would have been very sorry to have mentioned any of the circumstances that had transpired between her and Mrs. Seagrove, and which would, doubtless, have only been the means of making her very wretched.

CHAPTER XIII.

THE THREE VILLAINS.—THE QUARREL.

In a former chapter, in which we described the flight of our heroine and Patty, we stated that at the particular juncture when they were in the act of making their escape, the villain Chesterton was seen riding towards the Old Lone House, and but a minute or two later, and he would have been in the apartment, (for Emily heard him approaching,) and thus have completely frustrated their design. We will now return to him and his worthy colleague, Gerald Darnley.

It would be utterly fruitless to attempt to describe the astonishment, the rage, and disappointment of Chesterton, upon going to the apartment which Emily had lately occupied, and finding it vacated. He stamped and swore with passion, and then uttering the most bitter curses against Gerald and his own folly, (for he imagined he had been deceived by the ruffian,) he proceeded hurriedly to search every nook and corner in the place, but saw nothing of her. Her box, which was wide open, was emptied of its contents, and from that circumstance he concluded that she had fled. And now his indignation increased to such a degree that he could scarcely contain himself, and hastening from the rooms, he rushed along the gallery, and through the different apartments, the doors of which being left open, shewed the way of her flight, until he reached the chamber which opened to the terrace. The casement was standing wide open, and the rope ladder fastened to the balustrades of the terrace, left no room to doubt the manner in which she had escaped, but convinced him at the same time that she must have had an accomplice or accomplices. In a moment he concluded that Gerald had either deceived him, or that Will Darnley had borne her away.

"Curses, ten thousand curses light upon whoever hath done this!" exclaimed the steward, as he turned from the place, and made his way back towards the room in which he had left Gerald Darnley; "may every fatal spell, every damned misery that can attend mankind, pursue them. But it is all a trick, it is all the work of Gerald Darnley, or that braggart boy Will, and this ladder has been placed here to delude me; but I will have ample vengeance."

Thus speaking and uttering the most dreadful imprecations as he proceeded, Chesterton reached the room below, in which Gerald was seated alone, and the fury of his manner told the ruffian that something particular had occurred to arouse his wrath.

"How now, Chesterton," he exclaimed, "what has disturbed you?—Why do you look so fierce?"

"You may pretend to the contrary, but you will not deceive me, Gerald Darnley, or Luke Stanton, which you will;" said the other, fiercely; "you know well enough that the girl is gone!"

"Gone!" cried Gerald, starting hastily to his feet;—"gone!—fled!"

"Ay, fled, and through your means," returned Chesterton; "now pretend you know nothing at all about it, but it won't do for me, Luke Stanton."

"Why do you persist in calling me by that name?" demanded Gerald.

"Because it will serve most likely to remind you of a little circumstance which occurred some sixteen or seventeen years ago, and which being made public, you might be sorry that you ever aroused the vengeance of Miles Chesterton."

" Psha ! this is madness ;" returned the other, " by hell you wrong me, Chesterton ;—if Emily hath escaped—and I hope for both our sakes it is not true,—it is more than I was acquainted with, and must have been the work of treachery."

" Treachery !" returned Chesterton, ironically ; " you may well call it treachery."

" Gone, how, tell me quick ;" demanded Darnley.

" Escaped by a rope ladder," replied the steward, with a sneer, " placed on the terrace."

" Where is Will ?"

" How the devil should I know ? You ought to be the best judge of that."

" But may perdition seize me if I do know," retorted Gerald, " it strikes me that the boy has played me false."

" It does not appear very probable that he would use a rope ladder to effect his purpose," rejoined the steward, " when he could have taken her away by other means, when you was out of the way, and who was there to resist him ? It is a cursed trick altogether, you were afraid of offending your son, and have, therefore, connived with him to bear the girl off."

" May I mount the gallows to-morrow if it is not false !" returned Gerald ; " is it at all likely that I would run the risk of offending his lordship, of losing his reward, and that you were to give me ?—Psha ! you talk like a madman. But what is the use of standing here palavering ? While we are talking the bird is probably pursuing its flight. Let us first search every part of the house ; we may be mistaken, as we were once before, and perhaps we shall find her concealed in one of the chambers."

" Not much chance of that, I think," said Chesterton ; " it is not at all likely that the girl would suffer a rope ladder to remain suspended from the terrace without availing herself of it. Besides her chest is empty, and everything seems to make it certain that she has quitted the house."

" Damnation !" cried the ruffian Gerald, " this is bad news, and if she is not soon re-taken may place us in an awkward predicament rather. If it is the work of that headstrong boy, he shall pay dearly for his daring. Follow me, Chesterton, immediately."

Thus speaking, Darnley seized a couple of pistols, and led the way up stairs. They hastened over every room, and examined every spot likely to afford concealment, and every fresh disappointment they experienced drew forth from them the most dreadful imprecations ; but the open doors and casements, and the rope ladder from the balustrades, plainly convinced them that it was useless searching for the fugitive in the house, and they returned below, after having drawn the ladder in from the terrace.

" I think it is not likely that she can elude us long, if she has escaped by herself," said Darnley, " for where could she seek a retreat, without a friend or acquaintance in the world ? If we lose no time we shall most likely overtake her."

" How could she have escaped without assistance, think you ?" demanded Chesterton, fiercely ; " where was she to procure the ladder ?—How obtain the keys of the various doors ?"

" I wish I had been at the devil," said Darnley, " ere I yielded to your offer ; had I not, the girl would have been safe from troubling me or anybody else ere this."

" Then why did you not put her out of the way years ago ?" retorted the other villain, " why did you not do the business for both the brats ? You have no one to blame but yourself."

" You seem to take a delight in reminding me of the past," said Gerald, wrathfully; " but I would advise you not to go too far, I am not a man to take such remarks coolly."

" And I am not the man, I would remind you, to be frightened by a threat," returned Chesterton.

" Bah !" exclaimed Darnley, " we are two very fools for our pains, for while we are quarrelling we are losing the very object we wish to accomplish. Why did his lordship take any notice of the advertisement that appeared after the old woman's death? Had he left the girl to her fate, she would have been no farther trouble to us, but would have been an inmate of the workhouse, unknown and uncared for."

" His lordship, I think, acted very prudently," said Chesterton, " for how did we know but what the old woman in a moment of weakness might have divulged the whole story to her, and then we might all of us have been placed in no very enviable situation."

" If she is not re-taken, we are all lost, unless we take to immediate flight;" said Gerald; " doubtless she will make application to some magistrate, and give a statement of the whole affair, and the officers will be down upon us immediately. Come, come, no delay, but let's away in pursuit as fast as we can."

Chesterton, whose anger was somewhat now appeased by his fears, and who now began to think seriously that Gerald had nothing to do with the flight of Emily, prepared to obey him, when the door was suddenly thrown open, and Will Darnley entered.

" Ah! the very man we wanted to see," said his father hastily; " villain ! hast thou been deceiving us ?—Whither have you conveyed the girl?"

" The girl !—what girl?" demanded Will Darnley, fiercely.

" Emily !"

" Emily ?"

" Aye, Emily," returned Chesterton, with an impatient scowl, " you know full well what we mean, and your pretended ignorance is only a base subterfuge to mislead us ;—traitor, whither have you conveyed the girl?"

" Hoary-headed scape-gallows !" cried Will, while his eyes flashed with ungovernable rage; " by all the powers, if you say that word again, it shall be the last you shall ever utter in this world."

" Your passion is useless, boy," said Gerald, " tell me, I command you, do you know aught of the flight of Emily?"

" The flight of Emily !" reiterated Will Darnley, starting back in amazement;—" Ah! by hell, I see it all clearly now; but you cannot deceive me. The girl has been taken to some other place with your knowledge, for the purpose of preventing what you thought might have occurred, owing to the fancy I have formed for her. But if she be buried even in the bowels of the earth, I will find her out, and release her from your power, and then let those who have aroused my vengeance beware !"

" You speak very boldly, and threaten most manfully, hot-headed fool," said Chesterton.

" And thus do I prove that I can not only threaten but perform ;—down, old villain, and kiss your mother earth !"

As Will Darnley thus spoke, he clenched his fist, and dealt the steward a tremendous blow in the face, which felled him in the door-way, and completely stunned him for a few minutes ; and Will would in all probability have repeated his violence, had it not been for the interposition of Gerald, who stepped in between the prostrate man and his enfuriated son, and, in a determined voice, said,—

" Hold, Will ! or, by the infernal host, even though you are my son, I will blow your brains out !"

" A most affectionate parent; ha ! ha ! ha !" sneered the young ruffian, "however, I do not want the old dog's life;—there rise;—you see it is no use trifling with me; and now you may as well tell me where you have taken the girl, for I shall be sure to find her out, and then woe-betide you; even though I mount the scaffold myself, I will have my revenge on you."

".I tell you, Will," said his father, persuasively, "that neither myself or Chesterton know how Emily has escaped, and our suspicions fell upon you. We found all the doors of the different rooms leading from the girl's apartments, standing open, and the rope-ladder was fixed to the balustrades of the terrace, from which it appeared evident that she had descended."

"Is this true?" demanded Will, hastily.

"I will swear it;" returned his father.

"Where is Madge?—Where is Patty?" asked the son.

"I never thought to seek them;" replied Gerald, "but surely they have not betrayed us. What ho! Madge! Patty!"

"Ma conscience," ejaculated the old woman, toddling into the room, "I never heard sic a fuss in a' my life?—What be th' matter with ye a'?"

"Where is Patty?" hastily demanded Gerald.

"I dinna ken," said Madge, in reply, "I ha' na' seen her these twa hours or mair, an' then she went to Emily's apartments."

"Emily has fled!" cried Gerald, fiercely; "do you know anything about it?"

"Fled! ma conscience;" cried the old woman; "yer dinna say so?—But how should I know anything about it?—D'ye ken I be grown daft in my old age, to let a girl escape who has it in her power to set us a' by the ears."

"Where is Patty that she does not answer?" said Will.

"I dinna ken," returned Madge, "but if she be not in that part of the house where Miss Emily used to lodge, she be not in the other."

"Confusion!" cried the three villains in a breath, "then Emily and Patty have escaped together."

"I'll away in pursuit," said Will, snatching down his gun, "and I will never give it over until I have found them."

"Follow, follow!" cried Gerald, as he rushed from the house in a different direction to that which his son had taken, and accompanied by Chesterton, he was soon in hot pursuit of the fugitives.

While this quarrel and and colloquy was going on, of course, it gave our heroine and her companion an opportunity of completing their escape, and it was a fortunate job that it so occurred, for had it not, there can be very little doubt but that they would have been re-taken, their flight being discovered almost as soon as it had taken place; but before the three villains had started from the Old Lone House, Emily and Patty were far away from the spot, and, as has been shown, ultimately arrived at the place of their destination in safety.

All that night, and the following day, Gerald and Chesterton continued their pursuit with the most unremitting assiduity, but without the least success; they could not form any conjecture of the way the fugitives had proceeded, neither could they gain the least clue to them.

On the second night they returned to the Old Lone House, chagrined, disappointed, and alarmed, and determined to renew their pursuit in a different course on the following morning. In the meantime Will Darnley did not return at all; a week passed away, and then his father and the steward began to be afraid that Will had either been aware at the first where Emily was concealed, or else that he had since discovered her retreat and held her in his power, and this imagination gained strength when another week passed away, and they were still unsuccessful, while Will Darnley remained absent. The two ruffians were in a terrible state of

alarm; they dreaded the discovery of their guilt, and the numerous crimes in which they had been concerned, and the passions Chesterton had felt for Emily, were entirely superseded by the apprehensions that continually haunted his coward imagination, that she would by some means or the other, contrive to find out who she really was, and the villany which had been practised towards her and her parents, and that justice, though tardy, would ere long overtake them and their wealthy accomplice.

"She must be despatched, should she again fall into our power;" said the miscreant Chesterton;—"I see that we shall be in danger of the gallows every moment while she lives."

"I told you so, when you made your mad proposition to me;" said Gerald; "Patty, too, who may also discover who she really is, must be disposed of. She is far more dangerous than the other. However, when next they are within our power, if we are ever fortunate enough to discover them, Emily and Patty die!"

"They die," repeated the steward, in a hoarse voice, and they hastened to put fresh projects into operation, to discover the retreat of those they so much feared.

CHAPTER XIV.

THE TWO VILLAINS.—THE OUTRAGE.

SEVERAL more weeks passed away in the manner we have been describing, and still Emily and Patty suffered no interruption, and in the society

No. 17

of their kind friends began to feel comparatively happy. Through the means of Mr. Walton, they had become acquainted with the steps Chesterton and the other two villains had taken, in order that they might trace out some clue to their retreat; for they had sent a man to reside for a few days in the village not far from the Old Lone House, so that he might watch the movements of the ruffians, and give them timely notice of any threatened danger, so that they might be enabled to provide accordingly. With the steps that Chesterton and Gerald had taken, they were perfectly satisfied, for as yet they had nothing whatever to apprehend from them, but the behaviour of Will Darnley more alarmed them, for they knew well his crafty, designing, and determined character, and were certain that he would leave no means untried to find them out, and get Emily in his power; and so cunningly and secretly did he manage all his stratagems, that our heroine and Patty did not consider themselves safe from him for a moment; he might surprise them when they least expected, and once having made a discovery of their retreat, they well knew that it would not be long ere he contrived, by some means or the other to effect his object.

Thinking that the ruffians were less likely to look for them there, Emily and Patty, on the suggestion of Mr. Walton, took up their residence at the farm, an arrangement which greatly pleased all parties, as Mrs. Seagrove could be a daily visitor to them, and it did not put the honest family to the slightest inconvenience. But none were better pleased than the two charming daughters of Mr. Walton, and his son Henry, who had now the happiness to indulge in the almost uninterrupted society of those friends to whom they were so ardently attached. Frequently they would form a party, and wander among the beautiful and romantic scenery by which the neighbourhood was surrounded, after the labours of the day were at an end, and the calm of evening had set in. Sometimes the young people would form a party among themselves, and in the sweets of converse and harmless mirth, endeavour to forget their cares, and to give themselves up entirely to present enjoyment. In those moments, however, they were always careful not to stroll too far, and to keep a strict watch, so that they might not be surprised by the enemies they dreaded.

The sentiments of Patty and Henry Walton towards each other, daily increased, and never were two beings more worthy of each other. Henry possessed acquirements and natural abilities far beyond his station, and his intrinsic merits qualified him to shine in a far higher sphere of society. Warm, ardent, generous, and candid, he was the admiration and envy of all the young men of the village, who sought to emulate his virtues, and felt honoured by his friendship. When he heard Patty relate the many miseries she had been made to endure at the Old Lone House, his blood boiled with indignation, and he could not help giving vent to his feelings in no very measured terms, fully at the same time, concurring in the surmises of his lover, that the ruffian, Gerald Darnley, was not her father, such a connection appearing to him to be preposterous and unnatural.

"It cannot be," said the father,—"the bare idea is revolting. My Patty the daughter of a heartless villain, evidently familiar with every crime, is impossible!—But even should it unhappily prove to be so, nothing can ever alter my sentiments towards you, my dearest girl; I will continue to love you for yourself alone, and scorn to despise you for the vices of your guilty parent."

"I know you would not, dear Henry," said Patty, looking fondly in his face, "but alas! should it ultimately appear that I am positively the daughter of that dreaded man, whom I shudder to call father, what then would become of me; for he could force me back into his power, and would never give his consent to our nuptials; neither could I ever agree to your sacrificing your happiness and credit by connecting yourself with a family so abandoned, so degraded."

"Oh, talk not thus, Patty," said Henry, "we will forget that such beings ever existed, and retiring to some distant part of the country, where they would not be likely to discover us, live in that state of felicity the love we entertain for each other would be sure to engender."

"But surely your father would never sanction a union which, under those circumstances, might be productive of so much misery and disgrace;" said Patty, with a sigh.

"My father, I am certain would make any sacrifice, rather than crush my hopes," replied Henry; "besides, he is too fond of you, Patty, to refuse his consent, especially when he must be fully aware that such a refusal would be the cause of destroying our peace of mind for ever."

"Well, I do believe you, dearest Henry," observed Patty, fervently, and after all, I sincerely hope that something may occur to realize all our utmost wishes."

Henry remained silent for a short time, and then sighed deeply, and looked up in Patty's face with a most melancholy expression.

"What is the matter, Henry?" eagerly asked the damsel, "why do you sigh so; tell me, I beg?"

"A thought has just struck me, dear Patty," replied the youth, "which never before occurred to me. I have been thinking that, suppose it was to turn out as we have conjectured that you are not the daughter of Gerald Darnley, but the offspring of some noble parents, what hopes would there then be for me? Patty's rank would place her far above me, and the fond, the cherished hopes and visions of years, would be destroyed, and some wealthier suitor, who could not love you half so ardently as I do, would possess your hand, and Henry be forgotten for ever."

"Henry," observed Patty, in a tone of reproach, "I did not expect this from you. Is it possible that you you can think so meanly of my love, or place such little confidence in the sincerity of my protestations, as to believe me capable of such conduct as that you have described?—Think you that either time or circumstances can alter my sentiments towards you, if you do, then am I unworthy of your love, and here I absolve you from all the vows you have made to me."

"Patty," ejaculated Henry, vehemently, alarmed at the seriousness of her manner, "pardon me if I have been too hasty; I meant not to express any doubt of your sincerity towards me, but that you might be compelled to yield your hand to another."

"Oh, never, never," said the simple and candid girl, "nothing should ever force me to such a step; I would sooner suffer death than give my hand where it could not be accompanied by my heart; that heart which is and ever must be your's alone."

"Charming girl," exclaimed Henry, in a tone of rapture, and imprinting a warm kiss upon the glowing cheek of his lover, "could I ever doubt you, I should be a wretch unworthy of life."

At this moment they were joined by Emily, who had come forth from the farm to meet them, and they prepared to return home, as the sun was just sinking behind the western hills, and Mr. Walton had prepared a little extra entertainment on this occasion, it being the anniversary of his birth.

Engaged in agreeable conversation, the three friends were retracing their steps to the farm, when Henry suddenly felt Patty shrink back, and he eagerly inquired the cause, and whether anything had alarmed her?

"Observe those two gentlemen yonder, Henry," replied Patty, directing his attention to the spot on which they were standing, "they seem to have been watching us attentively all the way as we have come along; I have noticed them particularly, and am certain that their eyes have never been removed from myself and Emily for these four or five minutes. Who can they be? They are well dressed, and have the appearance of gentlemen."

Henry and Emily, astonished at Patty's words, looked eagerly towards the spot to which she called their attention, and beheld two men standing on a piece of rising ground, at no great distance from them, and evidently watching their approach with the deepest attention. Emily and Patty began to feel ashamed, for the lane they were proceeding along was very narrow, and they had no means of avoiding them without turning back.

"Oh, do not fear," said Henry, "their dress and general appearance denote that they are not any of the parties whom we have any cause to apprehend danger from."

"But what can be their motive for watching us so attentively?" said our heroine.

"I know not," replied Henry, "but it is certainly a piece of most consummate impudence. They wear the garb of gentlemen, and now we get nearer to them, I can see that one of them is an officer, and—oh, I see who they are now; the one in the military dress is Captain Bellingham, the nephew to the lord of the estate, of whom my father rents his farm, and the the other is his friend Sir Edgecumbe Sappington. They are on a visit to Bellingham Abbey, and have been for several weeks.

"Their boldness evinces anything but the manners of gentlemen," observed Patty, noticing that the two individuals just named, had not altered their position, but seemed as if they were resolved to wait until they came up to them.

"This is certainly most strange," said Henry, as a feeling of indignation took possession of him, "have either of you ever seen them before?"

Emily and Patty both answered in the negative. At that moment, the two gentlemen kissed their hands to our heroine and Patty, and turning round, walked on.

"This impertinence is almost unendurable," ejaculated Henry, his cheeks glowing with anger. "The puppies, I should like to demand an explanation."

"It is hardly worth while, Henry," said Patty, "and would, perhaps, only be met with scorn and insult by men who, doubtless, think their rank entitles them to outrage the feelings of the humbler classes with impunity. Let us make the best of our way to the farm."

Henry and Emily assented; but the circumstance had not only greatly surprised but vexed them, and Henry especially, felt very great resentment at the behaviour of the captain and his friend, particularly when he observed them, as they emerged from the lane, and turned towards the road which led to Bellingham Abbey, once more turn round, and repeat the familiarity they had before indulged in towards our heroine and Patty.

On their arrival at the farm, Henry made his father acquainted with their adventure, and the behaviour of Captain Bellingham and his friend. Mr. Walton gave full indication of the wrath he felt at the conduct of the two gentlemen, and when Henry had done speaking, he said in accents of severity which he was seldom in the habit of making use of :—

"The insolent puppies !—I know them both well. Sir Edgecumbe Sappington is a fashionable fop, wealthy and unprincipled; a most consummate ass, a *debauchee*, and a libertine of the first water. Captain Bellingham is possessed of all his vices, and innumerable others of his own. He is a military tyrant, whose greatest delight, apart from his intrigues, is in the lash;—and he exults in the sufferings of his fellow-men, over whom his gilt trappings, and not his virtues, stamp him superior."

"Indeed?" exclaimed Mrs. Walton, astonished at the unusual asperity of her husband's manner.

"Yes," remarked Mr. Walton, "all this is this *gallant* Captain Bellingham; "the eldest nephew of Sir Merton Bellingham, the lord of this manor, and I would not fear to tell him so to his face. Such as he call themselves soldiers and superiors! Psha!—I have seen something of these gingerbread striplings, and heard their character from old soldiers who have fought and bled for their king and country, and they all agreed that those who delighted most in seeing the streaming and lacerated backs of those under their command, were always the first to faint at a scratch, or tremble at the sight of an enemy's musket. Curses on that odious law which makes the condition of the brave protectors of our land, worse than that slavery they drain their dearest hearts' blood to abolish."

"You are right, father," remarked Henry, who entered into the subject with all the warmth of the former, "and it is to be hoped that the time is not far distant when the odious *cat* shall be taken out of the hands of such fellows, and only be used as a proper embellishment for the gibbet-post, an elevation some of its most zealous advocates deserve to attain."

"This Captain Bellingham, as well as his vile associate, as I before said," continued Mr. Walton, "is a rake, a libertine,—a heartless seducer. A fellow whose glory is the destruction of unsuspecting innocence, and the broken hearts of the unhappy victims of his vice. After this picture of the character of these two *gentlemen*, you will not feel surprised that I should take up the subject of their behaviour to Emily and Patty, this evening, so warmly; and you will likewise see the necessity of using the utmost caution in your future rambles while they remain in the neighbourhood, for, depend upon it, although you may not have seen them, they have beheld you before, and having been captivated by your charms, will use every endeavour to entrap you."

"The villains!" cried Henry, "by heaven, were they in a tenfold higher station than that they occupy, should they dare to make any attempt of the kind, I will not rest until I have had ample satisfaction for it. But perhaps, after all, there is not so much cause for fear as we all apprehend. They might have been taking too much wine, and knew not what they were doing."

"That they had probably been taking too much wine, Henry," said his father, "I perfectly agree with you in believing, for it is no more than they are constantly in the habit of doing; but that they did not know what they were doing, I decidedly think is an erroneous opinion. At any rate, let me again advise Miss Emily and Patty to use the utmost precaution, or they may fall into the hands of enemies as bad as those from whom they have recently made their escape."

Our heroine and Patty were extremely disgusted and shocked at the character which Mr. Walton had given of the two gentlemen,; but still they could not help being of the opinion which Henry had expressed, and meant what they did, more as a foolish frolic, than the serious construction which Mr. Walton had put upon it. Notwithstanding, they had considerable difficulty in banishing the circumstance from their thoughts during the whole of the evening, and determined to be even more particular than they had hitherto been in their walks, and most carefully to avoid any part where it appeared likely to them that they should encounter the two libertines.

Nothing particular occurred for two or three days after this, and the circumstance was almost forgotten, when one afternoon, Emily and Patty, who had only just been walking a little beyond the grounds of Mr. Walton's, suddenly rushed into the parlour in which the farmer, his wife, and daughters were sitting, pale and breathless, evidently very much alarmed, and although it was some considerable time before they could sufficiently recover themselves to give any explanation, they at length informed them, that a few minutes before they were surprised by Captain Bellingham and Sir Edgecumbe, as they were about to enter at the garden-gate; that they had grossly insulted them, first by pouring forth a fulsome tirade of nonsense, in which they protested a strong passion for them, and then attempting to kiss them.

Mr. Walton started up in a state of the utmost indignation.

"The scoundrels!" he exclaimed, "to dare to commit such an outrage, and upon the very threshold of my door. Where are they now?"

"We escaped from them with difficulty, sir," answered Emily, "and entering the garden, secured the gate after us, and, no doubt, they disappeared as soon as they saw us enter the house."

"I will not tamely brook this insult to two females to whom I have given my protection," said Mr. Walton, "I will see Sir Merton on the subject."

"Oh, no, that would be useless," said Mrs. Walton, "I do not think there is much difference between the character of the uncle and that of his nephew. He would probably be disposed to treat your complaint with levity, and instead of doing any good, it might be the means of making him your enemy, and he might, out of spite, turn you off his estate, which would be the ruin of us."

"Why, that is very true, my love," said Mr. Walton, "but yet, is it not really unbearable that these inordinate puppies should be allowed to carry on their vices with impunity?"

"It is indeed," returned his wife, "but all that can be done in the matter is, for Emily and Patty to be out as little as possible; at least, I would were I in their places, keep entirely to the house and gardens until these wild young men have quitted the neighbourhood, which, in all probability, will not be long."

"Your advice shall be attended to, madam," said Emily; "at least on my part, and I doubt not that Patty will also act as I do. I would not upon any account that you should risk the displeasure of Sir Merton through me and my friend, and I am also perfectly of your opinion that if the character of that gentleman answers the description you have given of it, that any appeal to him in respect to the conduct of his nephew would not be attended with any good result."

In these observations patty expressed her full concurrence, and after a few more remarks, the subject dropped, although both our heroine and Patty had been so shocked by the conduct of Captain Bellingham and Sir Edgecumbe, that they were very much discomposed all the rest of the afternoon, and could not succeed in obliterating it from their recollection. On the return of Henry, who had been out on a little business, and on his being made acquainted with what had taken place, his rage need not be decribed. He could scarcely contain himself, for, ready as he was to resent an insult when offered to himself, he was tenfold more exasperated when the object of insult was a woman. It was some time ere he could appease his wrath, but he highly approved of the advice which his mother had given them, and of Emily and Patty's determination to follow it.

This circumstance caused Emily and Patty much conversation, but as day after day passed away, and other topics occupied their mind, they gradually forgot it, and paid their attention to other subjects of more immediate importance. The principal that occupied their mind was their present situation. Although they had hitherto not been a burden to their friends, —at least Patty had not, the money she had saved not being yet ex-

Patty. "Wedding-ring — post-chaise — Gretna-green —hem! eh? Oh, positively, I'm the fellow!"

"Oh, forbear, forbear! If ye are men—if ye are gentlemen," implored Emily, "release us, and suffer us to proceed on our way homeward unmolested."

"Nay, the joy of meeting is too great to resign it easily," returned the captain, pressing our heroine's hand vehemently in his, in spite of her resistance. "Before I suffer you to depart, I must have a kiss from those pretty twin rubies, and likewise a promise to meet again."

"And, egad! so must I," said the consummate fop, Sir Edgecumbe; "and so, my exquisite little piece of fascination, make no more bother about it, but let me steal the nectar from your lips, and—"

"Off, sir!" exclaimed Patty, with an expression of indignation which for a moment abashed and staggered Sir Edgecumbe; "unhand me, sir, I insist! Your dress is that of a gentleman, but your behaviour proves you to be a brutal ruffian."

"Mighty complimentary, upon my word," said the fop, still retaining his hold of Patty; "but positively I am determined not to be defeated. Really you are the most delightful, charming, beautiful, demned creature I ever beheld, and——"

"Oh, help! help!" cried Patty; "Emily, let your cries rend the air! Surely some one will hasten to our assistance from the unmanly attack of these libertines."

"Emily!" observed Captain Bellingham, "what a sweet pretty name! —it is stamped upon my memory—engraven upon my heart for ever. Nay, silly girl, why are you so obstinate? Surely a kiss from a good-looking young fellow is no disgrace to you."

No 18.

PUBLISHER'S NOTE

pp.136-137 missing.

"Help! help!" shrieked our heroine; and with a most desperate effort she tore herself from the captain's hold, at the same moment that Patty also succeeded in releasing herself, and they both fled with the utmost precipitation, terror adding speed to their steps, and pursued by Captain Bellingham and Sir Edgecumbe.

They reached the back of the house, and here they ventured to look behind them, and were gratified to find that their tormentors had abandoned the pursuit.

They entered the parlour and fastened the door after them; then, each sinking in a chair, they were so overcome by fright that it was several minutes before they could give expression to their feelings.

"Heaven be praised!" at length said Emily, "we have outstripped our wild pursuers. Oh, Patty, that hateful captain has quite frightened me; his freedom and the levity of his manners are disgraceful to the character of a gentleman and a soldier."

"Yes, Emily," observed Patty, "I confess that I never felt more frightened in my life. What a pair of hateful beings they are to be sure. I thought they had quitted the neighbourhood, and I'm sure I shall not be easy for a moment while they remain in it."

"I wish that Mr. Walton or Henry had returned home," remarked Emily, "and the labourers have all quitted their work. I feel quite uneasy at our being left alone after this adventure."

"But you cannot surely think that the Captain and Sir Edgecumbe would venture here?" said Patty.

"They have boldness enough for anything, it is evident," returned Emily. "However, the door is fastened, and they cannot gain admittance to the house, if such should be their design."

"I do not think it is at all probable," observed Patty, "that they would attempt to approach the house, because they do not know whether or not Mr. Walton or the rest of his family are at home, and it is not likely that they would run the risk of encountering them, or have the boldness to attempt to commit so daring an outrage as that."

Emily shook her head.

"These fashionable libertines, I am afraid," she said, care little what they do, in order that they may obtain the gratification of their wishes, and they imagine that, being wealthy, they can do anything they like with impunity."

Emily was right in her conjectures, as will be seen by what follows. The Captain and his friend, although they did not keep up the pursuit, watched them enter the farm, and being aware that Mr. Walton and his family were absent from home, which information they had obtained from one of the labourers, they determined not to abandon their design so easily. The peculiar charms of Emily and Patty had made a very great impression upon them both, indeed, a much stronger impression than could have been expected from men who were accustomed to view female beauty with no deeper interest than what was excited by sensual desire; and ever since they had first seen them, they had determined to use every possible endeavour to gain possession of their persons.

They now walked slowly on towards the farm, and when they had arrived at it, they concealed themselves behind an angle of the building, and where they could observe them without being seen themselves.

"Egad, captain," ejaculated Sir Edgecumbe, speaking in low accents, "they have escaped us; the little faries are much too mercurial for us. However, they have entered the farm, and at yonder door, no doubt, however, taking good care to secure it after them. But eh, I declare they have left the window open, and, by Jupiter, there they are seated. What exquisite creatures! what forms! what features! what lips! what eyes! Positively the bare contemplation of them imparts a titilating sensation through my veins, with the exhilarating influence of a bottle of champagne or burgundy. I say, Captain, an excellent opportunity this. They are alone—hem, eh?"

Emily and Patty were seated with their backs towards the casement, absorbed in conversation, and totally unconscious that those who had so much alarmed them were so close at hand.

"That beautiful, but insensible Emily," observed the Captain, is a perfect icicle."

"And you are a complete ice-cream; or, demme, you would melt her in a moment," returned Sir Edgecumbe. "Fie, captain, you a soldier and talk in that manner? Why don't you copy my valour, my perseverance? Why don't you do as I intend doing? Since the enemy will neither capitulate nor yield at discretion, demme, storm the fortress, and carry off the prize by a *coup de main*. Ha! ha! I'm the fellow, positively demme, ha! ha! ha!"

"My dear Sir Edgecumbe," said Captain Bellingham, "you talk at random; think of the disgrace I should bring upon myself by such conduct; consider my *honour!*"

"Poh! honour!" retorted Sir Edgecumbe, contemptuously. "Demme, a bauble—a phantom we men of fashion can grasp at at any time for a cool thousand. Ha! ha! I'm the fellow. But, positively you seem to be quite smitten with this pretty little piece of prudery, Captain. Do you really love her?"

"I have told you before, Sir Edgecumbe, that ever since we first beheld them, I have felt that I loved Emily to distraction."

"Well, positively you astonish me," remarked Sir Edgecumbe. "This is much more serious than I expected it would be. And are you so far gone that you would marry her?"

"Why, no, that would be going a little too far," replied Captain Bellingham; "but could I persuade her to place herself under my protection (for I have learnt that she is completely friendless, and is not in any way related to Farmer Walton), I should be a happy fellow."

"So you doubt the power of your eloquence in persuading her?" asked Sir Edgecumbe.

"Why, you have had as much opportunity of judging as I have, Sir Edgecumbe," replied the Captain; "I have not spoken many words to her, but I judge from the manner in which she received my advances, that it will be as futile an attempt to make any impression upon her, as it would be to seek to batter down a fortress with a pop-gun."

"Well, now, I think quite different," observed Sir Edgecumbe, "and you know I am seldom mistaken. If you will follow the advice I will give you, Emily shall be your's as surely as I am resolved to get possession of her equally charming friend. I tell you, positively, that Emily is your's. I'll court her for you—I'll get her for you—I'll run away with her for you —I'll—I'll—oh, demme! I'm the fellow."

"What mean you?"

"Why, that if you'll only follow the instructions I will give you, you are a happy man. I have hit upon a rare scheme."

"Oh, tell me how to accomplish so desirable an object?"

"I will explain myself more fully by and by; but nothing can be more simple. You will only have to act the villain."

"The villain!"

"Yes, to be sure; that's nothing, you know, a mere every day business,

You'll do it capitally ; for you know nothing is more easy to we men of fashion than to act the tyrant and the villain. It is a mere school-boy lesson. Only a repetition of the practices of our forefathers. Oh, I flatter myself, with a few of my instructions, you will make an admirable villain. Positively, demme, I'm the fellow. But see, the lovely girls do not observe us, we can steal quietly in at the window, and surprise them. Now then, Captain, follow me."

As Sir Edgecumbe thus spoke, he approached the window, and climbing to it, was in the apartment in a moment, and without making the least noise. Captain Bellingham immediately followed him, but could not accomplish the task so quietly as he had done, and he had no sooner placed his foot in the chamber, than Emily and Patty were aroused, and hastily turning round, and perceiving the intruders, they uttered a loud scream, and became paralized to the spot. Bellingham was immediately on his knees at the feet of our heroine, and with a very well assumed appearance of sincerity, he exclaimed—

"Beauteous damsel, banish your fears ; not for the universe would I injure you. Hear me while I tell you that your numerous perfections have excited in my heart, the most ardent passion—"

"Begone, sir," said Emily, recovering herself, and speaking in a tone of dignity. "This intrusion, and from a stranger. Away, I cannot behold you without the utmost contempt and aversion."

"The devil, Captain," ejaculated Sir Edgecumbe ; "muster up your forces, or we shall be routed at the first attack But come, my pretty maiden, you positively must not follow the example of your cold, insensible friend."

"While justice and prudence direct the conduct of my friend," said Patty, with firmness, "I shall not differ from her sir ; surely it ill-becomes the characters of gentlemen to break like midnight robbers on the weak and defenceless. I thought too, Captain Bellingham, it was the province of a soldier to protect and not to insult a female."

"Wheuh !" exclaimed Sir Edgecumbe. "Egad, the lightning is as fierce as the thunder."

"Emily, dearest Emily," said the Captain, "on my knees I solicit your attention."

"No more, sir," cried our heroine, who had mustered up the most extraordinary fortitude, considering the circumstances, and the situation of herself and Patty, alone in the house, and entirely at the mercy of the two intruders ; "no more, sir ; for what purpose do you come hither ?—Why do you make your advances to one who is a stranger to you, but who knows sufficiently of you to tell you that she hates your presence as much as she abhors your principles."

"But a word," urged Bellingham, rising from his knee, and advancing nearer towards her, while Sir Edgecumbe endeavoured at the same time to embrace Patty, who, however, released herself from him with an air of the utmost detestation ; "but a word, dearest girl," repeated the captain, whom Emily's scorn seemed to make the more determined.

"Away, sir," said our heroine, "for should the master of this house return, great as you may consider yourself, from the station you bear in society, you may dearly repent your boldness in forcing yourself in here."

"By Heaven ! cold, insensible beauty, your scorn makes me desperate ; you shall be mine, and thus I——"

As he thus spoke, he was rushing forward to sieze Emily, when she with a courage which nothing but the danger of the moment could have called forth, snatched a couple of pistols from above the mantel-piece, where they had been hanging, and presenting them at Captain Bellingham and Sir Edgecumbe, held them both at bay, and completely astounded them with the unexpected action and boldness of her conduct.

"Captain Bellingham," she exclaimed, in firm and resolute tones, "Captain Bellingham and you Sir Edgecumbe, you see I am determined, I hold in my hands the instruments of death, and by Heaven, if you do not quit this house, your fate is sealed."

"Emily, hear me,"—ejaculated the captain, when his astonishment would allow him to speak.

"Not a word, sir," returned Emily, with a look which plainly evinced her meaning, "if you or your friend advance a single step towards myself or Patty, that instant shall be your last."

"Defeated, completely, and by a petticoat too, demme!" said Sir Edgecumbe Sappington, with a lackadaysical glance at his friend.

"Proud, scornful beauty," cried Captain Bellingham, scornfully, "I obey you, I leave the place, but remember, the next time we meet, it will be my turn to triumph."

As the captain thus spoke, he beckoned to Sir Edgecumbe, and they were about to retire, when there was a loud knocking at the door, and they started back into the room in a state of confusion.

"Damnation!" cried Bellingham, "we are surprised."

"Ah! heaven be thanked, it is our friends returned," said Patty, who had looked out of the window; "unfasten the door, Emily, and admit them."

Emily hastened to comply with this request, and in an instant Mr. Walton, Henry, and the other members of the family entered the room.

To describe the confusion and shame of Captain Bellingham and his friend, the surprise and indignation of Mr. Walton and his son, would be a task that we could by no means do justice to. They were all so much astounded, that it was several minutes ere they could give utterance to a syllable, but stood staring at each other in stupified amazement.

"How now, Captain Bellingham," demanded Mr. Walton, sternly, who was the first that recovered himself sufficiently to speak ;—"what means this intrusion?"

"How dare you thus intrude yourselves into this house, during the absence of its master?" added Henry; fixing upon the abashed and bewildered libertines, a look of the utmost resentment.

"Boy," exclaimed Bellingham, at last, in reply, and addressing himself to Henry, in a haughty tone, "methinks you forget yourself. A speech more humble would better become your lips, when you presume to address a superior."

"Superior," repeated Henry, contemptuously. "Hark ye, Captain Bellingham, I believe that is your name ; I am no more than a menial to you, I know, so fortune has willed it ; but still, I hold no man superior to myself, who does not seek to exalt himself by superior virtues ; and I deem him more despicable than the vilest wretch who crawls the earth, who takes advantage of his better fortune, to tyrannize over and persecute his fellow creatures. Now, sir, explain to me the purpose which brought you hither?"

"I scorn to answer to such an interrogator;" returned Bellingham, proudly, and biting his lips with vexation.

"Captain Bellingham," said Mr. Walton, in a determined voice, "I am the master of this place, I insist, therefore, in knowing the reason of your intrusion during my absence?"

"Oh, a mere frolic, old Perriwig," said Sir Edgecumbe Sappington, "positively, demme."

"Ah!" said Bellingham, "am I to be commanded to answer your impertinence?"

"The man whose intentions are honourable, Captain Bellingham," returned Mr. Walton, "will not shrink from an explanation of his conduct, but will rather court it, and let me tell you, sir, that I consider it disgraceful for men who are paid so handsomely by their country to protect its subjects, to be the first to insult that sex whose very weakness should be its bulwark."

"Be cool, I pray," said Mrs. Walton, who was fearful of the consequences which might follow, should he exasperate the captain.

"Nay, nay, wife;" replied Mr. Walton, whose indignation was excited to the utmost pitch, "I am a poor man, it is true, as plain in speech as I am humble in purse, and during many years of vicissitude, I have learned something of submission; but I never yet learnt to submit to unmanly insolence, especially when the object it selected was a female, and, damme if I would brook it, though I should suffer death for my temerity."

The captain remained silent for a few moments, being too much confused to make any reply, but at length in a subdued tone, and with a very well assumed look of supplication, he said :—

"Mr. Walton, I see you entertained an unjust opinion of me and my friend. The fact is, we have formed an attachment to these two young ladies, and would make honourable proposals, for which purpose we came hither to-day, and ——"

"Honourable proposals," interrupted Mr. Walton, with a look of scorn, "yes, such as ye gaudy butterflies, calling yourselves men of fashion, make to entrap the unwary and delude the humble victims of your villany."

"You are too warm, Mr. Walton," said Captain Bellingham, with great difficulty, stifling his rage at the manner in which the former addressed him, "but surely, the beauteous Emily will do me the justice to acquit me of——"

As he thus spoke, he approached our heroine with the most consummate boldness, and endeavoured to take her hand, and Sir Edgecumbe, who followed his example in everything, made the same advances towards Patty. Completely overpowered by resentment, Henry rushed forward, interposed between the villains and the two trembling and insulted girls, and, in a commanding voice, he said :

"Desist! Remember, as stout a heart oft beats beneath a peasant's humble jacket, as an officer's gold laced coat, and unprovoked insolence may render that heart doubly resolute. Forbear to repeat this boldness, unless you think you have a stronger arm than Henry Walton, a point I am ready this moment to contest with you."

"Well spoken, Henry," said Mr. Walton, "Captain Bellingham, I once more command you to quit this house immediately; you stand confessed, a heartless, bold-faced villain. And you, Sir Cockleshell Flash-in-the-pan, what's your name, make your exit directly by the door, unless you prefer a forcible ejectment from the window."

"Oh! dare you threaten?" said the captain.

"Dare I," repeated Mr. Walton, scornfully? "hark, ye—although I am not a military man, I am not to be frightened by the report of a pop-gun, like many of your feather-bed officers. True, your rank places you above me in one respect, but your vices sink you to a level which honest poverty can never descend to."

"Mr. Walton," said Bellingham, passionately, "this insolence is unbearable; mark me, you may repent this."

"I scorn you and your threats," returned Mr. Walton, "for the last time, will you quit this house?"

" Egad, captain." observed Sir Edgecumbe, who began to feel himself rather uncomfortable, " we are getting shamefully beaten in this attack, and I think it would be advisable to sound a retreat."

" Mr. Walton," exclaimed Bellingham, as he and Sir Edgecumbe advanced towards the door, " Mr. Walton, you have this night provoked an enemy who will pursue you to ruin. And you, Henry Walton, tremble, when next I behold you, it will be to triumph in your misery. Beware !"

With these words, fixing a look of resentment and revenge upon Mr. Walton and his son, Captain Bellingham and Sir Edgecumbe quitted the house.

It was several minutes after they had gone before any of the persons present could sufficiently recover themselves to speak ; at length, Henry, in a voice which fully shewed the wrath which filled his bosom, observed :—

" So, they are gone, the villains ! Oh, if it were not that wealth, rank, and power form a coat of mail to their puny carcases, I would have had ample vengeance for their insolence."

" Alas ; I fear that this will be the cause of some trouble to you," said Emily, " and never should I forgive myself should anything occur to disturb you, indirectly through me."

" In that respect, I perfectly agree with you, Emily," said Patty ; " already I am fearful it is gone too far, and the threats of Captain Bellingham fill me with the most serious apprehension. We will return to my aunt's, Emily, and———"

" Indeed you will do no such thing," said Mr. Walton, " I care nothing for his threats ; in what manner can he injure me ?"

" Mrs. Walton has already stated in what manner he might do so, my dear sir," said our heroine, " and you assented to the probability of it. Alas ! it seems to be my fate to bring misery wherever I go."

" Make yourselves contented, my dear girls," observed Mr. Walton, " for, after all, I do not think that Sir Merton would be prejudiced by what his nephew might say to him, nor has he any excuse to get me off the estate. I owe him nothing, and I have ever been, as he has himself admitted, one of his best tenants. Besides, he cannot so openly sanction the depravities of his profligate relative. I cannot consent to your leaving this place, for at Mrs. Seagrove's you would be more exposed to their villany, and without rendering me any good, for if the captain is determined to do me an injury, your removal from here would not prevent him,"

" You say right, father," observed his son, " here we can adopt such means as will frustrate the designs of Captain Bellingham and Sir Edgecumbe, and keep a vigilant eye over Miss Emily and my Patty. For my own part, I do not fear the fellows, the least in the world, and only wish I had the punishment of them for their boldness, they should not escape without their reward in full."

At the request of Mr. Walton and the others, Emily now related the manner in which they had encountered the captain and his friend, and their subsequent forcible entrance at the window of the parlor ; and Mr. Walton and his son, once more gave expression to the indignation which the behaviour of the libertines had excited in their bosoms.

When our heroine and Patty retired that night to the chamber in which they slept, they sat for some time conversing upon the adventures of the day, and now they were alone, they gave free expression to the fears that filled their minds.

" Patty," said Emily, " you and I are truly sisters in misfortune ; and no sooner have we escaped from one danger than we are threatened with another. I tremble when I think of the threats of Captain Bellingham, and I feel confident that he is not the sort of man to abandon any project he may have fixed upon, We are not safe in this neighbourhood, and whither can we go where we shall be free from danger ?"

"I know not, Emily," replied Patty, "and can give no advice upon the subject."

"Mine is a peculiarly hard fate," said our heroine; "I know not one friend upon whom I have any just claim, and I am a burthen and a cause of misery wherever I go. Surely it would be better to die than to live on in this constant state of care and anxiety."

"Endeavour to compose yourself, my dear Emily," ejaculated Patty, "and hope for better things ; Providence surely will not always suffer you to remain in this state of misery. No, no, do not despair, happier days are yet in store for you, depend upon it "

Emily shook her head and sighed.

" What I fear more than all is," she observed, " the trouble Mr. Walton and his family may be brought to through this last painful circumstance ; it would indeed be hard if they should have to suffer for their kindness."

" It would indeed," replied Patty, " but let us hope that such will not be the case."

But notwithstanding all that Patty could say, she could not succeed in banishing the apprehensions of our heroine, neither could she help feeling nearly as much alarmed herself. It was late before they retired to rest, for their minds were too fully occupied by what had taken place that day, to make them feel disposed for sleep.

The rage of Captain Bellingham at the manner in which he had been treated by Mr. Walton and his son, was of the most violent description, but Sir Edgecumbe treated the matter very lightly, being most sanguine of ultimate success, and pretending to treat the resentment of such " plebian creatures," (as he designated Mr. Walton and his family,) with the most superlative contempt.

"But to be thus scorned and insulted by the menial wretches," observed Bellingham, as himself and Sir Edgecumbe pursued their way towards the abbey ; " I tell you, Sir Edgecumbe, it is more than I can tamely brook; I will have revenge, as well as the gratification of my desires."

"Egad, captain," said Sir Edgecumbe, " now you are in the very mood to agree with my palate ; I am your friend to command ; say, in what manner shall we accomplish our revenge ? Shall we blow out old Walton's brains ; smother his wife ; ruin his two daughters ; hang his son—and—"

" Pray be serious, Sir Edgecumbe," interrupted Bellingham, " I am in no temper for mirth. I have, however, thought of a scheme by which I shall be able to gratify my revenge against Henry Walton, who I perceive is the lover of one of those lovely girls. Serjeant Lance will do anything for money; I will employ him to entrap this headstrong youth ; and once secured in the army, we shall have got rid of one of the principal obstacles to our wishes."

" Excellent ! excellent ?" cried Sir Edgecumbe, " I am all impatience until we commence operations ; we will see Lance this night, if you like, for the sooner he is made acquainted with the business the better."

" As soon as we reach the abbey I will send for him," said Bellingham ; " he is just the man for the purpose ; he has entrapped a number in his time, and is not at all particular what he does, so long as he is well paid for it. There could not be a better opportunity than the present for putting this scheme into execution ; it being the heat of war, the army wants men, and it don't do to stand nice about the manner in which we obtain them."

" To be sure not," said Sir Edgecumbe, " but there requires something more to complete our plot."

" What is that ?

"Why, the certain and easy possession of those two little divinities, to be sure," answered Sir Edgecumbe.

"That is sure to take place," said Captain Bellingham.

"Not so sure, unless caution is used," returned the knight; "it cannot be done in too much of a hurry; we must let the matter rest where it is for a short time, so that the fears and suspicions of the Waltons and the two girls may be lulled, and then they will fall easily into our power. We had better leave the abbey in a day or two, and pretend that we have quitted the neighbourhood, that will quiet all suspicions, and enable us to accomplish our purpose with greater certainty. What do you think of this? Isn't it an excellent suggestion? Positively, demme, I'm the fellow!"

"I approve of your suggestions, much," answered Bellingham, "an will take care to follow them. The day after to-morrow, we will leave th abbey, and take up our quarters in some obscure part of the adjacent town where we can have an opportunity of watching all that passes, and seize upon the first chance which presents itself to put our designs into execution. By Heaven! the beauty of this same Emily has so excited my passions, that I would willingly sacrifice a fortune to get her in my power."

"And the other is a most exquisite creature;" said Sir Edgecumbe, "what a splendid girl to ride out by your side, or to sport in a box at the Opera. Only let me get hold of her, and I'll warrant I shall soon win her to my wishes. It would be a marvellous thing, indeed, if any beautiful little, demmed angel, could resist me! Oh, positively, demme, I'm the fellow!"

"At first, I thought of endeavouring to work the old man some harm, by prejudicing my uncle against him, and getting him driven off the estate; which would in all probability, have been a ruinous job to him;" re-

No. 19

marked Bellingham, " but I think the loss of his son will be a sufficient punishment to him for the insolent manner in which he has this day treated us."

" Yes, I should rather think it will;" said Sir Edgecumbe; "most likely the military career of Henry Walton will be brief, especially if he is enlisted into your regiment, Captain ; continual hardships, disgrace, and punishment, will soon break his spirit, and the field of battle will do the rest."

" You have drawn an excellent picture of it, Sir Edgecumbe," remarked Captain Bellingham ; "what you have mentioned is exactly what I antici-pate will be the result of the plot."

" Ha! ha! ha! I think this fiery youth will have pretty good cause to repent letting his tongue run so glibly and so impertinently ;" said Sir Edgecumbe ; " but see, we are at the abbey."

" The two worthy friends now entered the abbey, and having made their way to the apartments allotted to their use during their visit, Captain Bellingham despatched his servant to request the attendance of Sergeant Lance.

The latter personage, was a shrewd, bombastical, cowardly, braggadocia, who, as the captain has described him, was fit for anything but an honest action, and a more appropriate individual to execute the designs of Bellingham, could not have been found. If he failed in anything he undertook, of a nefarious description, it would have been marvellous indeed ; for villany was his constant study, and he would have greatly reproached himself, had he, accidentally, found himself committing one act of integrity. He had been engaged in several rascally transactions with the captain, so that they knew each other very well, and Bellingham, from experience, therefore, was convinced he could trust him.

Sergeant Lance was not long in making his appearance. He was a tall, thin man, with a very red nose, and small, cunning-looking eyes ; there was always an artful grin upon his countenance, and his whole appearance fully denoted what his real character was.

"Sergeant Lance," said Captain Bellingham, " I would speak with you ; never mind the presence of this gentleman, he is my friend."

Lance touched his hat, and said, in reply :—

" I am all attention, captain—silent as a dead drummer, as my late gallant father of the South Warwick Militia used to say."

"You are a brave man, Sergeant Lance ;" observed Bellingham, with an affable smile.

" Brave, your honour," repeated Lance, " fierce as a thirty-six pounder, as my late gallant father of the South Warwick Militia used to say ;—look at my scars ;—see how I've been knocked about by the enemy, until my body's like the lid of a pepper-castor."

" Well, well," said Bellingham, impatiently, " a truce with prolixity, at present. You can serve me, serjeant, and I can amply reward you for such service; you are an old soldier, and——"

" A soldier !" interrupted Lance, tossing his head, and winking his eye conceitedly ; " ah, I fancy, captain, you are perfectly right, there. Consider the brave deeds I have done ; the glorious battles I have been in, the campaigning I have had, and you will, indeed, say *I am* a soldier. Why, I've been shot at by the enemy, and received three hundred lashes for the amusement of my officers, and if that don't constitute me a good soldier, drum me out of the regiment for a coward, as my late gallant father of the South Warwick Militia used to say."

" Hark ye, Lance," said Bellingham, "do you know farmer Walton, who lives not far from here ?"

" Ah! to be sure I do, and a hearty old cock he is, too ;" answered Lance,

"I have heard that he has been a sailor, and performed deeds that even I should be proud to be the hero of."

"You also know his son, Henry?"

"Aye, a stout, comely looking lad, he is, too; with a spirit that would make him a good soldier."

"True, true," remarked the captain, eagerly; "and now listen to me, but remember, I speak to you in secresy. You are at present in the possession of press orders to some extent, I believe?"

"I am, your honour."

"This Henry Walton would be a valuable man in the service."

"He would, captain;" coincided Lance.

"Well then, Mr. Lance, Sergeant Lance," said Bellingham, with a very bland smile, "knowing this, and what a remarkably loyal man you are, could you not contrive to add such a brave fellow to the service of your king and country?"

"What! your honour?" ejaculated Serjeant Lance, with affected surprise, "secret ambuscading? I—I—really I'm very tenacious of——"

"But suppose I were to reward you handsomely," said Bellingham, shaking a purse at Lance, who beheld it with an expression of delight; "would you have any objection then? This purse, and probably another to match it, for instance!"

"Why, captain," replied Lance, "I must confess, this materially alters the case. A noble action ought to be properly rewarded, and, as you say, I should be serving my king and country, by——"

"You consent, then?"

"Your liberality, captain, has made me your slave;" said Lance; "oh yes, I'll manage this affair with my usual ability and valour."

"Let it be done as quickly as possible, and mind he does not by any means escape."

"I'll take especial care of that;" said Lance, "perhaps, captain, you are aware, that I have agreed with the justices to pitch on a certain number of young fellows, who can most easily be spared from the country, and of whom I will take good care to clear it. Now, it so happens that, some time ago, Henry Walton seriously offended one of the justices, and he has accordingly marked him out for one of his victims; so you see, the affair can be managed with the greatest safety."

"The circumstance you have mentioned," observed Captain Bellingham, is indeed a fortunate one. Your promptitude has my thanks; but do not delay the execution of the plot. Perform your task well, and I will readily pay you for it."

"Never fear me, your honour," said the sergeant, "in the performance of bold and warlike deeds, I am a modern Alexander, as my late gallant father of the South Warwick Militia used to say. Good night, captain, sir, your most obedient."

"Good night, and success attend you;" said Bellingham; "I suppose in a day or two, we shall hear more about it?"

"It shall be done in the firing of a musket," said Lance; and he bowed himself out of the room.

"There is every prospect of the success of my plot," remarked the captain, when Sergeant Lance had retired.

"Egad, the serjeant is a most accomplished villain, certainly," said Sir Edgecumbe, "positively, he is a very devil of a fellow. But we had better join your uncle in the supper-room; he, perhaps, may otherwise think it strange. Oh, we shall finish this business in a twinkling; Emily will be yours, Patty will be mine; we shall be as happy as possible, and,—oh, positively, demme, I'm the fellow."

As the fop thus elegantly delivered himself, he took the arm of his *amiable* friend, and they left the room, very sanguine on the ultimate success of the nefarious stratagem they had concocted.

CHAPTER XV.

THE GUILTY PLOT.—THE SEPARATION.—THE DOUBLE ABDUCTION.

At the time they had resolved upon, Captain Bellingham, and Sir Edgecumbe Sappington quitted Bellingham Abbey, and retired to the town adjacent, where they had procured apartments, and remained *incog.* until they could complete their wishes. As may be supposed, Mr. Walton, our heroine and Patty, heard of the departure of the two libertines with the utmost satisfaction, and they began to hope that the matter would end there ; that they had abandoned their designs, seeing there was not the least chance of their succeeding in pursuading Emily or Patty to listen to their! guilty protestations. They were also in hopes that Captain Bellingham had forgotten his resentment, and, as they had not heard any more about it, that he would not think of putting the threats he had made in practice. They were very soon, however, fated to be undeceived ; the demon was at that time at work to render them miserable. Had they, indeed, been thoroughly acquainted with the dispositions of the two profligate gentlemen, they would have known that they never abandoned any design on which they had fixed their mind, until they had entirely exhausted all their ingenuity in vain, and that their artifices were too often attended with success.

A week elapsed after the departure of Bellingham and his companion from the abbey, and nothing occurred to cause any alarm in the minds of Emily and her friends. One, evening, however, Henry had occasion to go to the town, but as the business he was going upon would not detain him, he was expected back at the farm at an early hour. Contrary to such expectation, hour after hour passed away, and Henry did not make his appearance, they began to be alarmed.

"What can be the meaning of this ?" said Mr. Walton ; "something must have happened, for Henry is always very punctual."

"Some danger is at hand," said Mrs. Walton, in a voice of agitation, "my heart forbodes it. Oh, my son !"

"Nay, nay, do not be alarmed," observed Mr. Walton, "for, after all, there may be no occasion for it ; he may have met with some friends who have detained him. I will go forth and see whether I can meet him."

Mr. Walton reached down his hat, and took his stick in his hand as he spoke, and then quitted the house, but he had scarcely left it a second, and was proceeding across his grounds, when he heard a confused noise of several voices at the gate, and hastening to it, his surprise and alarm may be imagined, when he beheld his son, surrounded by several soldiers, by whom he was forcibly held, while Sergeant Lance was giving orders for them to force him along.

"Scoundrels !" cried the young man, struggling violently, "I will not go until I have seen my parents ! Unhand me ; I will not go !"

"What is the meaning of this ?" demanded Mr. Walton ; "what has he done to deserve this treatment ?"

"Ah, father !" cried Henry, "I am trepanned—duped—betrayed."

"Trepanned !"

"There, come, come, young man," observed Sergeant Lance, "it's no use being obstropolous ; the fact of it is, Mr. Walton, that your son is now a soldier; I have enlisted him; he must serve his king and country; he'll become a general before he dies, I shouldn't wonder. There, what's the good of making such a fuss about it? You ought to be proud of the honour bestowed upon you. No staying behind you; so, right about face, double-quick march, as my gallant father of the South Warwick Militia used to say."

"Surely you cannot mean what you say," cried Mr. Walton; "you will not drag my son away from me in this manner? Why have you had recourse to such cruel and violent measures as those?"

"Why, why, as for the reason," replied Lance, "that's my business; it is enough for me to tell you that your son is from this time, and must be, a soldier; and to-morrow morning he will be marched off to the depôt."

"Villain!" cried Mr. Walton, passionately, "you will assuredly be punished for this some time or the other; how can we expect men to meet the enemies of their country with spirit, when they are thus forcibly dragged from their homes and families, by a set of ruffians, who——"

"Come, come, Mr. Walton," said Sergeant Lance, "a little better language, if you please; learn to treat a military officer and a gentleman with a little more respect, as my late gallant father of the South Warwick Militia used to say. But I can't stand parleying here all night; double quick march, I say again."

"I will not be dragged along like a felon," exclaimed Henry; "ah! mother—sisters—Patty!"

Aroused by the hubbub of voices, Mrs. Walton and her daughters, with Emily and Patty, had hastened to the spot, and their astonishment and terror, when they beheld the situation of Henry, exceeded all bounds.

"Oh, God!" ejaculated Mrs. Walton, "my worst forbodings are realized; Henry, my son, what would these men do with you?"

"They would tear me from you, mother," cried Henry; "from home, sisters, Patty;—oh, I have been most basely, treacherously trepanned."

"Gracious Heaven!" cried the afflicted mother, "can it be?"

"It not only can be, but it is," said Serjeant Lance; "but we have staid here too long already; no more nonsense—away with him."

With a burst of the most intense agony, Patty now rushed forward, and throwing herself at the feet of Sergeant Lance, exclaimed in accents of the most earnest supplication,—

"Oh, mercy! mercy! spare my lover, my Henry!"

But in spite of the agony of all present, and the entreaties of Mr. Walton and his family, Henry was forced away; Mr. Walton following them until they arrived at the place where they intended to stay for the night, and where not being allowed to enter, he returned with a distracted heart to the farm.

It was with a heavy heart that Mr. Walton returned home, for he was well aware of the scene of bitter misery he would have to encounter from the agony of his family, and the distracted lover of his son. But he struggled hard with his feelings, and endeavoured to meet them with that composure and firmness which would enable him to advise with them, and soothe them under the trying circumstances. A scene of the greatest distress was the farm that night, and if there was one who could feel more than another, it was Patty, who, in addition to the unhappy situation of her lover, reproached herself with being the indirect cause of this affliction to the family of Mr. Walton, who had before experienced so much in the school of vicissitude, and had settled into a calm prior to herself and our heroine taking up their residence with them.

"Alas! my poor son," ejaculated Mrs. Walton, "how fatally realisedhav been my forebodings. This is a plot, depend upon it, concocted by Captain Bellingham, and his dissipated friend, Sir Edgecumbe."

"It is indeed," observed Patty, sobbing, "and had I not appeared in this neighbourhood, it would not, in all probability, have happened. Oh, Henry, dear Henry, how unfortunate is it that we should ever have met, then would you still have been happy in the bosom of your family."

"And I, too, " said Emily, "I have to upbraid myself with being partly, although inadvertantly, the cause of this trouble. Would that we had never come to this spot, or that we had remained with Mrs. Seagrove. Indeed, had it not been for me, it is most likely you would not have come hither; therefore, may I blame myself for being the primary occasion of all that has happened. Alas! it appears that a spell is upon me, and that it is my fate to bring misery upon all those with whom I have any connection."

"Henry, dear Henry," cried Patty, her anguish increasing, "and shall I never again behold you? They have torn you from me, and the villains who have contrived this nefarious stratagem, will, no doubt, take good care that we shall be separated for ever!"

"Be calm, dearest Patty and Emily," said the lovely Grace Walton, who with her sister, although, as it may be expected, they were, most poignantly affected, endeavoured to stifle their feelings, with that generous sentiment inherent in them, so that they might soothe the anguish of their parents, and those whom they loved with as much fervour as if they had been their own sisters; "you reproach yourselves unjustly, and, I think, take a wrong view of the matter. It appears to me that this is all the action of Lance, who is well known as a scoundrel, and is ready at any time to trepan all he can without any respect to individuals."

"Oh! no," observed Mrs. Walton, "villain as we know Sergeant Lance to be, I feel confident that he has had some stronger motive than that you would attribute to him, for trepanning my poor boy."

"What mean you?" demanded Mr. Walton.

"Why, that Captain Bellingham and Sir Edgecumbe Sappington are at the bottom of this base transaction," replied Mrs. Walton, "and that they have incited him to it from a feeling of revenge, and in order that the obstacle to their wishes might be removed."

"Oh, yes," ejaculated Patty, "such an idea is too reasonable to be refuted."

"Nonsense!" remarked Mrs. Walton, "your conclusions are formed too hastily."

"Did they not threaten us with vengeance, demanded Mrs. Walton?"

"They did," returned her husband, "but you know they have left the neighbourhood."

"They have pretended to do so," said Mrs. Walton; "but, depend upon it, it is only a scheme, the better to advance their villanous designs. Henry, my poor son, they have torn you from us, and never, never shall we meet again."

"But they dare not, by Heaven, they shall not commit such an act of villany," cried Mr. Walton, warmly; "they have enlisted him, it is true, but I can demand his release, upon application to the justice. They cannot swear him in without his own free will, if he has the means of paying the 'smart-money,' the technical term applied to a legal system of robbery."

"At the present time, they do anything with impunity," remarked Mrs. Walton, with a deep sigh; "and the justices are the very last persons who are likely to lean to that power whose name they arrogate. The horrors of war make a demand upon the country for soldiers, and they care little how they obtain them; full power is given to such heartless scoundrels as Sergeant Lance to entrap all that they can, and if inquiry is even instituted into their conduct, it is a complete mockery, and attended with no beneficial results."

"He must be brought before the justice in the morning," said Mr. Walton, "and I am, therefore, determined to make every effort in my power to obtain his release. Henry declared that he had been trepanned, and we have every reason to believe that he would not have voluntarily enlisted. If the magistrate will not yield him up upon the injustice of the circumstance being made apparent to him, he can have no possible pretext for ordering him to be detained, upon my paying the demand for a substitute."

"If you look for justice to Mr. Snoggins," returned Mrs. Walton, with a melancholy shake of the head, "alas! I fear me, how bitterly will you be deceived; it is foreign to his nature, and you well know it."

"I will admit that he is not one of the best or most impartial of men," replied her husband, "but still, he cannot, surely, so boldly act in opposition to all reason."

"It is well known,," said Mrs. Walton, "that he is a most abominable tyrant, who delights in the distresses of his fellow-creatures. He has also made himself very conspicuous of late in affairs of this description, and few that have been enlisted in a moment of folly or inebriation, have been suffered by him to escape. If that is the only hope you have, alas! all prospect of Henry's restoration to us is at an end."

Mr. Walton made no immediate reply; for although he endeavoured to calm the fears of his wife and the others, he knew too well what good reason the former had for the apprehensions she expressed, and he knew not what to say to combat them. He could not but see most forcibly through the whole of the villainous plot, and that it originated in Captain Bellingham and Sir Edgecumbe Sappington, and knowing the influence they possessed over the magistrate, he felt convinced that their triumph would be certain. Besides, Lance had told him that Henry would be taken to the depôt early in the morning, and it was, therefore, not at all unlikely that he would not be brought before Mr. Snoggins at all.

"Besides," remarked Mrs. Walton, after she had waited for a few minutes, expecting an answer from her husband; "you know that Mr. Snoggins is no friend of our son, and will, therefore, most likely feel inclined to gratify his petty malice against him, because he happened to give him a slight offence a short time back."

"I remember it very well," said Mr. Walton, "but it was a trifling affair, and I should not think that the justice would think it worthy of being taken any farther notice of. But endeavour to compose yourself tonight, and trust for a happier result in the morning than you anticipate."

No answer was returned to this, but the sighs and tears of Mrs. Walton and her daughters, as well as Emily and Patty, too evidently shewed how little they were disposed to follow the advice which he offered them. It was late ere the family thought of retiring to their chambers, for as may be expected after the circumstance which we have recounted, they none of them felt inclined for rest, and the misery which was depicted upon the countenance of every one, was too apparent to be mistaken. But no language can describe the intense agony of Patty, and when she and Emily quitted the others for the night, and retired to their own room, it was some time ere the latter could succeed in any way in calming her grief.

"Oh, Emily," she sobbed forth, "he is torn from me for ever; exposed to all the dread terrors of the bloody field of carnage, what prospect is there of his ever again returning?"

"Do not thus give way to the violence of despair," replied our heroine,

" even should your lover be forced away, does he not stand the same chance as others? and depend upon it, Providence, whose almighty arm is ever extended to protect the innocent, will shield him from the danger you apprehend."

" Would to heaven I could think as you do," returned Patty, " but I cannot divest my mind of the melancholy forebodings that beset it. Oh, Henry, dearest Henry, never did I know the actual strength of my love for you till now."

" I know not what to say, dear Patty," said Emily, " to console you; truly we are both the children of misfortune, and one common fate seems to attend us."

" It does, indeed," returned Patty, the tears gushing from her eyes, "and no sooner have we escaped from one disaster, than another befals us. That hateful Captain Bellingham, and Sir Edgecumbe, I am firmly of the opinion of Mrs. Walton that they are the cause of this."

" But have they not left the neighbourhood?" said our heroine.

" They have pretended to quit the abbey," replied Patty, " but I firmly believe that they are still secreted near the spot, and are only awaiting an opportunity to get us in their power. They are not the sort of men who would so easily abandon their designs, and they will not hesitate to commit any offence, in order that they may procure the gratification of their wishes."

" How unfortunate we are," exclaimed Emily, " no sooner have we escaped from one danger, than we are exposed to another; it seems, indeed, as if we were doomed to be the victims of persecution."

Thus in conversation of the most melancholy description, they continued till a late hour, before they thought of retiring to rest, and sleep long refused to descend upon their eyelids. They looked forward to the following morning to know the result of Mr. Walton's interview with Mr. Justice Snoggins with the utmost anxiety, although from the picture which Mrs. Walton had drawn of him, and which they had too much reason to believe was not exaggerated, they feared they had but little to hope from that quarter.

In the mean time, Sergeant Lance having seen Henry Walton in a place of security, hastened to Captain Bellingham and Sir Sappington, to inform them of the able manner in which he had effected his commission, and of the safe custody of their victim.

Captain Bellingham and Sir Edgecumbe had been anxiously waiting at the place to which they had removed, and where they were remaining incog, to see Sergeant Lance, and to learn from him whether or not he had succeeded, and consequently, it was with no little satisfaction they beheld him enter.

The *gallant* sergeant advanced to the centre of the room with a self important swagger, and placing his hand to his cap, uttered a still more self important and dignified "ahem."

" Well, sergeant," said Captain Bellingham, impatiently; "what success?"

" Glorious! triumphant! splendid! As my late respected and gallant father of the South Warwick Militia used to say;" replied Lance.

" Have you then succeeded in ——"

" The enemy is captured, captain," added the sergeant; "his chance of restoration to liberty may now be considered a forlorn hope, as my gallant father of the South Warwick Militia used to say."

" Bravo! capital! demme, he's the fellow, isn't he, Bellingham?" said Sir Edgecumbe Sappington.

" And you have got him in a place of security?" inquired the Captain.

" As safe as a gun, captain," answered Lance; "but you know I was sure to do that. I never fail—bless your heart, your honour, never. In the

performance of great and noble actions, I am myself alone, as my late gallant father of the South Warwick Militia used to say."

"Lance," observed Bellingham, in tones of satisfaction, "you have played your part to admiration, and I cannot sufficiently thank you."

"Positively, Lance, you are a most exquisite fellow; a thorough-going rascal!—A villain of the first water;" remarked Sir Edgecumbe Sappington, placing his quizzing glass up to his eye, and fixing upon him a lackadaysical look.

"Your honour highly flatters me," said Lance, "as my late respected and gallant father of the South Warwick Militia used to say, I am completely overwhelmed with these blushing honours, so thick upon me. In any clever and meritorious action like the one I have just performed, you will find Lance has not his equal."

"And how did you manage to entrap him?" inquired Bellingham.

"Oh, with my usual skill, captain," replied the sergeant; "met him at the 'Ploughshare,' partaking of ale with a few friends—joined their company; worked them into a good humour in my insinuating way—popt a shilling in the cuff of his coat—had him directly—he was flabbergasted—I was resolute;—swore positively that he had taken the money of his own free will;—I *can* swear, you know, your honour;—he began to storm and bluster, and so did his friends;—no use—catch any one frightening Sergeant Lance! Ha! ha!—Had my comrades handy—forced him off—but he didn't half like it; and a very determined young fellow he is too; but too hot and passionate ever to put up with the discipline of a soldier."

"So much the better," said Bellingham, "it will afford me a greater opportunity of gratifying my revenge. But did he see any of his friends?"

"Yes, captain," answered Lance; "you see, your honour, we had to pass near the farm of Mr. Walton, and Henry wanted permission to see

No. 20

them; but it wouldn't do, I knew better than to allow that.—Always got my eye upon the corporal, as my late gallant father of the South Warwick Militia used to say. However, he did see them;—they came out, I suppose, to look after him. The old man stormed;—the old woman begged—his sweetheart supplicated on her kness, and his sisters stood by in the most bitter agony. But they could make no impression upon me. I was invulnerable. Catch any one laying siege to my heart; poh! they may as well attempt to capture a fortress without arms or ammunition."

"Why, if I must tell you my opinion of you, sergeant," observed the captain, "I do not think you are overstocked with feeling."

"Feeling!" reiterated Lance, "stuff!—nonsense! What business has a person with feelings, I should like to know; especially a soldier? There's not such a word in the articles of war. But I say, your honour, that is a monstrous pretty girl, that Miss Patty, as they call her, and her and Henry do seem remarkably fond of one another."

"Doubtless they are, sergeant, "said Sir Edgecumbe, "but they shall never have each other, if I can prevent it; the girl is too rich a prize for such a rustic."

"True, your honour," coincided Lance, "and so I suppose your honour has made up your mind to have her yourself."

"The very thing I intend to do, positively," said Sir Edgecumbe, smiling upon the bombastical and conceited sergeant in a familiar manner.

"But there is that beautiful little creature, Emily, as they call her," said Lance; "she, I think, if anything surpasses in loveliness the object of your choice, Sir Edgecumbe."

"She does, she does," fervently cried Bellingham, "and never shall I rest until I have got her in my power!"

"Oh, oh," said the sergeant, winking his eye familiarly.

"But mind, Lance," continued Bellingham, "not a word to any person upon the subject."

"Your honour cannot doubt me for a moment, I'm sure," returned the sergeant; "always obey the commands of my superior officer."

"Very well; and if I should require your assistance again, you will be ready to do what I desire of you?"

"Certainly, your honour."

"But you must bring Henry before the justice in the morning to be sworn," said Bellingham.

"Yes, captain," answered Lance; "but that will be a mere matter of form, you know, as you are aware that I have press orders to an unlimited amount, and that Henry Walton having offended Mr. Snoggins, he has long been marked by him as one of the young men he wishes me to remove from the neighbourhood. The business will be settled in a tangent, and no money will buy him off; for Snoggins, you know, is a man who is not to be shaken from his purpose when he takes anything in his head."

"Well, get this business completed to-morrow to my satisfaction, and, as I promised you, I will find you another purse to match the one I have already given you."

"Your honour is very liberal," said Lance, touching his cap a great many times, and looking unutterable satisfaction, "and my gratitude will be ever unbounded. You may depend upon me; to-morrow morning, Henry Walton will be safely removed altogether. Has your honour any further commands for me?"

"Not at present, Lance; you will call upon me to-morrow, and let me know how the business has been settled?"

"To be sure, your honour," replied Lance. "Now, then, eyes right—right abou tface—Quick march!"

And having made his obeisance to Captain Bellingham and Sir Edgecumbe Sappington, Sergeant Lance shouldered his cane, and with much dignity, marched out of the room.

"Clever fellow! demmed clever fellow! a most devilish shrewd fellow!" exclaimed Sir Edgecumbe, when the sergeant had retired. "I declare he is the very pink of rascality—a villain of the first water! It was very lucky we happened to think of him, or it's a chance if we should have succeeded in our plot so easily. This same Henry will have good reason to repent having offended you, captain, or I am much mistaken."

"He shall, indeed," returned Bellingham, "the insolent upstart! He to presume to taunt and reproach me. By Heaven! I feel more satisfaction at having gratified my revenge in this instance, than anything I have done for some time before."

"Oh, yes, it was an exquisite plot, and has been performed to admiration," said Sir Edgecumbe. "But now that business is done, we must see about getting possession of the females."

"True; I, in particular, have no time to lose," remarked Bellingham, "as in a few weeks I shall be compelled to join my regiment, and it is uncertain when I may return again."

"Yes," returned Sir Edgecumbe, "and perhaps you may not come back at all. A field of battle is a very awkward place, and a gentleman may get popt off before he has time to look around him. For my part, I think it is devilish inconvenient, and it is very unreasonable for them to expect a gentleman to fight at all. I should not engage for any such thing, and if I were in your place, I should sell out without any more delay."

"What! and lose the friendship of my uncle, and be taunted with being what is technically called a feather-bed soldier," said Bellingham. "Oh, no, that would never do. The whole of it is, we must lose no time in getting the girls into our power, and when I am compelled to leave England—"

"Why," added Sir Edgecumbe, "you can place her under my protection until your return, you know; and, no doubt, I can manage to keep them both secure enough. Positively it is a very pretty arrangement, and I am all impatience until we set about the business."

"And so am I," returned Captain Bellingham, "and it is strange, indeed, to me, if it is many days before I succeed in devising some means of getting them into our power."

"Days," repeated Sir Edgecumbe; "oh, positively I cannot think of waiting days, my impatience will not allow me. Leave it all to me, captain, and in a very short time you may depend upon having the two angelic little creatures in our arms. Oh, positively, I'm the fellow—demme!"

"I will leave it to you, Sir Edgecumbe," said the captain, "and I have the utmost confidence in your success. They do not know that we are in the neighbourhood."

"Exactly!" returned Sir Edgecumbe, "and, therefore, they will not think it necessary to use the precaution they have hitherto done, but will indulge in their rambles as they used to do, in one of which we can surprise them, and having all in readiness, bear them away to a place of security."

"And whither would you propose taking them?" demanded Bellingham; "where do you think would be a place of safety, where we might keep them without any suspicions being excited that they were in our power?"

"I have before told you," replied Sir Edgecumbe, "at my beautiful little retired estate in the Isle of Wight—we couldn't have a better place."

"True," observed Captain Bellingham, "I had forgotten that; it is admirably adapted for the purpose, and once there, our triumph over them is certain. We shall, however, want some assistance in the plot."

"Certainly," replied Sir Edgecumbe; "and who can we employ better than Sergeant Lance?"

"No one that I am aware of," said the captain, "and it will not do to confide the business to too many. We will but suffer the excitement which the trapanning of Henry Walton has caused at the farm to abate, and then we will lose no time in putting our designs into execution."

Having come to this arrangement, they proceeded to converse upon different subjects, and after partaking of their usual deep potations, separated for the night.

The anguish of all at the farm continued to increase rather than abate, and Patty and Mrs. Walton in particular, were quite inconsolable. Mr. Walton waited with the utmost impatience until the morning, when he had fully made up his mind to hasten to Mr. Justice Snoggins, and, if possible, restore his son to liberty. Accordingly, he slightly partook of an early breakfast the next morning, and bidding his wife and the others not to give way to despair, as he was determined not to return without having obtained some satisfactory explanation, he took his stick in his hand, and walked from the farm towards the house of Mr. Snoggins.

It was, however, with a heavy heart (notwithstanding in the presence of his wife and family he had endeavoured to appear composed) that the honest farmer started forth upon his melancholy errand, and he foreboded no success.

Mr. Justice Snoggins was a very great man, indeed, in his way, and so the poor unfortunate delinquents who happened to be brought before him, knew too well from experience. We say the *poor* individuals, for Mr. Snoggins made a most praiseworthy distinction (as every honest and impartial magistrate should) between the patrician and plebeian offenders. The humble persons in the neighbourhood looked up to him with awe, and woe-betide those who offended him. Mr. Snoggins was a Solon, he considered, and frequently hinted so himself, and upon such unquestionable authority, who is there that would be bold enough to doubt? Mr. Snoggins was very highly connected, and consequently the fact was indisputable that he must be a gentleman of the most profound judgment, learning, and natural genius. They must be mad, indeed, who would presume to deny the sense and learning of those who happen to have the flood of a nobleman flowing within their veins. Some persons have the consummate impudence and ignorance to deny that genius is hereditary—at any rate, among the higher orders. Mr. Justice Snoggins thought different, and he said so, and having said so, the fact must be established beyond a doubt. Mr. Snoggins was also most zealously religious in public, and he frequently evinced the same, by incarcerating a poor man or two in gaol for a month or so, for the enormous crime of being able to earn no more than from four to seven shillings per week, and, consequently, not being able to purchase clothes sufficiently decent to appear in at church.

Mr. Justice Snoggins was certainly not very dignified in his appearance, however lofty his mind might be; for he stood only four-feet one and three-eighths, in his high-heeled shoes, and wig; his body was of a circumscribed description, and his left leg was considerably shorter than the other. His face was very thin; his features of the hatchet order, and his little grey eyes twinkled fiercely and cunningly from beneath his long grey eyelashes.

It was then to this man that Mr. Walton was going, and before whom he expected to see Henry brought to undergo the ceremony of being sworn in, and when it is recollected that the former had unfortunately offended him, it may be easily expected that the young man would meet with little, if any, mercy from the arbitrary Dogberry. When Mr. Walton arrived at the justice's, he was given to understand that, notwithstanding the earliness of the hour, Sergeant Lance had brought Henry there some time before, and the business being settled, the young man had been taken away to the depôt of the regiment, he having been duly sworn in to serve the king.

"This is a shameful outrage, I have no hesitation in saying," observed Mr. Walton, "and it reflects the utmost disgrace upon all parties connected with it."

"Eh! what? Can I be awake, and listen to such language in the magisterial office? Noddy, you hear what he says? You hear the insinuations he has thrown out against the bench and its dignity."

"Yes, your worship," said Mr. Noddy, who was the clerk to Mr. Justice Snoggins, and, therefore, a person of almost equal importance. He was a small-bodied man, with an immense head, a pale face, and a red nose; a large mouth; high cheek-bones; a low forehead; and a most awful squint.

"Put that down, Noddy," added Mr. Snoggins, looking broadswords instead of daggers at Mr. Walton; "I'll tell you what it is, Mr. Walton, you had better mind what you say, or the dignity of the bench may consider itself offended, in which case, you would stand a great chance of being committed for contempt,—contempt, sir, mind what I say."

"I repeat, that the whole of this affair is infamous," said Mr. Walton, looking on the miserable wretch, who fain would have appeared as a paragon of wisdom and sagacity, with an expression of the most ineffable contempt and pity; "and the magistrate who could be guilty of so gross an act of injustice, deserves not only to be disgraced from the office he so unworthily holds, but also to be severely punished, for thus trampling on the rights and liberties of the subject."

"You hear that, Noddy?" now completely shrieked Mr. Snoggins, so utterly astonished was he at the daring language of the farmer. "Set that down carefully, Noddy, and then I will take a few minutes to consider whether I shall commit him. Accuse me of injustice, me!—me!—Say that I ought to be disgraced!—punished!—By Heaven, this is nothing less than sacrilege! It is high treason! Insult me, one of his majesty's justices of the peace! It is a crime of the most heinous description. Put his words carefully down, Noddy."

"Yes, your worship," said Mr. Noddy, cocking his head on one side, and placing his eyes very close to the sheet of paper before him, on which he made certain hieroglyphics that were anything but creditable to the stenographic abilities of a magistrate's clerk.

"You may do as you think proper, sir," said Mr. Walton, "but beware that you do not overstep the bounds of justice and impartiality too far, or you may probably have reason to repent your conduct. My son has been most basely treated; in the first place, I am convinced he was trepanned, and you have given your sanction to the villany, by pretending to administer an oath, which I know very well he would not take of his own free will."

"You hear that, Mr. Noddy," said Mr. Justice Snoggins, "put that down carefully; he accuses me of sanctioning villany;—oh! the presumption of the man; put it down, Noddy; put it down!—Treason, libel, blasphemy! sacrilege!—Mr. Walton, you will put yourself in a very pretty situation, if you do not mind. You will please to bear in mind that I hold a high, responsible, and onerous office;—the law is the law; justice is justice; and a justice of the peace is a justice of the peace, and must be treated with proper awe and respect."

"I respect the office you hold, sir," answered Mr. Walton, "when it is exercised with impartiality and wisdom; but when an ignorant magistrate——"

"Ignorant magistrate!" croaked forth Mr. Snoggins, "take particular notice of that, Mr. Noddy; he calls me an ignorant magistrate. Put that carefully down. I do not hesitate a moment in saying that that is a felony. Mr. Walton, you are placing yourself in a very awkward dilemma."

"If a man is to be punished for raising his voice against a gross act of injustice," replied Mr. Walton, looking upon the ignorant Dogberry with the most superlative contempt, "I must admit that I have placed myself in an awkward situation. But let the consequences be whatever they may, I am determined that nothing shall prevent me from giving free expression to my sentiments, and, therefore, I again tell you, sir, that you have acted in a manner as disgraceful as it is unjust. My poor son has been regularly trepanned, and you have been one of the principal actors in the scheme of villany."

Mr. Snoggins stared at the farmer; he could scarcely believe the evidence of his senses; his ears certainly must deceive him; it could not be true that any individual should have the uncommon hardihood—nay, audacity—to address him, Mr. Snoggins, a right-down earnest, genuine justice of the peace, in such terms—in his own court—in his own chair—in his own wig. It was the very acme of presumption. Mr. Snoggins was horrified; Mr. Noddy was paralised; as for the parish beadle, he was ready to sink through the flooring with astonishment. The whole court was stultified. As for Mr. Snoggins, he was unable to conquer the power of his feelings for a few moments, and was incapable of giving utterance to a syllable, but he stared at Mr. Walton, and looked unutterable things; while Mr. Noddy, his clerk, gnawed one end of the pen, and stared at Mr. Walton with an expression of the most inexpressible horror and amazement. Mr. Snoggins not only looked, but thought terrible things. Such behaviour, such language, from a common farmer, and addressed to one of his majesty's justices of the peace, was not to be tolerated. A fearful example must be made of such a daring offender. He must take time to consider what punishment would be adequate to the offence which he had committed. Many persons had been hung, drawn, and quartered, for saying much less of royalty, thought Mr. Snoggins, and was he not in his official capacity, the great representative of the law, while the law was the support of the crown, and, consequently, an insult offered to the law was nothing more nor less than an insult offered to the crown. Mr. Snoggins thus argued mentally, and he half made up his mind to commit Mr. Walton forthwith; but having blown his nose fiercely, his indignation became greatly abated.

"Mr. Noddy," said he, turning to his clerk, "have you put down carefully all that this daring man last uttered?"

"Yes, your worship," replied Noddy.

"In my opinion it is high treason, Noddy."

"Yes, your worship," said the clerk.

"High treason, Noddy."

"Yes, your worship."

"I don't think I should be doing my duty if I did not commit him immediately."

"No, your worship," coincided the sagacious Mr. Noddy.

Mr. Walton smiled at the great official and his clerk contemptuously; and then turning to the former, he said—

"I have nothing more to say to you, sir, I have nothing to add to the opinion I have already expressed of your conduct. As I require justice, it would be useless my remaining here. My poor boy has been basely betrayed, and—"

" Your son was a daring rascal—an impudent rascal," said Mr. Snoggins.

" Such an opinion from a man like you is a compliment," said Mr. Walton, looking at the magistrate with pity and disdain.

" Did he not refuse to take his hat off to me when he met me in the village ?" said Mr. Snoggins; " yes, absolutely refused to bow to me, one of his majesty's justices of the peace."

Here the parish beadle and Mr. Noddy absolutely groaned with horror."

" He was a dangerous character; a terrible character," added Mr. Snoggins; " such a fellow as he is, might have caused a rebellion in the country. Refuse to take his hat off to me ;—a—a—a justice of the peace! Oh, shocking !"

" Oh, shocking," responded the beadle and Mr. Noddy; and then Mr. Snoggins once more blew his nose fiercely, and again he became more calm.

" Such a fellow as he is better out of the country than in it ;" observed Mr. Snoggins; " and, it's a glorious thing to be at war, since it is the means of ridding us of such vagabonds."

Notwithstanding the contemptuous source from whence it came, it was with the utmost difficulty that Mr. Walton could repress his resentment; but after darting upon the sapient magistrate a look of scorn; he said :—

" Mr. Snoggins, your observations are beneath contempt, and can excite no other feeling in my mind than that of pity for the weakness of humanity. While the power of oppression is placed in the hands of such jackanapes, it is not to be marvelled at, that flagrant acts of injustice are committed with impunity."

Having thus expressed himself, Mr. Walton made his way towards the door, upon which Mr. Snoggins arose ferociously in his chair, and in a voice shrill with passion, he exclaimed :—

" Noddy, Noddy, did you not hear that? And to be insulted in my official capacity with impunity? Is treason to be allowed to be uttered openly, and boldly, without any interference to suppress it? Muggs, Muggs, I say do your duty! Take this man into custody !"

Mr. Muggs swelled himself out to double his usual importance, and advanced desperately towards Mr. Walton, and made an attempt to place his hand upon his shoulder; but Mr. Walton pushed him aside, and then the beadle looked very fierce, and—walked back again, Mr. Walton quitting the house without obstruction, having left Mr. Snoggins, his clerk, and Muggs, completely flabbergasted.

Mr. Walton's state of mind may be readily imagined, and as he walked away from the house, his feelings almost overpowered him. He was at a loss what course to pursue; but to get Henry restored to liberty, he saw was completely hopeless. He dreaded to return home again to make his wife and daughters acquainted with the result of the interview with the magistrate; and he felt for the deep anguish he knew it would cause Patty, most severely. After he had proceeded to some distance, he determined to make his way to the depôt, and endeavour to get an interview with his son, and for that purpose he diverged from the road he had been proceeding, and hastened towards the barracks. Just before his arrival there, he met Sergeant Lance running from the place, and advancing to him, he demanded what he had done with his son.

" Oh, he's right enough ;—snug as possible,"—said Lance; " sworn—all regular ! He'll make a capital soldier after a few week's drilling."

" It is an act of villany that has placed him in the situation he now is," said Mr. Walton, with indignation, "and not his own free will. You know it, sir, and were it not that your numerous misdeeds have made you callous, you ought to be ashamed of the part you have acted in it."

"Come, come, better language, Mr. Walton," said Lance, "recollect who you are speaking to ; I am a soldier, and an officer ; and must not be insulted. I have only done my duty to my king and country, and demme if I wouldn't enlist my own mother, if she was qualified to serve in the army. I wish you good day, Mr. Walton."

"Mr. Lance," ejaculated the farmer, in a voice of agitation ; "if you have any pity for my feelings as a father, pray tell me how I may have an interview with my poor son ?"

"You stand no chance of seeing him, not any," returned the sergeant ;— "it's against the rules ; so you had better make up your mind to it. But bless my soul, Mr. Walton, what have you got to be unhappy about ?— What can be a more glorious life than a soldier's—Plenty of good clothes ; good living ; and sixpence a-day ! It's a gentleman's life, and if your son should happen to survive the engagement he will shortly be in, why he may come back a corporal at least. To be sure he's very passionate, but they'll soon cure him of that. Nothing like the army for moderating the temper. Good day, Mr. Walton ; eyes right ;—shoulder arms ;—quick march !" and the valiant sergeant marched off with much stateliness of demeanour.

Mr. Walton stood for a second or two after he was gone, undetermined in what manner he should act, but at last 'he resolved, notwithstanding he had too much reason to believe that what Serjeant Lance had stated was true, to hasten to the barracks, and endeavour to see his son. In this, however, as may be expected, he did not succeed, and the case being now decidedly hopeless, he turned his steps towards home with a melancholy heart, and not knowing in what manner he should endeavour to offer consolation to those whom he was well aware stood so much in need of it.

We will not attempt to describe the anguish of the unfortunate family, when they heard of the ill-success which Mr. Walton had met with, and Mrs. Walton was fearful from what had taken place between her husband and the sapient Mr. Snoggins, that out of revenge, the latter would adopt some means or the other to persecute and annoy them. This part of the affair, however, Mr. Walton treated with the utmost indifference ; the only sentiment he could feel towards the magistrate, being that of the most superlative contempt.

If there was one person that could feel more poignantly than another, that one was Patty who was completely inconsolable, and deaf to the words of Emily, who in the kindest and most forcible manner, sought to tranquillize her feelings.

"Alas !" she exclaimed, when they were alone, "we shall never meet again ;—exposed to the horrors of war, how little is the chance of his ever returning home again ; or even if he should, in the interval, what may not happen to me ?"

"Do not despair, my dear Patty," remonstrated Emily,—"Henry will stand the same chance as others ; and something seems to assure me that he will not only return safe, but that you will ultimately both be happy."

"Your kindness would flatter me with hopes that, I fear, will prove delusive," said Patty, sighing. "Oh, Henry, how little did I think we should thus be separated. And then, not even allowed to see him ; to have a parting interview with him ; or receive a few lines from him ; oh, this is indeed cruel."

Emily could not deny that ; and not knowing what answer to make, she remained silent.

"The manner in which the whole affair has been conducted," said Patty, after a pause, "convinces me that it was some preconcerted plot of villany; and I cannot help thinking that Captain Bellingham and his profligate friend knew something about it."

"They could never be so villainous, surely;" remarked Emily.

"Oh, I am of opinion that they are capable of almost any act," said Patty; "besides, did not the captain threaten both Henry and his father? and——"

"But then, they have quitted the neighbourhood?" interrupted Emily.

"They have pretended to do so," observed Patty, "but it is more than probable, that it is only a scheme to further their designs. Alas! I fear that we shall yet experience more trouble through them."

Emily could not help coinciding in the opinion of Patty; but she endeavoured to make her believe she thought otherwise, and tried all in her power to soothe her. In this, at last, she partly succeeded, and Patty put her dependence in Omnipotence, whom she trusted would interpose to frustrate the designs of the guilty, and protect her lover from the danger which she apprehended.

Mr. Walton determined to leave no means untried of getting an inquiry instituted as to the treatment of Henry, and by whose orders he had been so basely trepanned; but he met with no success, and in a few days after the circumstance took place, the regiment quitted the neighbourhood without their being able to get an interview with him, or even receiving a letter from him.

This flagrant act of injustice astonished all who heard of it, and it was in vain that Mr. Walton and his distressed family endeavoured to account for it, although it was very evident to them, that some person in power, and who had more than ordinary motives for his conduct, and the malevolent

No. 21

feeling he had displayed towards Henry, had been the principal cause of it all. Nay, the manners of Lance, and the behaviour of Mr. Snoggins, the magistrate, were sufficient to convince them that the plot had been preconcerted, and knowing the intimacy which subsisted between Mr. Snoggins and Sir Merton, Mr. Walton was at last fain to believe that the whole affair was to be attributed to the revengeful feeling of Captain Bellingham, who had held out threats to them to that effect.

"The dastard villain!" exclaimed Mr. Walton, in the warmth of his excited feelings;—"without the courage to become an open foe, he must avail himself of such cowardly means as those he has adopted, and then shelter himself from the chastisement due, under the shield of his rank. But I will seek him, and he shall find an injured father is not afraid to speak his mind, even were it to the king himself. I will find him out."

"But he is not in the neighbourhood;" said Mrs. Walton, "you know that he and Sir Edgecumbe quitted it some days since."

"A mere scheme; a base and crafty stratagem," remarked her husband; "I see through it all, now. But I will see Sir Merton Bellingham."

"Of what avail will that be?" demanded Mrs. Walton, "Sir Merton cannot be accountable for the actions of his nephew."

"But he can make me acquainted where to find the villain," returned Mr. Walton, "and through him, therefore, I will seek redress."

"Redress!" ejaculated Mrs. Walton, shaking her head; "alas! his rank protects him."

"Rank, dame!" exclaimed Mr. Walton, in a tone of impatience, "pshaw! is there not justice for the humble as well as the rich?"

"But he may be the means of working us further harm."

"I defy him."

"So you said before; but yet, if we judge rightly, he has succeeded in gratifying his malevolent feelings."

"The miscreant!" cried Mr. Walton, growing more indignant; "I will not rest until I have discovered him, and obtained satisfaction for this unparalleled outrage. My poor boy, to be thus forced from his home, his friends, his lover."

Patty sighed deeply, and the tears, in spite of her efforts to restrain them, gushed forth in torrents. Emily endeavoured to soothe her, and with the aid of Mr. Walton, and Grace and her sister, at length succeeded.

"Do not despair, dearest Patty," said our heroine, "afflicting as this circumstance is, it may at last turn out for the best. Providence will watch over and protect him, and he will escape the dangers of the battle field, and return once more to his native land, with honour and promotion."

The observations of Emily appeared to revive the spirits of the whole of the party, and Mr. Walton, although his ideas were anything but so sanguine as those our heroine expressed, encouraged them, and changed the tenor of his conversation from an expression of his resentment to giving utterance to hope.

"After all," he observed, "as Miss Emily had suggested, "it may turn out for the best, and the poor lad may get on in the world. I do not object to his being a soldier, for there are no individuals that I esteem more than I do the brave defenders of our land; but what I principally complain of is the clandestine manner in which he is smuggled into the service, and the cruel and arbitrary manner in which he has been forced away, without being allowed so much as a parting interview with those so dear to him."

"Ah! it was indeed a sad cruel job;" sighed Mrs. Walton.

"Well, well, cheer you, my dear mother," said the sweet Grace, assuming an expression of hope, which she was far from actually experiencing; "the clouds that at present obscure the horizon of our peace, may soon disperse, and we shall again be happy. Something seems to whisper me that Henry will survive the perils of the ensanguine field of strife, and will return with promotion, and make us all happy. Only think now, suppose it was to be that he was made a sergeant of, how grand it would sound. Serjeant Walton!—Oh, dear! the very idea sets my heart beating with a feeling of joy which I cannot resist. And then the fine tall and commanding figure of my dear brother, will look so handsome in regimentals, all lace and finery! Come, come, you must not despair, Henry will return safe; I am sure he will, and we shall all be happy again."

Smiles of such sweetness and hope, animated the beautiful countenance of Grace, as she thus expressed herself, that they were quite irresistible, and her father encouraged her by a smile of approbation, and coinciding with the opinion she had given utterance to, and being farther aided by the arguments and persuasive powers of Emily and Ellinor, Mrs. Walton and Patty became more composed, and they at length separated, our heroine and Patty retiring to the little room in which they usually sat together, and the windows of which commanded an extensive view of the surrounding country, verdant fields, pastures, and fertile vallies. Here they seated themselves, and our heroine endeavoured to chase away the deep grief which the melancholy and unexpected circumstance which had taken place, had naturally created in her bosom. But the shock which it had given to Patty's feelings, was too severe to be easily overcome, and although she endeavoured to encourage the hopes which the friendship and sympathy of Emily suggested, it was very evident that her bosom was overcharged with the most poignant anguish. Emily, however, pursued her efforts with the most unremitting determination, and Patty, who warmly felt the kindness of her attempts, endeavoured to calm her feelings.

While they were still engaged in conversation, Patty was suddenly startled by hearing our heroine utter an exclamation of terror, and, looking at her, she perceived that her countenance was very pale, and that her eyes seemed to be fixed upon some object which had drawn her attention from the window.

"Dear Emily," ejaculated Patty, "what is it that has alarmed you?"

"It is gone now;" gasped forth our heroine;—"but not a minute since it was there."

"What!—of what are you speaking?" demanded Patty, her eyes following the direction in which Emily was looking, but without being able to discover anything to create any alarm.

"Oh, Patty," exclaimed our heroine;—"not a minute since, I am almost certain I beheld the villain Chesterton, standing in the middle of the lawn yonder, and gazing direct towards this house."

"Chesterton!" said Patty, in a voice of excessive terror. "Oh, Emily, surely you must have been mistaken. It would be impossible for you to recognise him at such a distance."

"Oh, no, no;" returned Emily; "I feel almost certain that I was not deceived. I could not mistake the person of that man, which is too indelibly stamped upon my memory. The figure;—the height, the dress, and general deportment were the same. He stood in the centre of the lawn, as I have before said, but, suddenly, something seemed to startle him, and away he rushed down the declivity, into the valley beneath, and was in an instant hidden from my sight. Ah! see! there he is again!—Convince yourself, Patty!—Oh, God! it surely is the wretch we have both so much reason to fear;—look—look!"

With an emotion which we need not attempt to describe, Patty did gaze in the direction to which Emily pointed, and started with the most indescribable alarm when she beheld a man ascending from the valley on to the lawn, who, as our heroine had said, exactly resembled the villain Chesterton, in stature, form, and dress, but whose features she could not distinguish, he being at too great a distance. He came quickly up the hill, looking behind him two or three times, as if he was fearful of some one watching him, and having reached the same spot wherein Emily had seen him, he stopped, and having folded his arms across his chest, seemed to fix his eyes earnestly upon the farm house.

"There, Patty, there !" cried Emily, " do you not see him ?"

" I do," answered Patty, in a tremulous voice, and endeavouring, but in vain, to recognise the features of the man.—" I wish he would approach nearer, for although his person resembles the man of whom we are in dread, it is impossible for us to satisfy our suspicions by distinguishing his features at the distance he stands."

" It must be—it is him !" cried our heroine, in accents of the greatest alarm ; " it is impossible to mistake that fearful man ; and look, now he advances nearer. Oh, Patty, can there be any further doubt of his being the individual we apprehend ?"

As Emily spoke, the man approached several yards further towards the farm, and seemed as if he was half determined to come to the house altogether, and our heroine and her companion drew in their heads, fearful that he might observe them, although there was no possibility of his doing so, at the distance he was off, and the situation in which they were placed, the casement being nearly covered by a grape-vine, which spread itself entirely over the back of the house. They had, however, an opportunity of seeing him distinctly, and no doubt could any longer remain on their minds but that it was Chesterton.

" We are lost ! we are lost !" ejaculated Emily, " our retreat has been discovered, and what authority has Mr. Walton got for detaining us in his power ?"

" And to wrest us from Mr. Walton's protection, he must be guilty of a daring violation of the law ;" said Patty, who considering the care which she had already upon her mind, exhibited by far greater firmness than could possibly have been anticipated :—" Come, come, Emily, do not give way to fear, should Chesterton make any attempt to demand us, I will immediately apply to the justices for their protection. which they must give us."

" But should your father accompany this man," observed Emily, " he, at any rate, can insist upon your being delivered up to his custody."

" He will never do so," returned Patty ; " his conduct towards me has estranged every feeling towards him from my heart, and sooner than I would again be placed in his power, I would divulge all that I know, and ——"

" What !" interrupted our heroine, " reveal that which probably might place your father upon the scaffold ?"

" My father !" reiterated Patty, with a shudder ; " oh, no, no, he is not my parent ; my heart does not acknowledge the consanguinity. I repeat, should Chesterton, for he it certainly is, have the effrontery to demand us of Mr. Walton, I will throw myself upon the protection of the justices, and you, of course, will follow my example, Emily ?"

" Certainly," replied our heroine. " But alas ! I fear that we are destined to undergo a fresh series of troubles. You know full well, Patty, the desperate character of Chesterton and Gerald Darnley ;—I will not call him your father ; the title is foreign to my feelings and opinion ; and if they have discovered our retreat, which from the appearance of this man, there is no doubt they have, they will be sure not to leave any means untried to get us in their power. If they do not openly endeavour to gain possession of us, they will be certain to devise some stratagem or the other to get us in their hands, and accomplish the designs they have against us."

" But, as I before said," returned Patty, " the justices are bound to protect us."

" Justice," said our heroine, shaking her head, " is too often a mockery; and if we have no more impartial magistrates than Mr. Snoggins, according to the portrait which Mr. Walton has given of him, and which doubtless is a correct one, we have very little indeed to expect from them. Alas! I see fully the danger to which we are now exposed, and cannot form any idea of the manner in which we can extricate ourselves from it."

" It certainly is Chesterton," said Patty, apparently taking no observation of the remarks of our heroine; " I can plainly see the scar upon his forehead."

" And the same saturnine expression of countenance," rejoined our heroine, " which, once seen, can never be forgotten."

" We had better summon the attendance of Mr. Walton," said Patty, " so that he may see the individual of whom we are in dread, and be prepared to meet and answer him, should he make any application to get us in his power. Oh, Henry, dear Henry! now do I more than ever feel the want of thy protecting arm. But see—he moves : he is going back again. Quick—let us not miss the opportunity of Mr. Walton beholding him, for much may depend upon that simple circumstance."

Emily immediately rung the bell, and having summoned Mr. Walton directly, he was just in time to observe Chesterton before he descended again into the valley, and was lost to sight; and the glance he had was quite sufficient for him to be enabled to recognise him again under any circumstances.

" But are you certain this is the man whose evil designs you have so much reason to apprehend?" interrogated Mr. Walton.

" Oh, yes, we are quite sure of it," answered both Emily and Patty, simultaneously.

" Enough," said the former; " you have but to be cautious yourselves, in not rambling too far from the farm, and you may take my word for it that he shall not wrest you from my protection."

" Oh, sir," said Emily, " what a debt of gratitude we already owe you for the unexampled kindness you have shown us, and the many troubles we have been the cause of bringing upon you."

" Name it not," said the farmer; " Walton will always consider himself a happy man while he can be made the humble instrument in the hands of Omnipotence of protecting his fellow-creatures from injustice and persecution. But, after all, there may not be so much cause for alarm as you imagine. Accident only may have brought this Chesterton to the neighbourhood, and——"

" Oh, no, no," interrupted our heroine, " depend upon it he has gained a clue to our retreat, and that Gerald Darnley is not far off. I wonder that Mrs. Seagrove has not been here to-day. It is most likely that they have called at her house in the first instance, and probably she has been subjected to some coarse treatment."

" If they have been there," returned Mr. Walton, " it is all the better; for, not finding you there, they would most likely imagine that whatever information they may have obtained was wrong, and that you are not in this neighbourhood. At any rate, I cannot see how they could have any suspicion of your being here, as we are generally supposeu to be strangers to you."

" Oh, sir," said Emily, " had you any idea of their craftiness, you would not so readily come to that conclusion, Besides, by making any enquiry in the neighbourhood, they would soon be able to learn the place in which we are."

" And the appearance of the steward, and his so intently watching the house, shows that he must suspect, if he does not know for a certainty, where we are," observed Patty. " We are not safe in remaining here longer."

" But whither would you go? Where can you be more secure?" asked Mr. Walton.

" I know not," replied Patty, "unless we seek the protection of the magistrates."

" And then what power have they to withhold you from your father?" said Walton.

" Me they probably have not," replied Patty; " but what authority have they for their behaviour towards Emily ?"

" That of the nobleman under whose instructions it appears this Chesterton acts."

" Ah !" exclaimed Patty, " dare they plead that authority? Let them do so, and the dark secrets of many years would be revealed, the innocent righted, and the guilty parties brought to punishment. Ah, by Heaven I think to claim the protection of the law would be the readiest means of unravelling the mystery in which the history of myself and this poor girl is involved."

" But by doing so you might bring your own father and brother to the scaffold," remarked Mr. Walton. " Surely your gentle nature will not permit you to do that?"

Patty shuddered.

" My heart revolts at the idea of that cruel man being the author of my existence," she said ; " and yet my uncertainty upon that point alone prevents me from following that plan which justice seems to demand."

" And have you never heard the name of the nobleman to whom this Chesterton is steward?" enquired Mr. Walton.

" Never," answered Patty.

" Oh, name him not," cried our heroine; " whoever he is, (and certainly he must be closely connected with me, or he would not take so much trouble in my fate,) he must be a monster of the blackest dye, for by him was I doomed to death."

" Death !" repeated Mr. Walton, with a look of the utmost horror and astonishment.

" Ay, death," replied our heroine. " Gerald Darnley, the supposed father of Patty, was engaged many years since, it appears, to commit the hellish deed, but his courage failed him ; since then, it seems, he was employed by the same nobleman to perpetrate the hideous crime, for which purpose I was taken by the steward to the Old Lone House ; but the passion which the latter imbibed for me was the means of preventing it, although my secret enemy, it appears, imagines that I am no more."

" Is it possible," exclaimed Mr. Walton, " is it possible that there can be such monsters in existence? But how did you become acquainted with this, Emily ?"

Our heroine had never entered into a particular detail of the different conversations which she had heard between Gerald Darnley and Chesterton, to Mr. Walton, but she now did so, and the reader may easily conceive the horror with which he listened to them, and the emotion which poor Patty evinced at the recapitulation of the atrocities of the miscreant who claimed to be the author of her being.

" This at once," remarked Mr. Walton, " would be sufficient to demand a thorough investigation into the whole affair, and to unravel the dreadful mystery. Should Chesterton make any attempt to take you from beneath this roof, I would at once tax him with the same, and make known the circumstance to the proper authorities."

"Oh, no, that must not be," said Emily, "unless it should be discovered that Gerald Darnley is not really the father of Patty; sooner would I suffer anything than bring upon her that disgrace which the ignominious exposure of the crimes of her parent would be certain to entail upon her. Still I do not despair; I cannot help thinking that time will unravel everything, and bringing retribution upon the heads of the guilty, restore the innocent to those rights and that peace of mind of which they have been deprived. But Mrs. Seagrove, I am quite uneasy until I see or hear from her."

"I will immediately make it my business to call upon her," said Mr. Walton, "and if she has not seen anything of this man, Chesterton, I shall conclude that you have either been mistaken, or that accident alone may have brought him to the neighbourhood, without his having any idea of your living in it, in which case you have but to keep yourselves confined for awhile to the farm, and you will be perfectly safe, for he will find himself most egregiously deceived if he thinks to force you from my protection, unless he does it by stratagem."

"Oh, sir," exclaimed Patty, "what care, what trouble, what anxiety have we been the occasion of to you. Had it not been for us, poor Henry would not have been torn away from you, perhaps to meet with an untimely death in a foreign land, and—"

Mr. Walton interrupted her.

"It has been the will of the Almighty," said he, "and you have no cause to blame yourself. We must not murmur at the dispensations of Heaven. For you, Patty, I feel more than for myself; for should Henry fall upon the field of battle, all your young hopes will be blighted, and that become sear which should be fresh and blooming. But evening rapidly approaches, and I had better away to Mrs. Seagrove's without any more delay."

With these words, and not waiting to hear any further observations from Emily or Patty, Mr. Walton waved his hand to them, and quitted the room, and shortly afterwards the house, making his way to the residence of Mrs. Seagrave, wishing, if possible, to ascertain whether or not Mr. Chesterton had been to her.

When he had gone, our heroine and Patty entered into another conversation upon the subject, and their uneasiness became greater, as the certainty of its having been Chesterton they had seen more strongly impressed itself upon their minds. Already had their bosoms been sufficiently racked by the melancholy circumstance which we have been relating, and which had thrown the amiable family of Mr. Walton into a state of such distress; but this additional cause for anxiety and fear was almost more than they had strength to endure. They started at every sound they heard in the house, and waited with the utmost impatience the return of Mr. Walton from Mrs Seagrove's, anxious to know whether Chesterton had been there, and if he had, what had been the result of his visit.

Night at length sat in, and myriads of stars twinkled in the heavens, and the occasional bark of the faithful watch dog attached to the farm was the only sound which broke upon the stillness around. Our heroine and Patty left the room in which they had been so long sitting, and joined Mrs. Walton and her two lovely daughters below. They had already been informed by the farmer of that which we have been relating, and expressed a fervent wish that they might be mistaken, and that it was not Chesterton whom

they had seen at all; but that hope, although uttered with the best of feeling, had no effect upon Emily and Patty, they being too firmly convinced
within their own minds that it was the steward whom they had beheld
watching the house, and naturally judging from that, that he had came to
the knowledge of where they were, and would not miss an opportunity, by
some stratagem or the other, to get them in his power.

"So long is the time that has elaped since our escape from the old Lone
House without our being discovered," observed our heroine, "that I had
hoped we had eluded their vigilance; but this circumstance convinces me
that I was deceived. Alas! we might have been certain that our inveterate
enemies would not have rested until they had found us out."

"But knowing that you are acquainted with their misdeeds," said Mrs.
Walton, "it appears to me that they will be fearful to demand you; besides, this steward must show what right of jurisdiction he has over Emily,
also by whose authority he acts, and that might, and would, unquestion-
ably be the means of bringing to light certain facts which it would be dangerous for them to elucidate."

"That they would openly demand us, I do not think," said our heroine,
"but that they will devise some means to get us surreptitiously in their
power I have no doubt."

"And were they to do so, it would only place them in the same awkward dilemma," returned Mrs. Walton; "for we should be well convinced
who were the authors of the outrage, and take immediate steps to bring
them to justice, and thus would the whole of their crimes be brought to
light."

"So well contrived do all their plans appear to be," said Emily, "that I
fear they would manage to evade detection."

"Could we but find another retreat in a distant part of the country,"
said Patty, "we might baffle them; but alas! we know no one; and to go
amongst strangers would be almost as bad as enduring the cruelties to
which we know we should be subjected in their power."

"No," said Mrs. Walton, "here you must remain, and trust to fate;
and by using every necessary precaution, you may be enabled to frustrate
their designs. It is truly a painful situation for Patty, who cannot seek
redress and protection from the law, for herself and you, without bringing
her father and brother to punishment. Still I cannot, I will not believe
that these men of crime are related to her."

"Nature revolts at the idea," said Emily; "but oh, that we could ascertain the truth."

"Would to Heaven you could," said Mrs. Walton; "but the painful
mystery will not last for ever. Rest assured that something will ere long,
happen to unravel everything, and to gain retribution for the innocent."

They now endeavoured to change the subject of conversation, and to become more cheerful; but the effort was an ineffectual one; the trouble and
anxiety upon each one's mind was too great to admit of any alleviation.
That one, whose presence used to impart pleasure to every one around, was
gone, torn from them, and the idea of the intense agony poor Henry was
doubtless suffering, was sufficient, independent of every other care, to make
them truly miserable.

At length, Mr. Walton returned, and to the eager inquiries of them all,
informed them that Mrs. Seagrove had not seen or heard anything of
Chesterton or Gerald Darnley, until he mentioned the circumstance which
had so much alarmed them, and that her astonishment and alarm fully
equalled their own. He added, that, after all, he thought Emily and Patty
must have been mistaken, and however much the man they had seen might
have resembled Chesterton, that it was not really him.

Our heroine and Patty shook their heads, and expressed their firm conviction that it was the villainous steward, and that he was only waiting for an opportunity to seize them by stratagem. Mr. Walton endeavoured to assure them that while they remained under his protection they had nothing to fear, and he promised to take such precautionary measures that would be certain to render abortive any evil designs which their enemies might have in contemplation.

They did not separate for the night until a late hour, and previous to retiring to his chamber, Mr. Walton, accompanied by one of his male servants, went all over his premises to see that no one was lurking about, and that all was secure, and after laying strict injunctions upon those of his domestics who slept at the farm, to be watchful and wary, and to give immediate alarm if they saw or heard anything to create their suspicions, he hastened to his chamber.

The night passed away without the occurrence of any circumstance to create their alarm; all remained quiet, but Emily and Patty were too busily occupied with their own painful thoughts and apprehensions to suffer them to obtain much rest. They would fain have persuaded each other that their own disordered imaginations had deceived them, but the certainty of its having been the steward they had seen, was impressed too powerfully upon their minds to be easily removed.

"Alas!" said Patty, "how easily might you gain protection, and likewise an explanation concerning the dark mystery which hangs over your fate, were it not that a delicate feeling towards me, thinking as you do, that those who call themselves my father and brother, are deeply implicated in the guilty transactions. Would to Heaven that something would occur to prove that I am not related to them; what a relief would it be to my

No. 22

mind. I care not how humble, though honest my parents might be proved to be, so that it could be clearly shewn I am not related to those fearful men."

"Sincerely, my dear Patty," said our heroine, "do I respond to your wish; and nothing shall persuade me but that Gerald Darnley is not your real parent, neither that he is in any way related to you. The account Mrs. Seagrove has given of her supposed brother, tends to strengthen that belief, and the manner in which you were consigned to her care by him. There is one dreadful circumstance which I have frequently thought upon; and the occurrences, as related by your aunt, would almost induce one to believe that Gerald Darnley is in some way connected with it."

"I know to what terrible circumstance you allude, Emily," said Patty, "for it is one upon which my thoughts have often dwelt. The murder at the White Cottage, and the disappearance of the assassin, Luke Stanton, as he called himself, and the two children. Heaven forgive me if I wrong him by the supposition, for well am I aware that he has got too many heavy crimes to answer for already, but I have often thought that 'Luke Stanton, the assassin of the White Cottage, and the man whom I have been taught to look upon in the character of a father, are one and the same individual. The description of the man and Gerald Darnley, so well corresponding, and other things which I have heard my aunt mention, all serve to strengthen that opinion."

"It does not, indeed, appear at all improbable," observed our heroine; "and if it is indeed so, what a heavy catalogue of hideous crimes has this wretched man to answer for."

"My heart sickens with horror when I think of him," cried Patty. "Oh, Emily, how I shudder when I think of that Old Lone House; the skeleton of the murdered man, and the melancholy diary of his sufferings, revealed by the manuscripts now in your possession; and the several conversations you have related to me as having heard between Chesterton, Gerald, and his son. The poor murdered old man, whose hoarded riches you saw them counting and exulting over; oh, such events are too horrible to dwell upon."

"They are," returned Emily, "but is it not strange that no suspicion as to the real character of Gerald and his son should have been created?"

"It is, indeed," answered Patty, "but, inured to vice of every description, they were at no loss, you may be certain, to devise every plausible stratagem for their security. As I have before told you, they could play the hypocrite so well, that those into whose company they go are quite taken with their conversation, and believe them to be respectable men."

"But what profession do they imagine they belong to?" asked Emily.

"I know not," replied Patty, "but have no doubt they suppose them to be in the possession of an independence."

After breakfast they were visited by Mrs. Seagrove, who seconded warmly the opinion of Mr. Walton, namely, that our heroine and her companion had been mistaken in the person they had taken for Mr. Chesterton, and, although she strictly enjoined them to use caution, she endeavoured to divest their minds of any unnecessary alarm, and to persuade them to consider themselves safe from any outrage, while under the roof of Mr. Walton, for there was the law to protect them, and she did not believe that either the steward or Gerald Darnley would feel inclined to run the risk of getting within its fangs, and their conduct undergoing an investigation.

Emily and her friend could not subscribe to the whole of Mrs. Seagrove's opinion, although they did to the latter part of it, and after some further conversation upon the subject, it dropped, and their minds were fully employed in dwelling upon the circumstance which had been the cause of depriving them of Henry Walton ; and Mrs. Seagrove could not sufficiently deprecate the act, and was of the same opinion as Mr. Walton, that it had its origin in the revengeful feelings of Captain Bellingham.

" If there is a possibility of obtaining redress," observed Mr. Walton, " I am determined to have it. I shall not rest until I am satisfied on this point, and until I have ascertained for a certainty, whether or not the captain and his foppish friend are still in the neighbourhood, or were so, at the time. This very morning, it is my intention to go to Bellingham Abbey, and seek an interview with Sir Merton, inform him of the whole particulars of the manner in which his graceless nephew behaved to those under my protection in my own house, and the events that have since followed. Should he feel disposed to stand my friend, it might not yet be too late to get Henry released."

" Oh, think you so, dear sir?" eagerly ejaculated Patty, her eyes sparkling with sudden hope ; " do not then, I beg of you, delay any time in seeking an interview with Sir Merton at the abbey, and surely the eloquence of a father interceding for a son, who has been so cruelly and unjustly forced away from him, must have the desired effect."

" Alas, Patty," observed Mrs. Walton, " if you knew the real character of Sir Merton Bellingham, you would not say so, and it is useless to elate you with hopes that are not at all likely to be realized. Sir Merton Bellingham is haughty, callous, and austere ; and the last individual in the world who is likely to sympathise with the distresses of others, especially those who are in a more humble situation of life than himself. Besides, it is not likely that he will be disposed to listen to any complaints against his nephew, to whom he is greatly attached."

" By Heaven !" exclaimed Mr. Walton, warmly, " whether or not he is disposed to listen, he shall, for I will be heard ; and, notwithstanding his rank, if I hear anything which is calculated to strengthen my suspicions regarding his nephew, I will not be satisfied until I have learnt where I can find him, so that I may demand from him an explanation of his conduct, and redress for the misery which has been brought upon us."

" Well," remarked his wlfe, " I know it is useless to dissuade you from what you have fixed your mind upon ; but I only hope that you may not exasperate Sir Merton, who would prove too powerful an enemy to contend with."

" Leave everything to me, dame ;" returned Mr. Walton, " and depend upon it, if I do not obtain any satisfactory answer, it will not be attended with any bad results. I will hasten to the abbey without any further delay."

Mr. Walton accordingly put on his hat, and taking his stick in his hand, quitted the farm, and beat his footsteps towards Bellingham Abbey. The sound of the drum and the fife vibrated in his ears, before he had proceeded many yards, and when he reached the village, he found the consummate scoundrel Lance, beating up for recruits, and haranguing a number of gaping clowns who had gathered around him, on the glories of a military life ;—the splendour of a red jacket, and the blessings of sixpence per day. When Mr. Walton saw him, and recalled to his memory the villainous trick which he had served him, he could with difficulty repress his indignation ; but thinking it useless to get into any squabble with the fellows, he was about to take another direction in order to avoid him, when Lance saw him, and by a sign with his hand, having commanded the drummers and fifers to stop, with the most inconceivable impudence, he walked up to him, and extending his hand, said :—

" Ah, farmer ; on marching orders, as my late gallant father of the South

Warwick Militia used to say.   Glad to see you—fine morning.   See.
I'm on business, as usual—enlisted thirteen of em this morning! That's
something like doing the job, eh? Your son was a little qualmish, soon
get over that, he will make a capital soldier.   If he lives, I shouldn't wonder if he don't come back a corporal, at least.   There's glory, as my
late gallant father of the South Warwick Militia used to say."

"Were you not a wretch too contemptible for notice," said Mr. Walton,
fixing upon the sergeant a look of resentment, which even abashed him,
"I would inflict upon you such a chastisement, as would immediately put
your valour to the test.   You are a scoundrel of the blackest dye, and
many a man who has died by the hands of the public executioner, did not
deserve such a fate half so much as you do."

Sergeant Lance was completely astounded ; and the fifers and drummers
looked at each other, and then at Mr. Walton, in the most stupified amazement, and marvelled at the extraordinary courage the former must possess
to address such language to a recruiting serjeant, and that recruiting sergeant, no other than Sergeant Lance.

"Shade of my late gallant father of the South Warwick Militia, hear
this!" he cried at last; "I, Sergeant Lance, the modern Alexander of the
army, called a wretch beneath contempt, and threatened by a common farmer.   I—I—will be calm, and it is fortunate for you, Mr. Walton, that I
know how to act with forbearance, or——"

"Bah!" interrupted Mr. Walton with a look of the most ineffable contempt, and walking away, he took the direction which led to the abbey,
leaving Sergeant Lance and his companions to recover from the astonishment into which the boldness of the farmer had thrown them.

He soon reached the abbey, and having rung the bell, the porter made
his appearance, and upon Mr. Walton informing him that he requested an
interview with Sir Merton, he was told that Sir Merton could not then be
seen, as he was engaged with a gentleman.   Mr. Walton, however, requested that the footman should take his name up to the baronet, and inform him that his business was urgent, which, after considerable hesitation, he was at length persuaded to do.   Contrary to his expectation,
Sir Merton sent word back by the footman to shew him up stairs immediately.

Mr. Walton was ushered into the elegant apartment in which the haughty
baronet was sitting, but he started back with considerable amazement and
confusion when he beheld Mr. Snoggins seated by Sir Merton's side.   The
justice of the peace attempted to look very dignified and awe-striking, but
he most singularly failed, and Mr. Walton looked upon the poor pitiable
being with the most superlative contempt.   He, however, fully anticipated
the result of his interview with the baronet now, and was quite prepared
for what might take place.

Sir Merton Bellingham was by no means a prepossessing individual; he
was a very stout, red-faced, stern-looking man, and who, priding himself
upon his ancient pedigree, looked upon those in a more humble condition
as little better than serfs.   But Mr. Walton was not to be daunted by the
difference of their station in society from speaking his mind, and that
boldly, although, at the same time, not forgetting the respect due to his rank.

Sir Merton looked at the farmer with his usual sternness, and Mr. Justice Snoggins, having exchanged a significant glance with him, the baronet
gave utterance to a very loud ahem, and then in a haughty tone demanded—

"Well, Farmer Walton, what is your business with me?"

"My business is with *you*, Sir Merton, and you alone," answered Mr.
Walton, bowing respectfully, and looking expressively at Mr. Snoggins.

"Would not my steward have answered the same purpose?" demanded the baronet.

"Your steward, Sir Merton, could do nothing in the business I have come upon," said Mr. Walton; "would you allow me a few words in private?"

"I dare say what you have to talk to me about is not of such vast importance that it matters much about Mr. Snoggins hearing it," said Sir Merton; "if you think proper, therefore, I am ready to hear you."

"Oh, I dare say he has come to pester you, Sir Merton," observed Mr. Snoggins, "about that lazy fellow, his son, who, fortunately, has been got rid of in this neighbourhood."

"By a most villainous stratagem, sir," cried the farmer, resentfully, "in which you have taken an active part."

"There, Sir Merton, there, you hear that?" said Mr. Snoggins; "that's the way he abused me in all the dignity of my official chair only a day or two since, and it was only in consequence of my great clemency that I was induced not to commit him. He is one of the most insolent knaves I ever encountered."

"Insolent knave!" cried the farmer, indignantly; but recollecting himself, he added, "I beg leave to apologize to you, Sir Merton, if I have made use of language which you may consider indecorous, but you must allow that I have been provoked to it. I—"

"Well, well, well," interrupted the baronet, impatiently, "I have nothing to do with that, no more than to say that Mr. Snoggins, as one of his majesty's justices of the peace, ought to be treated with the most profound respect, and I have heard that you made use of the most unwarrantable language to him, on a recent occasion, in his own court."

"Oh, it was most awful," ejaculated Mr. Snoggins. "Why, would you believe it, Sir Merton, he absolutely called me infamous; accused me of being guilty of a gross act of injustice, and said that I not only deserved to be dismissed from the office I so unworthily filled, but also severely punished into the bargain."

"I have told you my opinion of your conduct," said Mr. Walton, "and I do not retract a single syllable."

"There, there! you hear that, Sir Merton; you hear how he addresses one of his majesty's justices of the peace, and—"

Mr. Snoggins could not finish the sentence, for his horror and indignation completely overcame him, and he looked at the baronet with an expression of countenance which sufficiently evinced the utter astonishment he felt at the effrontery of that man who could thus dare to address himself to a dignitary of his high and onerous situation.

"Mr. Walton," said Sir Merton, "I cannot allow such language to be made use of in my presence, and addressed to this gentleman. I should advise you to keep to the business upon which you say you have come to me, if not, I must desire you to leave the place."

"I should have mentioned the nature of my business immediately, Sir Merton," returned Mr. Walton, "had I not been interrupted; but I trust you will make some allowance for my feelings, when I inform you of the manner in which I have been served."

"Well, well, well—the business, the business?" impatiently demanded Sir Merton.

Mr. Walton then, as briefly as possible, related all the particulars of what had happened at the farm house, through the behaviour of Captain Bellingham, and Sir Edgecumbe Sappington, and the subsequent seizure of his son, which event he did not hesitate to attribute to the machinations of

Captain Bellingham, in consequence of the threats which he had held out to them.

Sir Merton listened to him with evident impatience, and when he had concluded, he said in a careless manner :—

"And is this all you have come to complain about ?"

" All !" repeated Mr. Walton, in a tone 'of astonishment, "and is it not enough, Sir Merton, that those who are under my protection should first be insulted, grossly insulted in my own house, and then my son basely torn from his family and friends, deprived of the means of purchasing his freedom, and sent clandestinely away, without so much as being permitted a parting interview with us ?"

" Tut ! tut ! tut !" ejaculated Sir Merton, " the country wants soldiers ; we have too many young fellows idling their time away at home, and I think it is a great mercy that there is such a law to rid the place of the lazy and the dissolute."

" To be sure it is, I perfectly agree with you Sir Merton," remarked the sapient Mr. Snoggins, " and as for Henry Walton, he was——"

" My son, although humble, was honourable, honest, and upright," said Mr. Walton, warmly," and I defy any one to bring the slightest blemish against his character."

" Oh, he was a sad young man ;—a sad young man," said Mr. Snoggins, " and it will be well for him if he does not come to some bad end.   What good can you expect a man to come to, who does not even take his hat off when he meets one of his Majesty's justices of the peace, and a lord of the manor, in the village ?   Oh, shocking ! dreadful !"

" Well, sir," said Sir Merton, addressing himself to Mr. Walton, " and what has all that you have been relating to do with me ?"

" I thought, sir," replied Mr. Walton, mildly, " that you would probably see Captain Bellingham upon the subject, and exercise your authority to prevent a recurrence of the outrage of which I have complained ; and moreover, that you might be induced, from feelings of humanity towards myself and distressed wife and family, to exert your influence to get him restored to us, by paying the sum usually demanded."

" I have no such influence," returned the baronet, " neither if I had, should I feel disposed to exert it for any such purpose.   I consider that you ought to think him very well off to have been trepanned, as you have been pleased to designate it, and if my nephew has been the cause of it, which appears to me to be a most unjust accusation, I can only say, that I think he has done both himself and you a very great service.   What do you think, Mr. Snoggins ?"

" Oh, I am decidedly of your opinion, Sir Merton," said the magistrate.

" To complain, too, because two gentlemen thought proper to say a few soft things, and steal a kiss or two, from two young girls, who happen to be living under your roof ; preposterous !"

" Monstrous !" said Mr. Snoggins.

" There could not have been more fuss made about it if it had been an elopement in high life," observed Sir Merton ; " I can do nothing for you, Farmer Walton."

The shame and indignation which the honest farmer felt, while the heartless baronet was thus speaking, choked his utterance, and he could only look the perfect disgust and contempt which he felt.

"After the opinion you have thus expressed, Sir Merton," at length he said, " it would be useless for me to say anything more upon the subject ; but perhaps you will inform me whether your nephew is still living in the neighbourhood, and if not, whither he has gone to, so that I may seek him out ; for from him I am determined to demand an explanation."

"Eh! what?" exclaimed Sir Merton, "seek an explanation from a gentleman, an officer in the army, and the nephew and heir apparent of one of the richest baronets in the country? Unexampled presumption!— Farmer Walton, you had better alter your tone and resolution, which ill become your situation in life, or you may get yourself into a dilemma you will have good reason to repent, probably, when too late. I am surprised at you, Mr. Walton; I am really surprised at you."

"I believe, Sir Merton, I have only acted and spoken as any other honest man and fond father would have done under similar circumstances. But I will not intrude upon your time any longer; Heaven, I trust, will grant me that justice which man may deny me. Good day, Sir Merton."

And with a polite bow, the farmer left the room, and quitted the abbey.

"Despicable wretch!" he ejaculated, as he walked away; "destitute of every feeling which should stamp you man. And this, then, is a specimen of the sympathy which the wealthy feel in the distresses of those to whose industry they are indebted for all they possess. Oppression is their delight, and virtue and female innocence they despise. Could the haughty baronet whose presence I have just quitted, see himself in his real character, how contemptible and hateful would he appear."

He soon reached the farm where he made them acquainted with the result of his interview with Sir Merton Bellingham, at which no one expressed any particular surprise, Mrs. Walton and Mrs. Seagrove having made them fully acquainted with the baronet's character. However, Mr. Walton determined to leave no means untried to find out the captain, and to gain that satisfaction he demanded.

That day passed away, and the next, without anything worthy of notice taking place, and as our heroine and Patty did not see anything further of the man whom they had taken to be Chesterton, they became more composed. A week passed away in the same manner, and at the end of that time they were delighted at receiving two letters, one addressed to Mr. Walton and his family, and the other to Patty, in the hand-writing of Henry. With a feeling of delight and anxiety which may be easily conceived, Mr. Walton broke the seal and read the contents aloud. Henry had embarked with the rest of the regiment into which he had been enlisted, the day before writing the letters at Portsmouth. From the tone of the letter he appeared to have become reconciled to the painful event which had taken him from them; and it expressed the most sanguine hopes that he should survive the perils of the contest in which he was about to be engaged, and that they should again meet in happiness.

Henry's letter to Patty was a most affectionate one, and as she read it, her tears flowed fast and she breathed the most fervent prayers for his safety and happiness. Happiness, however, while separated from her and his family, and without being able to to receive any intelligence concerning them, she felt convinced he could not experience, however much he might endeavour to conquer his feelings, and when the poor girl thought of the fearful dangers to which he would be exposed, despair of ever again beholding him almost settled upon her heart, and it was with the greatest difficulty that Emily and the others could succeed in imparting the least consolation to her.

The letters which had been received from Henry, were a source of great relief to the mind of Mr. Walton and his family, and they sought to yield without complaining, to the will of Heaven, seeing that they were unable to alter his situation, but must leave it to time and Providence to bring about that which they so much desired, and upon which their future happiness depended.

Week after week elapsed, and nothing having occurred to disturb them,

Chesterton was almost forgotten, and our heroine and Patty began to think, with others, that they had been deceived. The two young girls resumed their usual walks around the farm, without entertaining any apprehension of interruption or obstruction.

It was Patty's chief pleasure to stroll accompanied by Emily to those haunts which her and Henry had been accustomed to frequent, and every object she gazed upon brought him more forcibly to her memory, recalled every word that they had uttered, and in imagination she again held converse with him, and listened to his earnest vows of unalterable affection.

One afternoon when the two females had been thus engaged, they had been so deeply immersed in a conversation upon past days that they remained later than was their usual custom, and the night air which began to blow chilly, first aroused them, and they turned their steps towards home.

They had not proceeded many yards, when they heard a rustling sound in the bushes behind them, and before they had time to look round to see from what cause it proceeded, they found themselves seized forcibly and by the light of the moon, to their terror and dismay, they beheld they were in the power of Captain Bellingham, and Sir Edgecumbe Sappington.

Patty immediately fainted, and was borne by Sir Edgecumbe precipitately away in his arms, towards a post-chaise, which was waiting at a short distance from the spot; but our heroine struggling violently, screamed aloud for help; and seemed determined to resist Captain Bellingham with her life.

"Nay," exclaimed the libertine, endeavouring to force her along, "your cries are in vain; I have had trouble enough to get possession of you, and I will resign you now only with my life!"

"Oh, help! help!" again screamed Emily, almost exhausted with the power of her exertions to release herself, but the captain had succeeded in raising her in his arms, and was about to hurry after his friend, when, before he had proceeded any great distance, the report of a pistol was heard, the captain uttering an oath, declared he was wounded, and resigning Emily, fled as fast as he was able from the spot.

Our heroine heard somebody advance towards her, and not doubting but it was her preserver, she looked around, but she shrieked with terror, and immediately became insensible when she beheld the detestable villain, Chesterton standing over her.

"Ah! girl!" cried the wretch, in a tone of exultation, "you are again in my power! By the infernal host this is fortunate! Take her, comrades, and bear her away to the cottage, from whence we will all immediately make our departure for the Old Lone House."

These latter words were addressed to three desperate looking ruffians who accompanied him, and the unfortunate girl was immediately raised in their arms, and borne away with as much expedition as possible in the direction to which Chesterton pointed, and who followed close at their heels, unable to keep his savage delight within the bounds of reason.

CHAPTER XVI.

THE RETURN.—THE OLD LONE HOUSE.

WE left the two miscreants Chesterton and Gerald Darnley in a state of the utmost chagrin, terror, and disappointment, at the unsuccess which had attended their endeavours to find out whither Emily and Patty had fled, and

uttering vows of vengeance if they again fell into their power. The greater part of that night they sat up conversing upon the subject, and endeavouring to form some idea of in what course it would be best for them, in future to direct their search, and as they became more bewildered, so did their rage also increase.

"It is all your fault," observed Gerald, "had you not been so taken with the girl, she would have been despatched long since, and we should then have been perfectly safe."

"Well, well, I own you are right," returned the steward, "but of what use is it to upbraid me for it now; it cannot be helped. And then she is so lovely that——"

"Psha!" impatiently interrupted Gerald, "and are there not plenty more lovely girls in the world beside her? A *very* nice job we have made of it, and I should not be at all surprised to find the officers after us before long."

"But she knows nothing that can effect us materially," said Chesterton, "and as for Patty, it is not likely that she would divulge that which might place those whom she believes to be her father and brother in danger of their lives."

"And how can you know what Emily may not have overheard while she was here?" demanded Darnley;—"did she not discover the secret closet, and the skeleton, and——"

"But cannot we remove the skeleton and bury it?" said Chesterton, "and likewise destroy all the other circumstances which would corroborate the statements she might make. I cannot conceive why they were not removed years ago."

"Not for worlds could I touch again those mouldering bones," said

No. 23

Gerald, " I should imagine the eyes of the murdered man were again glaring upon me from their hollow sockets, and——"

" Psha?" cried the steward, " you were not wont to display these coward fears, Gerald. You evince an anxiety to murder the girl, and yet you express a fear to handle only a few crumbling bones. But we must do it, and the sooner the better: The girl, however, was bound by an oath not to reveal what she had seen in the secret closet."

" And of what avail, think you, is an oath administered by men like us, and, extorted under such circumstances? Reason and justice will absolve her from it, and she will not scruple to break it, depend upon it."

" You did not think so at the time," observed Chesterton, " or else what a mockery it was for you to administer it at all."

" I did not," said Gerald, " but then I did not give myself the trouble to consider it properly or the girl would never have had the opportunity to have escaped in the manner which she has now done."

" It is a cursed unfortunate job, as I before said," observed Chesterton.

" And all owing to you;" returned the other ruffian.

" Or, say rather to your mismanagement," said Chesterton.

" How so?"

" Why did you not confine her in a more secure apartment in the first instance?"

" I thought the one I placed her in safe enough."

" But did I not often tell you that I feared she would some day or the other slip through our fingers? and you only mocked at my fears. Besides, you granted her too much liberty; you should have kept her strictly confined to one room, and not have allowed her the range of half the building; and, above all things, you should not have permitted Patty to be her companion; that was madness."

" Ay, you can talk now, but you did not start all these objections before."

" But, I repeat, I did;" said Chesterton, " did I not on the night when I first determined to gratify my passions, and we found that the girl had escaped from her room? Had you then done as I suggested, my desires would have been gratified, and the girl still have been in our power."

" Had I acted with prudence, the girl would not have lived many hours after she was brought hither," said Gerald.

" And then you would only have got the money his lordship is to give you."

" And have destroyed one of the principal objects of my daily and nightly fears," added Gerald Darnley;—" the being who, ere long, may be the means of bringing us to the scaffold!"

" And why did you not think of this years ago, and have well perfor your task at first?"

" And why, let me ask did Lord——"

" Hush!" interrupted Chesterton.

" Why! there is no one to hear us, now."

" We do not know that, for certain," replied the steward, " and you know very well, we are bound by an oath, never to mention his lordship's name in connexion with this subject, for fear there might be listeners, and——"

" Well, well," observed Gerald Darnley; " I know that;—but, why, I say, did his lordship take any notice of the advertisement after the death of the old woman? The girl would then have remained unknown, and the secret would have been perfectly safe, for I have not the least doubt that old Nance never divulged anything."

" I know not that," said the steward, " for, as we were coming hither, she described to me the dying moments of the old woman, and from what she stated, it appeared that she expressed a wish to reveal some secret before she died, and——"

"But, did she tell the girl anything?" eagerly demanded Gerald.

"I questioned Emily narrowly upon that point," answered Chesterton, "and she replied that ere she could disclose what she wished, death stopped her breath for ever!"

"A fortunate job, or we should not have been here very likely at the present time to talk about it."

"But the girl might not have spoken the truth."

"Oh, there is no doubt but that she did, for had she been made acquainted with the terrible particulars of her history, there is every reason to suppose she would have made them known to those who would have afforded her protection, seen her wrongs redressed, and the heiress of the proud and wealthy estates which his lordship now unjustly holds, reinstated in her rights."

"True;" said Chesterton, " but after all, it was a bad job that the old woman was in the secret."

"It could not be helped!" returned Gerald, "she was necessary to our purpose; and I have often had my suspicions that she ultimately despatched the earl, to put an end to his lingering torments."

"Poor wretch! his sufferings must have been dreadful, indeed;" said the steward, in a hollow tone of voice;—"left to starve, and—"

"Hush! hush!" interrupted Gerald, suddenly grasping the steward's arm, and looking fearfully around the room;—"let us talk about something else;—not that—not that."

"And yet Emily and Patty have both seen the mouldering bones in the secret closet, and must, therefore, feel confident that murder has been committed."

"They have—they have—and should they divulge!"

"Aye, should they," observed Chesterton, "and those damning proofs remaining in the house, the whole of the fearful truth would be discovered. I repeat, that the skeleton must be removed from the closet and interred, and everything else destroyed that might excite suspicion."

"And you had better undertake to do all this pleasant business;" sneered Gerald, "since you have grown so wonderfully courageous. You did not exhibit your boldness on one occasion before, in a particular manner, when you were fearful of being left alone in the room, and when we missed Emily from her apartment."

"Fearful! aye, and was it not enough to try stronger nerves than either yours or mine? We were left in the dark with the mouldering bones of the murdered man, as you wanted to leave me by myself. But, the case is now desperate, and we, together, must remove them, and bury them in the vaults underneath the house. This night it had best be done."

"This night!" repeated Gerald, with a shudder of horror.

"Aye, this night," returned the steward, with a forced courage; "every moment that we delay we are in danger—they must be removed directly."

"Not to-night—not to-night," fearfully observed Gerald; "wait till daylight, and then,—"

"Bah!" cried Chesterton, "you are the most inconsistent fellow I have ever known;—one moment you have the courage of a lion, and ready to commit any terrible deed, and the next you exhibit as much weakness as a child, at the bare idea of removing to a place of safety the evidence of your guilt."

"Never, except by accident, have I entered that secret closet, in which Jerden met his fate, since the fatal period," said Gerald, "and call it cowardice, or what you may, Chesterton, I cannot, I will not go there in the solemn darkness of the night."

"Well, I suppose 1 must yield to your whim," said Chesterton; "but let us perform the task the first thing in the morning, and then we shall have less cause to fear."

"It shall be done."

'After which we must again resume our search after the girls," said the steward.

"And, I fear, with but very little chance of success."

"But how can they live? They must have some friends or place of shelter, or they would never have been able to exist, or to remain concealed so long. Know you not of any one with whom Patty is acquainted, and whose protection she may have sought?"

"I know of no one, except Mrs. Seagrove," replied Darnley, "and it is not likely that they would go thither, as they might rest assured that we should discover them with ease."

"But if they should seek the protection of the law?"

"They undoubtedly would do so," answered Gerald, "were we to discover them, and to openly demand them. Our only hope of getting them with any chance of success or safety is by stratagem."

"And, after all, I see nothing but the most dangerous prospects before us," said Chesterton, after a pause; "for, wherever they may be, it is not at all unlikely that they have made the persons who have befriended them, whoever they may be, acquainted with the particulars that have occurred to them, in which case, our real characters would become known, and should we succeed in getting the girls once more within our power, they would probably feel convinced who they were, and making the circumstances known to the proper authorities, not only get them restored to liberty; but also be the means of an inquiry being made into our conduct, which would prove anything but satisfactory to us."

Gerald Darnley traversed the room for a short time in silence, and immersed in deep meditation, and it was very evident that the coward fears of guilt were distracting his brain.

"I see we are not safe a moment scarcely while we remain here," he said at last; "and I am almost resolved to abandon the case altogether, and quit the country, where I shall be unknown, and may live without fear of detection."

"Pshaw! that must not be," said the steward, "that would be at once cowardly, and acting with treachery towards his lordship, for you know—"

"I do not want you to repeat anything," said Gerald, interrupting him, "the agreement we entered into is sufficiently impressed upon my memory. I think I have hitherto been found faithful to his lordship, and it is not at all likely that I shall turn traitor now; but when danger, like that which at present threatens us, stares us in the face, we know not what to say or do."

"True," answered Chesterton, "and we must, therefore, bestir ourselves, and devise some means to get possession of the girls again, and to avert the evil which we apprehend. I would that I knew where that headstrong boy, your son is, for should he have discovered their retreat, he would be sure not to rest until Emily was in his power, and he had put his determination regarding her into execution."

"And the time he has been away from the Old Lone House in search of her," said Gerald, "is of itself almost enough to convince us that he has met with some success in his researches. It is not likely, if Emily fell into his power, that he would bring her here again."

"Certainly not; and to be thwarted in my wishes by that boy—"

"Curses light upon him !" ejaculated Gerald; "I fear that some time or the other he will be the principal means of bringing us all to destruction."

"But he would never be the cause, surely, of bringing his own father to the gallows ?"

"And what affection think you a son brought up like he has been, and innured to every crime, can have for the father who instilled such vices into his mind."

"But we have a greater security against his betraying us," observed Chesterton.

"What is that ?"

"Why, that he himself has been implicated with you in crimes that would place his neck in the halter. The old man who you lately robbed, and who Will killed with his own hand !"

"Silence !" ejaculated Gerald Darnley; "I like not to talk of such deeds, especially at this solemn hour of the night. How dismally the wind howls through the crevices of this old house; a man might almost imagine it was—"

"Pshaw !" again impatiently interrupted Chesterton, "you actually take pains to create imaginary horrors to alarm yourself. We had better separate for to-night; it is getting late, and do not forget the morning. The earlier we perform the business the better, and when there is no one stirring. What time will you arise ?"

"Immediately you hear the old clock up stairs strike the hour of five, you will find me ready," answered Gerald; "would that the task was over."

"Good night," exclaimed Chesterton, taking no notice of the last observation of Gerald, who, having responded to his wish, he took up the lamp which Darnley had placed on the table ready for his use, and made his way to his chamber.

Having locked the door, Chesterton folded his arms across his chest, and for a few moments, traversed the room, while his contracted brows shewed plainly the deep and dark thoughts that were passing in his mind. At length he stopped, and throwing himself into an arm chair, he exclaimed :—

"Yes, it shall be so, should fortune ever place the girl within my power again. Sacrifice her life ! Oh, no; she has charms too great for that, and them would I possess ! And, then, the wealth to which she is entitled ;—ah! could I by any means contrive to make her my wife, I might, with the knowledge I possess, obtain a goodly portion of it, and then farewell to England for ever."

So pleased was the villain with this idea, that he forgot for awhile the danger himself and his atrocious colleagues were placed in, and almost fancied that Emily was already in his power; but he was soon aroused to a full sense of the delusion under which he was beginning to labour, and doubt, fear, and anxiety once more distracted his mind. One of his principal fears was that Will had succeeded in finding the fugitives out, and if that should be the case, all his hopes, and schemes, and anticipations would be foiled, and the most serious results were to be apprehended in several points of view,

Notwithstanding, Chesterton had affected no inconsiderable share of courage, in his recent interview with Gerald Darnley, he was very far from experiencing it, and although he knew the necessity of removing the fearful evidences of guilt that were contained in the secret closet, and the old gothic apartment adjoining; he dreaded the approach of morning, and would have been very glad if the business had been completed. There was something so terrible in gazing upon the ghastly remains of one who had met with so awful a death, that none but those who have been guilty of some frightful crime could imagine or describe it, and when the guilty Chesterton thought upon what he was going to do, and weighed every circumstance of the past in his mind, he was reduced to a state of the most unconquerable terror, and feared to look around the dreary chamber he occupied, lest his eyes should encounter some ghastly object.   He recollected the phantom of Mrs. Fitzormond, which he was convinced he had seen in that house, and which had interposed between him and Emily, at the moment when his sinful passions would have tempted him to commit an outrage upon her, and the words it had uttered ; and he could almost imagine he again heard the sepulchral tones of its voice, and gazed upon its fleshless bones, and unearthly eyes, the sight of which had before filled him with a sensation of horror, from which it was some time before he recovered.   He closed his eyes, and endeavoured to sleep; but in vain; and he lay tossing about in the bed for two or three hours, in the same agonizing state of mind ; now longing for the approach of daylight, yet, at the same time, dreading the arrival of five oclock, when Gerald and himself must set about their fearful task.

At length sleep did come to his temporary relief, if relief it could be called ; for frightful visions flitted before his busy imagination, and fancy conjured up even greater terrors than he had felt in his waking moments. The warm sunbeams streaming across his eyes, awoke him, and, starting up in bed, at that moment the old clock chimed forth the hour of six. Chesterton jumped out of bed in a moment, and before he could finish dressing himself, he heard the voice of Gerald at the door   He immediately let him in.

"We are beyond our time," said he, "but we are quite soon enough.   I have got a spade, and every thing necessary below.   But you look pale this morning ; I guess that you, as well as myself, do not much like the job we are going upon, although you tried to appear so bold over the matter last night."

"It is an unpleasant task," said the steward, "and I do not care how soon it is accomplished.   However, it must be done, and, therefore, the sooner the better.   I am ready."

Gerald Darnley and Chesterton then quitted the chamber, with the same noiseless steps as if they were going to perpetrate some fearful crime, and made their way, without speaking, to the old oak chamber, into which the secret closet opened.   Here Gerald Darnley paused, and his eyes rested on the bed.   A cold tremour appeared to come over him, and his face became pale.

"It was in this room," said he, "that hellish deed, which—"

"Hold your peace!" interrupted his companion ; "nor give way so soon to fear, which will entirely unfit us for the execution of our project.   Idiot that you must have been to have suffered this damning evidence of the deed perpetrated to remain here."

"See, the exact print of the hand of the unfortunate victim," said Gerald, still gazing appalled at the blood-stained bed clothes ; "I could almost fancy it was pointing in judgment against me   Oh, never shall I forget that night !"

"Are you going mad ?" cried Chesterton ; "I wonder if the sight of these things so affects you, that you are not afraid to live in this old house altogether.   Come, come, these sheets removed, and our business in this chamber is at an end."

Gerald, trembling, approached the bed, and averting his face, he made a snatch at the sheet, and as he did so, he imagined he heard a deep sigh issue from the bed. He started back to the further end of the room, with horror depicted in his countenance.

"What's the matter now?" demanded the steward, who had now become more collected; "why do you start, and what are you trembling in that voilent manner for?"

"Did you not hear that?" gasped forth Gerald Darnley.

"Hear what?"

"That pitiful sound!—that dismal sigh!" said Gerald.

"Nonsense!" returned Chesterton, "it was only your own timid imagination; I heard nothing. Come, come, arouse yourself. Here is an empty chest; we shall require it."

As Chesterton spoke, he raised the lid of an old empty chest, which stood in one corner of the room, and taking the blood-stained sheets from the hands of Gerald, threw them into it. He then, with the assistance of the former, removed it from the place where it had long stood towards the secret panel, behind the old clock, where they both paused again, notwithstanding all his efforts to the contrary, this time Chesterton, as well as Gerald, felt a sensation of dread stealing over him, which he found it difficult to conquer.

At length, however, he did, in a great measure, vanquish his fears, and touching the spring, the panel slid back, and a thick cloud of dust issued forth into the chamber, from the aperture. Gerald had involuntarily covered his face with his hands, on the opening of the panel, fearful of encountering the ghastly spectacle which the closet contained, and the dark deeds of many years past, came as vividly upon his recollection as if they had been enacted but the minute before.

Chesterton was the first that recovered himself.

"Come," he said, "assist me with the chest into the closet;—we shall never get done, old Madge will be up presently, and then we should have a third party in the secret as to where the remains of the earl are interred."

Gerald reluctantly took hold of one handle of the chest, which was very large and heavy, and they at once entered the closet. The frightful remains of the murdered man, who seemed to frown upon them from his eyeless sockets, struck an icy chill of horror throughout their veins, and they hesitated, and looked alternately at each other, and at the skeleton, with an expresssion which told the inward workings of their souls; and were for a short time unable to move or speak.

At last Chesterton pointed to the skeleton, and having made a desperate struggle to overcome their feelings, they both removed the chest nearer the skeleton, and the next moment the cold bones rattled in their arms, and were hastily deposited in the chest, and the lid closed down upon them, they hoped for ever.

They both paused to take breath, and to wipe away the drops of perspiration which the excitement of the moment had gathered upon their temples, and then Gerald cast his eyes towards the chair in which the unfortunate victim had formerly sat;—and next to the table, on which the pen and ink drew his particular attention,

"Ah!" he exclaimed, "I recollect once or twice when I visited him, he had a number of papers before him, and was busily engaged in writing; probably his life;—his thoughts. What can have become of these papers? They should be here. Should he have left a manuscript containing the melancholy particulars of his life, and the same have fallen into the hands of Emily, as the pocket-book did, it would probably reveal all, and then they would have us entirely in their power, and our destruction would be inevitable. My conscience seems to whisper to me the certainty of these conjectures."

"But you had been in the closet more than once after the deed, before Emily was brought to this house," said Chesterton, "and had therefore an opportunity of ascertaining whether or not there were any such documents, and to have secured them."

"The idea never occurred to me before now," said Gerald Darnley, "and—but what is this?"

His eye at that moment caught a piece of paper on the floor, under the table, and which had either escaped the notice of Emily, or had fallen from the packet when she took away the manuscripts, He picked it up, and the moment his eyes fell upon it, his countenance and his lips quivered.

"It is his hand-writing!" he exclaimed, "I can swear to it; and my worst surmises are verified; he has left behind him a memoir of himself, of which this is a portion, and which has, no doubt, fallen into the hands of Emily; if so we are lost. Read this, Chesterton."

Gerald placed the paper in his hand, and he hastily glanced over the following words :—

"Yes ;—my doom is sealed—never more from these dreary confines shall I be permitted to depart —— They have doomed me to death !—A dreadful lingering death !—Hunger, oh, then ——"

"This is no proof that there has been any more of the manuscript; "said the steward,—" but we delay time in indulging in vague fears and surmises. The chest !"

Gerald thrust the scrap of paper in his pocket, and with a trembling hand assisted Chesterton to raise the chest which contained the ghastly evidence of the bloody crime which had been perpetrated, and having closed the panel,—they left the room as speedily as the burthen they carried would permit them, and descending the stairs, they reached the parlour below, in which old Madge was not yet stirring. Here Gerald placed his spade across the chest, and lighting a lamp, opened a secret door in the wainscot, which revealed a flight of stone steps, and led to the vaults that extended for a long way under ground, from beneath the building. Through these dreary vaults they traversed, until they came to the last of the range, in which they stopped, and placed the chest on the damp earth.

The pent up air came in such noxious exhalations, that the light was several times nearly extinguished, but, at length it evaporated, and Gerald taking up the spade, commenced digging the grave.

"What a dismal place is this ;" said Chesterton, "and the air is enough to suffocate one ;—quick, quick, Gerald, with your work, or I shall leave you to it."

"Your bravery is again on the wane," sneered Gerald.

"It is many years since these vaults have been entered, I dare say, Gerald," observed Chesterton ; taking no notice of the remarks of Darnley.

"Ay," returned the latter, " it is indeed many years since, and no doubt it will be a great many more ere they will be entered by me."

"Had the body of the murdered man been buried here at first," said Chesterton ; "you would not now have been placed in the danger that you are of its having been seen. I am surprised that such an idea did not occur to you in preference to leaving him to rot in the secret closet."

"Hush! hark !—did you not hear ?" cried Gerald Darnley, suddenly dropping the spade, and clutching hold of the arm of Chesterton, he looked fearfully around him.

"Hear, what ?" demanded the steward ; evincing equal terror, although he endeavoured to conceal it.

"A groan !—it was such a one as the poor wretch who fell lately by the hands of my son, breathed in his dying agony ;"—said Gerald.

"Nonsense ! mere fancy ! mere fancy ! Proceed with your task."

"By hell! it was not fancy!—It proceeded from the chest.—Hark! there again!"

A deep groan was now plaiuly heard to issue from the chest, and the two villains stared at each other with the most appalled looks, whilst cold drops of perspiration bedewed their temples, and they were completely transfixed to the spot, trembling in every limb. Another groan, more dismal than the one before now smote their ears; and conscience-stricken, they rushed from the half dug grave, in their terror and confusion, extinguishing the light, so that they were involved in complete darkness, and were so much alarmed and bewildered that they could not find their way out for some time.

At length they did manage to gain the flight of steps which led to the vaults, and rushing up them as well as their trembling limbs would permit them, they once more entered the parlour, and closed the secret panel. Here they dropped into their seats, and gazed at each other for a few moments aghast, and with faces pale and livid, unable to speak a word, so great was the consternation which conscience had imparted to their guilty souls.

Chesterton was the first that found power to speak, and after having cast a fearful glance towards the secret panel, he said, assuming a voice of as much indifference as he could, but unable to disguise the horror which he still really felt,—

"We are a couple of idiots, to be so easily alarmed;—and have only been deceived."

"Deceived!" repeated Gerald;—"oh, no!—I heard it plain enough, and so did you; only you want to pretend to a great deal more courage and sagacity than you possess. I would not enter those dismal vaults again for all the universe!"

No. 24

"But is the chest to remain unburied?" asked the steward.

"For me it may."

"Then the skeleton might as well have remained in the secret closet."

"How so?"

"Why, is it not just as likely to be discovered where it is?"

"No, there are only two or three persons who know these vaults; myself, my son, his lordship, and yourself, and, therefore, it is not very likely that they will be found out. The mouldering bones will remain as safe there, as if they were buried in the deepest bowels of the earth."

"I fear they will not."

"'Psha! I tell you they will; and I have given you sufficient reasons for my entertaining that belief. At any rate, were I even certain that they would be discovered to-morrow, and myself have to mount the gallows for the crime, I could not again enter the place where they are."

"Madman!"

"I may be so; but if you are so very brave, you are at liberty to go to the vaults yourself and finish the job I have begun."

The steward could make no answer to this, but he walked several times across the room, and seemed to be deeply brooding upon the subject.

"'Tis strange," he partly muttered to himself, "and yet I could have sworn I heard it."

"Heard it!" reiterated Gerald Darnley; "to be sure; three times I heard it;—and it proceeded from the chest which contains the murdered Jerdan's bones. I have the courage to steep my hands in human blood; but I cannot without horror hear ———"

"Silence!" interrupted Chesterton, "why repeat it?"

"Just like that did he groan," continued Gerald, taking no heed of the observations of the steward; "just like that did he groan, when I listened to him, as he lay dying of hunger in the secret closet. I shall never forget him. It was a fearful crime!—It would have been a mercy to have despatched him at once. How terrible must have been his sufferings, and ———"

"Bah!" cried Chesterton; "my patience is exhausted!—Gerald Darnley affecting pity!—We shall next hear of the devil preaching a sermon. Come, come, the noxious air of those foul vaults has taken an effect on you; let us walk forth from the house for awhile; the morning air will revive us both."

Gerald Darnley, evidently glad to escape from the place for a short time, where his guilty conscience conjured up such terrors, assented, and old Madge not having yet arisen, they both quitted the house, and walked on to the heath, intending to return by the time at which they thought their morning repast would be ready.

They proceeded to some distance in silence, when Gerald Darnley was about to make some further observations on the circumstance which had so much alarmed them both, but the steward interrupted him.

"Let us change the subject," he said, "we have said quite enough about it, and have talked of it until we have made ourselves as frightened as a couple of children. It is necessary that we should talk further of the fugitives. What course do you now propose to pursue?"

"I know not," answered Gerald.

"The business must be settled soon, one way or the other," remarked Chesterton; "for his lordship will feel surprised at my long absence, and I must return to him."

"Aye, true, and he will expect you to render him a satisfactory account of the manner in which his instructions have been obeyed, and in what way the girl has been disposed of."

"To be sure he will."

"And of course, whether or not we succeed in discovering her, you will tell him that the girl is no more?"

"I shall. But is it not likely that some time or other his lordship may encounter her, and then all would be discovered?"

"He would not know her."

"Her features are so like those of her mother, that they must ever be indelibly stamped upon his memory."

"I do not fear that, it is many years since he saw her."

"And where was that?"

"Why, you know that he visited old Nance more than once or twice after she had taken up her residence at the White Cottage."

"And very imprudent it was of him to do so."

"Why, for my part, I cannot conceive anything wrong in his doing so," said Gerald; "she was too young at the time to take any notice of him, and it is not likely that she would recollect him, if she was to see him again."

"I know not that," returned Chesterton; "the memory of some children is very retentive, and there is something in the appearance of his lordship which was likely to make an impression upon a mind so susceptible as that which Emily possesses. I am not at all easy upon this subject."

"And what if his lordship were to discover that the girl still lives?"

"Why, his confidence in us both would be at an end at once, and he might seek revenge;" answered Chesterton.

Gerald smiled contemptuously.

"Seek revenge!" he ejaculated; "ha! ha! ha!—he dare not. Would not his own life have to pay the forfeit of his crimes as well as ours?"

"But he has wealth and title, and that is, at times, a security against the retributive hand of justice."

"I tell you he dare not betray us!" repeated Gerald; "nay, more, he would be fearful of even offending us."

"Well, well, I wish it may turn out as you predict," said the steward; "but I must confess that I have still my doubts upon the subject."

"You have no occasion to have any doubts at all;" observed Gerald Darnley; "no discovery will be made that way. All that we have to fear is, that they will divulge the particulars of what they have encountered and overheard in this place to the justices, and then, indeed, our situation would not be one of the safest."

"It would not, indeed," said Chesterton; "but yet, it does not appear reasonable or probable to me, that Patty, believing as she does, that you are her father, would do anything which would be sure to place you in such a perilous and disgraceful situation."

"I have often thought that Patty had some suspicion that I was not her father," said Gerald Darnley.

"But have you ever given her reason to imbibe such a suspicion?" interrogated the steward.

"Of course I have not," said Gerald; "I always, on the contrary, have used the utmost precaution."

"Then it is a mere idle surmise, and unworthy of a serious thought. But we must not lose any more time over this business; as I have before said, this very day we must re-commence our search in different quarters; and I am determined not to give up the pursuit until I have gained some satisfactory intelligence, either as to where they have concealed themselves, or that they are not in a situation to do us harm. Something strikes me that I shall, at last, meet with success."

Gerald Darnley shook his head.

" While Will still remains absent from the house, I have my doubts and fears upon that point ;" said he.

" Ah ! that daring boy will, I am afraid, ultimately be the ruin of us all. Would that he was out of the way, in some place where we might not have any cause to fear him."

" I would he were so too," returned Gerald ; "but I am fearful there is no chance of our obtaining our wish."

A short silence ensued, during which time Gerald Darnley seemed to be pondering over the last question in his mind.

" There is only one way of getting rid of him, should Emily once more fall into our power ;" said he. " The idea has just crossed my mind."

" What is it ?"

" It is this : to consent to his having the girl, on the condition that they both leave the country, and return to it no more ; neither to let any person know whither they are gone. That would prevent all further trouble, and save the shedding of human blood !"

" Will Darnley, the robber's son, allowed possession of the wealthy heiress !—her who hath inspired me with that fierce desire, which I still find it impossible to conquer ;" cried the steward, his eyes rolling wildly, and his whole countenance distorted with rage at the suggestion ; " never !"

" It is the only way we have of ridding ourselves of them both," observed Gerald, " about which you but just now expressed such an anxiety. But I am apprehensive that Will will manage to get possession of the girl, without being bound down to any such conditions."

" That thought is madness !" cried the steward. " We had better return to the house, and immediately after breakfast we will again renew our search."

Gerald Darnley made no answer to this, and they retraced their steps to the Old Lone House in silence.

They opened the door and entered the parlour, but instantly started back in amazement when they beheld Will Darnley, dressed as if he had just returned from a long journey, seated in a chair.

" Ah ! Will returned !" exclaimed the two ruffians in a breath.

Will started from his chair on their entrance, and his countenance expressed the most savage rage and disappointment.

" Yes," he exclaimed fiercely, " it is Will, come back to call you to a bit of a reckoning for the trick you have played him."

" What mean you ?" they demanded.

" What mean I ?" reiterated the young ruffian, " oh, you know full well. Where is the girl ?"

" You know she has fled," answered Chesterton, unable to conceal the satisfaction he felt to think that Will had not succeeded in finding her out, " and we have ever since searched for her in vain."

" Liar !" cried Will, in a voice of the most ungovernable rage. " It is all a scheme of your's and my father's. You have taken the girl to some place of security, and the story of her flight was only got up to get me out of the way and give you an opportunity of better furthering your designs. But I will be avenged."

" Rash fool !" cried his father, " why do you thus accuse us ?"

" Because I know that my accusation is just," returned the young man. " fool that I was to be cajoled to go on such a wild goose chase, while this hoary-headed miscreant has been enjoying the sport at home. But beware ! Will Darnley was never yet tricked without having ample vengeance !"

" Will," observed his father, in a milder tone, and feeling afraid that his son's ungovernable passions would involve them all in some fatal dilemma, " your suspicions are unjust. By hell, we know nothing of what has become of the girl ! Will nothing persuade you ?"

" No," was the answer; " I have been already duped too far ; but the next shall be my turn to triumph."

" What would you do ?" demanded Gerald Darnley.

" Tell me where you have concealed Emily and I will not do anything; but if I find that Chesterton has dared to—"

" Dared !" interrupted the steward, frowning dreadfully.

" Aye, dared," repeated Will, " I will not recall my words ; if I find that you have dared to make any advances towards the girl, I will not be satisfied until I have your life, even if in obtaining my revenge I bring myself and my father to the gallows."

" Will, again I caution you not to be too hasty," said his father, while Chesterton stood by, pale and trembling with mingled rage and apprehension. " We were not in any way privy to the escape of Emily and Patty, and we have in vain endeavoured to trace them to the place of their concealment, or to form any conjecture as to whither they are gone."

" It is false—false as hell," answered Will.

" Why do you waste words upon the boasting idiot ?" cried Chesterton. " Is he to treat us as children, and alarm us with his empty threats. I dare him to do his worst."

" Miles Chesterton," said Will, " provoke me not, or upon this spot will I convince you that I mean what I say, and you will have reason to repent the language you have made use of towards me. You know me well."

" I do," returned the steward, with a look of scorn and detestation ; " I know you to be a dastard knave, and a—"

Before Chesterton could finish the sentence, Will Darnley rushed fiercely upon him, and with one terrific blow with his clenched fist, he felled him to the floor, and then drawing a knife from his bosom, he was about to plunge it in the prostrate steward's heart, when his father darted forward, and presenting a loaded pistol at his head, exclaimed—

" Once more I command you to forbear, or by all the infernal host I swear that I will forget that my blood flows within your veins, and stretch you dead at my feet."

Will scowled frightfully upon Chesterton, and drawing back a few paces, said—

" Think not, father, that I yield to your threats, but I give him his life for the present ; but let him not cross my path, or that instant he dies. Get up, you old scoundrel, and quit the house immediately, or you shall never leave this place alive."

Chesterton gathered himself on to his feet in a dreadful state of rage, and turning to Gerald Darnley, who had interposed between him and his son, he said—

" Gerald Darnley, will you allow this, or—"

" It is like talking to the angry wind to attempt to reason with this rash boy," interrupted Gerald. " Leave the house, Chesterton, and I will meet you anon ; leave the house, or I see there will be bloodshed."

" Then it seems we are to be held at defiance by a beardless stripling," said the steward, gnashing his teeth. " But I warn you, that I will have retribution for this. This is the third time that I have received a blow from your son, and I will have revenge. I go according to your desire, but the time is not far distant when he will bitterly repent having thus assaulted Miles Chesterton."

" The time is not far distant," retorted Will, " when Miles Chesterton shall swing upon a gibbet, in the gaze of an exulting multitude."

"Ah!" exclaimed Gerald, "what would you do, Will?"

"Betray those who have deceived me, unless they endeavour to make me reparation by revealing to me the place where that girl, who I am determined to have, is concealed."

"Ha! ha! ha!" laughed Chesterton, scornfully, as he moved towards the door, "you hear how the fool talks. He forgets that before he can accomplish his threat, he must betray that which would place him in the same situation. I mock, scorn, and dare him to do as he says; Miles Chesterton will live to prove that he is a liar. Remember, Gerald, this evening I shall expect to meet you. You had better be true to your appointment."

As the steward thus spoke, he fixed upon Will Darnley a look of hatred and defiance, and glancing at Gerald significantly, he left the house.

Language cannot do justice to the nature of Chesterton's feelings as he walked across the heath, and ruminated upon what had taken place, and the blow he had received from Will, but those who have any conception of the worst passions of human nature, when excited, may form an idea. He swore a deadly revenge, and was resolved that unless Gerald would agree to assist him, he also should feel the weight of it. He did not consider at the time the great difficulty, if not the utter impossibility, without sacrificing his own life, of putting that threat into execution; he thought of nothing but the blows he had repeatedly received, and the insults and opposition that Will had ever given him, and he determined, let what would be the consequences, not to be satisfied without he had a fearful retaliation. One circumstance, however, amidst his anger afforded him the greatest satisfaction, and that was, the circumstance of Will having been equally as unsuccessful as himself and Gerald, in his search after our heroine, and he could not help encouraging a hope that she would yet fall into his power.

He walked across the heath to the nearest town, and entering a private parlour in the tavern there, he gave free indulgence to the variety of perplexing and conflicting ideas that troubled his mind. The return of Will Darnley, and that which had followed, would prevent him and Gerald from resuming their search after the fugitives that day, and in all probability the next; and that circumstance was of itself quite sufficient to occasion him much vexation, for with every delay his impatience and apprehensions increased. However, it could not be helped, and, therefore, he must endeavour to content his mind as well as he could.

In the meantime, after the departure of Chesterton, Gerald Darnley and his son got to high words, and the rage of both was equal; at one time their wrath having attained such a pitch that they almost got to blows.

"Father," observed Will, "you should know me well; when my determination is fixed upon anything, nothing can move me from it. I will encounter any danger in the accomplishment of it. Thus is it in the present instance. I have fixed my mind on Emily, and you have endeavoured to thwart my wishes in every way, and have at last connived with Miles Chesterton, and borne her and Patty to some place of concealment, thinking by that means to prevent the gratification of my desires, and—"

"It is false! Again, I tell you—nay, am ready to swear——"

"Swear, father," interrupted Will, with a scornful laugh;—"why, talk in that manner to me? We well know the value we both set upon an oath. I tell you again, that you are acquainted with the retreat of Emily, and unless you let me know, even though I should myself fall by so doing, I will instantly reveal to the world the secret on which your life depends, and drag his lordship from his usurped seat of power and wealth, and bring him to disgrace and punishment."

" Boy ! boy !" cried his father, with an expression of the utmost alarm,
"what is it you say ?"

" What I mean ;" answered Will, in as resolute a tone !—"the scoundrel
Chesterton, whom you are abetting, shall never triumph over me !"

Gerald Darnley walked across the room several times, in a state of great
agitation, and knew not how to act or what to say.

" Will," he at length demanded, " are you not my son ?"

" You tell me so," answered Will, coolly, " but I have no great reason
to be proud of the relationship."

" Would you then let your obstinate incredulity urge you to an act that
would bring me to the scaffold !" said Gerald.

" You have heard my determination," answered his son, "the voice of
Nature, as it is called, can have very little effect on me. You have the
means to prevent it, and if you persist in braving the consequences, be your
fate upon your own head."

Gerald Darnley fixed upon his son a look of fearful meaning, and placed
his hand upon his pistol. He was almost tempted to commit that terrible
and unnatural crime, which would at once have ridded him of the object of
his dread. But he recollected himself, and again traversed the room with
disordered steps.

" Curses light upon the girl," he at length exclaimed, " and upon my
weakness, which would not suffer me to despatch her years ago when I had
the power. Will, drive me not to madness !"

" I would bring you to reason, by convincing you of the folly of attempting to oppose my wishes ;" said the young man.

" Did I know where she was, and could once more more get her in my
power, I would no longer be an obstacle to your desires."

" A shallow artifice," returned Will, scornfully, " formed merely to appease my wrath, and to forward your own designs, and those of Chesterton ; but it will not succeed."

" Will nothing convince you that I speak the truth, when I tell you
again, that I know not, neither have I the slightest idea of where either
Emily or Patty have gone to ?"

" No. But, this is only a waste of time ; I will give you to day to make
make up your mind, and if to-morrow morning you still persist in refusing
to do as I desire, I shall know what course to take, and shall no longer
delay putting my threats into execution."

" By all the infernal host !" cried Gerald, unable any longer to control
his rage within anything like bounds ;—but at that moment he heard the
footsteps of old Madge descending the stairs, and lowering his tone, he
added :—

" Reserve this business for another opportunity ;—but reflect maturely
before you go to do that which will bring us all to inevitable destruction."

Will returned no answer to this, but his looks were sufficient to convince
his father that the young ruffian had fully made up his mind, and to assure
him that he must devise some means, and that speedily, of preventing him
from putting his desperate threats into execution.

The breakfast passed over in sullen silence, and as soon as it was concluded, Gerald fixing upon his son a look, which the latter perfecly understood, quitted the house, and hastened to meet Chesterton, knowing the
house at which he was likely to be found.

On his way thither, his mind endured all the terror and rage which the
interview he had had with his son, the desperate obstinacy of the latter, and
the threats he had held out to him, had naturally created in his bosom.
Again and again, he cursed the fate which had given him a son at all, who
was likely to bring him to ruin ; but he never thought, that it was to the

wicked and guilty precepts that he had himself instilled into his son's mind, that he had to attribute everything. Then again, he regretted that Emily had ever been brought to the Old Lone House at all; and cursed what he could not help thinking, the folly of his lordship in returning any answer to the advertisement, when Emily might have remained unknown, and would have been to them no cause of future dread. Some means must be adopted, and that without any delay, to quiet their fears, or he had not the least doubt but that Will would do as he had threatened. It must be done that very night; but what could they do? Will must be removed by some means or the other; but how was that to be accomplished, the wretched and guilty father could not form any idea. From shedding the blood of his own offspring, his soul recoiled with horror, but, yet, in any other way than his death he could not see any chance of their safety. Before he reached the house where he expected to find Chesterton, an idea had occurred to him, and which he was fully resolved to put into execution —that was one which, it will be seen, was the likeliest to afford them present security, without going to the horrible extremity of taking away his son's life, and when he thought of it, Gerald Darnley became more composed.

He found Chesterton pacing a private parlour at the tavern where he had expected to meet him, in a state of the greatest alarm and rage, and on his entrance, the steward's countenance underwent a variety of emotions, and it was very evident that he was burning with the most insupportable resentment.

"So you have come, then?" he said;—"I thought perhaps that daring boy of yours would not let you."

"Not let me?"

"No; it seems he is allowed to do as he pleases, and sets your authority at defiance;" replied the steward.

"We had better not talk here," observed Gerald, "lest we should be overheard. Let us walk forth, and then we can talk this matter over without fear, and I think I have something to propose, which will meet with your approbation."

"Nothing less than the removal of Will can afford me any satisfaction;" answered Chesterton; "and more than that, I must have revenge for the taunts he has so often thrown out against me, and the blows he has repeatedly struck me. Miles Chesterton is not to be insulted;—bullied, and struck with impunity."

"Well, well," said Gerald, impatiently, "we will talk of that anon. Will you attend me?"

Gerald Darnley left the tavern as he spoke, and was quickly followed by Chesterton.

"Now then, Gerald," said the steward, when they had got some distance from the house, and after looking round to be certain they were not observed, and that no one was watching them—"what is it you have to propose?"

"I will tell you; and it is the only plan which, under the circumstances, I think it would be advisable for us to adopt," answered Gerald.

"Had I the disposal of the young ruffian," said Chesterton, biting his lips, "he should not live long to put his threats into execution."

"That must not be," returned Gerald; "I cannot stain my hands with the blood of my own son."

"And yet that son would not mind sacrificing your life to his insatiate resentment," said the steward.

"But I have thought of a plan to render his threats futile."

"Name it."

"The vaults beneath the old house," answered Gerald Darnley.

"Ah! what of them," demanded Chesterton, with a shudder, when he recollected the circumstances that had so recently occurred to them in those dismal places, and in which the bones of the murdered victim of guilt and oppression were deposited.

"From what you have lately seen of them," answered Gerald, "you will feel convinced that they are places of security."

"They are."

"I would then, to prevent the possibility of the danger we apprehend from his headstrong obstinacy and vengeance," observed the villain Darnley, "confine him in one of them, until we have brought him to his senses, and convinced him of his madness in seeking, as he now is, to bring us to destruction."

"His death would be the readiest means of quieting all our fears," said the wretch Chesterton, and the expression of his countenance at the same moment was horrible and disgusting in the extreme; "whilst he lives, after the threats he has held out to us, though he be placed in confinement, I cannot consider that we are safe."

"Chesterton," said Gerald Darnley, and he fixed a look upon the steward which made him tremble, "no more of this, unless you would make me your mortal enemy. Villain—nay, monster I will acknowledge myself to be, but to imbrue my hands in the blood of that being to whom I have given life, I am not capable; my soul trembles with horror at the bare idea."

"Bah! base mockery! hypocrisy, nothing else."

"Call it so, or what you will," returned Gerald; "but such is my feeling, and any attempt to move me from it, makes us mortal foes. Already have I acceded too much to you."

"You are going mad!"

No. 25

"I should be mad were I to do as your blood-thirsty and inhuman propositions would tempt me."

"And yet you do not object to place your son in one of these vaults, where to exist many days, I should consider an utter impossibility," said Chesterton, "what call you that but murder, and lingering murder; assassination of the worst possible description? Answer me that."

Gerald Darnley seemed unable to do as the miscreant Chesterton requested him, and he traversed the spot for a few minutes in a state of the utmost agitation, and, apparently, deeply and painfully cogitating within himself. The steward watched him with much anxiety, and the feelings that were passing in his base mind, may be easily conjectured from the fact of the suggestions that he had made to Gerald. He looked into the countenance of the murderer closely, and noticed the movement of every muscle, in the hope that he would yield to his wishes, and commit the dreadful and unnatural crime which he had endeavoured to persuade him to perpetrate, but he saw nothing which gave him any reason to hold out an hope that he would gain the gratification of his desires, and he bit his lips.

At length Gerald Darnley, who had appeared to have had a strong contest with his feelings, turned towards the guilty steward, and while a look of the most determined description was expressed in his countenance, he observed, at the same time, that Chesterton trembled at his manner, and repented that he had said so much, and almost feared that he had proceeded too far.

"Miles Chesterton, you have hitherto found me too ready a tool—easily persuaded to yield to your wishes, without much consulting my own interests, and it is now time that you and I should understand each other better. Had it not been for my cursed folly in being persuaded by you to pander to your base appetite, the girl would now have been beyond the power to harm us. But the proposition you have just dared to hold out to me has almost tempted me to become your enemy, in which case you might have more to apprehend than you at present conceive. Murder my son!— The bare idea——"

"Psha!" interrupted Chesterton, who, although alarmed by the tone which his companion in crime assumed, was yet determined to put as good a face upon the matter as possible, "what nonsense you are talking. I did not mean to offend you; but after the numerous crimes you have committed, I did not think that you would stick about such a trifle."

"A trifle!" repeated Gerald, with a look of disgust and astonishment; "and call you then the murder of a son by his own parent a trifle?"

"To a man like you, familiar with deeds of blood, I do," was the cool reply of the inhuman wretch. "Recollect the murder of the unfortunate female, who——"

"Hush! hush, on your life!" cried Gerald, placing his hand before the mouth of the steward, and exhibiting the utmost terror; "that hellish deed will never be effaced from my memory—but I was urged to it by fear. I heard her in her sleep repeat the crimes I had perpetrated, and, fearful that she might betray me, I murdered one of the best of women that ever became the partner of a man. Poor thing, I——"

"There, there," impatiently exclaimed Chesterton, "let's have no more moralizing—I am completely sick of such cant and hypocrisy. Methinks it ill becomes Gerald Darnley to talk in this manner."

Gerald returned no answer, but it was very evident that he was suffering great agony of mind.

"I should not have recalled that circumstance to your memory, had you not been making a fool of yourself," said Chesterton.

"You had no occasion," returned Gerald, "for it is ever present to my recollection. But you have heard my determination. Would you make me your mortal foe ?"

" No."

"" Then why propose that which you see is decidedly foreign to my feelings ?"

" I did it without thinking, probably," said Chesterton, seeing, from the manner of Darnley, that it was necessary he should act with caution, and fearing that he had proceeded almost too far, urged on as he had been by his apprehensions of the revengeful determinations of Will Darnley.

" You mean that for an apology, I suppose," observed Gerald Darnley, with a bitter smile.

Chesterton nodded his head affirmatively, with something like a look of sarcasm, although he sought to disguise his real feelings as much as possible, dictated as he was by prudence, and fearful of the consequences that would in all probability accrue to him should he make an enemy of Gerald Darnley, with whom he had been associated in so many crimes, and who would be sure to adopt some stratagem to effect his vengeance, which he, with all his sagacity, might not be able to penetrate or to foil.

" Then you are willing to agree to the scheme I have proposed, are you ?" demanded Gerald.

" To make Will a prisoner in the vaults under the house where you reside ?"

" Exactly."

" Until we have sufficiently broken his spirit only, and are sure of his yielding to our wishes, and no longer seeking to oppose or obstruct our designs ?"

" Certainly."

" But how would you accomplish the task ?"

" It is not a very easy one."

" It is not. Will is a desperate fellow."

" It must be effected by stratagem. Madge must not know anything about it, or what has become of him."

" But might she not by accident find her way to the vaults ?"

" She knows nothing of them."

" That materially alters the case," said the steward, and he reflected for a few moments, and then added : " but might not his outcries reach her ears ?"

" It is impossible," answered Gerald ; " the vaults are so deeply buried in the bowels of the earth, as you are aware, that no sound could reach the ear."

" That is well," replied Chesterton, " but how could we convey him to them ?—The resistance he would offer, would be more, I fancy, than we could compete with."

" Were we to attack him for that purpose openly, it would."

" What, then, do you propose ?"

" That we seize him in his sleep."

" Ah !"

" I have a key that will unlock his chamber-door ; and when we are certain that he sleeps, we must enter cautiously, bind him hand and foot, and thus prevent him having the power to offer us any resistance."

" But his struggles, and the noise he would make, would alarm old Madge, and make her acquainted with everything."

" I have a scheme to prevent that."

" What is it ?"

" I will put a drug in her drink at supper-time, that will sufficiently steep her senses."

" And how would you account to her for his disappearance ?"

" That can be easily accomplished," answered Gerald.

" How ?"

" Why, old Madge will naturally conclude that he has gone off in the same abrupt manner that he did before, in search of Emily," said Darnley.

" But should she not ?"

" She dare not express any suspicions to the contrary," answered Gerald.

" Our fates rest in the power of too many persons, I am afraid," observed Chesterton ; " it is a pity that Madge should have been made acquainted with our secrets."

" Psha ! she is harmless ; she would not attempt to betray us."

" It is well that you have so much confidence in her," said Chesterton, " but, for my own part, I am not at all easy upon this subject."

" Well, enough of this ;" returned Gerald ; " do you agree to my proposition ?"

" I suppose I must."

" You can do as you please. If you do not, I shall decline having anything further to do in the affair altogether. The girl may take her chance, and I will leave Will to get her in his power if he can."

" Nay, what is the use of talking in that way ?" demanded the steward, " when you know that by so doing, you would bring destruction upon yourself as well as me and his lordship ?"

" I would chance it."

" But such a result would be inevitable."

" I know not that ; at any rate, I will make a bold struggle to prevent it."

" I will not put you to the test, if I can help it," said Miles Chesterton, " I will agree to what you have suggested. But you will not deceive me ?"

" How can I ?"

" The peculiarity of the circumstances under which we are placed, renders it necessary that we should be cautious."

" But we have known each other long enough, I should think," observed Gerald Darnley, " to render us less suspicious of one another."

" Well, well, there is enough of this," said the steward, " this is only a waste of time in words to no purpose. I repeat, I am ready to assist in the scheme you have proposed for the security of Will. But when shall it take place ?—It will not do to delay it any longer than can be helped. Every moment of procrastination is fraught with danger."

" It is."

" When, then, do you propose that we shall put our plot into execution ?"

" This very night."

" Ay, that is well ; at what time shall I come to the house ?"

" It must not be till after Will has retired to rest," replied Gerald, " for you know what he threatened, should you cross his path again, and you know, also, sufficient of his disposition by this time, to rest assured that he would not fail to put his threats into execution."

" The presumptuous varlet !" cried Chesterton, biting his lips ; " I shall not easily forget the blows he has struck me at different times, and my soul burns for vengeance. But at what hour shall I come ?"

" It will not be till after midnight," replied Gerald ; " I must also pretend to retire to my chamber, so that his suspicions may not be excited, but when you see a light at my chamber-casement, you may be sure that all is right ; whistle so that I may hear you, and then I will immediately let you in."

"It shall he so," said the steward, "and something strikes me that our plot will succeed. But those fearful vaults, Gerald, which you so solemnly protested that nothing should ever again induce you to enter; how is it that you have so soon been able to conquer your fears, and to come to this resolution?"

"Nothing but the most desperate necessity would persuade me to do so, and I can tell you that I by no means admire the job. Let that suffice you."

"No more do I."

"That ought to convince you what I may be tempted to do to serve you."

"And yourself too."

"Well, be it so, if you will have it; and, perhaps, it may not be altogether untrue."

"This night, then— "

"Will shall become an inmate of one of the vaults of the Old Lone House;" added Gerald Darnley.

"But what said he, after I quitted the house?" inquired Chesterton;— "does he still remain as obstinate as ever?"

"He does."

"And persists that we are acquainted with the retreat of Emily and Patty?"

"Yes."

"The headstrong idiot!"

"He also continues to hold out the same threats; swears to bring destruction upon all our heads, if we do not make him acquainted where Emily is concealed, and has only given me till to-morrow to consider of it, when he declares that he will put his threats into execution, even though he brings himself to destruction by so doing."

"The daring villain!" cried Chesterton; "I wonder you had patience to bear with him."

"Of what use would it have been for me to have acted otherwise?" demanded Gerald Darnley.

"And you are determined to act honourably towards me?"

"As long as you merit it—no longer."

"And to aid me all that you can in finding out Emily?"

"That, of course, for my own sake I am sure to do."

"And also in furthering my wishes with her?"

"How!" demanded Darnley; "did you not say that you would abandon them; and that to ensure our safety, the girl should die immediately, should she ever again fall into our power?"

"I said so; but suppose I cannot conquer my passions?"

"You must. We must not again involve ourselves in the danger we have already done by delay."

"And you are ready to imbrue your hands in the blood of that beauteous girl, and yet you pretend to shrink in horror from the bare contemplation of the assassination of your——"

"Chesterton," interrupted Gerald, "speak not to me again upon that subject. I will not, cannot, listen to you. Fain would I that this deed of blood might devolve upon other hands than mine; for had I not revolted from its perpetration with horror, I should have done it long ere this. But come, this interview has been protracted long enough."

"It has."

"To-night then?"

"I will do as you have instructed."

"Till then, farewell."

" Farewell."

Thus saying, the two villains separated ; Gerald Darnley retracing his footsteps to the Old Lone House, and Chesterton returning to the inn which he had quitted.

CHAPTER XVII.

THE SEIZURE.—THE STRUGGLE.

WHEN Gerald Darnley returned to the house, he found that his son was not at home, having absented himself almost as soon as he had done. From what Madge stated, he had questioned her very narrowly upon the subject of the escape of Emily and Patty, but, of course, as she knew no more about it than he did himself, she was unable to afford him any information, but she firmly opposed his opinion that Chesterton and Gerald had connived at it, and that they knew where the two girls were concealed ; for which Gerald very much commended her.

" That foolish boy seems to be determined to bring us all to ruin," said Darnley. " I wish he would again leave us, and never more trouble us with his presence."

" Ma conscience ! an' so do I," said Madge ; " I ken he will bring us into some bother or anither, an' a' through making sic a fuss about th' lassie."

" I am sorry that she ever came here, and I must have been mad to have yielded to such a step, but then I was fearful of offending his lordship."

" Ma conscience !" said Madge, " it were a unco bad job, an' I fear nae guid will come on it after a'."

" I need not warn you, Madge, to be cautious," said Gerald.

" Ay, mon, to be sure ye needn't," answered the old woman ; " I ken ye an' I ha' been acquaint long enough to render sic a caution unnecessary. But hark ! that is Willie's knock."

" It is," said Gerald ; " confusion light upon him, I wish he were at the other end of the world."

At that moment the door opened, and the young man entered, in the same mood he had been in when his father left him in the morning, and without exchanging a look with Gerald, he took a seat by the fireside, crossed his legs, folded his arms across his chest, and appeared for some moments to be absorbed in thought. His father watched him, but did not offer to interrupt him, and when he thought of the threats that he had held out to him in the morning, he could not help viewing him with a feeling of the utmost dread, and to wait anxiously for the arrival of night, when he hoped to succeed in executing the plot he had formed against him.

Madge having retired, Will turned to his father, and fixing upon him a savage look, he said, in a tone which evinced the feelings that were raging so furiously in his bosom—

" So, no doubt you think you have managed this affair very cleverly, and that you have entirely taken the girl out of my way ; but mind that you do not deceive yourselves."

" Well," replied his father, " I have already made every protestation in my power to convince you that you accuse both me and Chesterton wrongfully ; but you still obstinately refuse to believe me, and it is therefore useless to talk any more about it."

" But we shall have something more to say upon the subject," said Will ; " you know what I told you a short time since ; I shall only wait till to-morrow, and then if you still remain in the same tune, you may look out for the consequences."

"Do not try my patience too far, Will," said his father, swelling with almost ungovernable rage, "or you may induce me to do that for which I may afterwards be sorry."

"Ha! ha! ha!" laughed Will, scornfully.

"Damnation!" exclaimed Gerald; "am I to be mocked at, reviled;—scorned?"

"Nay, you may as well spare your wrath, father," said the young man, coolly; "I heed it not. It is very unpleasant, I know, to be told the truth at times; and I suppose that is the case with you in this instance."

Gerald Darnley walked across the apartment in a state of great excitement for a few seconds, and knew not in what manner to act. At length having stifled his rage as well as he could, trusting that a few hours only, would place Will entirely in his power, and prevent him from having any opportunity of putting his threats into effect, he resumed his seat, and did not offer to make any further observations. Will, however, seemed to be determined that the conversation should not drop so easily, and after a short time passed in silence, during which interval, he had remarked the emotion of his father with evident derision and exultation, he said:—

"Doubtless you laughed heartily in your sleeves, you and Chesterton, to think how nicely you had cajoled me into a belief of the tale you had told me, and by sending me away, had ridded yourselves of the principal obstacle to the success of your designs. But take care that it is not my turn to laugh shortly, and that you do not fall into the same snare you have laid for me."

"If fortune favours us," thought Gerald, "this night will place you in a situation that will deprive you of all power to do us harm."

He then observed aloud:—

"Will, why will you still persist in thus threatening me?"

"Because I know you have deceived me," answered the young man, "and unless you make me all the atonement you can, by making known to me where I may find Emily, and no longer opposing me in my wishes as regards her, by hell, although you are my own father, I will not rest until I have had ample vengeance, as I have before told you, even though I should myself fall in seeking it."

"You may thank my forbearance, Will," said Gerald, "or you would have to repent this conduct severely."

"Bah!" exclaimed Will, with a look of the utmost contempt and defiance; and quitted the apartment.

"Daring insolent!" cried Gerald, when he had gone;—"by the infernal host, I could almost be prevailed upon to do the deed which Chesterton would have urged me to, such is the manner in which he taunts me, and braves my authority. But no,—to-night, to-night, and all my fears shall be put to rest, so far as regards him, even though I run the greatest danger in endeavouring to accomplish my designs."

Will Darnley having partaken of dinner, once more left the house, and did not return again till the evening, when he was evidently flushed with drinking. Gerald had reason to fear him when he was in that condition, for he was usually most quarrelsome, and unmanageable; and excited as his feelings then were, he knew not to what excesses he might be led. However, it happened that he was completely stupified, and overpowered, and atmost immediately afterwards, he retired to the room in which he slept, and went to bed.

Gerald was glad to see that, for it was all in favour of their design, and he was in hopes that he might be conveyed, while in a state of insensibility to the vault, which was to be his future prison, with safety, and without his having the power to offer any resistance.

He had prepared himself with the drug, which he intended for old Madge, and he took the opportunity while her back was turned at the supper table, to mix it with her drink, and she quaffed it off, and soon afterwards complaining of being uncommonly sleepy, she hastily finished her supper, and hastened to her chamber.

Gerald also went to his bed-room, but first he opened the door of the room in which his son slept, and looked in. Will had thrown himself on the bed without undressing himself, and his loud snoring gave sufficient evidence of how soundly he slept. Gerald cautiously closed the door again feeling perfectly satisfied, but he was fearful upon second thought, as it wanted more than a couple of hours to the time when he expected the arrival of Chesterton, that he might have slept off the effects of the drink he had taken, and would awaken, and he regretted that Will had not partaken of supper, as it had been his intention, had he done so, to have administered a portion of the same drug he had mixed with the beverage which old Madge had drunk, to him. However, he had no other alternative now than to leave it to chance, and he resolved that he would succeed at all hazards.

He retired to his own chamber, in the gloominess of which, he passed the time very tediously until Chesterton's arrival. All the dreadful deeds he had perpetrated in former days rushed upon his recollection in fearful array, and the murderer feared to look around him, for fear of encountering the ghastly countenances of the victims of his guilt, and started at the slightest noise, which sounded to his ears like the dying groans of agony of those unfortunate beings who had fallen beneath his hands. Then the fearful adventure which him and Chesterton had met with in the morning in the vaults, and the dread of again entering them at that solemn hour, came to his mind with the most powerful and irresistible force, and he was two or three times partly resolved to abandon the guilty project he had in contemplation, and retire to his bed; but again the threats which Will had uttered against him, the certainty that he would fulfil them, and the bitter enemy he would be sure to create in the steward for having deceived him, darted upon his brain, and urged him on to the execution of the plot.

He had placed the light in the casement, as he had promised Chesterton, and he now listened anxiously for the signal, which was to assure him of his arrival.

The midnight hour had passed before he heard it, and then, taking the lamp in his hand, with a palpitating heart, he quitted his room, and descended the stairs. On arriving at the door of the chamber in which his son slept, he stopped to listen, and was gratified to hear him still snoring loudly. He hastened below, and cautiously unbolted the door, and admitted the steward.

"I am glad you have come," he said, in a low tone of voice, "for it is late, and I began to fear that something had occurred to prevent you."

"But, Will?" demanded Chesterton, impatiently.

"He sleeps soundly," answered Gerald, "everything is in favour of the success of our plot."

"And old Madge?"

"I mixed the drug with her drink," replied Darnley, "and there is no fear that she will have slept off its effects before the morning."

"'Tis well," observed the steward, "then we have no time to lose. Have you the cords ready with which we must bind him?"

"They are here."

"We must both pounce upon him in a moment, and secure him, and once bound, he will not have the power of offering any resistance."

"True! but I wish the deed was accomplished ;—those dismal vaults."

"Ah!" cried Chesterton, with a shudder; "I do not like the thoughts of entering them again. But we must not think about them, or we shall unfit ourselves for the task. Lead the way."

Gerald Darnley felt a shuddering sensation come over him, but he took up the lamp, and began to descend the stairs with silent steps, followed closely by Chesterton.

At the door of the young man's chamber they paused, and both listened attentively, and the heavy breathing of Will distinctly met their ears.

"He still sleeps," whispered Chesterton, in a voice of exultation; "fortune favours us; let us not delay a moment."

Gerald immediately opened the door, and they entered the room, where they beheld Will Darnley stretched sleeping upon the bed, in the same position as when Gerald had before seen him.

With the most savage and revengeful looks, Chesterton viewed his insensible foe, and the remembrance of the blows he had at different times received from him, rushed upon his brain, and rage, almost ungovernable, filled his bosom.

"Ah!" he suddenly ejaculated, advancing towards the bed, "now is he completely in our power: why should he live to endanger us further? Mine be the deed to——"

He had hastily taken a knife from his pocket as he spoke, and was about to plunge it in the bosom of Will, when Gerald starting forward, seized his upraised arm, and wrenched the murderous weapon from his grasp.

"By hell!" cried the ruffian, "if you make another such attempt, I

No. 26

will plunge the weapon in your own heart ! Is this the faith you keep towards me, when you agreed that there should not be any bloodshed ?"

" I was wrong ; I was wrong, Gerald ;" hastily replied Chesterton, " and I hope you will think no more of it. But to our purpose, for should he wake, we should probably be foiled in our attempt !"

The ruffians both rushed upon the sleeping man, as Chesterton spoke, and in a moment they had secured his legs and arms tightly with the cords. The action, however, awoke Will, who, opening his eyes, feeling the manner in which was pinioned, and seeing his father and the steward hanging over him, uttered a yell of rage, and made a desperate effort to release himself, but all to no purpose.

"Ah ! villains ! miscreants !" he cried ; " have ye then triumphed ? Unhand me ! release me ! or——

" Gag him !" exclaimed the steward, whose looks shewed how he exulted and gloried in the rage of the young man. " Gag him ! stop his noise, and then let us bear him to his new apartment, where he may probably learn whose turn it is to triumph now !"

Chesterton was obeyed, and then the two villains dragged Will from the bed, and endeavoured to raise him in their arms ; but he struggled with the desperation of a madman, and in vain endeavoured to burst the cords which bound him asunder, while his face was completely discoloured with the effects of his infuriate passion. The violence of his struggles, however, at length overcame him, and they succeeded in bearing him from the chamber, and conveying him down stairs. When they had entered the parlour they were compelled to pause to rest themselves, and to regain their breath, and they placed him in a chair. Here again Will, who was ready to choke with the power of his rage, made an endeavour to release himself but his strength was entirely exhausted, and he had no more power to offer them any further resistance. When he beheld his father approach the secret panel, a deadly paleness came over him, and he fixed upon Gerald such a look that he could not withstand, and he averted his eyes. Gerald hesitated, and when he thought of the awful place into which he was about to descend, and to which he was going to consign his son, a cold shuddering came over him, and he became irresolute.

" 'Psha !" cried Chesterton, " this is no time for silly fears ;—why do you hesitate ?"

Gerald made no answer, but after a severe struggle with his feelings, he touched the secret spring, and the panel slid back.

Will now appeared to have given himself up entirely to horror and despair, and he suffered them to do as they liked with him, but he fixed upon his father a reproachful glance, which was sufficient to make an impression upon the most callous heart.

The cold air came in a gust up the narrow and gloomy staircase, and froze the blood within the veins of Gerald Darnley and Chesterton, while the light they had with them would not penetrate into the darkness beneath. As they passed through the aperture and began to descend the stairs, Gerald, who proceeded first, almost imagined he beheld the ghastly countenance of the murdered man, whose skeleton was in the vault beneath, staring up at him, and he trembled violently in every limb. As for Will, he seemed completely paralyzed with horror, and remained in their hands as passive as a child. They descended very slowly, for the steps were broken in many places, and Will was a considerable weight, therefore, they were fearful of falling.

Chesterton pretended to a considerable deal more courage than he actually felt, and as a low, dismal, mournful sound, caused by the wind, came along the narrow passage into which they had now descended, he trembled, and almost fancied it was a repetition of those awful sounds they had heard in the morning.

At length they arrived in the vault where the skeleton was deposited, and when Will saw the half dug grave, and the chest by its side, which contained the sad remains of the murdered man, his fears seemed to overcome him, and he uttered a groan of horror, and glanced up in his father's face, with a look of mingled reproach and supplication. But Gerald noticed him not, his mind was too much absorbed by the terrors of the place, and not daring to cast his eyes upon the skeleton of the grave, he hurried on as fast as his trembling limbs would permit him, and opening an iron door at the farthest extremity of the vault from a bunch of keys which he carried suspended from his waist, they entered another cell beyond, and which Chesterton was not aware of. Here they placed Will upon the damp earth, and looked around them in silence. It was truly an awful looking place, and Chesterton could not help shuddering when he · beheld it. There was a heavy chain affixed to a staple in the wall, and in one corner of it was a heap of straw, upon which some poor victim of cruelty had, in all probability, stretched his limbs many years before.

Will cast one look around the dreadful dungeon, in which he had no doubt it was the intention of his father and the villain Chesterton to confine him, and he then uttered a deep groan, and seemed in a state approaching to apathy.

Gerald Darnley pointed to the chain, and the steward understanding him, they once more dragged Will to his feet, and secured him to it by an iron belt which went round his waist. During the time they were doing this, Will never offered to make the least resistance, and, in fact, he appeared to be nearly unconscious of what they were doing.

They now released him from the cords that had bound his arms and legs, and removed the gag from his mouth. All this time, Chesterton, notwithstanding the frowns and insignificant looks of Gerald, could not restrain the expression of his exultation at having thus securely got his enemy, and one whom he so heartily detested, in his power.

"Well," he exclaimed. in a tone of bitter irony, and looking round the place, " I must say that this is a very comfortable and healthy habitation, a very fit apartment for refractory boys, and those who threaten vengeance. I wish Will Darnley every enjoyment in it."

"Hold, Chesterton!" cried Gerald ; "hold, I say, unless you would make an enemy of me. Is it not enough that I have complied with your wishes by going to this extremity, but you must add mockery to the horrors which my foolish headstrong son will have to undergo in this place through his obstinacy ?"

"And have I not reason to exult at his misery after the many taunts, insults, and personal acts of violence he has offered to me ?" demanded the steward.

"Then keep the expression of it for your own private gratification," returned Gerald Darnley, scowling fearfully upon Chesterton. "Come, let us begone. Will, you may thank yourself for being placed in this situation, for had you not have held out threats that rendered your being at liberty dangerous, and not so obstinately have persisted that we knew what had become of the girl Emily, all would have been well. Here, then, you will remain a prisoner until you are brought to your senses, and we are convinced that you have abandoned your designs against us."

"Which you will have some difficulty in doing," added Chesterton, with a malignant grin.

Gerald once more fixed upon him a stern look.

" Will you hold your peace ?" he demanded.

" Dastardly miscreant !" exclaimed Will, in a hoarse voice, and his eyes flashing the utmost indignation and fury ; he had taken but very little notice of what his father had been saying, but had directed the whole of his attention towards the steward. " Dastardly miscreant," he repeated, clenching his fists, " dare but to approach me, and, shackled as I am, I will press your life out."

" Ha ! ha ! ha !" laughed Chesterton, in scorn, and his voice sounded awfully in that dreary place. Will became completely furious, and made a rush at him as far as the extent of the chain would allow him to do ; but finding that he could not reach him, he stamped with rage, and uttered the most terrible maledictions.

" Will," said Gerald, " this fury is all useless ; here you are powerless, and it is not by storming that you may expect to get your liberty."

" He shall never be restored to it again, if I can help it," said Chesterton.

" Enough," cried Gerald Darnley, impatiently, shuddering with the coldness of the place, and anxious to get away from the presence of his son, whose reproachful glances he could not bear to encounter ; " we have accomplished our task, and now let us begone."

He laid hold of Chesterton's arm as he spoke, and urged him towards the door, which Will observing, and his natural determined spirit being broken by the terrors of his situation, and the prospect of being left in that horrible place, in which it did not seem possible that any human being could exist for a few hours even, he was wound up to a complete pitch of despair, and turning his eyes towards his father, he exclaimed—

" Father, cruel as I know you to be, you cannot, you surely will not leave me in this dreadful place to perish."

" Did you not threaten me, boy ?" demanded Gerald.

" And was I not driven to it ?" said the young man ; " did not your conduct as regards that girl upon whom I had fixed my mind, drive me to desperation, and had you not have secretly conveyed her away from the house—"

" Liar !" interrupted Chesterton.

" Once more, perverse, obstinate fool," said Gerald Darnley, " once more I tell you that you accuse us wrongfully. But here you must remain until you have been brought to see your folly,"

" Father !" ejaculated Will, " hear me. You have brought me up to every vice and cruelty, and why, therefore, upbraid and punish me for displaying those feelings that have been instilled into my breast by you ? But cruel as you are, I cannot believe you monster enough to condemn me to a fate like this."

" Have you not threatened to do that which would have placed my neck in the halter ?" demanded Gerald.

" I will renounce that idea, I promise—nay, I swear to do so," said Will.

" You swear !" ejaculated Gerald ; " did you not treat me with scorn when I offered to do the same, to swear that neither myself nor Chesterton knew anything whatever of the girl ; and is your oath to be taken any more than mine ?"

" He must not—he shall not be believed," said the steward ; " were we to grant him his liberty directly, the first use he would make of it would be to go and impeach against us."

" Villain !" cried Will, gnashing his teeth, and shaking his clenched fist at him.

" Ha ! ha ! ha !" again laughed the steward ; " I can bear your taunts now. But come—why do we delay leaving this place? Good morning, William Darnley, and I wish you every pleasure that this place can afford you. Now Gerald, our business is completed, so let us away from hence, and take a glass of wine over the success of our plot. Come—come."

"Father, once more I ask you—nay, I even implore of you," cried Will, in a tone of frenzy, "do not leave me in this awful prison. Do with me as you think proper in any other way, since you will not take my promise not to betray you, but do not leave me here, and in the proximity of that ghastly skeleton, which——"

"Let us begone," said Gerald, hastily, in a low tone, and casting a fearful glance around him as he spoke—"let us begone! Will, you supplicate to me in vain. My safety demands your security, and your own folly has has alone brought this upon you."

"Oh, I will do anything to convince you of my sincerity," ejaculated Will, whom terror had made a complete child.

"Ha! ha! ha!" exclaimed the steward, ironically, "where is the desperate Will Darnley now?"

"Away!" cried Gerald, unable to meet the gaze of his son; and before Will could utter another word, he dragged Chesterton out by the arm, and, closing the iron door after them, he locked it securely, leaving his wretched, guilty son in darkness and alone.

Gerald and Chesterton both placed their hands before their eyes, to prevent them from beholding the skeleton, and hurried through the different vaults, and along the dreary passage towards the staircase as quick as possible, and without speaking a word. They were not long in reaching the steps, which having ascended, and finding themselves once more in the parlour, they were enabled again to breathe.

Gerald looked upon Chesterton, as he closed the secret panel, with a pallid countenance, and a quivering lip, and then sinking into a chair, he said :—

"There! now I hope you are satisfied after this unnatural job, of my readiness to serve you."

"'Psha!" ejaculated Chesterton ;—"what nonsense you talk, what have you and nature to do with one another; you have long, I should think, been strangers."

"To immure my own son in that vault of death," said Gerald, "and ——"

"There, there; no more of that ;" interrupted Chesterton, "it is done now, and you ought to feel satisfied that we have succeeded so well ; had we not done so, after the threats which Will held out, it is not at all unlikely that we should ere many hours have elapsed, been the inmates of a prison."

"I like not the deed."

"Nonsense! your own safety demanded it."

"He can never live long in that fearful place."

"So much the better," muttered the steward partly to himself; "then he will be beyond the means of working us any injury. But come, Gerald, I never saw you so dull and timid in my life before. Here is wine on the table I see, take a glass; it will revive your spirits."

Chesterton filled a couple of glasses as he spoke, and handing one to Gerald, he took the other himself, and they quaffed off the contents. It did seem to have the effect the steward guessed it would on his companion, and he became more composed.

"And now this task is accomplished," said Chesterton, "we must turn all our thoughts and energies to the discovery of Emily and Patty, and something convinces me that we shall at last be successful."

"And why do you think so?"

"Why, I have no particular reason for doing so, but, at any rate, we have got rid of one of the greatest obstacles."

"Ah!—And how do you purpose proceeding?"

"Did you not say that you had a relation living at ——"

"Mrs. Seagrove," added Gerald Darnley;—"she believes herself to be my sister."

"Believes herself to be, and is she not so?"

"She is not."

"Nor in any way related to you?"

"Not in the least."

"But you were brougtht up together."

"We were."

"And the parents of this Mrs. Seagrove ever behaved to you with affection, and called you their son?"

"True, they did so."

"That is strange, I cannot understand you."

"They knew not but that I was their own child;" said Gerald.

"How!—you surprise me, Gerald."

"Doubtless I do, but what I say is nevertheless true. My mother was wet-nurse to Mrs. Darnley, and was confined with me a few days only before that lady. The latter also was delivered of a boy, and which was compelled to be taken away from its mother, and committed to the care of mine a short time after it came into the world. It was a sickly child, and died when it was not more than a week old. Tempted by the hope of gaining a future reward, my parents pretended that it was their own son who had died, and palmed me off upon Mr. and Mrs. Darnley as their offspring."

"It was a cunning stratagem; but was it ever suspected?"

"It was not," replied Gerald.

"And your real parents never offered to betray you?"

"They studied their own interest too well for that; for when they made me acquainted with the truth, and I had every reason to believe that they were not imposing upon me, I well rewarded them."

"And are they still living?"

"They are not. They have been dead several years."

"And you do not think this Mrs. Seagrove, as you call her, has any suspicion that you are not her real brother?"

"Why, I can't say; if she has, she has never evinced it in her behaviour towards me; and neither do I see why she should entertain any surmises of the kind. You may be certain that she has never had the slightest hint of such a thing from me."

"Well then, this Mrs. Seagrove," said the steward.

"What of her?"

"After all, may not Patty, who she brought up, and Emily, have sought shelter with her? Especially as you have not corresponded much with each other lately, according to your own account," said Chesterton.

"No," replied Gerald, "I have before told you it is not at all likely. They would be sure to imagine that we should easily find them out there, and if they had gone thither, we should have heard something of them ere this."

"I think very different," said Chesterton; "at any rate, there will be no harm in going to the neighbourhood in which Mrs. Seagrove resides, and satisfying our doubts upon the subject."

"Well, you may do as you think proper," replied Darnley, "although

I think your errand will prove a fruitless one. I cannot leave this place; but must remain to take care of my prisoner."

"To-morrow I will start thither, and, lurking about the neighbourhood in which Mrs. Seagrove resides, be able soon, doubtless, to ascertain the truth or fallacy of my surmises. But, mark me, Gerald, while I am gone, look well to the security of your son. Do not let his entreaties prevail with you to grant him his liberty, or we shall be ruined."

"Much as I dislike the desperate scheme we are compelled to have recourse to," returned Gerald, "fear for my own personal safety, will make me cautious."

"'Tis well;" said Chesterton. "Come, drink again; we need something after the business we have been performing."

Chesterton once more replenished their glasses, and they drank off the contents.

"But," said Gerald, "Will must not be left there to starve, and we have not left him any provisions."

"And now is the only time, before old Madge is stirring," returned the steward, "to take him a supply."

"I cannot enter those vaults again at this hour," said Gerald.

"Psha!" ejaculated the steward, "you must conquer that weakness, or, if you would not leave your son to starve, as you have just observed, how are you to supply his wants?"

"It is a dreadful necessity," said Darnley.

"You will soon get used to it."

"I fear not; and although you pretend to so much courage, I do not think you would admire the job any more than myself."

"There is no time to argue upon the subject;—in a short time it will be daylight, and after old Madge has arisen, you will have no opportunity of going to him."

"I tell you again that I will not, I dare not go there again at this hour."

"Give me the provisions and the keys then," said the steward, mustering up all the courage he could assume.

"What would you do?"

"Why, I suppose, if you wont go, I must," answered Chesterton.

"Be it so," returned Darnley, very well pleased to be released from so unpleasant a task; "but, mark me, Chesterton."

"What would you warn me about now?"

"I would caution you not to play me false, nor to let your hatred and revenge against Will, urge you to commit any violence upon him," observed Gerald.

"More fears!—But you may trust me."

"If you deceive me, you shall pay dearly for it," said Gerald.

"Your threats are unnecessary; but come, the provisions and the keys; for time wanes apace, and, to tell you the truth, I do not care how soon I get this business finished."

Gerald filled a small basket with bread and meat, sufficient to last the wretched prisoner for two or three days, and then filling a pitcher with water, Chesterton, with his load, passed once more through the secret panel, which Gerald closed after him.

The steward cast his eyes fearfully below, before he ventured to descend the steps, and he felt a trembling sensation of dread stealing over him; but the thought of completing the misery of the man he so bitterly detested, served to encourage him, and he proceeded cautiously on his way.

When he had reached the vault in which the skeleton was deposited, he involuntarily paused, and in spite of all his efforts, he could not move from the spot, but remained with his eyes fixed upon the ghastly spectacle, while a feeling of the greatest horror pervaded his whole frame. At last, however, he turned away his head, and hastened towards the door of the cell in which Will Darnley was confined. He listened, and heard a low moaning from the inside of the vault, and the villain's base heart exulted when by that he was convinced of the suffering his hated enemy was already undergoing, and when he thought of that which was yet in store for him. He applied the key to the lock, and immediately he heard by the rattling of the heavy chain which secured him to the wall, that Will was aroused. The ponderous door flew heavily back on its hinges, and Chesterton entered the awful vault in which his victim was confined.

Having almost exhausted himself in giving vent to the expression of his horror, and in uttering the most fearful imprecations against his father and Chesterton, Will had sunk upon the heap of straw, and was giving way entirely to despair, when he heard the key turning in the lock, and as a sudden hope darted on his mind that his father had relented, and had returned to restore him to liberty, he started to his feet, and at that moment the door flew open, and his eyes fell upon the villainous countenance of the steward. It would be impossible to describe the expression of rage which distorted the features and flashed from the eyes of the young man, on beholding Chesterton, while the latter coolly placed the provisions he had brought with him on the ground, and looked at Will with a glance of exultation, mingled with the most perfect hatred.

Rushing to the full extent of the chain, and endeavouring to reach Chesterton, Will glared upon him with the fury of a madman, and in a voice rendered harsh by rage, he cried—

"Wretch! coward! villain! This, then, is your hellish work. Oh, that I could but get hold of you, you should not quit this living tomb alive! But think not that you will continue to triumph. Something will occur to release me from this fiendish confinement, and then beware, your life shall answer for it."

"Ha! ha! ha!" laughed Chesterton, "your impotent rage and threats serve to amuse me. This place, I am much mistaken, if you will ever again quit alive; and I have it now in my power to stretch you a corpse at my feet. But it does not suit my purpose to slay you yet; I will suffer you to live for some time longer, to enjoy the comforts of this sumptuous and commodious apartment, and to indulge in the pleasant sensations which, no doubt, your situation will excite."

"Damned scoundrel!" cried Will, bursting with indignation; "were I but released from this chain, you should not live another moment to give utterance to your cowardly expressions of triumph."

"I dare say not," answered Chesterton, with the most provoking coolness; "but fetters and chains are excellent things to curb such headstrong fellows as you, and no doubt a few weeks' retirement in this sequestered retreat will have the most beneficial effects upon your health and spirits."

Will could return no answer to this taunting speech, but he bit his lips with rage, until the blood came, and he groaned with the fury of an encaged wild beast. Chesterton folded his arms across his chest, and contemplated him with looks of the most unnatural satisfaction. Fearful, however, that Gerald would become impatient at the length of his absence, and recollecting that the time was passing quickly away, he took up the lamp which he had placed on the ground, and fixing upon Will a look of sarcasm, he said—

"I wish you a very good morning, Mr. William Darnley; I cannot honour you any longer with my company at present, which, no doubt, you much regret, as it is not very cheerful to be alone in this place, however much one may admire its other attractions. Good morning; I shall pro-

bably pay you another visit when I return from the place, where I have every hope of being able to find Emily."

Will Darnley uttered a dreadful execration, as the steward turned away from him with a malevolent grin of exultation, and Chesterton quitted the dungeon, and closed the iron door after him with a loud bang, taking care afterwards to lock and bolt it.

He was now again in the vault with the skeleton, but he had succeeded in somewhat abating his terrors, and he was hastening past the chest when he stumbled and fell over something on the ground—the lamp fell from his hand, and the light being extinguished, he was left in utter darkness in that awful vault, and prostrated near the grave which Gerald had dug for the reception of the skeleton.

Under ordinary circumstances, and with an unsullied conscience, his situation would have been awful enough; but, loaded as he was with crime, his terror may be easily conceived. However, he gathered himself up as quickly as possible, and endeavoured to find his way to the door, but in the confusion of the moment he continued to grope around the vault without being able to find it; and curses on the accident escaped his lips.

At length, however, he did manage to find his way out, and in a state of great trepidation he hurried along as fast as he was able through the different vaults, and the passage beyond, and at last succeeded in gaining the steps.

On his entrance into the parlour, he found Gerald Darnley seated in one corner of the room, apparently buried in deep meditation; but on seeing Chesterton the former arose, and looked at him inquisitively.

"So, you have come at last," said Gerald; " what have you been doing
No. 27

to detain you so long? Ah! you look pale, and tremble. What's the matter now? Have you again heard——"

"No, no," hastily interrupted the steward, "I have neither heard nor seen anything."

"Then why are you so much alarmed?"

"Psha! I am not alarmed," answered Chesterton, "only a little flurried. I had a fall in the vault where the skeleton is, and my light became extinguished, which rendered it rather a difficult matter for me to find my way out."

"Oh, is that all?"

"All!" repeated Chesterton; "and quite enough too, I think. I fancy you would not much like to be left alone in the dark in that place."

"No, no, I should not; but let us not talk any more about it," said Gerald Darnley. The boy—how did you find him?"

"How did you expect me to find him?" asked Chesterton;—"bursting with useless rage."

"You taunted him."

"And what if I did?"

"You promised me that you would not do so, and what necessity is there for it? He is punished enough already, without your increasing it by heaping upon him your tormenting irony."

"Nonsense!" exclaimed Chesterton; "it is only fair retaliation on my part for that which I have experienced from him."

"I would advise you not to repeat it."

"Well, you are foolishly particular, I think."

"May be so, but it is my will; and if you think my friendship worth retaining, you must submit to it. Your hot impetuosity would have led you to commit murder before we seized him."

"And what is the fate to which you have doomed him," demanded the steward, "but slow and deliberate murder? To have despatched him at once would have been mercy compared with it."

"I do not see the force of your observations," said Gerald.

"And do you think it possible that any human being can long survive in that damp and loathsome cell?"

Gerald made no answer at first, but after a pause he said—

"I do not think it will be necessary to keep him long there confined."

"And do you imagine, then, that whatever promises he may make, he will be sincere in them?" asked the steward.

"After the sufferings he will have to undergo, and which will break his spirit, I think we may trust him."

"Never!"

"I candidly tell you, then," returned Gerald, "that it is my intention to trust him."

"Are you mad?"

"No; but you will recollect that he is my son, and that, in spite of his conduct, and my character, I cannot help entertaining some feeling towards him."

"You will proceed with your folly, Gerald," said Chesterton, "until you ultimately bring destruction upon us all."

"If you only act with the same prudence and precaution that I shall, you will have no cause to fear."

"We shall see. But to-morrow I shall leave you in search after Emily, and then you will have to attend upon your son yourself, and I only hope that you may be found to act with the same prudence and precaution you seem to give yourself such infinite credit for."

"You will find that I do not give myself credit for what I do not possess," returned Gerald. "But see—daylight is just beginning to peep, and it will not do for you to be seen here, or something wrong will be suspected. You must begone, and I will retire to my chamber, until old Madge has arisen."

"Very well;" observed the steward; "but how do you mean to account for the absence of your son?"

"Leave that to me."

"Will not the old woman think it strange that he should have left the house so suddenly, especially after coming home in the state of inebriation which you have described, last night?"

"No, it will not much astonish her," replied Gerald; she is well acquainted with his character, and the strange manner in which he is sometimes in the habit of behaving, and will, therefore, only imagine that he has gone off in one of those eccentric freaks he is accustomed to indulge in. But, come;—do not delay!"

"I shall see you again by and by," said the steward, "till which time I shall bid you adieu; but mind and look safe after the prisoner."

"You have no occasion to fear me, in that respect," answered Gerald Darnley, as he cautiously opened the door for Chesterton, who at last took his departure. Gerald then crept silently to his own chamber; but not to sleep; no, his mind was too much disturbed for that, and throwing himself into a chair, he gave way to the numerous and conflicting thoughts that crowded upon his brain. He could not help reproaching himself for the fate to which he had consigned his son, and yet he had done it, he reflected through sheer necessity, and that Will had, in a great measure, brought it upon himself, by holding out threats to him, and he had every reason to believe, from the determined nature of his character, that he would have fulfilled the same. Then he regretted that he should have been tempted in the first instance to pander to the wishes of Chesterton, or that Emily had been the cause of so much trouble and uneasinesss. But more than all he repented not having, when he found that Will's inclination was towards Emily, resolutely refused to assist Chesterton in his plot, and have yielded to the wishes of his son. Chesterton might have stormed, and probably have threatened to betray him to his lordship, but he would have been afraid to have done so, because he must in so doing, have exposed his own conduct in the affair, and, if ever he had, Gerald had no more cause to fear his lordship, than his lordship had reason to fear him.

He could not think upon the terrible situation in which he had placed Will, without a shudder, and there were moments when he was almost inclined to trust to chance and the young man's promises, and to set him at liberty, but fear prevented him. He paced the chamber with disordered footsteps, and suffered these reflections to rack his brain, until he was completely bewildered and distracted. He was determined, however, let whatever might be the consequence, should the steward succeed in finding Emily, and getting her into his power, that he should never possess her for the gratification of his licentious passions, and that he would bestow her upon Will upon his consenting to take his share of the booty they had accumulated by their nefarious practices, and to leave the country. Thus he would save himself from shedding human blood again, and at the same time rid himself of a troublesome customer, in the person of Will, who, he had no doubt, if he once went away from England, would never return to it again; knowing that, while he was there, he was constantly in danger of being apprehended for the crimes he had committed, and to suffer an ignominious death. As for Chesterton, however chagrined and disappointed he might be at being foiled, and whatever he might threaten to do, he had no doubt but that his resentment would soon pass over, and that he would be afraid to attempt to put what he might threaten into execution.

Gerald next thought of the horrors of the vaults, and of the awful noises that he and Chesterton had heard in them, and when he reflected how often he must enter them in order to visit Will with the necessary provissions, he trembled with horror, and for awhile thought that he should never be adequate to the task.

In this mood he remained until seven o'clock had sounded, when he heard the footsteps of old Madge upon the stairs, and, therefore, left his chamber, after he had imagined she had prepared the morning's repast, and descended into the parlour.

"Ma conscience!" said the old woman; "an' where be Willie, I wonder? He's always an early riser, an' it be a wonder that he has not comed down stairs yet."

"Oh, it's nothing to be wondered at," answered Gerald, with apparent carelessness, "not at all to be wondered at, when you remember the state of intoxication he came home in last night. I don't suppose he has opened his eyes yet, and it would not be well to disturb him, until he has entirely slept off the effects of the liquor he had been drinking."

"Ma conscience!" cried Madge, "an' Willie certainly had had a wee drapie in his ee, an' it is, I dare be bound, as you say wi' th' puir laddie."

"No doubt of it," returned Gerald; "but, come, let us make haste with the breakfast; for I want to go out upon business."

The meal was, therefore, despatched as quickly as possible, and Gerald then arose from the table, and prepared to leave the house.

"If Mr. Chesterton should come while I am gone, desire him to wait till I return," said Gerald, as he quitted the place. But he had gone forth for the purpose of not being present when old Madge should discover that Will was not in the room, and lest he (Gerald) should by the confusion he might evince, betray himself to the old woman. He walked along for about an hour, unheedful of the way he was going, and buried in profound meditation, the nature of which we need not attempt to describe to the reader; and then when he thought it was most likely that old Madge had found out that Will was not in his chamber, he returned home.

The old woman met him at the door, with surprise depicted in her countenance, and immediately informed him, that, having waited and waited for a long time for Will to come down stairs, and still he not making his appearance, she became rather surprised, and alarmed, and at length resolved to go up to his chamber to inquire after him. She knocked at the door two or three times, and not receiving any answer, she at length opened it, when she found, to her surprise, that Will was not in the room, neither could she see him in any part of the house.

"Well," said Gerald, when she had concluded, with affected carelessness, "and do you consider that there is anything so very surprising in that?—Perhaps Will has gone out early in the morning, shooting, as he is sometimes you know accustomed to do; or he may have started off in search of the girl, Emily, and Patty, again, and there is no knowing what time he may return. He may be gone for weeks again."

"Ay, that be true," returned old Madge;—"Ma conscience! the puir laddie has been quite daft ever since that lassie were brought hither; an' I shouldn't wonder if he has ganged after her again."

"You know he will have his own way," said Gerald; "and, therefore, I never attempt to control him. He has gone where he thinks proper, and will find his way back again when his whim is over, no doubt."

"Ay I dare say he will," returned the old woman; "but he might bid a body good bye before he started."

"It's his way, and it's not worth while troubling oneself about it;" observed Gerald, and there the conversation abruptly terminated, although old Madge was far from being perfectly satisfied, but she was fearful to interrogate Gerald farther, as she knew that he did not like to be troubled with questions.

Soon after this, Chesterton arrived at the house, and Madge knowing that her presence was not required, retired up stairs to her own apartment.

"Well," said the steward, impatiently, "and how have you acted with Madge?"

"Hush!" replied Gerald Darnley, "she might be listening. We will walk out together for a short distance, if you please."

Chesterton nodded assent, and they left the house, when Gerald related to him the conversation which had taken place between him and old Madge, precisely as we have detailed it to the reader. Chesterton seemed to be satisfied that the old woman had no suspicion of the truth.

"How could she?" demanded Gerald.

"Why," answered Chesterton, "after the quarrel which took place between me and Will, I thought perhaps she might have imagined out of revenge you and I had contrived some means of putting him out of the way."

"And if she had, it would have been of very little consequence," said Gerald, "she would not have dared to have uttered a word of disapprobation respecting our conduct."

"Probably not," returned Chesterton; "but still I think it is quite as well not to let too many become acquainted with our secrets. We don't know what might happen to induce them, and afford them the means of betraying us, and it is always best to make security doubly sure; at least, that is the maxim which I always follow."

"Well, and perhaps it is a safe one, but I do not see that there is much necessity for it in this instance," said Gerald Darnley; "the old woman is pledged to keep all our secrets, and she has never yet given me any reason to doubt her. But we came not here to talk of her. Are you still in the same mind that you were this morning when we parted?"

"What, to hasten to the neighbourhood in which Mrs. Seagrove resides?" asked Chesterton.

"Yes," replied Gerald.

"I am; and something seems to tell me that my journey will not prove unsuccessful;" observed the steward.

"You are remarkably sanguine, sometimes, and when your suppositions appear to be the most improbable," remarked Gerald; "for my part, I think that you will be disappointed."

"I can't help it if I am; but, at any rate, I am resolved not to throw any chance away of finding out the retreat of the girl, and you ought to be as anxious as myself, when you recollect the danger we are placed in while her and Patty are suffered to be at large."

"And so I am," answered Gerald; "you must think me mad, if you suppose that I am not. But when do you intend to depart?"

"To-morrow morning."

"And should you find that the girls are there, what scheme do you mean to adopt to get them in your power?"

"Upon that I have not yet decided," replied Chesterton, "but I have no doubt that I shall be able to think of some plan or another to render my success certain. And now, Gerald, how do you feel after the affair of this morning? Have you yet got over your qualmishness?"

"I yet regret that necessity should have compelled us to have adopted such a course," answered Gerald, "and I hope before long we may feel ourselves at liberty to release him from his confinement."

"There is one thing which I should like to see done, before I leave here,' observed Chesterton,

"What is it?"

"The skeleton," answered Chesterton, "it would be much better and safer for us to see it buried."

"I shudder at the job."

"Nonsense! will you not have to enter the vaults often, now Will is there confined, and therefore, why should you be so fearful of assisting in this job?"

"Need you ask me," said Gerald, "after what we both heard there when we were going to inter the remains of the murdered man before?"

"But we have not heard anything since," observed the steward, "and after all, I strongly suspect that we suffered ourselves to be alarmed by mere idle imagination."

"Idle imagination!" repeated Gerald Darnley, "ah, you will never persuade me to that, Chesterton, nor do I believe you think so yourself, although you now pretend so to do."

"But I do," answered the steward, "and I am ashamed of myself for having shewed so much cowardice on that occasion. But it must be done, and this very day ; it will only be the work of a few minutes, and then we shall be comparitively secure. I cannot rest while that skeleton remains in any place where it is at all likely to be discovered."

"Where it now is, it is safe enough," said Gerald, "but in order to quiet your apprehensions, I will consent once more to accompany you for the purpose of placing the remains of the unfortunate Jerdan beneath the earth. But how shall we contrive to get old Mudge out of the way, while we put our scheme into execution?"

"Oh, that may be managed easily enough," answered Chesterton, "by sending her to the town on an errand'"

"Enough, it shall be so," observed Gerald ; "we will instantly re·turn to the house, for the sooner this unpleasant business is over the better."

"True, I am ready to attend you ;" and the two villains immediately retraced their steps to the Old Lone House, where Gerald acted according to the suggestions of Chesterton, and despatched old Madge to the town. She had no sooner departed, then they set about the business, although it was with a quaking heart that Gerald did so, and the steward, although he endeavoured to conquer his feelings as much as possible, revolted at the disagreeable task.

When they had descended into the vault, Gerald cast his eyes towards the door which opened into the wretched place where his son was confined, and he trembled, and was afraid to approach it ; but the steward, who felt all anxiety to know in what situation Will was then, advanced towards the door, and listened. All was quite still.

"I do not hear any one stirring," he said to his companion, "he must sleep."

"Sleep, sleep in such a dreadful cell as that," replied Gerald, "it is im-possible, unless it is in the sleep of death."

'It would be better if he did, " returned the steward ; "but the consti-tution of Will is too robust, to sink under a few hours of incarceration. You have the key of the door with you, have you not? Let us satisfy ourselves."

"No, no!" replied Gerald ; "I cannot bear to look upon him again just yet."

"Why," ejaculated Chesterton, "any one would suppose that Will had ever been to you a most affectionate and dutiful son, to see the manner in which you are affected, instead of his having threatened to be the means of bringing you to the gallows."

"Hush!" cried Gerald, glancing round with a look of terror;—"oh, let us get out of this dreadful place as soon as possible; come, come, quick! Or, I shall never be able to assist you in this task. Even now, I could almost fancy I heard—"

"Fool!" interrupted Chesterton, "you are again suffering your idle terror to overcome you. Close the lid of the chest."

Gerald averted his eyes from the chest as he approached it, and hastily shut down the lid. He then, assisted by Chesterton, raised the chest from the earth, ahd after some labour it was deposited in the grave, and the earth thrown over it, and trampled down, so as to prevent its having the appearance of having been disturbed, as much as possible. The disagreeahle task was at last accomplished, and both Gerald and the steward felt more easy than they had done for some time before. The former would then have retired immediately from the vaults, but Chesterton laid hold of his arm and prevented him.

"No," he said, "it may be some time time before I shall have another opportunity, and I cannot leave this place until I have once more gazed upon our prisoner, and seen the effect which confinement has already had upon him. Come, Gerald, what have you to fear?"

"Why will you be so obstinate," asked Gerald, "and what gratification can you feel in thus exhibiting yourself to your enemy, and exulting in his misery? If I comply, remember——"

"I know what you would say," interrupted the steward, "and there is no necessity for you to proceed farther; unlock the door."

Gerald, with a trembling hand, complied, and the door flew open, and revealed to them their wretched prisoner, who was stretched on the heap of straw, and apparently asleep. The noise which they made in entering, however, awoke him, and raising his head, and beholding his father and the steward, he uttered a wild cry of mingled anguish and resentment, and then arose hastily upon his feet, and fixed upon them a terrible look, trying in the wild frenzy of his despair and rage, to release himself from his chain.

"Wretches!" he cried, "again do ye come hither to mock me, and exult in the misery you have inflicted upon me?—Father! if, by such a name, I ought to call you; think you for this unnatural crime you will go unpunished?"

"And would you not have been guilty of a still more unnatural crime," demanded Chesterton, "by placing your father beneath the hands of the public executioner?"

"I was goaded on to threaten so, by believing, that you and my father had both deceived me;" answered Will, "and that you knew where Emily was concealed. As for you, Miles Chesterton, mark my words, much as you may think you triumph now, I shall yet live to see you mount the scaffold! and to exult in your fate!"

The steward returned no other answer to this than a smile of contempt, and the young man turning to Gerald, who had shrunk beneath the power of his glances, said—

"Father! once more I appeal to you! If you would save yourself the perpetration of one more terrible crime, the murder of your own son, relent ere it is too late, and release me from this terrible place. Do this, and I promise to abandon all the designs I have conceived, and——"

"Will," exclaimed Gerald, in a softened tone of voice, but at the moment Chesterton caught hold of his arm, and interrupted him;—

"Idiot!" he cried, "would you be deceived by specious promises?

Listen to him not ; the hour after that which gave him liberty would consign us all to prison."

" Oh, villain ! villain !" exclaimed Will, and Gerald was once more about to speak, when the steward interposed to prevent him.

" Nay," he observed, " listen not to him, I repeat, but leave him to his wild raving.   Come, let us away ; Madge will return before we have made our way from the vaults."

Thus saying, Chesterton pulled his companion away from the vault, and closed the door after them, fastening it as before, and as they hastened towards the steps that led to the parlour, they could hear the loud maledictions of the infuriated Will, which came in hollow reverberations along the passage.

Chesterton regretted that he had persuaded Gerald to enter the cell, as he was fearful that the appeal which Will had so forcibly made to him might cause him to waver in his determination, and that, after he, Chesterton, had departed upon the journey he intended, he would be prevailed upon to release him from incarceration.

When they had once more reached the parlour, they found that old Madge had not yet returned.   Gerald was in a considerable state of agitation, and Chesterton suffered him to give free indulgence to the excitement under which he laboured for a few moments without interruption, thinking that, when it had in some degree abated, he would the more easily be persuaded to promise to do as the steward requested, and which seemed so indispensable to their safety.

" After all," at length said Gerald, " I think the punishment to which we have consigned Will is too severe."

" What, for threatening to bring you to an ignominious death ?" said Chesterton.   " Psha! any one would think you were mad to hear you talk."

" I cannot think that he would have put his threats into execution, and—"

" Nonsense !   You know full well the desperate and determined character of your son, and must be aware that he would not hesitate to commit any crime to gratify his revenge.   I think we have adopted the wisest and the only safe course, unless we had taken his life away at once."

" If we had put him in a less awful place of confinement," said Gerald, "that would have answered every purpose, and he would have been equally secure."

" You'll remember it was your own proposition," said Chesterton ; " but where else could you have confined him ?"

" In one of the strong chambers of the house," answered Gerald.

" From which he could easily have effected his escape," added the steward, " or have made his situation known."

" That would have been impossible, except to Madge, for the rooms I speak of are so remote, that it would have been a fruitless task for him to have attempted to have made his escape, or to make his situation known to any person."

" He cannot be better than where he is," said the steward, " and if you attempt to alter his situation, we shall be ruined.   I am afraid, Gerald, that when I am gone you will, in a moment of weakness, destroy all that we have taken so much difficulty to accomplish, and by liberating your son, place us all in a most dangerous dilemma."

" I have given you my word that I will not," answered Gerald, after a pause, " and I will not break it."

" And you will not attempt to remove him from his present place of confinement ?" asked the steward.

"I will not," was the reply.

"Enough—I am satisfied," said Chesterton; and at that moment, as old Madge passed the parlour casement, the conversation dropped.

During the day, Gerald Darnley, notwithstanding he tried all he could to conquer his emotion, suffered the most acute agony of mind; but towards night, the arguments of the villain Chesterton had so far succeeded with him, that he became quite composed, and after weighing every circumstance in his mind, felt convinced that there was no dependence to be placed in the promises of his son, and thought that he could not have adopted a more prudent or secure plan, to set all his fears at rest as regarded the threats of Will.

When Madge found that Will did not return the whole of the day, she concluded that Gerald's surmises as to his having started off in search of Emily were correct, and both Darnley and Chesterton, of course, encouraged her in that supposition.

The two villains did not separate until a late hour, but sat together talking over their future plans, and the manner in which they thought it would be most advisable for Chesterton to proceed in his search after the fugitives. It was agreed between him and Gerald, that three ruffians, acquaintances of the latter, and with whom they had often been engaged in various nefarious transactions, should be despatched after the steward, to be in readiness to assist him, should he find the objects of his search in the neighbourhood where he was going to, and Gerald promised to make every arrangement with them to that effect.

"Should I be fortunate enough to find them there," said Chesterton, "I must not be too precipitate, or I may be thwarted in my endeavours to get them in my power. I must use stratagem, watch a most favourable opportunity, and when they fancy themselves the most secure, then can I surprise them, and bear them away witnout much difficulty."

No. 28

"True," returned Gerald, "and you will not delay any longer than you can help on the road, I suppose, but come direct hither?"

"Certainly," answered Chesterton; "what shall I have to detain me on the road unless it is some accident? You have everything in readiness here for their reception, and we must take especial care that they do not again have an opportunity of escaping from us."

"I will take care of that," said Gerald; "but you are almost too sanguine, as I have told you before, although I hope that you may be able to prove that I am mistaken."

"I hope so too," returned Chesterton; "but come, it is late, and I must rise early in the morning, as I have many things to arrange for my journey. In the first place, I must send some plausible excuse to his lordship for my protracted absence, although he is, doubtless, so occupied in entering into the pleasures of the metropolis, that he seldom, if ever, thinks about me."

"Perhaps not," snswered Gerald; "although it will be as well to send an excuse, as you say, lest his lordship might entertain some suspicion. You had better remain here to-night."

"I will do so," said Chesterton, "and care not how soon I retire to my chamber."

Gerald and the steward now separated for the night, and hastened to their chambers.

CHAPTER XVIII.

THE CONFLAGRATION.—THE ESCAPE.

The next morning, all the arrangements being made, Miles Chesterton took his departure from the Old Lone House. We shall not trouble the reader with an account of his journey, as nothing occurred on the road of any interest; and in due time he was set down within a few miles of the place of his destination. He walked there, and put up at an obscure inn, where he thought his appearance was less likely to excite any curiosity or suspicion, and determined to commence operations in the morning.

The persons who frequented the inn while Chesterton was there were very few; and after he had taken sufficient time to rest himself, therefore, he walked from the house, and took the direction which he had been given to understand led to the residence of Mrs. Seagrove. Night had set in when he arrived there; and although he did not expect to see anything of them, if they were there, at that hour, he felt a sort of gratification in taking a survey of the house in which the object of his search might, in all probability, be secreted. He walked around it and examined every window, but he did not perceive any light in either of them; and he was, therefore, compelled to believe either that Mrs. Seagrove was from home, or had retired to rest. After waiting on the spot for a few minutes without any prospect of his gaining any intelligence, he left it and returned to the inn, still indulging in the hope that he should at last succeed in finding Emily and Patty in that neighbourhood.

On his return to the inn, there were several persons assembled in the coffee-room. and in order that he might not appear singular, and might also gain some information from their discourse which might be of service to him, he took his seat in the same room.

The conversation was of a general nature, but principally devoted to the subjects more commonly discussed than others in the parlour of a country inn—namely, the state of the crops, the markets, &c.; and Chesterton was beginning to yawn, and was thinking about seeking his own chamber, when he heard one of the company mention the name of Mrs. Seagrove. His ears were open in a minute, and being seated near the individual who was speaking, he listened attentively, but without appearing to be paying any attention.

" They were two fine girls, from London, I think," said the person alluded to.

" Yes," said the man to whom he was addressing himself, " the wenches were well enough, but they were too simple, I think, to be from the great metropolis."

" Why neither you nor I had much chance to judge of them," observed the other, " for Mrs. Seagrove used to keep them so close in the house that no one hardly ever saw them. I can't think what could have been her motives for that, unless it was that she was afraid some one would run away with them; and I confess I shouldn't have minded making love to one of them myself, for I was quite smitten with them at first sight."

" I remember one of them from quite a child," said the second speaker, " she was brought up by Mrs. Seagrove, who is said to be her aunt— Patty, I think they call her. The other one I do not remember to have seen before, although they are so very much alike that I should take them to be sisters."|

" Yes, there is a great likeness between them," returned his friend; " but they have left Mrs. Seagrove's."

" Yes," said the gentleman, " they have; so I suppose they only came upon a short visit. Have you any idea whither they have gone?"

" I have not," answered the other; " but it strikes me that they are in the neighbourhood, and that they have some reason for being so sly in their movements, and in not letting the place of their destination be known."

" Why, as for that, I do not see anything at all remarkable, seeing that it was of no business to any persons but themselves and their friends."

" Very true; but these two girls. somehow or the other, have excited such an interest in my breast that I cannot help feeling that I should like to see them again, and to become better acquainted with them."

" Which it is not very probable you will ever do," observed the previous speaker's companion, with a smile; and there the conversation dropped. But it would be utterly impossible to describe the feelings of Chesterton during the time it was going on. His agitation was so great that he had much difficulty in concealing it from the observation of the persons present. Here, then, his surmises were confirmed. Emily and Patty had sought a shelter at the house of Mrs. Seagrove, but had gone again; and had he not have been so long before he left the Old Lone House for that neighbourhood, he might have at once achieved the object of his journey, and got Emily, at any rate, once more within his power. It was singular that he should be guided to a house where a conversation upon the subject should take place on the first night of his arrival there, and he could not still help thinking the same as one of the speakers, namely, that the girls were yet concealed somewhere in the locality, and he determined to leave no stratagem untried to find them out.

Not being disposed, after having gained this information, to listen to, or join in the common-place conversation which was going forward among the guests, Chesterton now retired to the chamber allotted to him, and he there indulged in meditation upon the subject which had so long occasioned him the utmost care and anxiety, and endeavoured to devise some scheme which would be likely to bring his efforts to a successful issue.

He was surprised that Emily and Patty had not used more caution than, it was evident, they had done, and that they had not taken more care not to be seen ; but above all he regretted that the idea had not suggested itself to him sooner to search for them in that quarter—then they would have been certain to have fallen into his power.   However, he fully resolved that he would do all that ingenuity,-perseverance, and promptitude could accomplish, in order that he might still meet with success ; and hope suggested to him that he should yet triumph.

So elated was he with what he had heard, that he could not sleep for thinking upon it, for some time after he had retired to his bed, and when he did, dreams of the most flattering description haunted his imagination. He fancied that he had succeeded in his stratagems—that he was once more at the Old Lone House, and that Emily was again in his power.   He thought, moreover, that he had triumphed over the objections of our heroine —that she returned his passion—that he held her in his embraces, and pressed warm kisses upon her lips, which she returned with the same ardour ; and in the midst of his ideal happiness he awoke to the reality of disappointment.

The visions that had flitted before his imagination increased his energy and determination, and he made up his mind to lose no time in prosecuting his enquiries and researches ; but it would be necessary to do that with the utmost precaution, lest suspicion should be excited, and, if Emily and her companion were in the neighbourhood, it would afford them an opportunity to escape. · In the course of an hour or two he had well laid all his plans, and was resolved not to lose any time in putting them into execution.

After he had partaken of his morning's repast he left the inn, and made his way towards the place where he had appointed to meet the men whom Gerald Darnley had provided to aid him in the plot, and who had started at the same time as himself, but by a different coach.

He found that they had arrived, and were at the cottage which belonged to one of their friends ; and here Chesterton informed them of what he had heard, cautioned them to keep a sharp look out, and to bring him any information they might obtain, immediately.

They had not been many days in the neighbourhood, ere they succeeded in so doing ; they first ascertained that Mrs. Seagrove was on intimate terms with Farmer Walton, and they afterwards learnt decidedly that the two girls who had first resided at the house of that lady, were then sheltered beneath the roof of the farmer.

The extacy of Chesterton at this information, and the success, so far, of his stratagem, knew no bounds, and he already considered his complete triumph as all but certain.   But to get them in his power immediately, it would be impossible, he must devise some scheme to do so without endangering himself, and it therefore became indispensably necessary that he should not act with too much precipitation, lest his plans should be frustrated.   We have already shewn the reader how he watched about the farm, and was at last gratified by seeing Emily and Patty at one of the windows ; and we need not say what were his emotions at the moment. He could scarcely contain himself for joy, at the good fortune which had hitherto attended him ; but fearful that the girls might have observed him, he hurried away, and returning to the place where he had put up, he sought to consider what it would be best for him to do.   If they had seen him, there was no time to be lost, for they would, doubtless, immediately quit the neighbourhood, and find some means to elude him ; but he could not make an attack on the house and bear them off, and all that they could do would be to keep a strict watch round about the house to see whether they ventured to walk out, and if they did, it would be very easy for him and his companions to seize them, and convey them speedily from the spot.

At one time he had a good mind to go boldly to the farm and demand them; but then again he abandoned that idea, being afraid that they would appeal to the magistrates for protection, and that would be the means of the whole of the villany practised by himself and his infamous associates being found out.

He placed his companions in different parts of the neighbourhood, and they all four kept up a constant watch all day, and to a late hour every evening; but Emily and Patty being certain that it was Chesterton they had seen, kept themselves so closely confined to the house, as we have before described, that the opportunity they were so anxious for, was not afforded them.

In the meantime, Chesterton accidentally became acquainted with the sentiments of Captain Bellingham and Sir Edgecumbe Sappington towards our heroine and Patty, and he had not the least doubt but that it was their determination to elope with them, the first chance which was offered them, consequently he had no time to lose, or they would succeed in thwarting his scheme, and getting possession of the prize it had cost him so much care, trouble, and danger to obtain. How he succeeded, we have already shewn the reader, and we will now, therefore, return to our unfortunate heroine, whom the ruffians conveyed according to the orders of the delighted steward, to the cottage, without meeting with any interruption. Chesterton was, however, very much vexed and somewhat uneasy that he had not succeeded in getting Patty into his power as well as Emily, but his unbounded joy at having succeeded so far as he had done, soon drove that idea from his thoughts.

Emily had became insensible immediately after her seizure, and as Chesterton gazed upon her, and pressed his lips rapturously to her's, he thought the poor girl looked more lovely than ever.

We will pass hastily over this scene, and merely state that, when our heroine again recovered her senses, she found herself in a post-chaise seated by the side of Chesterton, and the vehicle was proceeding at a most rapid rate. The terror she felt needs no description; but she clasped her hands in despair, and knew it was useless to give way to lamentation, or to appeal to one who was callous to all sense of feeling. She fixed upon him a look of the most searching inquiry and horror, and the savage glances of triumph with which the steward was eying her, were not at all calculated to lessen the fears she experienced. That she was being conveyed to the Old Lone House again, she had not the least doubt, and when the horrors she had already endured there, and the fate which seemed likely to be in store for her, rushed hastily upon her brain, she felt she had but too good reason to despair.

Chesterton, however, did not give her much time for reflection, and during the brief interval that had elapsed since her recovery, he had been eying her with looks of the utmost boldness, while at the same time his delight was so powerful that he could not help giving full expression to it.

"Beauteous Emily, need I tell you the extacy your restoration has imparted to me?" he observed. "Oh, did you but know the state of anxiety, of distraction which I have been in since your flight, you would no longer doubt the power of the love I feel for you, and might be inclined to lend a favourable ear to the asseverations of my passion."

Emily turned upon the villain a look of the most ineffable disgust and contempt, but recollecting she was in his power, and that if she exasperated him he might be induced to act with violence, she lowered her indignation as much as possible, and, in a voice of the most impressive supplication, said—

"Oh, Chesterton, and will pity for ever remain a stranger to your bo

Why will you not suffer me to remain at liberty, or if you have the power
to detain me, prove to me the authority by which you act? Whither are
you now conveying me? Oh, in mercy do not again take me to that fearful place, but suffer me to remain at liberty, and all that you and Gerald
Darnley have previously inflicted on me, I will freely forgive, and never reveal to any one that might be the means of working you harm."

Chesterton shook his head.

"And think you, Emily, after all the trouble I have taken to find you
out again, and the passion with which you have inspired me, I will so
easily resign you?" he exclaimed. "No, no—you are mine now, and we
part no more."

"Alas! Alas!" groaned Emily, wringing her hands, "what will become
of me? Oh, God! do not suffer, I beseech you, the guilty to triumph over
me!"

"I seek your affections," returned Chesterton; "those obtained, every
happiness that the world can afford you, shall be at your command."

Emily made no answer to this speech, but she clasped her hands vehemently together, and raising her eyes, she breathed a prayer to Heaven for
its Almighty interference.

"And whither are you conveying me?" she demanded, after a pause, and
during which interval she had become more composed.

"To the house from which you made your escape," answered the
steward.

"Alas!" sighed our heroine, "to endure a repetition of those horrors I
have already undergone there?"

"To enjoy every happiness but liberty, if you will not obstinately oppose my wishes," returned Chesterton.

"Happiness with you!" cried Emily, with a look of disgust.

"Yes, happiness with me," replied Chesterton. "I tell you again, that
if you will but look with favour upon my suit, there is no comfort which I
will not study to procure for you."

"The bare idea of such a thing fills my mind with horror," said Emily,
and she covered her face with her hands to shut out the bold and disgusting glances which the steward fixed upon her.

"Nay, Emily," observed Chesterton, who bit his lips with vexation at
the hatred and disgust which she expressed towards him, "it is useless for
you thus to seek to exasperate me by insulting speeches, and treating my
vows with scorn. To obtain possession of you I have run every risk, and I
am determined, let the consequences be whatever they may, that, in spite
of your opposition, I will gain the gratification of my desires, and if you do
not yield to my solicitations, force shall compel you."

"Heaven will, I trust, interpose to prevent you," ejaculated our heroine.
"Oh, Patty, kind-hearted and equally unfortunate girl, what has become
of you? Perhaps your fate is as terrible as mine."

"Ah!" exclaimed the steward, "it was a very unfortunate job that Sir
Edgecumbe succeeded in bearing her away, for should she betray us, we
are lost."

The whole circumstances of their seizure by Captain Bellingham and Sir
Edgecumbe Sappington now recurred to the memory of our heroine, and
she suffered her anxiety for the fate of her friend to make as great an impression upon her as her own. And yet her seizure by Sir Edgecumbe,
Emily could not help thinking was preferable to her having fallen again
into the power of Gerald Darnley, as she might be able to escape from the
former, and be the means, by divulging all she knew to the proper authorities, to rescue her (Emily) from the danger which threatened her.

Finding that it was completely useless for her to complain, or to appeal to Chesterton for pity, Emily at last resolved to remain silent, and throwing herself back in the vehicle, and covering her face with her handkerchief, she gave herself up entirely to the gloomy meditations that her situation gave rise to.

It was now getting rather late at night, but still the chaise proceeded on its way, only stopping occasionally, in some retired spot, to give the horses temporary rest. Emily having completely abandoned herself to despair, took no notice of what was passing, and Chesterton did not offer to interrupt her in her meditations, which were of the most pleasing description, having once more got into his power that girl who was at once the object of his fears and his admiration. He pictured to himself the astonishment which Gerald Darnley would experience when he found that he had succeeded in discovering Emily and Patty, and in bringing the former once more to the Old Lone House; but he was determined that the dreadful deed which Gerald had expressed his resolution to perpetrate should Emily ever again fall into their hands, should never take place, unless absolute necessity, and to save their own lives, should render such a dreadful alternative unavoidable.

He was very anxious to return to the Old Lone House, in order that he might ascertain whether Will Darnley was still in confinement, and he reflected with double gratification upon the additional torture which the knowledge of Emily being in his (Chesterton's) power, would be sure to inflict upon the young man's mind. This would afford ample means for the satiation of his revenge, and his soul panted for the time to arrive when he could taunt him upon the subject, which he determined to do, in spite of the injunctions of Gerald Darnley, and in the manner in which he had threatened him to do.

They continued to travel the whole of the night, and nothing worth noticing occurred. The steward never offered to engage our heroine in conversation, after the one we have described, and after travelling for an hour or two, buried in deep thought, he at length fell asleep; and Emily was thus released from the resentment and disgust which his discourse would have occasioned her.

The sun had only just began to peep above the eastern hills, when the vehicle reached the heath upon which the Old Lone House stood, and in a short time afterwards, Emily beheld that dismal place, from the window of the vehicle. Her heart sunk with the most indescribable terror, as she gazed once more upon that lonely building, in which she had suffered so much, and encountered so many terrors, and she dreaded to meet again that guilty man, whose soul was stained with so many crimes, and who had undertaken to become her murderer.

Gerald Darnley had not been apprized by the steward of what had taken place, so that when the vehicle drew up to the door, he was much surprised and alarmed, thinking it was his lordship, whose suspicions and doubts having been excited by the long absence of Chesterton, he had come there to ascertain the cause, and he felt at a loss to invent a story to satisfy him as to the disposal of Emily, and whither the steward had gone. He came to the door, and when he beheld Chesterton alight, and immediately afterwards assist our heroine to descend from the carriage, his astonishment and satisfaction may be very easily conjectured.

Emily trembled violently and hung down her head when she once more beheld the detested Gerald Darnley, while the latter uttered an exclamation of gratification, as he hastened towards her, and taking hold of her arm rather savagely, assisted Chesterton to lead her into the house.

"Ah!" he exclaimed, "by hell, this is a fortunate job! The girl once more in our power! She shall escape no more. Welcome, young lady, to your old quarters ! Chesterton, this business does you credit. But, where is Patty ?"

"She is not with me!" answered Chesterton.

"Ah! has she then escaped?" cried Gerald, "confusion! Our danger is then not at an end!"

"I know not that;" returned the steward, "but I will explain everything to you, presently."

"And so," exclaimed Gerald, with a fearful scowl, "you thought to elude our vigilance, girl, did you! But you find you have deceived yourself, and I will take good care that you shall never have another opportunity of releasing yourself. Had you acted differently, you might have averted your fate, but now——"

"Hold, Gerald Darnley," interrupted Chesterton; "it is no time to talk in this manner. We must confer together anon upon the subject."

Completely overcome by the terrors which the words and demeanour of Gerald Darnley had created in her bosom, Emily threw herself at the feet of the two villains, and, with tearful eyes, implored their pity and forbearance.

"You supplicate in vain, girl," cried Gerald, fiercely; "you have proved by your conduct that you are not to be trusted, and our own safety demands that we——"

He was interrupted by the entrance of old Madge, who, upon seeing our heroine, clasped her hands together, and exclaiming—"Ma conscience!"—stared at her with the greatest amazement, and seemed to be scarcely able to credit the evidence of her eyes.

Emily continued on her knees, and still looked up imploringly in the stern countenances of Gerald Darnley and the steward; but she implored to them fruitlessly, and Chesterton having raised her from the posture she had thrown herself into, turned to Gerald and said—

"Come, come, Gerald, there has been enough of this; myself and my companions here are hungry, for we have not stopped to partake of anything upon the road. Let us have some refreshments, therefore, without any more delay, and Madge can see Emily to her apartments, and look to her wants."

Gerald ordered the old woman to spread a repast upon the table, which having done, she motioned Emily to follow her, and led the way to a different part of the building to that in which she had been previously confined.

Gerald waited with the utmost impatience while Chesterton and the others partook of of their meal; which having at last despatched, and the three ruffians taken their departure, Gerald turned to the steward and said—

"And now, Chesterton, do not keep me any longer in this confounded state of suspense, but furnish me with all the particulars of what has occurred to you since you have been away, and by what means you so fortunately contrived to find the runaway?"

"Well," answered Chesterton, "I will no longer tire your patience; and I think, when I have made you acquainted with everything, you will acknowledge that I have acted in this affair with great judgment and precaution."

"I have no doubt you have," observed Gerald; "but proceed."

Chesterton then related every particular with which the reader has already been made acquainted, and Darnley listened to him with the greatest attention and the deepest interest.

"How cursed unfortunate it is," he exclaimed, when Chesterton had concluded—"how cursed unfortunate it is that Patty should have escaped."

"It is," returned the steward, "but it could not be helped. If we had pursued the captain and Sir Edgecumbe, we might have been surprised, and the girl Emily taken from us."

"Should Patty contrive to escape from this Sir Edgecumbe Sappington, as you call him," added Darnley, "we shall still be in danger of our evil deeds being discovered."

"Had you not been either thoughtless or obstinate," said Chesterton, "and have mentioned the fact of Mrs. Seagrove, or your sister, as you call her, being living, and have agreed in my opinion, that Emily and Patty had sought refuge there, they would both have been in our power long ere this."

"Yes, I will own I was to blame," returned Gerald; "but it can't be helped now. We must not fail to use every exertion to discover where she is, and to get her into our power."

"True; but I am doubtful of our success," said Chesterton. "But what of Will? Is he still in the same place of confinement?"

"He is," replied Gerald, "and expresses great regret for the threats he held out to us. But now that Emily is again in our power, I have a scheme by which we may release him, and without being under any apprehension for the consequences."

"Psha!" ejaculated the steward with a frown, "nothing but his safe custody ought to satisfy us. But what is your scheme?"

"Give him up Emily, and compel him to banish himself with her, from the country for ever," answered Gerald.

"And think you I will agree to this?" interrogated Chesterton.

"If you are wise, you will," replied Gerald.

"What!" exclaimed the steward, "and do you suppose, then, that after I have had all the trouble I have to get the girl into my possesion, I

No. 29

should be that egregious ass to bestow her upon my rival?—Ha! ha! ha!
—You must be mad to think of such a thing, Gerald."

"But you must consent!"

"Must!—that is a bold word, but I tell you I will never consent!"

"Then the girl dies!"

"She shall not!"

"How!—would you oppose the will of his lordship?" demanded
Gerald.

"I have fixed my mind upon the girl, as you know," returned Chesterton; "and I am determined to have her. I think, after all the trouble I
have been at, I am fully entitled to her."

"While the girl lives, or is in this country, we shall not be safe a single
hour," said Gerald.

"Nonsense!" said the steward; "I will be bound for her security.
Come, Gerald, you and I must not quarrel over this business. It is necessary for us both that we should remain friends."

"I have no wish that we should be otherwise," observed Darnley; "but
upon this point we cannot, unfortunately, agree. I think I have suggested
a very good plan for the ensurance of our mutual safety, and to prevent
the shedding of human blood."

"The proposition is unreasonable, and one to which I cannot accede."

"You had better take time to consider of it," remarked Darnley.

"Well, well, I agree, but I do not think that anything will alter my determination;" replied the steward. "What apartments do you think of
confining the girl in?"

"Two in the left wing of the building," answered Gerald. "I think
they are more secure than any of the rest."

"'Tis well," observed Chesterton, "we must keep a strict eye upon her
this time, for should she again escape, it is a chance if we should be able
to get her in our power again, and she would, in all probability, seek the
protection of those authorities who would afford her redress, and bring us
to punishment for our crimes."

"I will take care that she shall not have such an opportunity."

"To-morrow or the next day, I must leave here for London, to join his
lordship," said the steward, "but as soon as I can I will return hither,
and during my absence, I shall trust to your honour in taking proper care
of the girl, and not to endeavour to act in regard to her derogatary to my
wishes."

"Oh, you may trust to me," answered Gerald, while at the same time
an expression passed over his countenance, which escaped the observation
of Chesterton, or his suspicions would have been excited. "But do you
not think it is likely that during the time Emily and Patty have been under
the protection of this Farmer Walton and Mrs. Seagrove, that they have
made them acquainted with the treatment they have received under this
roof?"

"No," replied Chesterton; "if they had done so, we should have been
called to an account for our conduct from another quarter before this, you
may depend upon it."

"But they must have given some good substantial reason for their being
driven to take the course they did, in eloping from this place," said Gerald.

"True," coincided the steward, "and no doubt they did invent some
plausible excuse; although I think that fear would prevent them from
telling the truth."

"And now that they have disappeared so suddenly from the place,"
added Gerald, "they may conclude that they have again fallen into our
hands, and if they really feel so deeply interested in the fate of the girls,

as the shelter and protection they afforded them would make it appear they are, they might institute such inquiries as would prove anything but pleasant to us."

"It is folly for us to alarm ourselves with these useless surmises;" said the steward, after a pause; "I do not think that we have any occasion to encourage them."

"I hope what you say may prove to be true," returned Gerald, "but I am far from easy upon the subject."

Madge now entered the room, having conducted our heroine to the apartments allotted to her use, and the conversation was abruptly terminated.

Madge took up some refreshments to the fair prisoner, who, on her entrance into the room, she found on her knees, earnestly supplicating the mercy and protection of the Supreme Being. She stood a few moments and gazed at her in silence, and, for the first time, the old woman could not help feeling a ray of pity stealing to her heart; it was only transient, and placing the provisions she had brought with her on the table, she quitted the room.

Although it was several hours since Emily had eaten anything, her mind was too much distracted to suffer her to partake only but very slightly of the repast which Madge had brought her; but the little she did eat, refreshed her, and recruited her exhausted strength.

Again then, she was in the power of those cruel men, whom she had so much cause to dread, and when she remembered the words that Gerald had uttered, it seemed pretty evident to her that her doom was sealed. Even if she was saved from the murderer's knife, had she not everything to dread from the loathsome passion of Chesterton?—And would not death, even in its most terrible shape, be preferable to such a fate as that? —Oh, yes, it would;—misery, shame, degradation presented far greater terrors to her than the grave.

"And why should I wish to live?" she soliloquized, "why should I, the poor friendless one, who has never known anything but sorrow, wish to prolong this wretched existence?—Oh, no, rather let me court death as a friend, whose unerring dart will release me from all my heavy afflictions."

Tears here came to the poor girl's relief, and she became silent and abstracted for some time, a living statue of despair and misery.

Madge had informed her that Will Darnley had quitted the house some days before, and it was supposed that he had gone in search of her. Our heroine was pleased to hear this, as it would relieve her from the odious persecution of one of her oppressors, and she hoped that something would occur to prevent her ever seeing him again, as his very name was sufficient to fill her with disgust and horror.

The situation of our heroine was now, if possible, worse than it had been before when she was a prisoner in the Old Lone House, for then she had a gentle companion in Patty, who was ever ready to sympathise with her in her distresses, and to offer her all the consolation in her power. But now she was alone, surrounded with nothing but enemies, and with the knowledge of that dear friend being also exposed to misery, without any certainty as to her fate.

These reflections were sufficiently agonizing, and Emily wept most bitterly as they distracted her mind.

The apartments she was now confined in were large and gloomy, but comfortably furnished, and there were several books upon a shelf in one corner of the inner room; but Emily could not attempt even to abstract her thoughts from her own sorrows by reading, and the time, therefore, passed heavily and tediously away.

Chesterton did not offer to visit her that day, and after her first being brought to the house, Emily saw no one but old Madge, who only came to her when she came to bring her her meals, and then seldom made use of more than one or two observations, which always fell listlessly upon our heroine's ears, and were seldom replied to by her.   It was the intention of Chesterton, she undertood, to lodge in the house, which served to increase her alarm, especially when she recalled to her memory the different events that had taken place when she was before a prisoner there.   She examined the rooms around, but there was nothing to afford her the least hope that she would be able to make her escape, the doors and windows being too well secured.   Towards night, however, she became more composed, and having committed herself to the care of Omnipotence, feeling fatigued, she retired to rest, and sleep came to the relief of her agitated mind.

After the conversation, which we described in a few pages previous to have taken place, had concluded, Chesterton having some business to transact with the three fellows whom he had employed to assist him in bearing Emily away, quitted the house, and, on being left alone, Gerald having sent old Madge to another part of the building, lighted a lamp, and opening the secret panel, began to descend the steps, with a determination to visit his wretched son in his horrible place of confinement.

"Trust to my honour," he soliloquised, as he proceeded; "ha! ha! ha! What a mockery!   He shall find that in this instance Gerald Darnley will have his way; if the boy agrees to my proposition, as soon as Chesterton shall have departed from London, I will release him, and let the girl be the companion of his flight.   It will be better than shedding her blood."

Gerald Darnley had now become so used to the terrors of these dismal places, that he could enter them without the slightest feeling of dread, and he passed through the different vaults without bestowing the least attention to their horrors, until he arrived at the door of the one in which Will was incarcerated.

The young man, whose constitution was greatly impaired from confinement, did not make any effort to arise from the pallet of straw on which he was reclining on his father's entrance, and he stood looking at him for a few seconds earnestly and in silence.

"Will," at length said Darnley, "has the punishment you have received, yet brought you to your senses, and would you still put your threats into execution?"

"Father," replied Will, in a subdued tone, "why do you come to torture me?"

"I came not for that purpose, boy."

"Was it then to give me death?   It would be far preferable to this lingering state of misery," said Will.

"Answer me my first question."

"It is useless; I have so often assured you that I would abandon such designs, but you would not believe me."

"I am inclined to trust you now."

"Ah!" exclaimed the young man, in a tone of joy, and starting to his feet as well as his almost exhausted strength would permit him, "can you really mean what you say, or do you only mock me?"

"I am sincere," answered Gerald, "I have only to exact certain conditions from you, and then, to-morrow or the next day, I will give you liberty!"

"Can I hear aright?" cried Will Darnley, "or do my senses deceive me?"

"You do not deceive yourself, nor are you deceived, Will," replied his father. "I will not only release you from this awful dungeon, but give you Emily."

"Emily!"

"Ay, Chesterton discovered the place of her retreat, got her in his power, and she arrived here this morning," answered Gerald.

"Emily an inmate of this house again, and you offer her to me! What is the meaning of this change in your resolution? You bewilder me!"

"I would defeat the designs of the steward," said Gerald, "and save the life of the girl. It rests with you whether those wishes shall be accomplished or not."

"How!"

"You must promise me that you will depart with the girl to some foreign land, and never more return to this country," said Gerald Darnley.

"Promise," said Will, "oh, willingly—sincerely."

"You must also promise that nothing shall ever induce you to reveal any of the circumstances that have occurred to us, or the crimes of which we have been guilty."

"My own safety will, of course, prevent me from doing that," answered Will.

"Enough, then; to-morrow night, or the next, you may expect me."

And before the young man could make any reply, Gerald had departed from the vault, and fastened the door after him, leaving him in a state of the greatest astonishment, to reflect on the singular proposition which he had made to him.

A suffocating smell suddenly awoke our heroine, and starting up in the bed, on which she had laid down without undressing herself, she was horror-struck at beholding a large glare of light in the apartment, and beheld flames forcing their way through the panels of the bed-room door. She screamed loudly with terror, and starting from the bed, rushed towards the casement, and tried to open it, but it defied all her efforts, and completely distracted, she turned her eyes towards the door, but all hopes of escape that way seemed futile, as the room beyond appeared to be involved in flames, and the poor girl wrung her hands, and looked despairingly towards Heaven, as nothing but the prospect of a horrible death was before her. The crackling of the burning timber, the roaring of the destructive element, and the falling of different portions of the building, formed a concatenation of noises that were awful in the extreme; while the dense clouds of smoke that filled the room, almost took away her senses. Wound up to a pitch of desperation, at last Emily made a rush towards the burning door, and forcing it in, dashed madly through the flames until she reached the passage beyond, (the outer door having been destroyed), without sustaining any material injury. Here, however, all further egress seemed to be entirely cut off, for the staircase was in one mass of flames, and to have attempted to have descended it would have been certain death. She had not a moment for thought, but turned towards the left, believing that it led to a small gallery, and with which a staircase communicated. Here the flames seemed not yet to have reached; and Emily hurried hastily on. She was just about to descend the stairs, when a portion of the opposite side of the building fell in, and she plainly distinguished the form of a man, who appeared to be clinging to the rafters, fall with it, and sink into the raging gulph beneath. She had but a moment to look, but that was enough to convince her that the form she had seen was that of the wretched, guilty Gerald Darnley. She hurried down the stairs, and making her way towards an opening in the building, in spite of the flames that roared and hissed around her, gained providentially the outside of the house, and hurrying to a short distance across the moor, where she was in safety, she sunk on her knees, and returned her thanks to Heaven for her miraculous preservation. She could yet see the livid glare reflected from the conflagration in the Heavens, and when she thought of the awful death of Gerald Darnley, although it ridded her of one of her bitterest enemies, she could not help shuddering with the intensity of her horror. Had the villain Chesterton met with a similar fate; she strongly suspected that he had, and dreadful was the retribution with which they had been visited. But these ideas shot with the speed of lightning through her brain, and then she had to devote her whole thoughts to the future course she should pursue. Her situation was, indeed, awful, without any friends, protectors, but such as she might find in the Walton family, or from Mrs. Seagrove, and she revolted at the idea of again intruding upon the kindness of these benevolent people, upon whom she had not the slightest claim, and to whom her and her equally unfortunate friend, Patty, had already brought so much trouble; besides, what means had she of prosecuting the journey to them, destitute of money, and when she considered the length of the same? Her thoughts were, however, for the present diverted from the subject, by the idea of where she should direct her steps that night. To remain upon the barren moor, she could not bear to think of with any degree of patience; and yet where could she seek a shelter, being entirely without money, and as the hour was such an unseasonable one.

Although the reflection of the flames must have been seen from the nearest village or town, no one came near the burning pile, and the Old Lone House was, therefore, suffered to fall a prey to the devouring element, without any person offering to render assistance to try to save it.

At length, after racking her brain for some time, in uselessly endeavouring to think of some place where she would be likely to obtain a shelter, Mrs. Burton, who had so kindly treated her and Patty on their escape from the Old Lone House, recurred to her recollection, and, although it was some distance from the place where she then was, as her only prospect of a lodging for the night rested there, and probably of advice in what manner it would be best for her to prcceed in future, she determined to make the best of her way thither. After having once more, therefore, offered up her thanks to the throne of mercy, for having rescued her from the power of Gerald Darnley and his infamous colleague, she pushed on her way across the moor, as fast as the fatigue she had already undergone from her exertions would permit her.

It was long past midnight when she arrived at the cottage of Mrs. Burton, in neither of the casements of which did she perceive a light. She poused at the door, and could scarcely find courage to knock, although she knew not what reason she had to fear, and especially after the behaviour she had experienced on a former occasion, from Mrs. Burton and her daughter. She had not a doubt but that they had retired to rest, and it was a pity to disturb them; but there was no time for reflection, or for hesitation. The time was waning away apace, and Emily knew not the danger with which delay might be fraught. She at last knocked at the door of the cottage, but she had to repeat it two or three times before any notice was taken of it, but at length she observed a glimmering light in one of the casements above, and almost immediately afterwards it was cautiously opened, and the head of Mrs. Burton protruded itself, and in a timid voice demanded who was there, and what they wanted at that hour of the night. Our heroine answered her as laconically as she could, and Mrs. Burton uttered an exclamation of astonishment as she recognised Emily's voice.

"Bless my soul! is it possible?" ejaculated the old woman, "whatever can have brought the poor child into this neighbourhood again, and alone? Stay there, my dear, and I will come down stairs immediately and let you in."

"Oh, thanks! thanks!" cried our heroine; but Mrs. Burton had taken in her head, and was already descending the stairs; therefore she did not hear her. Emily had not to wait many minutes before the cottage door was opened, and Mrs. Burton made her appearance in her night-clothes, and immediately recognising Emily, embraced her with all the same affection as if she had been an old and intimate friend, and welcomed her to the cottage.

"Ellen has gone to service," said the old woman, "and, therefore, I can very well accomodate you, and shall be very glad of your company, for it is remarkably lonely here by one'self. But bless the child, what has again brought you to this neighbourhood, and alone;—and what has become of Miss Patty?"

"The story is too long to tell now," answered our heroine, "but I will furnish you with every particular in the morning. In the meantime, it may be enough to inform you for the present, that I know not what has become of my unfortunate friend, Patty; that I once more fell into the power of my enemies, and was conveyed to the Old Lone House again, which this night was totally destroyed by fire, and I believe that Gerald Darnley, Chesterton, and Madge, have all three perished in the flames."

"Heaven's will be done!" piously exclaimed the old woman, clasping her hands together, "what a terrible visitation of the vengeance of the Almighty; and to think that I should not see or know anything of the fire. Well, for certain it is a very good job that that old House is destroyed; for it was a nasty, dreary, frightful looking place, and I am much deceived if there have not been deeds perpetrated within it, equally as black as its aspect."

"Oh, yes, indeed there has; too well have I experienced the truth of these surmises," returned Emily.

"I do not doubt it," returned Mrs. Burton; "but I will not put another question to you to-night, for I am certain you must be fatigued and require rest. Come, child, you will find the bed in which you reposed before, in the same room where I sleep, and I am very happy indeed to think that I should have it in my power to render you this trifling assistance."

Emily was about to return her acknowledgments to the good woman for her kindness, but Mrs. Burton would not hear her, and smiling a welcome upon her, she led the way to the clean little sleeping room, and having placed the lamp on the table, she requested our heroine to make the best of her way to bed, and to leave all further explanation till the morning.

Being, of course, very much overcome by the fatigue she had undergone, Emily did not raise any objection to this, and having undressed herself and bid Mrs. Burton good night, she hastened to the humble, but extremely clean couch, and sleep was not long before it visited her pillow. Strange dreams, however, disturbed her imagination, and presented to her fancy several fearful and tormenting scenes. which upon waking, she racked her brain in vain, to unravel, although she had no doubt that they foreboded to her much future misfortune.

As was her usual habit, she awoke at an early hour in the morning, notwithstanding which, she found that Mrs. Burton had already arisen, and had descended down stairs to tidy up the parlour, preparatory to their taking their morning's repast. Mrs. Burton greeted her with much kindness, and inquired whether she had rested well; to which Emily answered in the affirmative, and once more returned her acknowledgments to the good woman for the manner in which she had behaved to her, an absolute stranger as she was almost to her.   Mrs. Burton impatiently interrupted her, and desired that she would favour her with the particulars which she had promised to furnish her with on the previous night, with which request Emily instantly complied, and made her acquainted with all that had happened to her and the unfortunate Patty, since the last time she had seen them, until her being re-captured by Chesterton, taken to her old place of confinement, and the subsequent destruction of that house of crime by fire, and her own hazardous escape from the burning ruins.

Mrs. Burton listened to her with the deepest attention and interest, and when she had concluded, she enquired of our heroine what she thought of doing under the awkward circumstances in which she was placed.   Emily informed her that she intended once more to return to Mrs. Seagrove and the Waltons, and to solicit their protection for the present, or until something could be done for her, hoping that she should be able to obtain a situation.   Mrs. Burton would have persuaded her to remain for awhile with her ; for, she said that she had the means of supporting her well enough, as she had recently had a little property bequeathed to her, and that moreover, she would be society for her, now that Ellen was away from home : but after expressing her full sense of the kindness of the good-hearted woman, she begged leave to decline it, stating as one of her reasons, that it was too near the scene of her late misery, and that should not both of her enemies have perished, or, Will Darnley, who she did not know was in the house at the time of the conflagration, return to the neighbourhood, they might discover where she was, and it was not at all unlikely that she would thus again fall into their power.   Mrs. Burton in vain endeavoured to combat these objections, but there was one thing she would insist upon, and that was, that Emily should accept of a small sum of money to pay her expenses to where the friends who had behaved so kind to her resided, and to supply her with any little necessaries that she might require on the journey.   Emily reluctantly availed herself of this offer, shrinking from laying herself under an obligation to a person who was almost an entire stranger to her, and not having, at present, at any rate, the least prospect of having it in her power to repay her ; but the unaffected freedom with which Mrs. Burton pressed this favour upon her, at length overcome her scruples, and she accepted two or three guineas with much thankfulness.

Before she departed from the cottage of Mrs. Burton that day, the latter contrived to make all the enquiries about the fire which she could, and as nothing had been seen or heard of Chesterton and the old woman, although the remains of Gerald Darnley, dreadfully burnt, had been taken out of the ruins, it was fully believed that they had also fallen victims to the flames.

The deaths of Gerald and Chesterton now absolved our heroine from the oath which had been extorted from her, and as it would be no difficult mat-ter to discover who the master of Chesterton was, the long hidden and dreadful mysteries might be unravelled, and Emily restored to those rights which she had now every reason to believe she was unjustly deprived of. But how was she, a poor, friendless girl, without even the means of a bare subsistence, to proceed against one who possessed both wealth and power, and would laugh her accusations and her claims to scorn ?   She saw more difficulty surrounding it than she had first imagined, and she almost gave up the idea in despair.

In the afternoon our heroine left the cottage of Mrs. Burton, and having taken her place in the coach, was soon on her journey.   Alternate hopes, doubts, and fears, racked her mind as she proceeded, and her anxiety to know whether or not anything had been heard of Patty became most in-tense.   We will not detain the reader by any tedious detail of Emily's

journey, but at once set her down at the place of her destination, from which she had so recently been forced away by the wretch Chesterton, who she had every reason to believe had now paid the penalty of his numerous crimes. But terrible was the disappointment she was fated to experience; the Waltons had been driven from the farm by the hard-hearted and ignorant Sir Merton Bellingham, and instigated thereto by Mr. Justice Snoggins, and no one could give her information of whither they were gone to; and Mrs. Seagrove had been seized with a fit a short time after her disappearance in which she had suddenly expired.

It would be useless our attempting to describe the astonishment, disappointment, and grief of Emily when she received this melancholy intelligence; it was so powerful that it almost overcame her, and had not a paroxysm of tears come to her relief, she must have sunk beneath their influence. Poor Mrs. Seagrove! Alas! what would be the agony of Patty, did she but know of her fate? Of Patty, too, nothing whatever had been heard, nor could the least clue be found to her, nor any one imagine what had become of her.

There, then, was our heroine left alone in the world, and knew not what would become of her, or whither she should turn her steps. She had but a very little money left, and when that was exhausted, she must starve or beg. She wrung her hands and wept bitterly. The woman at the little inn where Emily gained this melancholy intelligence, behaved with much kindness towards her, and evinced much commiseration in her fate, and invited her to remain at her house during the time she thought of staying in the neighbourhood. Situated as she was, Emily could not but express her warmest gratitude for the woman's sympathy, and decided upon accepting of her invitation; but it must be only for a short time, as she must, before many hours had elapsed, endeavour to devise some plan for her future conduct, and whither she should go. Miserable, truly wretched, indeed, was

No. 30

the poor girl's fate, and the more she reflected upon her situation, the more bewildered did she become. The bare idea of applying to the poor-house for relief made her shudder with horror, and she thought she could almost endure anything rather than do so. But, alas! what other prospect was there before her?

At last she remembered the pressing offer which Mrs. Burton had made her, and seeing no other means, much as she dreaded laying herself under an obligation, she made up her mind to return to her, and remain beneath her humble roof until such times as she could get a situation, which she hoped, through Mrs. Burton or her daughter, shortly to be able to do.

The next day, Emily started on her way back to the village in which Mrs. Burton resided, knowing that any longer delay, and for which there was not any necessity, would exhaust the slender means she had of returning.

The poor woman was much surprised to see her come back so soon, but more astonished and grieved at the dismal account she had to give her ; but after the first ebullition of her own grief, she sought to tranquilize the feelings of our heroine, and after some considerable time spent in expostulation, she succeeded better than she expected she would have done.

We will now pass over a period of two months, during which time Emily remained at the cottage of Mrs. Burton, and was treated with every kindness, but was unable to learn anything of her friends, neither did she see any prospect of her obtaining a situation. She became daily more uneasy, although Mrs. Burton sought all in her power to make her comfortable, but our heroine's heart revolted from the bare idea of eating the bread of idleness, and her anguish daily became more insupportable.

At length a circumstance took place which promised a change, and once more inspired Emily with hope. A lady came down on a visit to a family in the neighbourhood, and during the time she was there, she visited the cottages of the poor people to see on whom she could bestow her charity, and her name was soon spoken of in terms of the highest esteem, she being regarded as a female of the most benevolent and philanthropic disposition. She was a lady of about forty years of age, stout, with good-looking and insinuating features, and of the most amiable and prepossessing manners.

Among others that she visited, was Mrs. Burton, and immediately on beholding Emily, she appeared to be greatly struck with her, and put several questions to the former about her. When Mrs. Burton had answered her, Mrs. Eldridge, for such was the lady's name, paused for a few minutes, and seemed to be buried in thought, at length, turning to Mrs. Burton, she said—

"The story you have told me about this poor girl deeply interests me, and I should like to do something for her. Would she, think you, have any objection to go to service?"

"Oh, no, madam," answered Mrs. Burton, eagerly, "that is the very thing she wishes to do, and most happy should I feel could I but hear of one for her. Poor thing! there is something about her appearance of a superior description, and she seems to be too good for a menial situation."

"That is very true," observed Mrs. Eldridge; "I am quite taken with her appearance, and as I am in want of a female companion, being a widow, and if she has no objection to go with me to London, to which place it is my intention to depart the day after to-morrow, I shall be happy to engage with her."

"Oh, madam," answered Mrs Burton, joyfully, "I am sure Emily will be delighted at the offer, and feel eternally grateful to you for your kindness. I will immediately go to her, and make known to her your proposition."

"Ay, do so, my good woman," returned the lady, "and I will wait here to hear her answer. There is no time to lose, and the sooner business of this kind is settled the better."

Mrs. Burton curtseyed very low, and proceeded up-stairs to our heroine, to whom she imparted the proposition of Mrs. Eldridge, As Mrs. Burton had anticipated, Emily expressed much pleasure at the offer, although it was mingled with pain at the thought of leaving Mrs. Burton, from whom she had received so much motherly attention, and at entering, as it were, upon a fresh life with a female of whom she had no knowledge, but who certainly appeared to be possessed of every amiable quality. She quickly, however, in a great measure stifled those feelings, and, drying up her tears, accompanied Mrs. Burton to the parlour below, where Mrs. Eldridge was impatiently awaiting her answer.

When she was made acquainted with our heroine's determination, she evinced much satisfaction, and behaved to her with so much kindness and urbanity of manners, that Emily was quite captivated with her, and mentally blessed the good fortune which had thus opened a prospect of relief from her difficulties.

Mrs. Eldridge having desired Emily to hold herself in readiness to leave for town the day after the morrow, and repeated her promises, took her departure from the cottage, and left our heroine and Mrs. Burton to converse upon the circumstances.

Emily had very few preparations to make, and by the time appointed she was in readiness. But as the hour of her departure arrived, her heart palpitated, and she felt a sensation of dread, mingled with the other anticipations in which she had ventured to indulge. She had heard much of the follies and vices of the gay metropolis, and dreaded being exposed to them ; yet surely, under the protection of a lady like Mrs. Eldridge she had nothing to fear.

The parting between her and Mrs. Burton was a most affectionate one, and they promised to correspond frequently with one another, and the former to send our heroine any information which she might obtain of the Waltons or Patty. Emily then stepped into the post-chaise along with her future mistress, and the vehicle was driven off.

CHAPTER XIX.

THE DECOY.—THE PLOT.—THE DISCOVERY.—THE ESCAPE.

As they proceeded on their journey, Mrs. Eldridge endeavoured to divert Emily's thoughts in agreeable conversation, and in pointing out and describing to her the different objects they encountered on the road ; and although she at times succeeded, yet when Emily reflected upon the sufferings of the past—the mystery of her birth — the cruel persecution she had been subjected to—the death of Mrs. Seagrove, the mysterious disappearance of the Walton family, and the abduction of Patty—it is not to be supposed that she could help feeling the most poignant anguish; and which was not a little increased at the thoughts of going amongst strangers, and entering upon such a different course of life to that which she had hitherto been used to. As they approached, however, nearer to London, the novelty and variety which her eyes encountered, for awhile estranged her ideas from such tormenting subjects, and she listened with much pleasure to the vivid and graphic description which Mrs. Eldridge gave of the manners of the inhabitants of the metropolis, and the different amusements with which it abounded.   At times it struck our heroine, however, that there was a certain tone of levity about some of the pictures which Mrs. Eldridge drew of the fashionable vices and frivolities of that "overgrown wen," which would have been as well avoided; but this did not make any serious impression upon her, as she imagined that the life of seclusion and simplicity which she had hitherto led, might cause her to put a wrong construction upon that which was really harmless; and by the time they had arrived in London, she had so far conquered her melancholy feelings as to be in better spirits than she had for some time experienced.

The vehicle at length stopped at the door of a handsome house in a fashionable street at the west end of the town; and our heroine, looking up, beheld two or three very gaily attired, but, as she could not help thinking, rather bold looking young ladies, fixed at the drawing-room windows, to whom Mrs. Eldridge nodded very familiarly, while the post-boy gave a loud double knock at the door.

"These young ladies are my nieces," said Mrs. Eldridge, as she prepared to alight from the chaise; "and you will find them very agreeable and amiable companions, my dear."

Emily made no reply, but she felt a trembling sensation come over her, as a servant in livery handed her out of the vehicle; and when she entered the hall, and the door was closed upon her, such a powerful feeling of dread came over her that had not Mrs. Eldridge taken her arm, she actually would have sunk.

"You are flurried, my dear, I see, at entering a strange place," said Mrs. Eldridge, in a voice of kindness; "but come, come, you must not be timid or bashful—you will soon see that you have no occasion for it."

"I hope you will pardon me, madam," replied Emily, in a tone of simplicity, "but indeed——"

"Yes, yes, I know what you would say, my love," added Mrs. Eldridge; "but compose yourself; I can make every allowance for your feelings, but you will soon recover yourself, I have no doubt—at least, it shall not be my fault if you do not."

They had now ascended the drawing-room stairs, and at the door the three young ladies before mentioned met them, and, with many exclamations of pleasure, embraced their aunt, and welcomed her return home. They then eyed our heroine with glances of curiosity and boldness that very much disconcerted her, and, blushing, she hung down her head, and again a deadly sickness came over her. The thought immediately struck her, that it was rather singular Mrs. Eldridge should require a companion, when she had the society of these three young ladies; but she had not much time given to her for reflection.

"Well, my dears," observed Mrs. Eldridge, "you see I have returned, and no doubt you are very glad of it. I have the pleasure to introduce to you another companion, Miss Emily Fitzormond, for whom I bespeak your warmest affection."

The young ladies smiled very graciously, and each expressed the pleasure they should feel in conciliating Emily's esteem, to which the latter returned a suitable reply; and thus the ceremony of introduction ended. But still our heroine felt ill at ease, and there was something in the manner of the young ladies, which created a sensation of shame in her bosom.

The apartment they were now in was elegantly furnished, and everything which Emily beheld seemed to denote the wealth of Mrs. Eldridge. That lady frequently smiled very blandly upon her, and said many sweet things to her, but at the moment she was about to become more composed, a vulgar giggle among the young ladies, would completely disconcert her, and when she gazed with a timid look of astonishment, she frequently noticed Mrs. Eldridge fixing upon them a significant glance, which she was at a loss to understand. She could not suppress a sigh, when she thought of the friendless state she was in, amongst strangers, and in a place like London, where she knew not by what snares she might be surrounded, nor could be acquainted with the various schemes that are adopted by the guilty and unprincipled to entrap the unwary. Two or three times she regretted that she had so readily accepted the offer of Mrs. Eldridge, without having previously heard more of her character; but when she remembered the many acts of benevolence she had performed in the place where they came from, and the great kindness with which she behaved to her on the journey, she could not but think her exactly what she appeared to be, and reproached herself for having entertained a suspicion which was in the most remote degree calculated to do the lady an injustice.

Having partaken of some refreshments, the three young ladies made themselves very agreeable, although there was something in their conversation and general deportment altogether, which our heroine could not approve of; however, she imagined that they only conformed to the rules of London life, and that the difference of it from that simple life she had hitherto been used to, made it appear strange and unnatural to her.

Emily felt very much confused when she observed them frequently eyeing her rustic dress, which contrasted so strangely with their showy and fashionable apparel, with looks of derision, and she would have given anything, had it been in her power, could she have retired to have indulged the feelings that perplexed her mind, alone.

" You must excuse Miss Emily, my dears," said Mrs. Eldridge, " if she appears strange in company with you; but, having always been brought up in the country, of course it cannot be expected that she can know much of the manners of London life. No doubt, however, under my tuition and yours, we shall make a wonderful alteration."

" Oh, I have not the least doubt but that we shall, my dear aunt," said one of the young ladies, and then there was another titter amongst the three, which made our heroine blush, and no doubt it would have been prolonged, had it not been for Mrs. Eldridge, who gave them a look which enjoined them to forbearance.

" In the first place, we must see to an immediate alteration in her dress," resumed Mrs. Eldridge; " this unseemly rustic garb must be thrown aside, and, until we can get some clothes made for her, I must get you, Lucretia, —for I think your things will fit her,—to lend her one of your dresses, and then, when her hair is properly dressed, and she has that pretty little gold watch, and those diamond bracelets of mine, which I intend to lend her, she will look charmingly, and *fit to see company.*"

" Oh, my dear madam," said Emily, " you will overwhelm me with so much kindness; such finery will ill-become your servant and dependant, and indeed I would prefer wearing the humble dress I—"

" Nonsense, child !" interrupted Mrs. Eldridge, " when I engaged you, it was to be my companion, and to treat you as one of my own family, and I insist, therefore, that you conform to my wishes. I shall introduce you to my circle of acquaintance, but there is one request I trust you will comply with, especially as it is meant for your own welfare."

" Oh, name it, madam," uttered Emily, eagerly, and anxious to show her willingness to comply with the wishes of her new found benefactress.

" I will tell you," answered the lady; " as you might not be so well received in society, were your real circumstances made known,, I have thought of introducing you as the daughter of my late brother, and, therefore, desire that you will assume the name of Rosina Deloraine."

"Oh, madam," exclaimed our heroine, who felt a repugnance to adopt such a course ; "I would rather that were avoided. I like not to tell an untruth; and, therefore, if it is your opinion that such is the kind of reception I am likely to meet with in my real character, pray excuse me, and do not introduce me at all."

Lucretia and her two companions again giggled, and they exchanged glances with one another, which Emily saw, but could not understand.

"My dear girl," returned Mrs. Eldridge, " I must persist in my request ; I ask it as a particular favour, and I trust you will not refuse to grant it me."

Emily made no immediate reply, and recollecting the singular glances of the young ladies, she felt very much confused, and far from comfortable in her situation.

"Into what am I to construe this silence, Emily ?" demanded Mrs. Eldridge.

" If it is your will, madam," answered our heroine, " of course, it is my duty to obey; although I must confess that I would much rather it could have been done without."

"Tut, tut, you will think differently, by and by," observed Mrs. Eldridge; "however, remember, from this time, you are Rosina Deloraine."

"I will not forget, madam," replied Emily, and the conversation was changed to a different topic. Mrs. Eldridge seemed to exert herself to the very utmost to render herself and her companions agreeable to our heroine, but she felt far from comfortable, and there was something in the behaviour of the young ladies which she could neither understand nor admire. Early in the evening she was glad to avail herself of the excuse of being fatigued with the journey, to retire to the chamber which was to be allotted to her use, and to which she was shown by a female servant, a young girl with a very red face, and excessively vulgar appearance and manners altogether. But Emily, although she immediately retired to bed, did not, by any means, feel disposed to go to sleep, and she lay for some time revolving in her mind the circumstances of the last few days, and the reception she had met with at the house of her benefactress. Notwithstanding the kindness of the latter, there was something in the general conduct of the young females whom she had introduced as her nieces, which, so far from prepossessing, had filled her bosom with a sentiment bordering upon disgust, and imparted to her mind strange misgivings, which she could not shake off; but, nevertheless, she did endeavour to conquer the feeling all in her power, thinking that, in all probability, she might be imbibing a wrong prejudice against them.

The chamber in which Emily was, was immediately above the drawing-room, so that she could hear all that passed therein ; and, it was not long after she had rested, that she heard several loud knocks at the street door, and from the noise which proceeded from the room below, it seemed pretty evident that company had arrived. Soon afterwards the sound of several voices met her ears, in which she distinguished those of men, and then followed loud laughter, and other noisy demonstrations of mirth.

Emily knew not how it was, but she could not help trembling violently, and she almost feared to remain in the chamber, though for what reason she had no distinct comprehension. Several hours elapsed, and the party, for such it evidently was, had not broken up,—when Emily, at last overpowered by sleep, yielded to the influence of the drowsy god, and soon became insensible to all that was passing.

In the morning she was awakened by a knock at her chamber-door, and, on requesting the person who knocked to enter, Lucretia, as Mrs. Eldridge had called her, made her appearance, *en deshabille*, with a dress of the most elegant description hanging across her arm, and greeted our heroine with much apparent cordiality; but she could not help thinking that her eyes looked heavy and bloodshot, and her countenance pale and wan, like one who had passed the previous night in dissipation.

"Now, my dear Rosina," she said, putting on a most bland smile, "if you feel disposed to arise yet, I will assist you to dress; and, according to my aunt's request, I have brought you one of my dresses; for we shall have company to-day, and my aunt intends to introduce you to her friends."

"Mrs. Eldridge is very kind," said our heroine, "but I wish she would suffer me to occupy only the place for which I thought she had engaged me—that of a servant. Indeed, I dread entering into the society of those above my station, for which I am not qualified, and by no means ambitious of."

"Nonsense," said Lucretia, "you will soon brush off this timidity, I have no doubt; and you will find the acquaintances and friends of my aunt, the most agreeable people in the world. To-day we only expect Sir John Darlington, Mr. and Mrs. Bevington, Captain Romaine, and one or two more."

"Are the parties of your aunt generally formed principally of gentlemen?" inquired our heroine, with a look of astonishment.

Lucretia appeared to be rather confused at this question, but at length she assumed an air of perfect indifference, as she replied—

"No, not always; but then these are such very fine gentlemen, particularly Sir John Darlington, who, although not by any means a young man, is the very epitome of gallantry. I am certain he will be quite struck with you, Rosina, for you will really, without any flattery, look remarkably lovely when you have on this dress, which, I am certain will fit you to a T."

Emily blushed deeply, and was at a loss for words to express herself as she would wish; she, therefore, made no reply, but suffered Lucretia to assist her to dress, and to place the watch which Mrs. Eldridge had mentioned, by her side, and the bracelets on her wrists. When this was completed, Lucretia declared she looked most charming, although our heroine had really never felt more uncomfortable in her life; and, as she caught a glimpse of her person in the mirror, she felt the crimson blushes suffuse her cheeks, and she would have given anything to have been allowed to have resumed her humble clothes again.

After some few observations of no interest, made by Lucretia, they descended the stairs, and on entering the parlour, beheld Mrs. Eldridge and the two other young ladies, seated at the breakfast table, and only awaiting their arrival. On seeing our heroine, Mrs. Eldridge and the others exchanged the most significant glances, and then the former launched forth into the most fulsome compliments to Emily upon her beauty, and the elegance of her appearance, which confused her the more, and left her in a state of perturbation which was deserving of the utmost pity. The morning's repast passed over without anything worth recording taking place, but Emily was forced to listen to the extravagant compliments that were so lavishly bestowed upon her by Mrs. Eldridge and her nieces, until she was heartily sick, and already began to feel that her situation under the roof of Mrs. Eldridge would be more irksome, and less agreeable than she had at first anticipated it would be. We will pass over the state of trembling suspense which Emily endured in the interval which elapsed prior to the arrival of the expected guests, and introduce the company to the reader, as they were introduced to our heroine.

The first was Sir John Darlington, a dark, swarthy-looking man, about the middle age, who, notwithstanding he endeavoured to make himself appear a very amiable gentleman, and did the gallant to perfection, he had sufficient in the expression of his countenance to show that he was familiar with vice. Emily no sooner beheld him than she started back in amazement, and he seemed no less struck than herself, and was unable, apparently, to speak for a minute or two. The countenance which Sir John bore, was one which was stamped indelibly on our heroine's recollection. She was confident she had seen it before, but where it was, for the moment, she could not call to mind. At length, it darted upon her brain with the rapidity of lightning, he was the same individual, who, upon one or two occasions, when she was a child, had called upon her supposed grandmother, but who, she was now confident, had not been in any way related to her, and the words he had made use of to Mrs. Fitzormond, had ever since been most vividly present to her recollection. Could it be? or was she mistaken? No, she could almost have ventured to swear that it was the same man who then stood before her. The baronet also evinced considerable emotion, and his lips quivered, and he turned pale, but he quickly recovered himself, and went through the ceremony of introduction with greater ease than might have been supposed. Emily, however, could not help shuddering when he took her hand, and she felt a sensation at her heart, which she found it impossible to subdue. In spite of his emotion, the extreme beauty of our heroine appeared to excite his warmest admiration, and he fixed upon her a look which brought the blushes, deep mantling to her cheeks, and trembling, she cast her eyes to the floor, and was violently agitated.

There were two other gentlemen, and a lady, only, named Mr. and Mrs. Bevington; the former a tall, ordinary, and extremely stupid looking personage, and the latter a female, fat, vulgar, and unprepossessing; and Captain Romaine, who had all the appearance of a finished *rone*.

We will not capitulate all that took place on that, one of the most wretched days which Emily ever recollected to have passed. The manners of the company were bold, and even indelicate; lewd jokes were bandied freely about, and Mrs. Eldridge and the other females seemed to enjoy them with as great a relish as the gentlemen. Disgust, terror, and indignation, filled the bosom of Emily: could this be the amiable, the benevolent Mrs. Eldridge? She could scarcely believe the evidence of her senses! But, alas! it was too true; and horrible ideas began to take possession of her mind, which she found it impossible to conquer. What added to the anguish and disgust of Emily was, that Sir John Darlington seated himself by her side, and kept urging his conversation upon her, and every time she gazed in his countenance, and listened to the tones of his voice, she became still more convinced than ever that he was the same individual her suspicions had first lighted on. Whenever she caught the eye of Mrs. Eldridge, she saw her watching the baronet and herself, with an earnestness and anxiety of demeanour that not a little added to her astonishment and distress, and the expression of her countenance was so changed that she could scarcely believe it was the same woman.

Emily made but few observations, but her heart was almost full to bursting, and her agony was not a little increased, when the company, with the exception of Sir John, arose, and left the apartment, and she was about to follow their example, when the knight seized her hand, and placing his back against the door, prevented her.

" Stay, beauteous Rosina," he observed, " I must have a word with you alone."

" Sir!" exclaimed the indignant damsel, and she attempted to withdraw her hand.

"Nay, frown not, lovely Rosina," cried the baronet, and an alarming expression glowed in his countenance; "those looks ill become such transcendantly charming features! Rosina, listen to me while I confess the sentiment with which you have inspired my heart. I love you, Rosina, and would fain convince you of the strength of my admiration. Ah! not one look of kindness? By Jupiter, this must not be! On those ruby lips, that invite the amorous kiss, let me——"

And, as he thus spoke, he attempted to throw his arms around our heroine's waist, but she broke from him.

"Hold, sir," she exclaimed, with a look of offended modesty and resentment; "this language I must not listen to. Why am I left alone?"

"Do not be rash, Rosina," continued Sir John; "I will soon explain everything."

"I seek no explanation from you, sir," retorted Emily, "but an apology for the insult you have offered me. If Mrs. Eldridge sanctions such conduct as this, she shall find that the poor friendless girl has the spirit to resent it. Let go your hold instantly, sir, and suffer me to pass unmolested."

"Not until you have sealed my forgiveness with a kiss!" ejaculated Sir John, attempting to throw his arms round the maiden's waist; but, wound up to desperation, and offended virtue adding strength to her, Emily broke from him, and, rushing out of the room, she hastened up the stairs, entered her own apartment, and locked the door; and, throwing herself into a chair, burst into a violent paroxysm of tears.

"Good God!" she cried, "into what description of house have I been trepanned? What is the woman into whose power I have been betrayed? Oh, can one who could plainly sanction such conduct as that to which I have been subjected, be sensible to any feelings of shame or virtue? Mer-

No. 31

ciful Heaven! protect me—direct me how to act. Am I for ever to be made the sport of fortune, the victim of guilt?"

She was aroused from these painful reflections by hearing some one ascending the stairs. She trembled with apprehension, and once more tried the door to ascertain for certain whether she had fastened it. Immediately afterwards she heard a knock at the door, and then the voice of Mrs. Eldridge demanding admittance. Emily trembled, but she feared to disobey her, thinking that if she refused, she would use violence, and she might be subjected to the most painful consequences. She slowly unlocked the door, and Mrs. Eldridge entered the room. Her looks were not angry, but there was an expression of confusion in her countenance which did not escape the observation of Emily, who now beheld her with very different feelings to those which she had formerly done.

"What a silly girl you was to be so alarmed at what was only intended by Sir John as a harmless frolic, my dear," said the lady; "certainly he was too forward, and I have chided him severely for his conduct, and he is ready to offer you any apology in his power. Sir John is a very gay man, and his extreme gallantry sometimes leads him to overstep the bounds of prudence, but I assure you he means no harm."

"Oh, madam," cried our heroine, "how little did I expect, so soon after my entrance into this house, to be subjected to insult. Why was I left alone with the knight?"

"That was purely accidental," replied Mrs. Eldridge, "but I will take good care that the behaviour of Sir John shall not be repeated. Come, come, pray return with me to the drawing-room, where you will find all my guests anxious for your return, and Sir John Darlington perfectly contrite."

"Oh, no, no, my dear madam," ejaculated Emily, "pray excuse me; I cannot—I dare not again encounter that man, whose very looks fill my soul with horror."

"You surprise me," observed Mrs. Eldridge; "why, I am sure Sir John is a very good looking man, and if his admiration of your beauty did lead him into an act of indiscretion for which he is now extremely sorry, I do not see why you should feel such a strong sentiment of disgust towards him. Once more let me prevail upon you to attend me back to the drawing-room."

"Do not think me obstinate or disagreeable, madam," said Emily, "if I again beg to be excused from complying with the request you have made to me. But I cannot conquer my feelings at present, and my presence would only interrupt the harmony of your meeting. Indeed, madam, I aspire not to the station you have placed me in, and would rather be one of the humblest of your servants than to be placed in a situation for which I feel myself not in the least qualified."

"This seems to me like mere affectation," said Mrs. Eldridge, in a crosser tone of voice than Emily had before heard her assume; "but I yield to your request, trusting that you will endeavour to conquer such ridiculous feelings for the future."

With these words Mrs. Eldridge, much to the relief of Emily, left the room; and the latter, again locking her door, seated herself by the side of her couch, and gave herself up to the melancholy and perplexing thoughts which the adventures of the day naturally gave rise to in her breast. Her doubts of the integrity of Mrs. Eldridge's real character, gained strength; and yet it seemed scarcely possible that deceit and hypocrisy could lurk beneath such a specious mask. So much was she shocked, however, by what had happened, and so greatly had her fears been excited, that she regretted having ever entered the house; and such was the power of her apprehensions, that she would not have hesitated to have quitted it again, could she have found any opportunity to escape. Her situation was truly lamentable, and she could not dwell upon it without the most intense anguish, and fears for the future; for should she quit the house of Mrs. Eldridge, whither could she direct her steps?—Where flee for protection?—How exist?

The company passed the time away in the same noisy revelry that the party had done on the day before; and every now and then, as the loud tones of the ever-to-be-remembered voice of Sir John burst upon Emily's ears, she felt such a dreadful sensation at her heart that she could scarcely contain herself. She was afraid to retire to rest while the noisy guests were still in the house, and it was not until a very late hour that the bustle from below made her imagine that they were at length about to depart. In order to make sure that her surmises were correct, she arose from her seat, gently unlocked the door, and stepped cautiously on to the landing to listen.

Their voices, bidding each other good night, convinced her that she was correct, and hearing the street door closed, she imagined that they had departed; when suddenly she heard a footstep on the stairs, and, trembling with terror, she was about to re-enter the chamber and close the door, when the voice of Mrs. Eldridge arrested her purpose, and she was constrained to listen.

"No, Sir John, hold!" she heard her say; "not to-night. To make such an attempt would be to frustrate all."

"Psha!" answered Sir John, "what nonsense. I do not see why there should be any delay. You have grown very particular of late, Mother Eldridge."

"I am not particular," returned the woman, "but I think it would be highly imprudent to be so precipitate. I have taken a good deal of trouble to get possession of the girl, and I should not like to allow any chance to lose her. She is now secure, and if you will only let the matter rest for a few days, until she has got over the alarm into which your conduct has thrown her, you will be able to accomplish your wishes without the least danger."

"Well, well," returned the knight, in a reluctant tone of voice, and after a pause, "I suppose I must yield to you. But mind, I will not wait longer than three days, or I shall not fulfil the agreement which has been made between us."

"In three days from this," replied Mrs. Eldridge, "I promise you that the girl shall be yours."

"Enough," said Sir John. "Remember!—Good night."

"Good night!" responded Mrs. Eldridge; and immediately afterwards Emily heard the street door opened and closed again; and, half dead with horror, she rushed back into the chamber, locked the door, and, throwing herself on her knees, groaned aloud in the agony of her feelings, and implored the protection of the Most High! The truth, the danger of her situation, was now confirmed—she had fallen into the power of an infamous female panderer to the vices of the libertine, and unless she could effect her escape, her ruin was certain.

We must pass over the mental sufferings that poor Emily endured after this terrible confirmation of her worst fears, for our pen could not sufficiently pourtray them; but after a severe struggle, she somewhat regained her composure and self-possession, as it was necessary that she should muster up all her fortitude to give her the least chance of escaping from the fate with which she was threatened.

She slept but little that night, but by the morning she had so far conquered her emotions as to appear more composed than could have been
anticipated, and when she descended to the breakfast-room the following
morning, there was nothing in her appearance and behaviour which could
excite the suspicions of Mrs. Eldridge, or the fallen creatures whom she
called her nieces.

That day passed away without anything particular occurring, but Emily
determined at all hazards to make an attempt to escape from that infamous
house that very night. Mrs. Eldridge behaved to her with greater kindness
than she had ever done, and it was astonishing how Emily could stifle her
real feelings, now she knew the character of the diabolical woman who
had trepanned her away from the cottage of Mrs. Burton for such vile
purposes.

Night came, and Mrs. Eldridge having made an appointment to go to
the theatre, the opportunity appeared propitious to Emily for her purpose.
The three girls remained at home, and when Mrs. Eldridge requested our
heroine to accompany her, they pressed her so warmly to allow her to remain at home to keep them company that she yielded.

The time which our heroine was compelled to pass in the society of
these unfortunate girls, was a period of the greatest suspense and anxiety;
and she was very glad when, about eleven o'clock, they declared themselves
to be very tired, and proposed to go to their chambers. Emily stifled her
feelings, and bidding them good night, hurried to her own chamber, where
she knelt down, and implored the protection of Heaven in the attempt she
was about to make. She arose with more confidence and firmness than
she had thought she could have mustered, and hastily stripping off the
finery with which she had been attired, and resuming her own clothes,
she then extinguished her light, and stepping on the landing, listened to
hear whether any one was stirring, but all was still. With noiseless steps
she now began to descend the stairs, and although her heart throbbed violently against her side, she reached the hall in safety, and, silently opening
the door, the next moment was in the street, and at liberty! She paused
not to look around her, or to think upon what course she should take,
for all places were alike to her, but hurried on with the speed of lightning,
heedless of the different streets she passed along. It was a fearful night—
a perfect deluge of rain descended upon the earth, and the wind blew a
complete hurricane. Poor Emily was soon drenched to the skin, but still
she proceeded on her way without any fixed purpose, and without the
prospect of a shelter for the night. She had proceeded in this manner for
about an hour, when she felt her strength suddenly fail her, and she sunk
exhausted and fainting on the step of the door of a large mansion. Here
she had not been long when the watchman came up, and seeing her
wretched condition, was about to convey her to the watch-house, when, at
that moment, two meanly but cleanly-dressed young women who happened
to be passing at the time, interceded, and requested the watchman to allow her to be removed to their humble residence, which was in a court
close by, where she should receive every attention, and that he could make
any further enquiry into the matter which he should think proper. The
watchman, who was a humane man, and liked the appearance of the young
women, assisted them with our heroine to their humble dwelling, which
had a very clean appearance; and having laid her on the bed, and the
watchman having seen that they were using all their endeavours to restore
her to sensibility, and also ascertained that Emily was entirely destitute of
money, left her in their care.

We will not seek to describe the feelings of our heroine when she was restored to consciousness, and found the novel situation in which she was placed. From this time to that period at which we commenced this tale, our heroine's history may be very briefly told. The young women who had acted so kindly towards her were sisters, and had been very early left orphans. Illness, and a long series of misfortunes, had reduced them to such a painful extremity that they had no other means of obtaining a living than by ballad-singing. This precarious avocation they were pursuing when they met with Emily; and from their cleanly appearance, and possessing excellent voices, they were enabled to make a better living than they could probably have done by any other means.

Emily related to them a portion of her melancholy history, but took care to conceal from them the name she had hitherto gone by; and they, compassionating her completely destitute condition, offered her an asylum in their humble dwelling, and that she should share with them whatever they got, if she would attend to the domestic duties of their home. Emily at first shrunk ashamed from such an offer; but recollecting the situation she was in, and also thinking that, by remaining for awhile in this place, where no one would think of seeking her, she might elude her enemies, should any of them still be in existence, or until fortune might reveal the deep mystery which hung over her, she at last consented, much to the delight of Martha and Susan Palmer, which were the names of the two young women that had befriended her.

She wrote a letter to Mrs. Burton, informing her of all that had occurred to her since she left her, and informed her of her present safety, but did not let her know where she was, as the kind attention of the two sisters to her made her more willing to remain with them than to encroach upon the goodness of that kind-hearted woman.

We have now but little to add to what we have already related of the circumstances and vicissitudes, almost unparalleled, that brought the unfortunate Emily Fitzormond to the deplorable situation in which she was introduced to Sir Felix Mandeville and his lady, at the commencement of this narrative. She had never been able to learn anything of the Waltons, or of Patty, and she had almost made up her mind that she should never see them again.

She had not been many months with the ballad-singers, when they were unfortunately attacked with a most malignant fever, of which they died; and Emily, who had formed as great an attachment to the poor girls as if they had been her own sisters, thus found herself once more alone, and without a friend in the world; for Mrs. Burton, she had heard, was dead, and her daughter Ellen was married, and had gone abroad with her husband. She buried the two sisters as decently as she could, with the small trifle of money they had saved up between them, out of their precarious livelihood, and then was left without a farthing, or the means of obtaining a subsistence, unless she adopted the same course that they had done. Her nature revolted from the idea, but she had no other alternative than to starve, and at last desperation drove her to it; and Emily Fitzormond soon afterwards became known about the different streets of the metropolis as the pretty ballad-singer.

We have now brought this narrative down to that epoch from which we have so long digressed.

CHAPTER XII.

HAPPIER DAYS.

SELDOM had Emily slept more tranquilly than she did on the night when a shelter was granted her in the hospitable mansion of Sir Felix Mandeville. Something seemed to whisper to her that happier days were in store for her; and the kind and gentle manners of Sir Felix, his lady, and their lovely daughter Arabella, had quite overwhelmed her. Emily had long been very ill, and had been forced to part with almost every article of her humble furniture but the mattrass she slept upon; and she felt confident that she must shortly fall a victim to heavy sorrow, and the constant exposure to inclement weather, if she was not placed in another and more comfortable situation.

In the morning she arose much refreshed, and found her old clothes removed, and some clean things placed by the side of her bed, in which she dressed herself; and hope having once more taken possession of her heart, the roses had resumed their place in her cheeks, and she looked as lovely as ever she had done.

She had not been risen long, when there was a gentle tap at her bedroom door, and, on opening it, Arabella tripped lightly into the apartment, and with a sweet smile, requested to know how our heroine had rested, and upon being answered, she informed Emily that her father and mother requested to see her in the parlour. Emily curtseyed and obeyed, and Arabella leading the way, they quickly entered the room where Sir Felix and his lady were seated at breakfast. Emily entered with a timid air, and they seemed forcibly struck with the alteration of her appearance, but there was another individual who at that moment entered, and upon whom the extreme beauty and interesting countenance of Emily seemed to make even a more lively impression, if possible. This was Augustus Mandeville, the only son of Sir Felix and his lady, a young gentleman, possessed of the greatest personal and intrinsic merits, and was in all things the very counterpart of his amiable parents. He thought he had never before gazed on so lovely a creature, and the simplicity of her dress, and the peculiar circumstances under which she had been introduced to the family, rendered her an object of still greater interest than she would otherwise have been. Emily blushed as his eyes met her's and with an air of modesty she held down her head.

"Come hither, my poor girl," said Lady Emmeline in her usual gentle tones, "be seated, and partake of some refreshment. Be not afraid;—your answer to the questions we put to you last night, have greatly interested Sir Felix and myself, and as you do not look like one who would attempt to practice deceit, we have a wish to assist you."

Tears of gratitude trembled in the eyes of Emily, and she was for some moments unable to return any answer, but when she did, she expressed her sincere acknowledgments for the kindness of Sir Felix and his lady, in a manner which more than ever convinced them that she was no imposter. She was, however, too bashful to avail herself of the honour which they had offered her, until they pressed the invitation, and to which were added the intreaties of Augustus and Arabella, and at length Emily did take a seat at a small table, near that at which Sir Felix and his family had taken their places. The breakfast passed over in silence, and when it was finished Emily was requested to relate her melancholy story, which she did, in nearly the same words in which we have detailed it in the previous pages of this story.   As she proceeded, it would be utterly impossible to pourtray the deep interest, sympathy, wonder, and horror, which it created in the minds of her auditors, and they frequently interrupted her to give expression to their feelings, which were excited in such an extraordinary manner. When she had concluded, there was a simultaneous burst of commisseration escaped the lips of them all, and Sir Felix, after a pause, during which he had been reflecting deeply upon the remarkable facts they had heard, arose, and kindly advancing towards our heroine, and taking her hands, said—

"If what you have related be true, my poor girl, and I have every reason to believe that it is, you have been one of the most unfortunate of Heaven's children, and shall henceforth find friends in me and Lady Mandeville, who will do all in our power to unravel the mystery of your birth, and to bring to condign punishment those who have been guilty of such atrocious crimes.   You shall remain here, under my protection, and if I find that you merit it, you shall never have cause to regret the day when you sought charity at the door of Sir Felix Mandeville.   The deserving child of misfortune shall never cease to find a sincere friend and benefactor in he who now addresses you."

Emily sunk on her kness, overpowered by her feelings, and clasping her hands, looked up in the face of Sir Felix, with looks that expressed more than a volume of words could have done.

"Oh, sir!" she cried, "this goodness; it is more than I can or do deserve, and——"

Sobs choked her utterance, and she could say no more.   Sir Felix gently raised her, and smiled benevolently in her countenance, and Lady Mandeville, approaching her, said,—

"Your tears, my poor girl, convince me of your sincerity—and, wild and romantic as your story is, it was told with that artless simplicity which was sufficient to convince any one who heard it, that it was no fiction. Yours has been a most unparalleled career of vicissitude, and they must be heartless indeed who would not, if they have the means, stand up for the protection of the innocent and oppressed, especially for one of that sex, which commands the respect of all.   Here, my poor girl, you may throw off all restraint, and endeavour to make your life happy, and to look forward to the future with hope.   While you merit it, you shall be treated with every kindness, and my daughter Arabella, I am certain, will not think it any disgrace to have such a companion."

"In that supposition, my dear mamma spoke her daughter's sentiments," said the sweet girl, with a gentle smile, while Augustus, whose eyes had never scarcely for an instant been removed from our heroine's countenance, now fixed his eyes upon his sister, and their expression told plainly the manner in which he approved of her feelings, and how much they were in unison with his own.

Again did Emily endeavour to speak her thanks, but her voice failed her, and once more sinking upon her knees, her attitude sufficiently told the sentiments of her heart.

"And you think then, that this Gerald Darnley and Miles Chesterton, the steward, both perished in the ruins of the Old Lone House?" said Sir Felix.

"Both, sir, I have every reason to believe," answered Emily.

"That is unfortunate," said the baronet, "for had either of them escaped, there would have been some chance of their apprehension, and then the whole mystery would be unravelled.   But the young man, William Darnley, he was from home at the time."

"So I was given to understand, sir," replied Emily.

"Then he may still be alive, and search must be made after him. And in all the conversations which you overheard between Gerald Darnley, his son, and this Chesterton, you never could ascertain the name of the noble miscreant who employed them in their principal nefarious transactions?"

Emily replied in the negative.

" But probably he might be traced through the name of his steward;" observed Lady Mandeville.

"No, I do not think that," returned Sir Felix, "because it is most likely that the name of Chesterton was only an assumed one; he would be sure to take the precaution to do that. Have you the manuscripts you say you discovered in the secret closet?"

" Unfortunately, I left them at the house of Mr. Walton," replied Emily.

" That is indeed unfortunate," returned the baronet, "for they are a material part of the evidence against the guilty party. However, it will be better for us not to make any stir in the matter, at present, but to use every precaution, and something may possibly transpire to forward our inquiries."

Every one agreed as to the propriety of this suggestion, and after some further conversation upon the deeply interesting subject, it was dropped, and our heroine was engaged upon other topics, upon all of which she shewed such quick perception and superior understanding, that they all became more charmed with her, every moment they conversed with her.

We will now pass over a period of nine months, during which interval, Emily had so ingratiated herself into the favour of Sir Felix and his family, as to be looked upon with almost the same attention as one of their own. The adventure which had introduced our heroine to the family in so remarkable a manner, and the conduct of those benevolent people towards her, caused no little gossip and excitement amongst the servants, and the persons in the neighbourhood for some time, but it gradually wore away, and Sir Felix and the others had taken particular care not let any persons become acquainted with her singular history, and they also took precaution to go in an assumed name, so that there might be no chance of the inquiries they were were secretly making being frustrated.

Augustus every day became more and more enamoured of Emily, and he was never happy but when he was in her society, and the passion he had imbibed for her soon became known to our heroine, whose heart beat responsive with his own. She, however, endeavoured to subdue her love for one, to whose hand she had no prospect at present of being able to aspire, and sought by absenting herself from his presence as frequently as she could, to drive her image from his heart. But, alas! the very means she adopted, but served to increase the flame, and affection was too deeply implanted in their hearts to be easily eradicated.

It was on the anniversary of Arabella's eighteenth birthday, that Sir Felix determined to celebrate the joyful event at his mansion; and accordingly, cards of invitation were issued to a considerable number of the nobility and gentry, and the day was anticipated to be one of unusual festivity. At an early hour the guests began to assemble in the saloon, where Sir Felix and his family awaited to receive them, and Emily was also one of the party. This ceremony was gone through with all the usua formalities, and our heroine was an object of universal curiosity and admiration, and there was not a person present, who could help acknowledging her exquisite beauty and her captivating sweetness of demeanour.

"Lord Egremond, allow me to introduce to you, my fair ward, Miss Hollingbrook," said Sir Felix, introducing our heroine to the nobleman he addressed. Emily raised her eyes, but they no sooner rested on the coun-

tenance of the lord mentioned, than she gave utterance to a half stifled scream, and tremblingly clung to Sir Felix, scarcely able to save herself from falling. Her astonishment and terror will not be wondered at, when, in Lord Egremond, she recognised the villain, Sir John Darlington, as he had chosen to call himself, when she had met him at the house of that infamous woman, Mrs. Eldridge.

Lord Egremond seemed no less thunderstruck than she was, and started back a few paces, and gazed at her with looks of mingled surprise and incredulity unable to speak.

Before either of them could recover themselves, or Sir Felix could inquire the reason of this extraordinary emotion, a person standing by his lordship, informed him that his steward desired to speak with him immediately on business of importance; and he had only just given this intimation, when a man was seen making his way across the saloon towards his lordship, and when he had got within a few paces of the spot where they stood, our heroine fixed her eyes upon him, but immediately screamed aloud, and exclaiming :

" Chesterton ! Chesterton !" fainted with terror in the arms of Sir Felix Mandeville.

" Confusion !" cried the steward, for he it was ;—" Emily Fitzormond here ?"

" Damnation !" vociferated Lord Egremond, his eyes flashing fire, and his whole frame convulsed with the most powerful emotion ;—" Emily Fitzormond, say ye, and alive ? Villain ! wretch ! traitor ! You have deceived me ? But you shall suffer for it ! Die, infernal scoundrel, and with you the secret you would probably some time or the other reveal !"

As the enfuriated lord gave utterance to these words, he snatched his hanger from his side, and before any of the astonished guests could interpose, he plunged it twice into the body of the guilty steward; who

No. 32

fell bleeding on the floor, but was quickly raised in the arms of one of the bystanders.

Lord Egremond, seeing that Chesterton still lived, would have rushed upon him again, but he was seized and held back by several persons, and Chesterton with a ghastly look, cried:—

"Hold him back! hold him back! let him not complete his bloody work until I have had my revenge, and disclosed a tale of blood which will make the murderer tremble. Bear me hence—quick! Bind up my wounds, or I shall bleed to death ere I can make the only atonement in my power. But let not yon usurper escape; I repeat he is a murderer! Oh—"

Miles Chesterton was quickly taken to another apartment, where his wounds were bound up, and a surgeon was sent for; and Lord Egremond, upon whose brow madness and guilt were stamped, was conveyed to a room, in which he was for the present confined.

All this was the work of less than five minutes; in that time, the author of all our heroine's misery was revealed, in Lord Egremond, and he had partly admitted his guilt in the words he had uttered, and the sanguinary vengeance he had inflicted upon his wretched myrmidon.

It was some time before Emily recovered her senses, but when she was made acquainted with what had happened, her feelings may easily be conjectured, but cannot be properly described. The whole was so sudden, that she could scarcely persuade herself but that it was a dream; but when she was convinced of its reality, astonishment, and admiration of the wonderful ways of Providence filled her breast, and she waited with the utmost impatience for the return of Sir Felix and other persons, who had gone with him to bear witness to the dying confession of the unhappy Chesterton.

There, propped up by pillows, the dying wretch with difficulty gave utterance to the dreadful tale of crime, while his horror-struck listeners attended to him with the most painful interest.

We shall not attempt to give it in the precise words of the dying man; but it may be thus briefly detailed:—

The present Lord Egremond was the first cousin of the late Lord Jerdan Egremond, and being his only relative, and the next heir to the titles and estates, if Lord Jerdan died unmarried, or without issue; they had been brought up from infancy together, both the parents of the former having died when he was very young. When boys together, John Harlington, which was his family name, exhibited none of those unfortunate traits in his character which afterwards distinguished him, and ultimately led him on to the perpetration of the most horrible crimes; but, on the contrary, his disposition was very mild and affable: but beneath all, secretly lurked the hypocrite, and it only required excitement, as was found in his after career, to render him capable of the basest deeds. Towards Lord Jerdan, who had ever behaved to him with the kindness of the most affectionate of brothers, he secretly nurtured the most envious and inveterate feelings; jealous of his superior fortune, although he had shared it freely with him, he only waited an opportunity of gaining full possession of it, and, consequently, his greatest dread was that the former should get married, and he endeavoured by every means in his power to prevent it. It was with that object in view that he avoided the company of the female sex as much as possible, and as Lord Jerdan was seldom out of his society, he hoped by that means to bias his inclinations, and to lead his mind to other objects. Whenever the fair sex became a subject of discourse, Mr. Harlington had ever some argument ready to excite prejudice against them, and being very eloquent and forcible in his observations, they had a very dangerous tendency. Lord Egremond, however, was a man of too powerful a mind to be influenced by anything which Mr. Harlington could say ; and he frequently discussed the subject with him with much ability, and warmly reprobated his unnatural prejudices. Lord Egremond was a most enthusiastic admirer of woman, and always the first to champion their cause, and, therefore, that Harlington should meet with a strong opponent in him is not at all to be wondered at. When alone, this was the source of much uneasiness to Harlington ; he would curse the warmth of his friend's temperament, and, although in reality no one could be more attached to the sex than himself, he secretly cursed all womankind. Proud, haughty, and ambitious, the principal hopes of Harlington were fixed upon the coronet of he to whom he pretended to be a warm friend, but who, in fact, he utterly detested, and would have been happy had some accident occurred to deprive him of life ; indeed, there were not any means, however base, scarcely, that he would have hesitated from adopting to further his wishes.

Beneath a specious exterior, John Harlington nurtured every vice that can render a human being hateful. A more fawning hypocrite, a more despicable sycophant could not be, and his base mind was capable of con-ceiving the most abominable vices, and also of carrying them into execution. Gold was the deity he principally worshipped, and to obtain it there was no crime which he would have hesitated to perpetrate. Once offended, he was a most implacable enemy, and he would not rest until he had obtained his revenge ; and yet this was all managed with such consummate ability, and so secretly, that it came upon the victim unawares, and without his being able to imagine the source from whence it sprang. But in society, no person could be more agreeable and insinuating than Mr. Harlington, and his company was universally sought after. Such was the character of the man who was afterwards destined to bear so prominent and revolting a part in this narrative, and whose crimes were fated to bring such lamentable and utter misery upon a family, and for so many years to de-prive the members of it of their rights. But we have given but a very faint portraiture of him ; a full conception of his baseness will be easily formed by the reader by the circumstances we are about to record.

But how very different was the character of his friend, Lord Egremond. Every manly virtue had a place within his mind, and his greatest delight was in performing acts of pure charity and benevolence. A most warm and enthusiastic friend, he was the admired of every one ; and his general affa-bility engendered the highest esteem of all ranks and classes. The Christian and the philanthropist were exemplified in him to a most eminent degree, and he was looked upon by all who knew him as the general friend of man-kind. The poor and unfortunate in him ever found a friend ; humble and striving talent a supporter ; and genius a most enthusiastic admirer. He was a liberal patron of the fine arts, and his taste was of the most refined order. To all these virtues and accomplishments, Lord Egremond also added a most noble person, and handsome, manly countenance ; and it was not to be wondered at, therefore, that he should be as great a favourite among the fair sex as he was with his own. Thus Harlington saw all his hopes crushed that way, and he set his base mind to work to devise some other means to obtain the object of his ambition.

" By all the infernal host I swear," he frequently soliloquized, when alone, " that the title and wealthy estates of Egremond shall be mine, in spite of everything, and even though I purchase the possession of my de-sires by the most fearful crimes. I am no despicable coward to tremble at the performance of trifles to attain the object of my ambitious wishes ; nor was I made to linger on in this manner, the mere dependent on the bounty of another. No ! I will achieve the object for which my soul has so long

panted, and which I am ready to run any risk to accomplish. It may take
time, and I will not by precipitation frustrate my designs ; but, ultimately,
I am convinced that I shall triumph. Would that death would release me
from the only obstacle to my becoming possessed of rank and title. But
it must be—the time must come, and something whispers me that all my
wishes will be gratified."

Thus would the villain give expression to his hopes and intentions when
alone, and his determination increased every day. But at the same time,
the affable manner in which he behaved towards the object of his detestation and envy, completely blinded the latter, and added to that fervent,
brotherly attachment which he had always felt towards him. Noble and
virtuous himself, he could not suspect others, especially that man with
whom he had been brought up from childhood, and who had ever evinced
an equal affection to that which he (Lord Egremond) had shown towards
him. But little did he dream the guilty plot which the villain Harlington
had in contemplation against him, and that he would ultimately bring him
to destruction, and cause such complicated misery in his family.

Lord Egremond frequently rallied Harlington on his prejudices against
the fair sex, and the latter, fearful that he might by his constant perseverance in speaking against them, at last create no good feeling in the
bosom of the former towards him ; and likewise perceiving that all the
arguments he could make use of were not likely to alter his lordship's
opinion, he at length affected to be convinced of the force of Egremond's
observations, to abandon his own prejudices, and to become a convert to
the opinions of his friend, although, in fact, as we have before observed, he
was always of the same, and not only a warm admirer, but, in private, a
zealous devotee at the shrine of beauty. This, although it caused Harlington no little regret to be compelled to adopt, was a wise plan, inas-
much as it strengthened the attachment of Lord Egremond towards him,
and, consequently, afforded him greater opportunities of forwarding his
infamous designs.

Thus passed away several years, and so well did the hypocrite play his
part, that Lord Egremond had not the slightest suspicion of the guilty intentions he had towards him, and little thought that, at the very time when
he professed for him the greatest friendship, he was actually endeavouring
to conceive the readiest means to get rid of him. Murder he trembled to
commit himself ; he was too great a coward for that ; but he would willingly have employed any other wretch to have waylaid his intended victim,
but he feared to make the proposition to any person, neither did he know
of any individual who was at all likely to undertake the foul deed.

It was soon after this that Harlington became acquainted with the villain,
Woodthorpe, who has hitherto been known to the reader only in the name
of Chesterton ; and he took him into his service as valet, and well knowing
the depraved character which he possessed, he was enabled to prevail upon
him to aid him in his diabolical wishes.

It was, however, not for some time after Woodthorpe, alias Chesterton,
had been in Harlington's service that the latter ventured to unburthen his
mind to him, and it was not then, until after he had bound him by a
heavy oath of secrecy, that he did confide his thoughts to him, and ventured
to propose to him to murder Lord Egremond, promising him at the same
time, a very large sum of money for the performance of the deed. Guilty,
however, as Woodthorpe most assuredly was, his hands had never then
been stained by human blood, and he, therefore, shuddered at the bare
mention of such a deed, and although he promised that he would do all
that was in his power to get some miscreant to undertake the bloody crime,
and in which he said that he had no doubt he should ultimately succeed in

doing, as he was acquainted with several fellows who were perfectly familiar with crime, and who, upon the promise of a good reward, would not hesitate to perpetrate any deed, however enormous it might be.

With this Harlington was forced to be content, finding that it would be useless to endeavour to prevail upon Woodthorpe; but he severely reproached him for his cowardice, and enjoined him by a more stringent oath than before to secresy. He placed but little dependence in the promise of Woodthorpe, and he was rather fearful of it also, for he would then be left entirely at the mercy of the ruffian, who, in the hopes of being better rewarded, might divulge the whole to Lord Egremond, and thus all his infamous plans would not only be frustrated, but himself brought to expoposure, disgrace, and punishment.

For several years more the villain was compelled to linger on, impatiently wavering between hope, fear, anxiety, and disappointment; and still he saw no more prospect of his being able to accomplish his designs than he had done at first; neither had he been able to persuade Woodthorpe to commit the deed, nor had the latter seen any one yet to whom he could venture to submit their designs, and to propose the assassination of Lord Egremond. The friendship of the latter towards the villain who was plotting his destruction, increased, and there was nothing in the behaviour of Harlington which could in the least tend to excite suspicion : indeed, his friendship appeared to keep pace with that of Lord Egremond, and they were looked upon, by most people, as brothers. Lord Egremond had hitherto remained single, and thus far the hopes of Harlington were somewhat encouraged; but he was very quickly doomed to be disappointed, and to have his alarm excited in a considerable degree, and not without sufficient cause.

Lord Egremond proposed travelling for some time upon the continent, to which Harlington readily gave his consent, trusting that abroad some opportunity might present itself of putting the designs he had so long had in contemplation into execution, and, he secretly vowed that Egremond should never return to his native country alive. They left England, and having settled for a short time in Italy, there became acquainted with an English gentleman, resident there, whose family only consisted of himself, his lady, and an only daughter, of great beauty and intrinsic acquirements, of whom, it was very evident that Lord Egremond soon became deeply enamoured, and Harlington perceived, to his chagrin and alarm, that the lady reciprocated his sentiments, and the gentleman, her father, who had noticed their attentions towards one another, seemed to approve of their attachment. We need not attempt to describe the feelinge of rage that filled the bosom of Harlington on this discovery, and a thousand times he cursed the ill-fortune which had introduced them to the family of Mr. Beaumont, which was the name of the gentleman, but his indignation was greatly increased when his surmises were confirmed by Lord Egremond confessing to him the impression which Adeline Beaumont had made upon his heart, and that it was his determination to make to her a confession of his love, and to seek from her a return. But fearful that he might excite the suspicions of Egremond, if he offered any opinion regarding the lady contrary to his own, he affected to approve of his taste, and Egremond, encouraged by the behaviour of Mr. Beaumont, and that of the lady, sought an opportunity of confessing to the latter the passion with which she had inspired him, and had the felicity to receive from her an acknowledgment of a return, and a request that he would apply to her father. On the wings of love and hope, Egremond flew to the feet of Mr. Beaumont, and informing him of the sentiments which himself and the beauteous Adeline entertained for each other, supplicated his consent to their union,

which was granted without hesitation, and a day appointed for the ceremony to take place.

Harlington, who now at once saw his hopes partly destroyed, was in a
state of rage which needs no description from us, and he secretly determined, at all hazards, to destroy the lady ere that which he had so much
reason to apprehend should have taken place.

Towards Adeline, however, he behaved with the same hypocritical
urbanity of manner which he ever evinced towards Lord Egremond, and
she, as well as others, completely deceived by them, thought him a most
estimable man, and was delighted to think that Egremond possessed such a
devoted friend.

Harlington and Woodthorpe had frequent conversations upon the subject, and consulted what was to be done, but when the former proposed the
murder of Adeline, Woodthorpe shuddered at the bare idea of it, with the
same horror as when his master had hinted to him about the death of Lord
Egremond, and positively refused to have anything to do with it. Cowardice, and not humanity, made him revolt at the thought, for although
there was scarcely a crime besides of which he had not been guilty, from
the perpetration of that he shrunk with a feeling of horror which we cannot adequately describe.

Harlington was terribly enraged at the refusal of Woodthorpe; but he
was afraid to offend him, knowing that he was entirely in his power, and
trusting that he should be able in time to wean him to his purpose, and
persuade him to become a ready instrument towards effecting the accomplishment of his wishes.

The day appointed for the solemnization of the nuptials, was agreed to
be celebrated with much splendour, and there was to be a grand banquet
given in the mansion of Mr. Beaumont. A thought suddenly suggested
itself to the mind of Harlington, and a sanguine hope of its success sprang
up in his bosom.

"Ah!" he muttered to himself, when he was alone; "it shall be so;
success seems certain to attend it, and I will muster courage sufficient to
perpetrate the deeds, for, upon me suspicion can never light. Poison might
easily be mixed with her refreshment at the banquet, and thus at once I
shall rid myself of one of whom I have such cause to be in fear." This
deed too might work a double effect, for the sudden death of Adeline might
so shock him, that he might never recover from the effects of it; and thus
he should have got rid of every obstacle to wealth, rank, and title, and that
without drawing down upon himself the least suspicion. The wretch
actually prided himself upon this idea, and exulted in the anticipation of its
success. He confided his diabolical intention to Woodthorpe; who would
fain have dissuaded him from it, but he found it was of no use to endeavour
to do so, and, therefore, he said nothing about it.

As the day of the nuptials approached, the determination of Harlington
became stronger, and having banished from his mind all the former scruples
he had felt, he awaited for the moment when the crime should be accomplished, with the greatest impatience. Woodthorpe, cruel as he was, could
not think upon the dreadful and heartless murder of so beautiful and innocent a female as Adeline, without shuddering with horror, and several times
he was half inclined to divulge all he knew; but then again, fear of the consequences to himself, prevented him, and the miscreant remained faithful to
his inhuman master.

At length the auspicious day arrived, and Lord Egremond and Adeline
Beaumont were united in the indissoluble bands of matrimony. The ceremony was over, and the time fixed upon for the banquet had arrived. The
guests were all seated at the table, Harlington near his intended victim ;

whom he watched with eager and malignant eyes. The villain had watched his opportunity, and had contrived to mix a subtle poison with her drink, and he knew that if she quaffed off the contents of the glass, she would be no more in a very few minutes, and that no remedy could save her life. It was a moment of the most terrible suspense to the intended murderer; but his rage and disappointment were beyond all description, when she declined taking any wine, and thus his villanous design was, very happily, frustrated. He was fearful, however, that some other person would drink the contents, and, therefore, he, as if he had done it by accident, upset the glass, and spilt the contents upon the floor. No one took any particular notice of the action, and suspicion was not, therefore, in any degree excited. But Harlington was glad when the guests arose from the table, and he had an opportunity of retiring, for he was afraid that he should not be able to conceal the emotions that filled his bosom from the observation of the persons present. He walked into the garden, and there alone, gave vent to the fierce and ungovernable feelings of rage that filled his bosom in the most violent manner. It appeared to him as if a spell was upon him, and that he was to be foiled in all his evil designs.

"But I will not," he ejaculated to himself; "no, by hell! I will not be entirely thwarted, even though I lose my own life in making the attempt."

The day passed over without anything more, worthy of particular notice, taking place, and the day after the ceremony, the happy couple, attended by Harlington, Mr. Beaumont, and one or two more of their friends, set out to some little distance in the country, to spend the honeymoon; and in anticipation of the most unbounded and uninterrupted happiness.

We will pass over several months, during which time Lord and Lady Egremond had returned to England, and Harlington had made two or three attempts to put his diabolical designs into execution, and at every fresh failure, his rage increased until he could scarcely contain himself within the bounds of reason and prudence. But yet, in his behaviour to Egremond and his fair bride, he never gave even the slightest sympathy of hatred or jealousy, but, on the contrary, acted with the same strict urbanity which had before so firmly established him in their regard. But now there was another circumstance to add to his alarm and rage. Lady Egremond proved to be *enceinte*, and in the birth of a child, if it should live, Harlington saw, of course, an end to all his ambitious hopes. In the due course of time, Lady Egremond presented her delighted lord with a lovely girl, which had every appearance of health, and thus the villain Harlington saw another obstacle to the gratification of his desires. He, however, resolved to use every possible endeavour to remove it, and to place himself in a fair way to the possession of the wealth and title he coveted.

Another year elapsed, and yet Harlington was unsuccessful in all his stratagems. Lady Egremond had given birth to another daughter, and the happiness of her and her husband was unbounded. Little did they imagine that they nurtured a serpent in their bosoms, and that he was, under the mask of brotherly affection, contemplating the most atrocious crimes.

A short time prior to this event, Woodthorpe had become acquainted with Gerald Darnley, just after he had ruined himself in acts of dissipation, and quickly finding that he was a man, who would not shrink from the perpetration of any deed for money, he introduced him to Harlington, and who, after some hesitation, thinking at last that he might trust him, he imparted to him his wishes, and offered him a most handsome reward if he would undertake to remove the different obstacles to the gratification of his ambition. Gerald readily agreed, and it was not long ere he concerted a plot with Woodthorpe to remove Lord Egremond first, and then the others afterwards. A favourable opportunity was soon afforded them. Lord

Egremond was compelled to go a journey to a distant part of the country upon business, and Harlington excused himself from accompanying him, by pleading indisposition. Of this opportunity, Gerald Darnley determined to avail himself to put his nefarious scheme into execution.

We have before mentioned in the course of this narrative, that the Old Lone House was the property of Lord Egremond, but it had been deserted by the family for several years, and suffered to fall into decay. In this place Gerald Darnley and two or three others, who lived by plunder, had taken up their residence, and also an old woman, who was the mother of one of them, and who was introduced to the reader, at the commencement of the tale, as Mrs. Fitzormond, and the pretended grandmother of our heroine. Gerald Darnley had not been married more than two years, and his wife had presented him only with one child, a boy. She was a poor, delicate, gentle creature, and worthy of a much better husband. Gerald brutally ill-used her. This old house was promised to Gerald by Harlington, as part of the reward he was to receive, if he executed his plot well; and he was, therefore, the more anxious to meet with success.

From where Lord Egremond was at that time residing, the Old Lone House was situated about fifteen miles, and they could, therefore, calculate from the hour he had fixed upon to start on his journey, what time he would cross the moor. There Gerald, with his companions, determined to surprise him, but not to take his life, according to the express command of Harlington, though for what reason they could not very well imagine, as he had before been so anxious to have him removed altogether. They were instructed to convey him, a prisoner, to the Old Lone House, and there to await his (Harlington's) further orders.

We need not say what success attended this design; the reader has seen it from what has transpired in the course of this narrative. The unfortunate Egremond was only attended by one servant, and was surprised, and quickly overpowered, according to the plan laid down. He was conveyed to that dismal place, the Old Lone House, where he was destined to meet a horrible, lingering death, as described by him in the manuscripts which our heroine had found.

We need not attempt to describe the agony which Lady Egremond endured at the disappearance of her husband, and for some time her grief was so intense that Harlington began to entertain strong hopes that death would put a period to her existence, and thus save him the trouble of getting rid of her by forcible means. He also pretended to suffer much anguish at the uncertain fate of his kinsman, and affected to go in search of him, but he went no further than the Old Lone House, where he taunted the wretched victim of his cruelty in the most fiendish manner, and exulted in the dreadful suffering he was undergoing, and the awful fate to which he had consigned him, although he had never behaved any otherwise than as a most affectionate brother towards him, and had not given him the slightest reason to entertain such feelings of deadly revenge towards him.

We will not harrow up the feelings of our readers by detailing all the sufferings that the wretched Jerdan underwent in his place of confinement in the secret closet, until death mercifully terminated them; the manuscripts, and other events that have been recounted in the course of this tale, have sufficiently explained them. After his death, the closet was fastened up, and never afterwards was entered above once or twice, until Emily was accidentally led thither.

All search after Lord Egremond having, of course, proved fruitless, it was at length concluded that he had been waylaid and murdered, and that the assassins, in order to escape detection, had buried the body. Lady Egremond was for some time inconsolable at her heavy and irreparable

loss, but at length, time somewhat mellowed her grief, and she turned her whole attention towards her two children, whom the wretch Harlington had also marked out for his victims, on the first opportunity which should present itself.

A few months only had elapsed after the dreadful and melancholy event which we have been relating, when both the children were missed from the nursery, where the nurse had only left them for a few minutes, alone, while she went to fetch something from another apartment, and, although a strict and immediate search was made after them, and large rewards offered to any person who could give any information concerning them, they could never be heard of afterwards.

Harlington had taken good care to be from home at the time of their abduction, and when he returned, and was informed of the circumstance, he affected such violence and apparent sincerity of grief, that not the least suspicion attached itself to him.

This terrible event was a final blow to Lady Egremond; she was seized with an illness from which she never recovered, and died of a broken heart only a few months afterwards.

Nothing afterwards being heard of the children of the late Lord and Lady Egremond, it was concluded that they were also dead, and Harlington, after waiting some months, took upon him the title and estates of his murdered kinsman, according to the will of that ill-fated nobleman, and flattered himself that he was secure from detection.

In the meantime, Gerald Darnley had the two children safe in his power, although Harlington imagined they were no more, and had given Darnley a large sum of money for the inhuman part he had acted in the plot. Their innocence had touched even the flinty heart of that guilty miscreant, and unable to do the hellish deed he had been instructed to commit, he

No. 33

took them to the Old Lone House, where he placed them under the care of his wife, and old Nance, as she was called, otherwise Mrs. Fitzormond. Having afterwards, however, committed an extensive robbery, and being fearful of being discovered, and that the children would also then become known, he disguised himself and his wife, assumed the name of Luke Stanton, and removed to the White Cottage, where he took up his residence until such time as he thought he could return to the Old Lone House with safety. Several times he had nearly made up his mind to murder the children, but Providence always arrested his hand, and their innocence protected them. In this manner, having disguised one of the children as a boy, the better to prevent suspicion, he continued to live at the White Cottage, until the night of the dreadful event recorded in the second chapter of this tale. He had quarrelled with his wife, and fearing that she would betray him, he savagely murdered her, and fled the place, taking with him the two children. He returned to the Old Lone House, no one there being acquainted with where he had been during the time he was away, and having informed them that his wife had died suddenly, he left one of the children (our heroine) in the care of old Nance, who had taken charge of his son during his absence, and then took the other (Patty) to Mrs. Seagrove, on whom he prevailed, as has been seen, to take her under her protection, upon the supposition that she was his child.

For some time afterwards Emily remained at the Old Lone House, taken care of by Mrs. Fitzormond, as she afterwards called herself, and was seldom suffered to quit that dismal apartment, which has been so frequently described, and was ever afterwards so strongly impressed upon her memory.

At length, however, Harlington discovered that Emily was living, although he knew not but that Patty was no more, and immediately hastening to the Old Lone House, he upbraided Gerald for the manner in which he had deceived him, and demanded that he should commit the atrocious deed for which he had received the reward. Gerald firmly refused, but promised that the secret of her origin should never be divulged by him; and, on Harlington still insisting on the perpetration of the crime, he threatened to reveal the whole affair, in consequence of which, the villain became alarmed, and was forced to accede to the resolution of Darnley, and moreover, was glad to present him with another reward, in order that he might secure his silence. After some altercation, however, Darnley yielded to the wishes of Harlington, namely, that Emily should be removed from the Old Lone House, in care of Mrs. Fitzormond, who she would be taught to believe her grandmother, and that, on those conditions, and a faithful promise from all connected with the plot, that she should never be informed who she really was, he would permit her to live, and allow a certain sum annually for her support.

Old Nance was glad of the proposition, for she was tired of living at the Old Lone House, and really felt an interest in the fate of the poor child: and Gerald Darnley was by no means sorry to get rid of the child, without being compelled to do so by a violent death, so the plan was finally agreed to, and Mrs. Fitzormond, as she now called herself, left the house with her charge, and, by a strange accident, took up her residence in the very cottage where Gerald Darnley had lately dwelt, in the name of Luke Stanton, and committed the horrible murder on the body of his wife.

We have now very little to relate concerning the sisters, with which the reader is not already acquainted. Emily, or, as the right name and title of our heroine was, Lady Olivia Egremond, was attended to with much care by the old woman whom she believed to be her relation, and Harlington called two or three times at the cottage, and gave Mrs. Fitzormond the money he had agreed upon. But these visits caused him so much mental torture, from the great likeness which our heroine bore to her murdered father, that he afterwards discontinued them, and resided principally in town or on the continent; where, in extravagant scenes of folly and dissipation, he endeavoured to drown the loud voice of a guilty conscience. But he was in a constant state of apprehension lest Olivia should discover who she really was, and often did he wish that she was no more.

Mrs. Fitzormond also passed a life of the greatest misery, and her mind was continually the abode of horror, when she reflected upon the guilty deeds with which she had been connected. Frequently was she upon the point of confessing the whole truth to the child, and thus making all the atonement she could for the part she had acted in the guilty affair; but fear prevented her, and the dreadful secret was left to be revealed in the miraculous manner we have described.

The most singular circumstance connected with the conduct of Harlington, was, that he should have taken any notice of the advertisement which was published in the newspapers after the death of the old woman, as he was running a great risk by so doing; but his conduct could only be accounted for by his entertaining a fear that if no person had claimed her, and she should have been taken to a poor-house, there would have been such strict inquiries made into her origin, that, by some means or the other, facts would have been elicited, and all his villany detected.

However, as has appeared by the circumstances that have been described in the course of this narrative, he had once more formed the determination to quiet his fears altogether, by her death, and for that purpose he despatched his steward to the White Cottage to take charge of her, and to convey her to the Old Lone House, where Gerald was to receive an extra reward to despatch her. It has been shewn that the guilty steward was forcibly struck with the young girl's beauty, and immediately formed the resolution to deceive his lord, and to endeavour to gratify his libidinous passions. What followed has been amply detailed.

The usurper had been very uneasy at the lengthened absence of Chesterton, and was sometimes fearful that treachery had been practised between him and Gerald Darnley; but Chesterton wrote him so plausible a letter, in which he described the manner in which our heroine had been despatched, and the reason of his delay, that he became perfectly satisfied, and, at last, concluded that the object of his terrors was at an end, and that all evidence of his guilt was safe from discovery; but the avenging hand of the Most High, never suffers the guilty to escape a most terrible retribution, and, even at that time it was impending over the inhuman monster's head.

He launched forth into every scene of debauchery and vice, little thinking how brief his career was to be, and that his crimes were to be revealed in so miraculous a manner.

On the night of the fire at the Old Lone House, Chesterton contrived to escape, after having witnessed the end of Gerald Darnley; but he concluded that Emily and Will Darnley had both perished in the ruins.

He hastened to London, where he sought out his master, who felt great satisfaction at the circumstance, as one of the principal actors in his inhuman designs was safely removed from the power of betraying him, and he would not have cared had the steward shared the same fate, as he then thought that he should be perfectly safe. Little, however, did the villain imagine that both the daughters of the victims of his barbarity still existed, or what a perpetual hell would his mind have been.

Lord Egremond, as he called himself, in his amours, assumed his former title, namely, Sir John Darlington, and as has been seen, it was under that title he was introduced to our heroine by Mrs. Eldridge, who was an infamous procuress, pandering to the worst vices of the wealthy and the depraved, and who was frequently employed by the usurper of the rights of Emily and her sister.

Her extreme likeness to the late Lady Egremond most forcibly struck him when he first beheld her, and chilled his heart, and our heroine, as we have before stated, immediately recognized him, although so many years had elapsed, as the individual who had called at the White Cottage, when she was under the care of Mrs. Fitzormond, and who had made so powerful and lasting an impression upon her mind. But still she could not be certain that he was really the same person, and had she ventured to accuse him, she would have at once discovered herself, and he would have been certain to have taken care that she did not escape the fate which he imagined she had already met with.

The unfortunate female that had been murdered in the chamber adjoining the secret closet, and whom the ill-fated Lord Egremond had imagined to be his wife, was a woman who Gerald Darnley, having ascertained had been taking a large sum of money, waylaid at night, as she crossed the heath, and forced her to the Old Lone House, where he perpetrated the hellish deed, in the immediate vicinity of the other wretched and expiring victim.

Lord Egremond had never more than the initials of his Christian names engraven on his jewellery, or marked in his memorandums, and hence the initials J. D. (Jerdan Dorrincourt), which our heroine had observed in the pocket-book, and on the ring, which she found in the manner we have described.

Our readers are well acquainted with all the particulars which followed these events, and, therefore, it is unnecessary for us to tire their patience by a recapitulation of them. We have recorded the particulars of the dreadful confession of Miles Woodthorpe, alias Chesterton; but it would be utterly impossible to do adequate justice to the feelings of astonishment, horror, and wonder, which pervaded the minds of all who were interested in it; but more especially our heroine, through whose veins the tide of horror at the deplorable fate of her parents, and surprise at the discovery which had been brought about in so mysterious a manner, rushed with an impetuosity that almost overpowered her. In Patty, then, she discovered a sister, and the interest which had connected their hearts, was at once accounted for. Oh, that she had then been present, that she could have enfolded her to her bosom, and called her by the dear, dear title of sister; but when she reflected upon the uncertainty of her fate, her anguish was greatly increased, and she threw herself into the arms of Lady Mandeville, and wept bitterly.

The guilty steward also confessed about the removal of the remains of the murdered Earl of Egremond from the secret closet, by himself and Gerald Darnley, and their interment in the vault underneath the building, and, therefore, he gave every possible means for the confirmation of his statements, had there been any doubts of the truth of his confession on the minds of those that heard it, which it was almost impossible that there should be, so clearly was everything stated, and only a minute before he expired, he appealed to Heaven to attest that he spoke the truth, and affixed his signature to the written document which had been taken from his own lips.

The termination of his confession finished the earthly career of the guilty steward, and he was summoned to answer for his manifold crimes at the bar of his Almighty Judge.

CHAPTER XIII.

THE DEATH OF THE MURDERER.

SCARCELY had the breath left the body of the guilty steward, than a message was sent to Sir Felix Mandeville from the persons who had been left in charge of Sir John Harlington (for such was his actual title), that he was seized with strong convulsions and appeared to be dying.

Sir Felix and the medical attendants immediately hastened to the chamber of the wretched man, and there found him in a most awful state. He had recovered from the convulsions, and, in spite of all the endeavours of his attendants to prevent him, had forcibly raised himself up in the bed, and with bloodshot eyes, and ghastly countenance, was staring wildly around him.

Upon the entrance of Sir Felix and the medical gentleman, he fixed his eyes upon the former, and in a terrible voice, in which all the intense agony of a guilty conscience, and a hopeless soul, were expressed, he shrieked out—

"Ah! see—'tis he! 'tis the phantom of the murdered Egremond! —His filmy eyes are fixed upon me!—Envenomed snakes issue from his mouth, and hiss and spit at me!—Horror! horror!—how frightful he looks!—The dreadful torment of hunger is upon his fearful brow!—He comes nearer to me!—Oh, do not let him touch me!—Keep from me those bony fingers!—Keep him off, I say!—Keep him off!—I am not more than human, and cannot bear it!—Oh, still he approaches me!—Oh, save—save me!—I do confess I murdered him!—It was I—it was I— Keep him away—oh, horror!"

And then, his strength exhausted, the wretched man sunk back on his pillow, and drew the bed clothes over his face, as if he would shut out from his sight the ghastly object, which his conscience conjured up.

It was very evident that he was seized with death, and the doctor gave not the least hopes of him as soon as he had seen him. He ordered him to be kept as quiet at they could, but that was impossible; for he was only calm at intervals, and those were very short, and nothing could then restrain the violence of his ravings.

About five minutes elapsed, and once more throwing the clothes wildly off him, he jumped up in the bed, and with looks more awful even than before, he cried,—

"Ah! he is there again!—He is standing at the bed-foot!— Wretches! why do you not move him from my sight?—Send for a clergyman;—But no!—No holy man must enter here!—What have I to do with God or Heaven?—Have I not been a monster all my life?— I—I have—I have!—and the deep gulph of perdition is yawning to receive me!—See—see—how the flames rage!—And hark, the wailing cries of the damned!—Look! look!—what hideous forms are those, with fiery eyes?—Oh, save me from them!—Do not let them touch me!—Oh, horror! can nothing save me from this dreadful doom?"

"Repent, repent, unhappy man," said Sir Felix Mandeville, in a solemn tone of voice; "unburthen your conscience of the weight of guilt which oppresses it, it is not yet too late for forgiveness!"

"Forgiveness! forgiveness!" cried the poor hopeless wretch, "who talks of forgiveness to a monster like me? It is mockery; mockery! such as the fiends of hell alone could utter."

"Acknowledge your crimes; the only earthly atonement you can make, and endeavour to make your peace with God; before whose dreaded tribunal you must shortly appear;" added Sir Felix, in the same tone of solemnity.

"Appear before him whom I have so highly offended," exclaimed the dying sinner, and the expression of his countenance became more awful then ever; every muscle of his frame was violently convulsed, and large drops of perspiration stood upon his temples; "oh, no, no, no, I cannot die, I dare not die! I must not appear before that awful Being. Let me not die! let me not die! Doctor, do not leave me; do not neglect me! Try all that your skill can perform; I must not die!—you shall have riches unbounded if——Fool! what riches have I to bestow? None; none! every fraction was usurped; I am a very beggar! But still, doctor, have pity upon a poor miserable wretch, and out of charity attend to him!"

"Compose yourself," observed the doctor, who was a very humane man! "all the assistance that medical skill can render, depend upon it, you shall not lack."

"Oh, thanks! thanks!" said the dying man, with a look of gratitude; snatching eagerly the doctor's hand, and pressing it vehemently; "Oh, thanks! thanks! then you will not let me die?"

"Not if human power can save you, I will not," answered the medical gentleman;—"it is to be hoped that you may yet live to repent."

"Live to repent," ejaculated Harlington, staring wildly, and his countenance changing; "live to repent!—No, no!—to die an ignominious death upon a scaffold; amid a gaping and exulting mob!—Ah!—I see the hangman now!—He claims his victim! See, see—the fatal scaffold is erected!—The people are collected!—They ask, where is the murderer? —They scoff, they revile me! Oh, anything is preferable to that terrible fate! Do not resign me into the hands of the public executioner!— Death! death!—how terrible art thou; and yet I have no means to fly thee!—Oh, that I had never sinned!"

With a groan of the most indescribable agony, Harlington once more sunk back on his pillow, and again covered his head with the bedclothes.

"He may become more tranquil when we are not present," said the doctor; "let us leave him for awhile, Sir Felix."

The dying man in a moment caught the doctor's words, and starting up in the bed, as if nothing had been the matter with him, he cried—

"Nay, do not leave me! do not leave me! The fiends will tear me piecemeal if you do. Even now they are grinning and spitting at me! Do not leave me—I must not be alone! I confess all—I am the murderer of Lord Jerdan Egremond! It was by my instructions that the two girls of the deceased countess, Olivia and Amanda, were stolen away from the nursery by Gerald Darnley, and ordered by me to be assassinated. Providence, however, has saved one of them, the eldest, but the other—"

"Was also saved," added Sir Felix; "Darnley did not murder her, and she most likely still lives."

"Ha! ha! ha!" hollowly laughed the dying man; "you would deceive me—you would deceive me! Both girls living—oh, impossible!"

"They were both saved from the murderer's knife," said Sir Felix.

"Repeat those words again," exclaimed Harlington—"both saved?— You would not torture me—you would not deceive a poor dying sinner?"

"By Heaven I would not!" solemnly ejaculated Sir Felix.

"Oh, God! I thank thee!" fervently cried the dying man, clasping his hands vehemently; "another dreadful, hideous crime is saved my heavily-burthened conscience!"

He sunk back on his pillow, continued his hands clasped together, raised his eyes towards Heaven, and his lips moved as if in prayer. Yes, even that man of guilt dared to ask for that mercy from the Supreme, which he had never granted to his fellow-creatures.

After this a pause ensued, and Harlington remained silent; he seemed to have exhausted himself, and gradually sunk to sleep. The doctor nudged the arm of Sir Felix, and they silently quitted the chamber together.

That sleep was but the prelude to Harlington's everlasting one. According to the statement of his attendants, he awoke about an hour afterwards, looked wildly round the room, gave two or three convulsive struggles, and before they could ring the bell for assistance, with a deep groan his soul quitted its mortal tenement to be ushered into the presence of his immortal Judge.

The news was quickly conveyed to Sir Felix Mandeville, and the other members of the family, who, spite of his numerous crimes, dropped a tear of pity over the ghastly corpse of the murderer.

CHAPTER XIV.

THE RUINS SEARCHED.—THE SISTERS.

The funeral obsequies of the late Sir John Harlington were performed with all the pomp befitting his rank; but the execrations of the multitude followed his remains to the tomb. The body of Woodthorpe was also decently interred.

Mercy was one of the predominant passions of our heroine; but when she recollected the terrible fate of the author of her being, she could not but think upon the memory of his murderer with terror and detestation. She pictured to herself all the torment which her unhappy father must have endured, confined in that fearful closet without food, without hope; and scalding tears came to the relief of her greatly overcharged bosom. Then the uncertain fate of her sister, and the chance whether they should ever behold each other again, filled her bosom with the most painful and indescribable feelings, and she knew not which way to turn for consolation.

The acquisition of wealth and rank which she had now suddenly obtained, was treated by her with indifference, when those agonizing thoughts tormented her mind.

Lady Mandeville and her fair daughter, Arabella, tried every means in their power to console her, but they only partially succeeded; for her grief was of too powerful a nature to be easily eradicated, and they almost gave up their task in despair.

One thing, however, tended more than all to pacify her, and that was a lengthy advertisement which was inserted in all the papers every day, by Sir Felix, giving a full description of Patty, alias Amanda, detailing every particular of her abduction, and offering an immense reward to any one who could furnish any information of her. He would also immediately have hastened to Sir Merton Bellingham, and demanded of him an explanation, and whither his reckless nephew had gone; but he heard that he was on the continent, and, therefore, it would be no use following him there.

If there was one who tried more than the rest to console our heroine, and who succeeded better, it was Augustus. To his gentle and impressive arguments, Olivia, for such we must now call her, listened with peculiar pleasure; and it was very evident that love had gained a place within her heart, which time would best serve to strengthen. Augustus was not a being who could be very well resisted by a pure and susceptible female like our heroine; and strange as she had hitherto been to the passion, she now felt and mentally acknowledged it; nor sought she to destroy a sentiment which was founded in virtue, and which she felt confident was as warmly returned by the object who had inspired it.

Augustus soon perceived the conquest he had made, and his ecstacy knew no bounds; Olivia was just the gentle, beauteous being, which his warm imagination had long since pictured as the woman upon whom he could fix his whole soul, and he only awaited to see her restored to tranquillity, to be superlatively happy.

There was another subject now upon which our heroine expressed the greatest and most natural anxiety, and that was, that the ruins of the Old Lone House should be searched, to see whether the remains of her unfortunate parent were still in the vault, where they had been removed by Darnley and the steward; in order that they might have Christian burial, and of course there was no time lost in complying with this request.

The vaults underneath the Old Lone House had suffered but little by the fire, and the mouldering bones of the murdered earl were found in the chest, as described by the steward.

It was an awful sight for those who beheld those ghastly remains of what was once noble and virtuous, and there was not a dry eye present.

Olivia, who would insist upon being one of the melancholy party, no sooner beheld the ghastly remains of her father, than she knelt down, and prayed a blessing upon his soul, and invoked the protection of his spirit for her and her sister for the future. She then arose, and with more calmness than might have been anticipated, she took the offered arm of Sir Felix, and walked from the place, after having first seen the remains of her father deposited in a splendid coffin. It seemed as if her mind had been relieved of a great weight; she had performed a sacred duty, and she felt happier than she had done for some time before.

The persons employed in the search, by orders of Sir Felix, proceeded to examine further, and bursting open the door of the adjoining vault, there discovered the corpse of Will Darnley chained to the wall. He was not in the least burnt, and had probably died either of suffocation, or starvation, after the destruction of the Old Lone House.

The remains of the late Earl of Egremond were deposited in the family vault of his ancestors, and were followed by a vast concourse of persons, many of whom were old people, who very well remembered the earl and his lady, and had resided on his wide domains from childhood.

The Manor-house of Egremond was a fine old gothic pile, and covered an immense space of ground, having a handsome park of several acres attached to it.

Sir John Harlington had resided but little in it, since he had become so unlawfully possessed of the estates and title of Egremond, but it had been properly attended to, by his orders, and was, therefore, in excellent repair, and the park in good order.

Olivia was quite charmed when she beheld it; but yet a gentle melancholy stole over her senses, when she thought upon her parents, and

the blight which had been cast upon the fortunes of her noble house, by the hand of villany, and her tears began to flow.

In spite of the persuasions of Sir Felix and the others, who would have prevailed upon her to return to London, Olivia expressed her determination to take up her residence for some time at the Manor-house, and finding it would be useless to endeavour to alter her determination, they yielded, but insisted upon remaining with her, to which, of course, she willingly assented, and had always contemplated.

The persons who resided on the estate, and who had ascertained all the particulars, were delighted when they heard of our heroine's restitution to her rights, and were anxious to congratulate her upon her accession to wealth and rank; but their modesty under Olivia's peculiar circumstances, prevented them for the present.

A few weeks passed away without anything of particular importance occurring, and our heroine had somewhat regained her tranquillity; and in the society of Lady Mandeville and her amiable family, she seemed likely to be soon restored to all but complete happiness.

Augustus was one of the visitors at the Manor-house; and in his society, Olivia felt happier than any of the others.

Two months had elapsed after the interment of the remains of the late Earl of Egremond, that Olivia and Augustus were seated alone in the grand drawing-room of the Manor, when they heard the sound of carriage wheels rattling along the avenue, and going to the casement, they beheld a very elegant carriage hastening towards the Manor, the livery of the servants of which was entirely unknown to either of them. It stopped at the gothic portal, and no sooner was the door opened, than alighted from it the graceful form of a gentleman, who handed out a lady most elegantly attired, who was immediately escorted into the house by the gentleman.

No. 34

Olivia felt a trembling sensation come over her, and she was obliged to lean upon Augustus for support. Something of a particular nature, she was certain, was about to happen.

She was not long kept in suspense; Lady Mandeville hastily entered the room, and addressing her, said :—

"Olivia, my love, compose yourself I beg, and prepare yourself for a surprise !"

"Ah !" ejaculated our heroine, and her heart bounded to her lips; " I know what you mean ! My heart presaged it ! Let me fly !"

And before Augustus and his mother had recovered from their astonishment, she darted from the room with the speed of lightning, and bounded down the stairs, followed by Lady Mandeville and her son.

She did not pause a moment at the parlour door; but rushing into the room, uttered a scream of joy when she beheld Patty and Henry Walton !

She uttered a frantic cry, and exclaiming :—

"Sister! Dear sister!" She rushed into the arms of Patty, and immediately fainted !

Yes, it was Patty, otherwise Amanda, looking more lovely than ever, and Henry Walton, the alteration in whose appearance was most remarkable.

For a few moments the persons present seemed to be completely paralysed to the spot, with astonishment, and Amanda, who supported her sister in her arms, wept tears of joy upon her pallid cheeks. No one could look more beautiful than did Amanda, the former companion of our heroine in her misfortunes, and Augustus could not help gazing upon her with looks of the most enthusiastic admiration, and with feelings of the deepest interest, when he heard his beloved Olivia address her by the name of sister. But even if she had not done so, the great likeness that existed between them, and the conduct of both, would have convinced him of their consanguinity. He could see at a glance that she was the same fair, and gentle, and affectionate being that Olivia had described her to be, and his heart immediately warmed towards her.

Augustus, however, remained silent, and did not offer to interrupt Amanda, who continued to press warm kisses upon the lips of our heroine, and to weep tears of extacy and affection upon her cheeks. From her, his eyes rested on Henry, whose fine commanding and graceful figure, which the difference of dress set off to the best advantage, and the intelligence of whose handsome countenance, which was the index of a mind where every honour and virtue presided, caused in his breast no less admiration than that of his fair companion. Could this be the Henry Walton he had heard Olivia describe? If so, what strange freak of fortune had so altered his circumstances ?

He was thus lost in the chaos of conjecture, and Amanda, aided by Henry, was still supporting the insensible form of her sister, when Sir Felix and Lady Mandeville, who had been apprised of the arrival of the strangers, entered the apartment.

Amanda was so fully abstracted by her own thoughts, that she did not at first notice the entrance of the kind protecters of her sister, and, in a voice almost inarticulate, she said ;—

"Sister! sister! oh, blessed sound! Oh, yes, dear girl, well am I convinced of the truth of that which I have heard. Always did my heart whisper to me that we were related, and that time would unravel the dark mystery which had so long hung over our fate. Almighty God ! wonderful indeed are Thy ways ! Let not erring mortals arraign the justice of Thy decrees ; for Thou never failest to restore the innocent to their rights, and to visit the guilty with Thy terrible retribution !"

"And do we, indeed, behold the beloved sister of the much-injured Lady Olivia, whom we have so long been anxious to see, and whom we had begun to fear we should never behold again ?" said Sir Felix Mandeville, advancing with his lady towards Amanda as he spoke, and gazing with admiration upon one of the most lovely beings, with the exception of our heroine, that he had ever beheld.

Amanda, with the assistance of Henry, gently laid Olivia (who still remained insensible) upon the sofa, and turning round hastily, seemed to be for the first time conscious that she was in the presence of any one but Henry. Deep blushes suffused her cheeks ; she curtseyed very low, and endeavoured to speak, but failed, and stood trembling, the very picture of confusion and powerful emotion.

Lady Mandeville smiled affectionately upon her, and endeavoured to re-assure her.

"Dear Amanda, for such your countenance convinces me you are," she observed, "compose yourself, and think only of the joy that is in store for you. Need we say that we, who have fortunately been enabled to prove the friends of your sister, greet you with the utmost pleasure ? And this gentleman—"

"Mr. Walton, my husband," added Amanda, in a timid voice, and blushing still more deeply.

"Yes, Sir Felix," said Henry Walton, "the happy husband of one of the best of wives. No longer the rustic Henry Walton ; but, if money could add to my bliss, the now wealthy Major Walton, who trusts that he may prove himself not unworthy to be honoured by your friendship."

"The husband of Amanda must be worthy of our warmest regard ;" answered Sir Felix Mandeville, approaching Henry Walton with an air of warm friendship, which could not fail mutually to conciliate his warmest esteem, and taking his hand he pressed it as vehemently as if they had been friends for many years. Lady Mandeville then went through the same ceremony with the same cordiality and the same grace, and she evinced by her amiable and bland demeanour, how welcome Henry and Amanda was to them. There was yet another too, had been waiting anxiously to be introduced to Henry and the beauteous sister of our heroine ; that was Augustus, who saw in the open countenance of the former, something that he could esteem with the order of brotherly affection. And it was not long ere his wishes were gratified, Sir Felix introduced his son, and the young men greeted each other with a freedom which would make any one imagine that they had been intimate friends and companions from their childhood.

"But pray see to the recovery of my poor sister ;" exclaimed Amanda, at length, and it was evident from her manners, that the urbane reception she had met with from Sir Felix and his lady had made her become more confident and composed.

"It is only the power of her feelings that have overpowered her ;" observed Lady Mandeville, "she will soon be restored. See, even now she opens her eyes— she recovers—she revives !"

At that moment Olivia heaved a deep sigh, and opening her eyes, she looked anxiously and vacantly around her, her eyes first rested upon Sir Felix and his lady, and in a melancholy voice of disappointment, she exclaimed :

"Where is she ? gone ! It was only a dream then ? Oh, it was cruel to deceive me ! It was very, very cruel to play with my feelings like that ;

they were agonized sufficiently before. Patty! sister! Will you ever be restored to me? Or shall we meet alone again in Heaven?"

"Emily, dear, dear Emily; look up; behold me;—I am restored to you; your sister, your own fond sister is here!" cried Amanda in a voice of the most indescribable emotion, and throwing her fair arms round our heroine's neck. Olivia uttered a cry of the most frantic delight.

"Ah! 'tis her! It was then no deceptive vision!—Amanda, sister!—Oh, happiness supreme! Oh, bliss unutterable!"

We must draw a veil over this scene; it would be impossible to describe as it deserves, the feelings of transport that throbbed the bosoms of the lovely sisters as they embraced again and again; their tears mingled together, and for some time they were unable to give utterance to a syllable.

None of the persons present, who were deeply affected, offered to interrupt them; and a profound silence reigned, which was only ever and anon broken by the sobs of the sisters.

At length they partially recovered themselves, and Olivia, in a voice of the utmost sweetness, said:—

"This happiness is so great and so sudden, that I can scarcely persuade myself even now that is reality. Patty, for still is that name most familiar to me, most dear to me, being the one under which you was first introduced to me; after being separated from me so long to be once more restored to me, and after such a marvellous change in circumstances; it seems scarcely possible. And you are looking so well, too;—and—Henry Walton—what does this mean?"

"In Henry, my dear sister," said Amanda, in a more collected tone of voice, "in Henry you now behold my husband!"

"Your husband!" ejaculated Olivia; "Wonderful!—Oh, what a deal have we to tell each other. But our kind friends; our best friends; Mr. and Mrs. Walton, and their amiable daughters; oh, say, what has become of them?"

"Oh, dear Emily," observed Henry Walton, "they are all quite well, and will be here to-morrow, or the next day."

"Oh, happy news," fervently ejaculated our heroine; "I shall never be able to support such an accumulation of joys!"

"For the present, my dear girls," affectionately observed Lady Mandeville, "pray endeavour to compose yourselves, and by and by all will be explained, and you will then be entirely happy."

"But tell me, Patty," said Lady Olivia, "for you appeared to be acquainted when we met with the manner in which we are related, how did that come to your knowledge?"

"Why, my love," answered her sister, "your advertisement, and the lengthy accounts given in most of the daily papers, afforded me that knowledge. But it is four days since they first met my eyes. I will not attempt to describe my emotions when I perused them; you, my dearest Emily, will thoroughly understand them."

"Our's has, indeed, been a most miraculous fate," said our heroine; "but, after all, many as have been the sorrows that we have had to endure, and painful as have been the trials that we had to undergo, we must not repine, for the goodness of the Almighty is made manifest in the wonderful manner in which He has unravelled the dark mystery, and not only restored us to our rights, but to each other. Oh, my sister, how grateful to the all-merciful Supreme ought I to feel for the manner in which He preserved me from the base and sinful designs of that awful man, Chesterton, and for so often having saved me from the assassin's knife, when aimed at my life by that guilty man, Gerald Darnley. Even now, as the scenes in the Old Lone House pass before my retrospection, I shudder with horror."

" Come, come, my dear Olivia," said Sir Felix, gently taking her arm, and Augustus offering to take the other, which, however, she declined, and suffered Amanda to retain possession of it; " I must entreat that these melancholy ideas be banished for the present, and let to-day be given up to the happiness which this blissful restoration has given rise to. If you please, we will retire from this apartment, and Lady Olivia and her sister, if they think proper, can enjoy each other's society together in private until dinner-time, when they may have succeeded in composing their excited feelings."

The sisters returned their acknowledgments, and gladly availed themselves of this suggestion, and hastening to the chamber of our heroine, Lady Mandeville and the gentlemen made their way to the principal sitting-room.

There Henry Walton and the others, soon became as familiar, and as much at home, as if they had been acquainted for many years, and in answer to questions, although he said it was his intention to leave Mrs. Walton to relate her history herself, he said, that when he had been trepanned in so shameful a manner, through the base designs of Colonel Bellingham, he was hurried off to Portsmouth, and from thence, in a very short time, sent with the remainder of the regiment into which he had been enlisted, abroad, where he was in several actions, and was wounded. At the end of two years he returned to England, found out his parents, and discovered, that, by the death of a distant relation, of whom they knew nothing, they had come into the possession of immense wealth, and, that handsome fortunes had likewise been bequeathed to himself and his sisters. Of his subsequent meeting with Amanda, in what way, and their marriage, he would say nothing, as he thought they would be more gratified to hear it in the narrative which Amanda would give them. He added, that having imbibed a great taste for the army, he had purchased a commission, and now held the rank which he had previously told them.

Sir Felix and his lady were extremely glad to hear of the fortunate change in the circumstances of the amiable family of the Waltons, and were quite prepossessed in favour of Henry; who evinced all the manners of a gentleman of education, notwithstanding the situation of society he had formerly moved in. He possessed intrinsic virtues that could not fail to make themselves apparent, and which must excite the admiration and esteem of all who noticed them.

The sentiments of Augustus Mandeville and himself, it was soon very evident, entirely corresponded, and as soon as they beheld each other, their hearts throbbed with an ardent feeling of friendship.

In the meantime, the two lovely sisters, when alone, gave unrestrained indulgence to their feelings, and for some time their bursts of transport took precedence of all conversation.

At length, they became more calm, and then our heroine so far conquered her emotions as to be enabled to detail to her sister every particular that had happened to her since their last separation, and finally came to the discovery which had been made of their origin, and described the fearful confession of the guilty steward, and the fate of him and his base master.

We need not occupy the time of our readers by attempting to pourtray the feelings of horror, astonishment and grief, with which Amanda listened to this eventful narrative ; and when her sister had concluded, it was several minutes before she could find power to speak. She traversed the chamber in the most agitated manner, and frequently torrents of tears rushed to her eyes, and streamed down her cheeks. The horrible fate of their father, left in that secret closet to perish of hunger, and afterwards his emaciated corse to moulder away to a skeleton, filled her bosom with the utmost terror, and left her scarcely any room for consolation.

Olivia sat and watched her with an agonized bosom, but she offered not to interrupt her; she knew well her feelings by her own, and had been prepared for the expression of them. At length, however, Amanda became more calm, and throwing her arms round the neck of Olivia, they remained for some time locked in each other's embrace, and gave themselves up entirely to the indulgence of their own feelings.

"Oh, my beloved sister," at last said Amanda, "what a dreadful recital is this you have been giving me! Our unfortunate parents; and that bloodthirsty monster, Sir John Harlington. I tremble while I give utterance to his name!"

"He has gone to answer for his crimes," ejaculated Olivia, solemnly;— "may the Almighty Judge grant him more mercy, than he did to he unfortunate beings whom he murdered."

Amanda responded to the prayer, and then, after an effort, became more tranquil.

"I cannot relate my adventures since our separation, now," said Amanda; "I do not feel my strength adequate to the task; besides, it is rather lengthy, and, therefore, my dear sister, I must claim your indulgence until to-morrow."

"Anxious as I am to hear it, dearest Amanda," answered our heroine, "of course, I cannot but agree with so reasonable a request. To-morrow morning then, and shall look anxiously for your eventful narrative."

"I will then give it you; and you may expect to hear many things that convince you, I have had my share of troubles as well as yourself;" said Amanda.

"Oh, my sister;" observed Olivia, "how surprising it is to look back upon our past life, and to reflect upon the manner in which we were introduced to each other; and how soon our hearts warmed towards each other with the instinctive throbbings of consanguinity!"

"The retrospect is astonishing," returned Amanda; "but, from the first moment we met, something whispered to me that we were connected together, and I could have sacrificed my own life to have saved you from danger."

"Your conduct proved the truth of your assertions, beloved Amanda;" replied her sister,

"Death would have presented no terrors to me," added Amanda, "if the sacrifice of my life would have saved you from destruction!"

"I do believe you, Amanda," answered Olivia, "and Heaven knows that my feelings towards you were reciprocal."

"Oh, yes, that I know they were;" said Amanda; "well am I acquainted with my Olivia's heart, which, in every respect, is the counterpart of my own. But now we have discovered our origin, and are once more restored to each other, we will never again part!"

"We will not! we will not!" energetically cried Amanda, and tears of mingled joy and sorrow coursed each other down her fair cheeks; "and, in each other's society endeavour to forget the horrors of the past, and to look forward to the future with hope."

"And Heaven, if we rely upon its holy will, will not fail to reward the evening of our days with the brightness of peace;" said Olivia, with a look of reliance in the beneficence of the Most High.

A pause ensued; during which our heroine seemed buried in deep reflection.

"Poor Mrs. Seagrove, too," she observed; "her's was a melancholy fate."

"It was, indeed, to die so suddenly," said Amanda; "how delighted she would have been had she lived to witness this discovery; and to have learnt the consanguinity which subsists between us."

"She would indeed," coincided Olivia; "and much do I regret her loss; for a more amiable friend it has never been my lot to encounter."

"No doubt you were much surprised at the disappearance of the Waltons, in so mysterious a manner;" said Amanda.

"Indeed I was, when I heard of it," replied our heroine; "and am now anxious to know what could be the occasion of it."

"I shall explain everything in the narrative which I shall give you to-morrow," observed Amanda "and, indeed, you will be informed of many things that will excite your astonishment."

"I have no doubt I shall," returned Olivia; "and I am most eager for the arrival of to-morrow, that I may ascertain the particulars."

"You shall be made acquainted with everything, dearest Olivia," said Amanda; "and you will then perceive that I have had my share of troubles, as well as yourself, since we were last separated."

"I dare say you have endured plenty of hardships, my dear Amanda;" said Olivia; "but I trust that our troubles are now over, and that the future will be redolent of happiness."

"Heaven send that your anticipations may prove correct," exclaimed Amanda; "for certainly we have had our ample share of misfortunes. But, my dear Olivia, how fortunate you were to meet with such amiable friends as Sir Felix and Lady Mandeville. What you have told me of their behaviour to you, and their urbane manners, convince me that they are most worthy people."

"You do but do them justice by such an opinion, my dear sister," answered our heroine; "they have been to me the kindest of benefactors, and I owe them a debt of gratitude which I shall never be able to repay."

"And their son appears to be a most amiable young man;" observed Amanda.

Olivia blushed, and appeared to be very much confused; but Amanda took no notice of it, and she seemed to await impatiently for the answer of her sister. Olivia soon recovered herself, and replied—

"Augustus Mandeville is worthy of being the son of such amiable parents," she replied, "but there is another to whom you have not yet been introduced, and for whom I can ensure your esteem."

"And pray who is that, my Olivia?" interrogated Amanda.

"Arabella Mandeville," answered our heroine, "the beauteous and virtuous daughter of the excellent people of whom we are speaking. You will, I am sure, be delighted with her."

"Surrounded by so many generous and virtuous hearts," said Amanda, "our happiness will, indeed, be complete."

"It will," returned Olivia, "and the future will, I trust, fully recompense us for the many vicissitudes we have encountered."

At this moment a domestic knocked at the door, and informed Olivia and her sister that their friends awaited their presence in the dining-room, and they prepared to attend the summons.

On their entrance, the company were much pleased to see the alteration in their appearance; for they had completely tranquillized their feelings, and even attempted to meet them with smiles. Here Arabella was introduced to Amanda, who was much struck with her extreme beauty, and the sweetness of her demeanour, and returned her salute with much enthusiasm.

The dinner passed off very agreeably, and there was nothing said in reference to the past, so as to harrow up the feelings of Olivia and her sister. The evening, too, was passed away in conversation upon general subjects, and when they separated for the night, they all felt as happy as if they had known each other from their childhood.

At the earnest request of the Lady Olivia, her sister agreed to sleep with her for a night or two; and, indeed, now that they were once more restored to each other, they could not be happy for a moment out of each other's presence.

They lay awake for some time, and in sweet conversation the hours passed almost unconsciously away.

Such was the difference of the circumstances under which they now met, that they could scarcely believe that it was anything but a dream; and when they recalled to their memory the many misfortunes they had encountered, they could not but lift up their hearts in the most unbounded gratitude to Heaven, for the manner in which it had preserved them from so many unparalleled dangers, and restored them to each other, and to those rights that had been so long and surreptitiously withheld from them.

The sisters felt a most indescribable sentiment of awe when they reflected that they were now beneath the roof of their ancestors, and it brought with it a feeling of the utmost gloom when they thought upon the dreadful fate which their father had met with. They looked around the spacious apartment, and could almost imagine they saw the shades of their parents gazing upon them. They mutually invoked the blessing and protection of the sainted authors of their being. After that they became more tranquil, and the melancholy thoughts that had before tormented them were banished from their minds.

" But Bellingham," enquired Olivia, as a sudden thought crossed her mind—" what has become of him ?"

" He is where he cannot again work any one harm," replied Amanda.

" Ah!" ejaculated our heroine, " what mean you ?"

" He is no more," answered Amanda.

" No more !" repeated Olivia, with astonishment.

" He has been long since dead ;" said the former ;—" he never recovered from the wound which he received from Chesterton."

" Unfortunate, guilty man !" ejaculated Olivia; " may Heaven pardon him his numerous errors."

" He died truly penitent ;" said Amanda.

" And most happy am I to hear it ;" observed our heroine, fervently ; " but what has become of that most egregious fop and libertine, Sir Edgecumbe Sappington ?"

" He also has gone ' to that bourne from whence no traveller returns !' " answered Amanda.

" Sir Edgecumbe also dead ?" ejaculated Olivia, with a shudder of horror.

" It is true ;" returned Amanda; " he was slain in a duel about six months since. But pray wait until the morning, dearest Olivia, and you shall be informed of all the particulars."

" Certainly, my dear Amanda," said our heroine ; " I do not wish to put any questions that might torment your mind."

It was getting late, and both the sisters feeling tired, once more committed themselves to the care of Providence, and embracing each other, they dropped off into a tranquil sleep.

Dreams of the most blissful description flitted before their imagination, and the night passed away most tranquilly, and the morning dawned, and the sisters awoke refreshed and composed.

It was a lovely morning, and the sisters arose, and having dressed themselves, they agreed to ramble over the building, our heroine undertaking to

shew Amanda the different beauties of the fine old gothic seat of their ancestors.

The manor-house was a most spacious edifice, and was celebrated for the beauty of its gothic architecture; it contained innumerable apartments, and they were all fitted up and furnished in the most costly manner. As we have before said, Sir John Harlington, although he did not inhabit the house himself, for it reminded him too much of his crimes, had taken especial care to keep it in thorough repair, in order that he might prevent suspicion, and no person could take a survey of the interior of the mansion without feeling the most lively admiration for the taste and magnificence of everything upon which the eye rested.

Its gothic style had not been in the least altered, and it had still its loan chambers, and long winding galleries, as of old, and all the other particulars that gave it an air of feudal splendour.

With what feelings did our heroine and her sister Amanda traverse every apartment, and, as they recalled to their memory the sad fate of the authors of their being, whom they had never beheld, the melancholy with which it inspired them, found vent in tears.

If possible, Amanda was more violently agitated than our heroine; for the latter, during the time she had been at the mansion, in the society of those kind friends, Sir Felix Mandeville and his amiable lady, had had an opportunity of mellowing the violence of her grief, and she had succeeded far better than could, under the circumstances, have been anticipated.

"Oh, Olivia," said Mrs. Walton, after a long pause, during which she had been giving free indulgence to her emotion; "had those unfortunate beings, to whom we owe our existence, been living, what a delightful charm could everything we now gaze upon have possessed. But now, alas! they serve but to harrow up our feelings, and to recall more vividly to our recol-

No. 35

lection, the dreadful fate to which our father was doomed, and the premature death of our unfortunate mother."

" 'Tis true, dearest Amanda," replied her sister, " but still, it is both sinful and useless for us now to repine.   It was the will of the Almighty, and terrible, indeed, has been the retribution with which He has visited the guilty.   They are all now summoned before the awful bar of eternity, where they will have to answer for the manifold crimes they have committed during their earthly career.   Let us, my dear Amanda, by our future conduct, prove ourselves worthy of being the children of parents whose virtues yet live in the memories of all who knew them."

" We will, indeed, my sweet sister," said Amanda, conquering her feelings, and appearing almost completely tranquillized; " fully, indeed, do I appreciate the excellence of your advice.   Blessed in each other's society, and that of our dear friends, we will endeavour to forget the melancholy of the past, and look forward to the future with hope and resignation."

" And Heaven, I trust," exclaimed our heroine, " after the many heavy trials we have had to endure, will not suffer our hopes to be disappointed.   We shall yet live to be happy.   Oh, Amanda, when we come to reflect only for a moment upon the many dangers by which we were formerly beset; how frequently our very lives were threatened, and yet the Supreme Being has rescued us from all, and reinstated us in onr rights, how thoroughly grateful ought we to be.   We should never cease to pour forth to Heaven, our thanks for its mercy."

" True, Olivia," replied her sister, " we can never be sufficiently grateful.   But say, have we not yet traversed the whole of the manor-house ?"

" No, my love," answered our heroine; " we have yet several apartments to visit, and while we are about it, we may as well see them all."

They now moved across a wide and lofty corridor; ascended a wide staircase, and entered a spacious gallery, hung round with portraits of the ancestors of the noble house of Egremond.   A lofty casement of stained glass at the further end of this gallery, shed a mellow and solemn light upon every object; and added to the awe which both our heroine and Amanda felt on entering it.

They walked slowly along, Olivia leading the way, a little in advance of her sister, but she suddenly paused, and pointed significantly towards two portraits, in an excellent state of preservation, in silence.

They represented the likenesses of a lady and gentleman, and Amanda no sooner beheld them, than her heart bounded to her lips, and, with clasped hands, she sank on her knees, and raised her eyes towards Heaven. She needed no one to inform her whom these portraits were meant to represent.   Olivia followed her example, and the two sisters prayed fervently to Heaven, and invoked the blessing and protection of their sainted parents.

They remained in this posture for several minutes ; but at length they arose, and they both felt more composed than they had done for some time before.   They gazed leisurely upon the portraits, and their admiration and veneration increased every minute.

The portrait of Lord Jordan Egremond, represented a fine, handsome man, apparently of about thirty.   His features were noble and regular ; his eyes brilliant and expressive, and his lofty and expansive forehead bespoke the wisdom with which he had been endowed.   The whole expression of his countenance was mild, bland, yet commanding, and there was something peculiarly impressive about the smile which played around his lips.

The countenance of Lady Egremond, was loveliness itself.   The complexion was fair and transparent ; the features soft and beauteous as nature ever moulded ; the lips just parted sufficiently to exhibit her teeth of pearly whiteness, and incomparable regularity ; her eyes were a radiant blue, and the brows that surmounted them, were finely arched. Her hair hung in beautiful and natural tresses about her neck and bosom, and altogether there was something in the portrait, which represented her as a being almost too bright for this sublunary scene.

Our heroine and Amanda could have gazed for ever, without being tired, at these portraits, but Olivia remembering that it was getting late, and that their friends would expect them at the morning's repast, gently drew her sister away, and they hastened over the other part of the mansion, in which they did not observe anything else particular to attract their attention ; so they made their way to the apartment in which their friends were awaiting them for the morning's repast.

The demeanour of the beauteous sisters was so tranquil that Sir Felix, Lady Mandeville, and the others were quite delighted, and they fondly hoped that a short time would tend to make them forget the melancholy events that had marked their early life, and that their subsequent days might be those of uninterrupted happiness and prosperity.

The whole of the amiable family of the Mandeville's were quite pleased with Henry Walton, whose intrinsic merits became the more apparent the longer a person was in his company, and no one could help rejoicing at the singular good fortune which had suddenly elevated him from a state of comparative indigence, to one of affluence, and to that station in society he was so well calculated to adorn.

During the night and that morning, Amanda had fully prepared herself for the task she had imposed upon herself, namely, that of relating her adventures after her abduction bp Sir Edgecumbe Sappington, and the separation between her and our heroine.

The Mandeville's and Ohira were most anxious to hear the narrative, and therefore, as soon as the breakfast was over, they requested her, if she found her strength adequate to the task, to favour them by fulfilling the promise she had made them, without any further delay. Amanda acceded, and after having taken a minute or two to collect her thoughts, she commenced her narrative, as will be found in the succeeding chapter.

CHAPTER XIV.

AMANDA'S STORY.

" I NEED not, my dearest Olivia, seek to bring to your recollection that fatal evening when we were both seized by Bellingham, and his ignorant and unprincipled associate. It is, no doubt, impressed upon your memory in such vivid colours, that nothing will easily efface, for well can I judge your feelings by my own. The whole was like a frightful dream to me !—I remembered Bellingham seizing you in his arms, and endeavouring to drag you forward ;—I recollected hearing the report of a pistol, and I knew no more. I became at once insensible.

" When I recovered, I found myself in a vehicle, which was proceeding at a rapid pace, and by the light of the moon, which streamed in at the window of the carriage, I beheld myself in company with Bellingham and Sir Edgecumbe Sappington. The former was groaning deeply, and apparently in great agony, and was holding his arm ; from which I concluded that he had received the contents of the pistol, the report of which I had heard, though by whom it had been fired, I had not the means of forming the slightest conjecture.

"On beholding my situation, my terror became excessive, and I demanded to know, whither they were conveying me, and what had become of you, Olivia.

"'Oh, curses light upon her,' groaned Bellingham. 'I wish I had never beheld the proud beauty ; it is through her that I have received this confounded wound, which, I fear, will be productive of the most serious consequences to me.'

"'The oppressors of innocence never fail to meet with their just punishment,' I exclaimed in a solemn tone, and with a sudden air of firmness, which, however, soon vanished, and I added ;—

"'But whither, I repeat, are ye conveying me? and why am I thus unjustly and brutally torn from my friends?'

"'To be taken to the arms of one who has long adored you, my little divinity,' replied the detestable Sir Edgecumbe.

"'Unmanly villain!' I exclaimed, spiritedly, 'release me, and let me return to my friends, or, humble as I am, dearly shall you have to pay for this deed.'

"'Now do not put yourself in a passion, my little angel,' returned Sir Edgecumbe, with the most provoking coolness ; 'you will be as happy as the days are long, if you will only wait patiently.'

"'Wretch!' I ejaculated, 'I will make the air resound with my cries.'

"'And a great deal of use that will positively be to you, my love,' answered Sir Edgecumbe, with the most consummate impudence and indifference, 'where there is no one to hear you!'

"I clasped my hands together in an agony of despair, and remained silent ; but scalding tears coursed each other rapidly down my cheeks. The vehicle continued to roll on at the same pace, and Bellingham's pain appeared to increase. He rocked himself to and fro in the carriage, and looked as ghastly pale as if he was dying. A silence of some seconds ensued, and finding that it was useless to speak to them, I leant back in a corner of the vehicle, and gave myself up to the melancholy thoughts which my situation naturally gave rise to in my breast.

"'How much further is it to the nearest village, Sir Edgecumbe?' at length interrogated Bellingham, in a faint voice ; 'if we do not quickly have some advice I shall expire.'

"'We are now in the Elm Tree Wood,' said Sir Edgecumbe, 'and it is only about half a mile, to the right, to the village of B——. Do you think you could reach there with the assistance of one of the servants?'

"'Is there a surgeon residing there?' asked Bellingham.

"'There is,' answered Sappington ; 'Doctor Beauclerk, a very eminent man.'

"'Then I will endeavour to reach him, without delay,' replied Bellingham ; 'I think I shall be able to accomplish it, with the aid of one of the men. You need not wait for me, for I shall not return ; but put up at the first place of convenience I can meet with there. Should I recover, I will lose no time in rejoining you at the place to which you are going.'

"Bellingham, although evidently very weak and faint, now descended from the vehicle, and leaning on the arm of one of the men who were outside the carriage, he bade Sir Edgecumbe farewell, and slowly departed as the latter had directed him towards the village.

"The vehicle was now again driven forward with great speed, and Sir Sappington threw himself carelessly back in his seat, and picked his teeth, without taking the slightest notice of me. This, however, was more of a relief to me than otherwise, and I was left to free but melancholy indulgence of my own thoughts.

" Distracting indeed they were, and my brain whirled round with agony. My dear Olivia, I know, will do me justice to believe that in these she held a most powerful and dismal part. In vain I sought to imagine what had become of you, and how it had happened that you had become released from the power of Bellingham. Sometimes a hope sprang up that my father had rescued you; but that idea was quickly banished, and I became lost in the chaos of conjecture.

" The deep anguish which I knew my friends would experience at my, perhaps both your's and mine, mysterious disappearance, I was convinced would be intense, and I felt more for them than I did for myself, fearful and alarming as my situation was.

" From picking his teeth, the insensible baronet fell to humming a portion of a song, and in the midst of that, he fell off to sleep, and snored as loudly as if he had been some noisy roisterer in a tap-room.

" I looked from the window of the carriage, but the prospect beyond was dismal enough. We had emerged from the Elm Tree Wood, and were travelling over a wild and uncultivated waste, which, as far as my eye could stretch, presented not a single habitation or individual.

" For several hours we continued to travel in this manner, only stopping once or twice, for a short time in secluded places, for the horses to rest themselves; and then the vehicle proceeded with greater rapidity than before.

" Sir Edgecumbe frequently addressed himself to me, but I returned him no answer, and knowing it was no use appealing to his humanity, I stifled my feelings as much as I possibly could; committed myself to the care of Omnipotence, and determined to await the issue of my fate with becoming fortitude, entertaining a cheering hope that something would occur to rescue me from the villain's power.

" I will pass over the remainder of our journey, which in detail might appear very tedious to you. You can all very well imagine the state my mind was in, and, therefore, it is unnecessary for me to repeat it here.

" The grey mists of early morn were gradually fading from the horizon, when the carriage stopped, and looking from the window of the vehicle, I beheld a handsome-looking villa, situated in a romantic spot, and surrounded by rich fields and pastures, that were shortly to be irradiated by the morning's sun.

" ' Well,' said Sir Edgecumbe, ' it is fortunate that our journey is at an end, and without any obstacle, for, confound me, if I was not almost tired of it. I do not like such damned fatigue, positively. Now, my little captivator, allow me the honour to hand you out, and to introduce you to your future residence, which, take my word for it, you will find to be a perfect palace; and, if you only act wisely, you will be treated the same as if you were a little queen.'

" I returned no answer to this fulsome and ridiculous speech, and looking around, and seeing no person near but the fellows of Sir Edgecumbe, I knew it was useless to remain obstinate, and, therefore, passively suffered myself to be handed from the vehicle by the detested and contemptable baronet, scarcely, however, at the same time, being aware of what I was about, and before I had exactly been restored to consciousness, I was led into the house, and was ushered by Sir Edgecumbe into a very elegantly furnished apartment. Several domestics were in the hall when I entered, and they eyed me with much curiosity, but the baronet waved his hand, and they quickly made their exit.

" I threw myself on a sofa, and, overcome by the power of my emotions, could not restrain my tears. Sir Edgecumbe with an affectation of sympathy advanced towards me, seated himself by my side, and attempted to take my hand. His touch was like the bite of some loathsome reptile to me, and hastily withdrawing my hand, I conquered my tears, and jumping quickly to my feet, I retreated to the further end of the room, and, with the utmost indignation expressed in my countenance, in a voice of firmness exclaimed :—

" ' Forbear! touch me not ; lest the vengeance of offended Heaven descend upon your head. It is true, you hold me in your power, but if you attempt any unmanly outrage, Omnipotence will, I trust, give me strength to resist it, and will heap its terrible retribution upon your head.'

" ' How confoundedly apt all you young ladies are at preaching a sermon;' said Sir Edgecumbe; ' but positively, although it may be very pretty, I have no particular taste for such things. And now, my little divinity, I must tell you one thing, which I hope you will bear in mind ; and that is, that I am one of the best fellows in Christendom, until a person becomes obstinate with me, and then I am a ve—ry devil! I am positively! But I don't see what you have got to make yourself uneasy about ; here you have got a sweet little residence with everything at your command, and of which you can reign the sole mistress ; plenty of books to read; servants to wait upon you, and a man who will adore you like anything ; he will positively !'

" It was some moments before I could make any reply to this speech, and my resentment was so great that I could scarcely contain myself ; but at length it changed into pity and contempt, and looking scornfully upon the empty-headed baronet, who prided himself upon having said some marvellous pretty things, I said :—

" ' And is this the language of a man who calls himself a gentleman, to an unprotected female, whom he has basely torn away from her home and friends, and who seems determined to hold her in unjust confinement? Shame on you ! shame on you !'

" ' Very pretty—exceedingly pretty,' said Sir Edgecumbe, with the most provoking coolness; ' the very thing, positively, for a romance, or it would fetch down thunders of applause in a play, that it would. But it is quite out of place here, although I shall have no objection to hear it now and then, for it will be positively very amusing occasionally. As for being taken away from your friends, you will soon find that you have no cause to regret that circumstance, for you will be as happy as a little princess here, that you will, positively, my little angel.'

" I returned no answer, for I found it was completely useless talking to a man who was quite insensible to pity or feeling, and I placed my trust entirely in Omnipotence.

" ' Well,' said the baronet, after a pause, in his usual careless manner, ' confound me if the journey has not made me devilish hungry, and, therefore, we will take our breakfast.'

" He rung the bell as he spoke, and a female servant appeared, to whom he delivered his orders, and then lounging on the sofa, without taking the least notice of me, he took up a book and pretended to scan over its pages, although I do not believe that he read a syllable.

" The servant quickly re-appeared with the morning's repast, which, having placed on the table, at a motion from Sir Edgecumbe, she retired. He then immediately seated himself at the table, and requested me to join him, but I refused, for I felt not inclined to eat, and I need not say that, in his presence I was truly miserable. Finding that all his powers of persuasion were of no avail, he abandoned the attempt, and proceeded to eat his own breakfast, which he did apparently with an excellent rellish, for he eat as much, and as greedily, as if he had been a farmer's servant.

" During this time, I was allowed to indulge in my own thoughts, the description of which need not be mentioned ; and when he had concluded, I requested him to allow me to retire to the apartments that were to be appropriated to my use, as I was tired, and wished to rest myself for awhile. With this request Sir Edgecumbe could not but comply ; and ringing the bell for the female servant I had just seen, and with whose appearance I was much pleased, he desired her to conduct me to my suite of apartments.

"Letty, which was the name of the young woman, curtseyed and obeyed, and smiling kindly upon me, she led the way, and I followed her with a light heart, much pleased at being released from the presence of the ignorant and unprincipled baronet.

"The rooms were very handsomely furnished and displayed every comfort that a person, placed in other circumstances than my own, could desire.

"I will not tire your patience by detailing all that happened to me while I here remained a prisoner ; the importunities of Sir Edgecumbe, the various attemps he made to obtain the gratification of his sinful desires by force, and the fortunate manner in which I was enabled to resist him. Providence never forsook me, and my gratitude is for ever due for the shield it threw around me. Letty behaved to me with the greatest kindness, and it was a great source of relief to me under the many trials to which I was subjected.

"Bellingham never came to the house ; the wound he had received proved mortal, and he gradually sunk under it, until he died ; which he did, as I understand, very penitent, and endeavoured to send word to my friends by one of his attendants, to inform them of the whole circumstance, and the place where I was concealed. But it was too late ; he had not strength to do as he wished, he never rallied again, and expired before he could scarcely give utterance to a syllable.

"His death had little or no effect upon Sir Edgecumbe Sappington, and in a very short time he evidently forgot that such a person had ever existed, or stood in the situation which the libertine and the unprincipled falsely denominate a friend.

"Ten months elapsed in this manner, without any change taking place in my situation, and it is astonishing how I contrived to prevent the villain Sappington from effecting the designs he had formed against me. One evening, by the connivance of Letty, I effected my escape from the house, Sir Edgecumbe being from home at the time. But fate was against me ; I had not proceeded far, when I met the baronet returning, and, in spite of my resistance and outcries, he succeeded in forcing me back to the house again. Fortunately, however, Letty escaped suspicion, and my escape was believed to proceed entirely from accident.

"Sir Edgecumbe became more importunate than ever, and there were times when I almost despaired of being enabled to escape the fate with which he threatened me ; but the Almighty supported me, and, notwithstanding I remained in the baronet's power for six months more, I was enabled to defeat him.

"Whilst I was in his power, Sir Edgecumbe continued to carry on the same course of folly and profligacy which he had ever done, and, at length, Heaven visited him with its just retribution. One of his wild associates, in a fit of jealousy, demanded of him satisfaction. He granted it ; fell by the shot of his rival, and was brought home a corpse. Here then was an end to the libertine's guilty career, and he fell unpitied and unmourned by a single individual.

"This, as you may be certain, was the cause of my immediate liberation, and the following morning, I and Letty departed together, my mind in a state which there is no occasion to describe to you. The first place we went to was the cottage of Letty's mother, who received me very kindly, and would have persuaded me to have remained with them for a few days, until I had recovered myself; but I was too anxious to return to my friends to agree to such a proposal, and I determined to depart the next morning.

"Accordingly, the following morning, almost as soon as it was daybreak, I bade Letty and her mother farewell, thanking them for their kindness, and promising to see them again, and quitted the cottage on foot, not having the means to travel any other way, and, with a palpitating heart, hastened on my way to that neighbourhood, from which, so many months before, I had been so unjustly and cruelly forced.

"As I proceeded, a number of melancholy forebodings crossed my mind, of which I in vain tried to divest it, and I could not get rid of the impression that fresh misfortune was in store for me.

"I had but a very small sum of money, and was, therefore, compelled to live very scantily on the road, but I did not despair over it, thinking that I should shortly be restored to my friends, where my wants would be at an end.

"I was two days in travelling, but at length the tall spire of the village church met my eager gaze, and my heart bounded more violently than before. Alas! what a terrible shock awaited me!—I reached the farm where, my dearest Olivia, we had experienced so much kindness from our more than friends. It was in the possession of strangers. I inquired for the Waltons; they had long since disappeared, and no one knew whither they had gone. I asked for you, my sister;—you had not been heard of since the night of my abduction. I was distracted!—But there was yet another, one more, one dear friend; a more than mother. I hastened towards the house formerly occupied by Mrs. Seagrove. That was also the property of a stranger! It was then I heard of Mrs. Seagrove's sudden death. My God! how shall I seek to describe my feelings on receiving this melancholy intelligence? It was wonderful that I did not immediately expire. I need not seek to describe to you what I suffered on that occasion. I was released from confinement only to find myself alone in the world. I was, for some time, the very epitome of despair, and wrung my hands, and wept, scarcely knowing how to contain myself. Whither was I now to turn my footsteps; for I was almost pennyless, and had not a friend that I knew of, in the world. I had no other alternative but to return to the cottage of Letty's mother, where I might find a shelter until such time as I might form some plan for the future. But, in the meantime, fatigued as I was with travelling, and such a distance, on foot, it was not likely that I could venture to return until I had duly rested myself. My money was so limited, not amounting quite to a guinea, that I should be compelled to act with the strictest economy, or it would never last me to the end of my journey. I sought out a little decent tavern, which I knew was not much frequented, and was kept by a kind-hearted widow; and there I determined to take up my lodging until such time as I should be able to resume my journey.

"The woman, who had some slight knowledge of me, evidently pitied my condition; for she saw that I was fatigued and foot-sore, and she behaved to me with the greatest kindness. From her I learnt the particulars of the strange and sudden disappearance of Mr. and Mrs. Walton, and their family, and the melancholy and sudden death of the amiable and beloved Mrs. Seagrave. I need not inform you of the torrents of tears that coursed each other down my cheeks, as I listened to her dismal recital, for you, my dearest Olivia, can form a just conception of the intense agony which I must have felt.

" From the same source also, I was made acquainted with the destruction of that fearful scene of our misery, the Old Lone House, and as was supposed, all who were in it. Little did I imagine that you, my sister, was an inmate of the place at the time ; or, how great would have been my agony ; what bitter, what poignant misery should I have endured ; what terrible suspense should I have been left in ; but as it was, I felt something like satisfaction, for I was released from the bitter enemies who had so long and so maliciously pursued me. That they were relatives, I had long since ceased to believe, and therefore no feeling of pity, unless it was for the terrible account to which the wretches were so suddenly called, entered my mind. Such a rapid succession of terrible events, however, gave me a severe shock, and made a most powerful impression upon my feeling. The destitute and completely friendless situation in which I now found myself, was sufficient to cause despair in even stronger minds than mine, and I was for some time, quite lost and bewildered in what manner I should act.

" To the kind hostess I related the particulars of my situation, and from her I found every commiseration ; she had been the mother of a large family, most of whom she had buried, and she knew how to sympathise with my misfortunes. In vain did I endeavour to account for the singular disappearance of the Waltons ; I could not conjecture the slightest reason which they could have for such extraordinary behaviour, and I the more wondered that they had not left word with some confidential neighbour, whither they were gone, in case that either you or I should return to the vicinity, and that we might know where to find them.

" The only course which I saw that I could at present adopt, was to return to the cottage of Letty's mother, upon whose benevolence, although I knew she could ill-afford it, I must intrude for a short time, until I could obtain a situation, and something seemed to assure me that it would not be long before I should prove successful.

No. 36

" Notwithstanding the state my mind was in, the fatigue I had undergone, made me sleep soundly that night, and in the morning I arose refreshed, and prepared to commence my melancholy and dreary journey. The good landlady of the house where I had made such a brief stay, and who had treated me with so much kindness, bade me adieu most affectionately, and promised, if she should hear anything of the Waltons, to let me know, and also to inform them of what I had told her ; of the many troubles I had endured, and of my ultimate return to the neighbourhood under such dismal circumstances.

" I had not proceeded far, when I had occasion to look in the little handbasket which I carried with me, when my eye was attracted by a small paper parcel, and unfolding it, you may judge of my astonishment, when I beheld a sum of money, amounting to half a guinea in silver, and inside the paper was written, in the hand-writing of the kind hostess, the following words :—

" ' The widow's mite ; accept it, and welcome, and may Heaven prosper you on your journey, and in your future undertakings.'

" This unassuming and unostentatious instance of philanthropy, affected me to tears, and I was obliged to pause on the road to recover myself ; I reflected that the money was more than the poor woman could afford, and at first I thought of going back, and returning it to her ; but then again I thought that she would probably feel herself hurt, and with the hope of being able before long to return it, and some acknowledgment of her kindness, I retained possession of it, and resumed my journey.

" I will pass speedily over that journey, which to me was a most weary one, but which, in detail, cannot possess any interest to you. In three days I arrived at the cottage of Letty and her mother, by whom I was received with the most honest and unbounded kindness, and they expressed in terms which I could not mistake, their sorrow in the disappointment, and the unexpected news which I had met with. They endeavoured to convince me by every means in their power, how welcome I was to remain with them, while they had the slightest means in their power ; and they sought to encourage me with hope that it would not be long ere I should either hear something of my friends, or be placed in a situation to obtain my own living until something more fortunate should turn out. With these hopes I appeared to be satisfied, and concealed all I could the abhorrence which I really felt at the idea of being beholden to almost entire strangers to me, and especially to those who I was convinced could so ill afford it.

" Three weeks, however, had only elapsed, when I was fortunate enough to hear of a situation, and left the residence of my kind friends. The situation offered to me the most favourable prospects ; it was with a widow lady, who had an only son, a young man about my own age. Her residence was in a distant part of the country, and there were only two more servants besides myself.

" For some weeks all went on well enough ; my mistress behaved to me with much kindness and indulgence, and I was beginning to think myself very fortunate, when the delusion was suddenly put an end to, and I became truly miserable.

" The son of my mistress was a young man of extremely weak mind and vicious principles, and being her only offspring, she had treated him with too much indulgence, and never corrected, but entirely overlooked his errors ; the consequence was, that they had grown upon him, and what with the tuition of the depraved characters he was in the habit of associating with, and his own base propensities, he had, at length become a thorough blackguard.

" This man imbibed a guilty passion for me, thinking, no doubt, from the menial situation which I held with his mother, that he would make an easy conquest.

"I will not disgust you, or your patience, my dearest friends, by detailing to you all the miseries I had for some time to endure from the importunities of this young libertine, in which he was encouraged by his parent, until, at length, fearful of the worst consequences, I effected my escape from them, and, with very little money in my purse, once more bent my footsteps in the direction of the residence of Letty's mother, even with a heavier and more melancholy heart than when I had before intruded upon their kindness. Fresh misery was here destined to attend me: Letty and her mother had quitted the neighbourhood, and no one could inform me where they had gone.

"I was now, indeed, in a most deplorable condition, and had nothing but the prospect of a poor house before me: my money was nearly all gone, and I had not a friend to whom I could apply, or a shelter beneath which to place my head. I wrung my hands in despair, and I cannot possibly do justice to the agony of my mind. I left the place, and wandered, I scarcely knew whither.

"It was on the second evening that my money was entirely gone, I had had no food, and ill and exhausted, I could with difficulty proceed on my way. To add to my misery, the weather was most inclement, and the rain descended in torrents. At length, as night came on, and I saw not the least prospect of a shelter, I was driven to desperation, and seing a handsome house before me, I knocked at the door, and piteously implored relief and a lodging for the night. The female servant who answered the door to me, looked upon me with compassion, conducted me to the kitchen, and then went to inform her master and mistress of the circumstance, and my deplorable condition and request. In a short time she returned, with a message that she was to conduct me to them. I followed her with a palpitating heart, and, on entering the drawing-room, and recognising the master and mistress of the place, I uttered a wild and frantic cry, and immediately fainted. Will you be astonished, my dear friends, when I inform you that chance had led me to the very house of those dear people from whom I had been so long separated, and whom I had never expected to see again, Mr. and Mrs. Walton.

"I must draw a veil over the scene which followed;—it is more than I can describe! Mr. and Mrs. Walton and their lovely daughters were almost delirious at my wonderful restoration to them; and shed torrents of tears at the sufferings I had undergone, and the uncertainty of your fate, after whom they had made the most indefatigable inquiries, but without meeting with any success. They had been compelled to quit the farm so abruptly to attend the death-bed of that relation from whom they derived all their wealth, and had not returned to it since.

"The regiment to which Henry belonged was on its way to England, and with the hopes that he had survived the horrors of war, they awaited with the utmost impatience for that time to arrive. In the meantime they used every endeavour which they could, to learn what had become of you, but to no purpose, and we were at last compelled to imagine that you were no more!—Oh, Olivia, what hours of agony did that idea cause us all!

"At the expected time, the regiment to which Henry belonged, returned; he came back in safety.—What a scene of transport was his meeting with his parents, his sisters, and myself! Imagination must depicture it, for I cannot pourtray it!

"Henry has informed you of his fortune;—his purchasing a commission, and his present rank, I have little to add; three months after this, finding that our sentiments for each other were unchanged, I became his wife! I will leave to your own conceptions our emotions when the articles in the newspapers met our eyes, informing us that you were still living; your altered circumstances, and that you were my sister! You know the rest; my narrative is at an end!"

CONCLUSION.

AMANDA had scarcely concluded, and Olivia and the others had not time to give utterance to their feelings, when a post-chaise was driven along the principal drive, and Mr. and Mrs. Walton and their daughters were announced. With a cry of delight, our heroine rushed forth to meet them, and the next moment was clasped alternately in the arms of those dear friends she had never expected to behold again.

A few words will suffice to close this "strange, eventful history;" nothing but happiness now reigned at the ancient Manor House of Egremond, and the melancholy events of the past were forgotten in the present bliss.

It was several days, however, before they were quite restored to tranquillity, when they returned to London to the mansion of Sir Felix Mandeville, where for some time they had determined to take up their residence. In a few weeks after these events, Augustus Mandeville confessed the passion with which our heroine had inspired him, and having received from her an acknowledgment of a reciprocal sentiment, he hastened to his parents to solicit their consent to their union. This was gladly granted, and two months afterwards, Lady Olivia Egremond was led to the altar by Augustus Mandeville.

The sisters continued to reside together, having made a vow that nothing but death should separate them, and the old Manor House was soon rendered as cheerful as it had been in the life-time of the late unfortunate Earl and Countess of Egremond.

FINIS.

www.ingramcontent.com/pod-product-compliance
Lightning Source LLC
Chambersburg PA
CBHW081146020726

47504CB00009B/2019